I0715464

OTHER BOOKS BY
V. S. HOLMES

NEL BENTLY BOOKS
Travelers
Drifters
Strangers
Heretics
Fugitives
Emissaries

BLOOD OF TITANS
Smoke and Rain
Lightning and Flames
Madness and Gods
Blood and Mercy

SHORT FICTION
"Nowhere Fast" *(We Came to Dance)*
"Starfall" *(Vitality Magazine)*
"The Tempest" *(Out of the Darkness)*
"Disciples" *(Beamed Up)*
"Familiar Waters" *(Love and Bubbles)*
"Mere Primordium" *(poem, Mystic Blue Review)*

EMISSARIES

STARS EDGE: NEL BENTLY BOOK 6

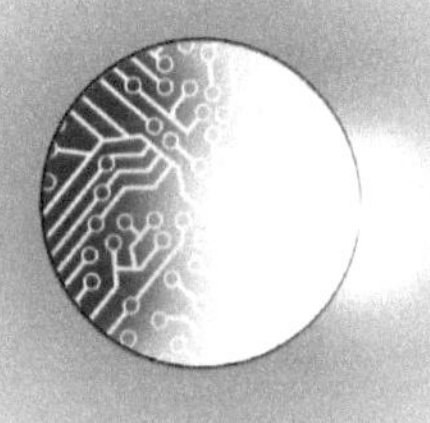

V. S. HOLMES

AMPHIBIAN PRESS

Amphibian Press

13820 NE Airport Way
Suite #K471902
Portland, OR
97251-1158
United States

www.amphibianpress.online
www.vsholmes.com
ISBN : 978-1-949693-64-5

For the runners,
may you find someone who
runs as fast as you.

AUTHOR'S NOTE

This series combines archaeology with science fiction. This book is a work of fiction, and something to be enjoyed as entertainment. I wholeheartedly believe we are far from alone in the universe.

That being said, I am an archaeologist by trade, and I know humans are ingenious and resourceful enough to build pyramids and other architectural wonders all on their own. I strive to turn the stereotypes of "ancient aliens" on their heads—and portray a world as complex and nuanced as the humans that forge our future.

ONE

Dawn was brilliant, even from 500 million miles. Light lanced through the thick acrylic of the transport's windows, reflected off the mighty blue belly of the alien gas giant. Nel couldn't tear her eyes away. After months of dodging through the dark asteroid field, she almost believed the sun no longer shone.

Granted, this wasn't her sun.

Nel perched on the edge of her thin bunk, listening to the creak of the shuttle, the rattle of the crew preparing for landing. Gurgling systems. Whispering ghosts.

"Hello," she whispered back.

She grabbed her leg and lined it up with her thigh before going through the almost-familiar motions of hooking it up and rolling the final silicone sleeve over the place where flesh met prosthetic. They'd spent the better part of the last few days prepping for this flight and briefing those who followed Lin from IDH. The discussions hadn't included anything past getting to a safe place to regroup, but Nel still scarcely had time to sleep, let alone speak with Emilio. And the weight of the ghosts and their whispers seemed too heavy for a passing conversation.

Her comm beeped. Nel finished zipping her electrosuit before jabbing at her wrist.

Sender: MBently
Morning Honey!
We're all packed, scheduled to land—dock?—tomorrow afternoon. See you soon.
Love you!
XO, Mom

It was meant to comfort, but Nel's stomach churned. She tapped out a response wishing for safe travels and raked her hair back, wishing she looked more presentable. *I bet Dar has space-pomade made from some glittery—*she stopped herself. Dar was comatose, riding safely in their transport's single cryo-med bay, and while his hair gel was probably still impeccable, Nel wasn't about to ask if she could borrow any.

The Recursive and the other ships would catch up over the next several days. This shuttle, however, was the van guard—and icebreaker. Nel just hoped that they didn't break so much ice there was nothing left to stand on.

She slipped from her room and headed toward the tiny kitchenette in the fore of the shuttle.

Water steamed and sputtered as she pumped the pedal of the rehydrator, watching the instant coffee burble in her insulated mug. The bittersweet aroma filled the tiny cantina. For a moment, she could pretend she was in her own kitchen in Jasper Hill, waiting for her French press to steep.

Another bunk door slid quietly open then shut. A moment later Emilio stepped up beside her and set about making tea. "Morning."

"Morning." Nel pumped the rehydrator for a second cup and stepped out of his way. "Dar?"

"Stable."

The shuttle wobbled slightly as she downed the last of her coffee, spilling it onto the breast of her suit. *Fuck.* At least electromesh didn't short circuit.

"Can you tell this thing's autopilot transition hasn't been calibrated in months?" Emilio sighed.

"I think we're all in need of a tune-up," she muttered, glaring at her front. "Besides, what's a little coffee stain when you're trying to make a first impression?"

He snorted and jerked a nod toward the cockpit. "Should be coming into view, if you want to see."

"Fuck yeah." Nel followed him through the door and into a wash of blue light. Emilio took one of the spare seats, offering the pilots a quick nod. They were still dressed in their IDH uniforms, but the most obvious badges had been ripped away.

After months of running from them, the sight still made Nel's skin crawl.

Nel eyed all the buttons she could so very easily accidently press and stayed on her feet, looping one hand through the cargo webbing against the rear wall. Squinting against the brilliance, she asked. "So what is *Vīrya* exactly?

"Home."

Adrenaline zinged up Nel's spine as the tall woman breezed in. She took up a wide, stable stance on the other side of the doorway from Nel, gripping the netting in one delicate hand. The space between them constricted, the cockpit feeling suddenly airless. Nel had hoped, the few times she allowed herself to hope at all, curled in the warmth of Lin's arms on *Odyssey*, that when she did see Lin's home, it'd be her hand that Nel gripped in her clammy fingers. Not rough canvas webbing. Another shudder of turbulence shook Nel back to reality.

The satellite ahead was shaped like a gleaming top. A dome protected the living area, which currently faced the sun. The manufactured atmosphere was brilliant blue-green, brighter than Nel expected. They hurtled closer. The structures and landscape below were warped beneath the thick layers of translucent titanium, but spindling antennae and massive ports studded the satellite's dark, rough underside. The whole looked like ridiculous flat-earthers concept art, a gleaming disk with water plummeting off the sides into vapor. A thrill went through her at the sight.

"I thought you were raised on *Odyssey,*" Emilio remarked. "At least, that's what Dar said."

"We grew up in a lot of places. Dragged on diplomatic missions. Later on, I stayed on *Odyssey* mostly, and he followed Ibu to Samsara when he was old enough to study at the flight school there. But when we could, we'd return here to the family estate."

If Nel dared to look at Lin at all, she'd do a double take. She had always known Lin was wealthy. Or whatever passed as such in the faux egalitarian guise of IDH. Somehow, though, she hadn't realized that meant owning one's own satellite. "So you fucks are like, rich-rich."

Emilio chuckled.

"Our parents are very influential and have high-contract skills," Lin began to argue.

Rapid chirping rose from the instrument panel and the co-pilot shot a glance at the chattering viewers, before barking into the comm: "All personnel, secure yourselves for docking."

Nel wordlessly dropped into the seat beside Emilio and buckled the five-point harness. No one else had bothered to don helms, but she wished they had.

"Hold tight," Emilio murmured beside her.

She renewed her grip on the armrests as a metal eyelet opened in the satellite's underside and they rocketed into its dark, mechanical belly. Nel flinched. *Way too fast.*

The panel shut behind, sealing them within. Air roiled into the vacuum through nozzles circling the airlock. The shuttle's thrusters screamed against the sudden gravity as another circular eye opened and they dropped into the atmosphere of the interior.

Brilliant lights shone across the stone landing pad as they settled, featherlight. Landing gear whispered them to the ground. Their air mingled with the atmosphere for another few moments, then the computer dinged.

Their pilot sat back. "Welcome to *Vīrya*. You may move freely about the transport."

Emilio unbuckled himself and headed for the cryo bay to check how Dar fared in landing. Lin's gaze was still fixed straight ahead, her hands fiddling with her now-defunct badges.

Nel sneered as she snapped her own seatbelt off. "Embarrassed to be seen with us?"

Lin blinked away the snark. "A lot has changed since I last saw them."

"Guess no one expects their daughter to be the enemy, no matter how much writing was on the walls." Nel lurched into motion before one of them decided to draw a weapon again and swayed towards the ramp. Walking was easier than it had been, but she doubted she'd ever have her former ease.

Light and air billowed in. Nel hesitated in the doorway, watching as Emilio handed Dar's cryotube off to a group of medics. She fidgeted with the handle of her duffle and tried to place the scent wafting in. *It doesn't smell fake.*

"Nove!" Lin strode across the landing pad with an increasingly rare smile.

Nel turned, expecting to see a whole welcoming committee of Nalawangsas. Instead, a single figure awaited them. She hoped her smile didn't slip when she set eyes on the senti-comp. Everything about Phil had been utilitarian. Kasanove lived up to his namesake. The gleaming acrylic housing his only remaining flesh was treated with something that diminished the glare. His dark skin still had an almost life-like sheen. The container itself perched on a hovering brass column that set his eyes at about the level of Nel's own.

"Lin, welcome home."

"Thank you. Where are our parents?" Lin's brows arched.

"We'll discuss that later."

"That gives the rest of the fleet time to settle in, I suppose."

"Indeed. I've had the docks below prepared." He let out a soft electric cough. "Perhaps you'd like to introduce me to your flight mates?"

"Of course. Nove, this is Emilio Sepulveda of Los Pobledores, and Dr. Nel Bently, both terrestrial." Lin introduced with an impatient gesture at the two of them. "This is Kasanove, steward of *Vīrya* and head of security."

"Munashi Sepulveda, your insight is most welcome." A hatch opened in his front and an intricately articulated limb extended to shake Emilio's hand, then reach for hers. "And Dr. Bently, my cousin Philos told me much about you. I hope we'll all have a chance to talk in depth."

Nel hesitated, but took the hand. It was stiff and hummed with electricity. She had been uncomfortable with the idea of senti-comps, but now her own cobbled together electric limb strained beneath the weight of her flesh. Perhaps they were all on some great spectrum of integration. When she smiled, it was genuine. "Thanks, Kasanove. I look forward to getting to know you better."

"Do let me know if there's anything I can do to make your stay more comfortable. It's currently 1632 and we are in the summer phase of our cycle. Perhaps you'd like a tour of the place?"

"I'm going with the medics. I want to be there if he wakes up." Lin left without another word, loping toward the elevator into which her brother's cryotube had descended.

Emilio cast a lingering glance after them, but turned back to the senti-comp. "Thank you for your hospitality, Kasanove. A tour sounds good, but I imagine we'd both enjoy it more after we got our bearings and rest."

Nel flashed him a grateful glance and nodded.

"Well, we'd be happy to show you about when you're more comfortable. I know Lin is all business, but truly, any friend of a Nalawangsa is a friend of mine."

Friend. The word felt strange in Nel's ears. As much as she had balked at the various labels into which Lin tried to squeeze their nebulous relationship, "friend" hadn't been the alternative Nel really wanted. Granted, neither had "enemy."

She reached for her bag, only to find it nestled beside the rest on a small platform hovering behind Kasanove.

The walk through the wide halls was a miniature tour in itself, and despite their earlier protestations, Nel found her steps slowing as they rounded corners, peering at the signs carved in the walls.

"Is this stone?"

"Indeed, Dr. Bently," Kasanove replied, rotating in place to look back at her. "The bones of *Vīrya* were carved from an existing moonlet orbiting Thalassi—the gas giant above."

It looks like silicate. Nel mused, grateful that, beyond his brief answers, Kasanove was content to make most of the journey in silence. They made another few turns before the senti-comp led them into a small chamber at the end of one hall. The floor was carved in a mandala of sorts, and the walls bore well-worn grooves.

"Much of what you've seen houses the satellite's inner workings, mechanical systems etcetera," Kasanove explained. "All the actual living quarters are outside, on the surface. You'll spend your time there. You may find your eyes take some time to adjust."

Nel glanced at Emilio, mouthing "outside?"

His response was cut off, however, when the floor beneath them quivered and began to rise. The elevator was fast, but far smoother than the lurching ascension of those on *The Recursive*.

Or the shafts on Lahifa, Nel recalled with a wince. Her neck and back were still stiff from her and Dar's plummeting attempt at escape. The elevator must have risen several dozen floors, but it was only a few moments later that they rocketed through another iris and into brilliant light.

Nel winced, realizing Kasanove's remark about the light was not hyperbolic. She riffled through her battered field pack, grateful for her unwillingness to ever, truly, clean the thing out, and pulled out a pair of scratched sunglasses. Shoving them over her watering eyes, she finally got a good look around. "Holy shit."

Crisp whitewashed stone buildings jutted from a dense leafy, emerald canopy. The air was heavy with plumeria, and the fresh bite of lemon. Rushing water echoed from countless sources, even on the broad medallion of the elevator pad.

"Dr. Bently, this way—" Kasanove protested as she stepped toward the trees.

"I need a minute," she rasped out. New gravity—real gravity—dragged at her bones, every step pulsing with the adrenaline and endorphins of exercise. She shuffled across the carved pad, relishing the imperfect texture that resonated through her bones. Hot leaves. Baking earth. Ratcheting insects. Cork branches swayed overhead in an honest-to-fuck breeze, humidity hazing the view of dozens of other transports outside the dome. Nel turned slowly in place, grateful the sunglasses hid the tears she blinked away. Peace swept over her like an evening wind, heavy in the way she now recognized as Samsara's ghosts. Did they miss the sun on their skin as much as she?

Kasanove caught Nel's gaze as the archaeologist turned to look up at the nearest building. "I enjoy seeing this place through new eyes, Dr. Bently. It renews my love for its beauty."

She nodded wordlessly, and finally fell into step beside Emilio. The gardens were not so much manicured or contained as they were in balance with the more human, manufactured elements of the satellite. She would always be moved by human ingenuity, by the drive they had to carve not just survival, but beauty from their world. The Los Pobledores leader seemed similarly in awe, though his appreciation was gentler than her own.

White washed flagging cut through the vibrant undergrowth all the way up to a steep ramp. A gleaming rail embedded in the center bore a large metal platform. They stepped aboard and Kasanove's pedestal hummed up and clicked into place, triggering the platform's ascent. If the walk through the fabricated jungle hadn't awed her, the view as they rose a few hundred meters above the towering trees toward the first main level of the stepped pyramid would have. Nel wasn't sure what exactly she expected of Lin's parents, but a private satellite hadn't been in the running.

"Are there many forests where you two were raised?" Kasanove asked.

Emilio chuckled weakly. "Not particularly, more rocks and scrub brush. Nel?"

"A lot—we joke you can't see any of the mountains because there are too many trees. But they aren't like this. Our winter lasts as long as our summer—sometimes longer, it seems."

"I look forward to hearing more about it. Sant enjoyed his time on Earth, as did Lin when she was younger. I think the people fascinated her more."

"Me too, sometimes." She floundered between good manners and honesty, finally settling on vagueness. "I'm very grateful to be here. And see this."

The platform glided smoothly to a halt at the first, broad landing. Here, the ogee arches led into a deep covered walk, which held benches and planted containers. The floors above, each slightly smaller than the lower, climbed for another dozen meters. The whole was topped with a sweeping roof, steeply pointed at each end, the gables carved with intricate designs she recognized from Samsara. Dread popped like a bubble in her gut.

She glanced at Emilio, watching his thoughtful expression flutter from curiosity to concern. Did he, too, wonder if they were walking into the belly of the beast?

Kasanove seemingly didn't notice their hesitation, humming under one of the larger arches into the building itself. "I apologize, Lin only sent word that you would be joining us the day before yesterday. If there's anything missing from your room, just let me know."

"I'm used to pretty cramped quarters," Nel promised. With a last, lingering glance at the impossible engineering outside, she followed the senti-comp into the depths of *Vīrya*. "Three hots and a cot are more than enough."

Kasanove's laugh was oddly reverberant despite his lack of chest cavity. Did senti-comps record the entire breadth of their reactions prior to integration? Or were their voices a fabricated version of their speech? "I think we can manage that. You'll be in our guest wing, near to the Nalawangsa private quarters."

"What about the others on the ships?" Nel wondered abruptly, turning to look back across the network of paths and buildings.

"Though *Vīrya* is only home to approximately ten thousand people at any given day, its actual capacity far exceeds the population of your fleet," Kasanove's tone warmed at the last word. "Such as it is."

"A lot of folks took shuttles elsewhere," Emilio interjected. "Many had ties outside of IDH, or Earth, or saw this as a new beginning, I suppose."

"Regardless, we're happy to host those who haven't yet decided where their path leads," Kasanove demurred. "Those not involved with our continuing investigations will be housed in some of the villages, placed mostly based upon their skillsets." He paused, looking over Nel for a moment before offering: "If you're looking for someone in particular, I can have a copy of our passenger manifest sent to your personal comm."

She flashed a sheepish smile. "Thanks, yeah. My mom." She hesitated, realizing it wasn't, actually just her mother. What about Xand? Or Jem, and Big Rig, and Zeda? Would they even be here at all? Or maybe they hopped the first transport back to Tersa Eth or the *Natasha*-whatever that Jem mentioned. She almost ran into Emilio's back as they halted in front of a broad, mahogany door.

"Munashi Sepulveda, this is your apartment, and Dr. Bently, yours is the next down." Kasanove explained.

The senti-comp's hand emerged again, this time holding a slim piece of metal. "This will serve as your key while you're here. As long as it's on your person, you'll be able to enter most areas as you please, including your chambers. Your private system is loaded with maps of the grounds as well as a variety of entertainment. Should you wish to do any research during your stay, you'll find a substantial database in the library the level below."

"Wow, thanks," Nel answered, already itching to view the maps. The sheer size of the place was astounding. "If I need something, do I just say your name? Like on *Odyssey?*"

"I answer to 'Kasanove,' 'Nove,' or just 'Computer,' if you'd prefer, though I'd rather you didn't. And please make yourselves at home. I will gladly give you a tour, but you are welcome to explore the breadth of the satellite on your own, save for a few of the mechanical sectors for safety reasons."

"You're not gonna tell me to stay out of the west wing or anything?" Nel drawled.

Kasanove's dark eyes fluttered under their lids within the tank. "*Vīrya*'s secrets keep themselves, Dr. Bently. Should you have any questions, you need only ask. Unless you have need of anything else, I'll take my leave. Enjoy your stay, Munashi Sepulveda, Dr. Bently." His pedestal reversed a few meters, then rotated and disappeared down the hall with a faint, comforting hum.

"That was a joke, right?" Nel asked. "About the secrets?"

Emilio snorted, looking over the electronic key in his palm. "I think we've both been around these people long enough to know the unfortunate answer to that." He jerked a nod to his door. "I'm going to get settled. Maybe see you later?"

"Sure thing," she offered two thumbs up and pulled a smile onto her face. Her own arched door opened silently when she tapped the key against its panel. Aside from the incongruous panel, the surface was carved in Samsari, though she wasn't certain of the words.

It opened onto a large room. An open archway led out onto a balcony, screened only with billowing womb-red silk curtains. Carpets covered the flagging. A broad wooden desk was centered on the balcony doorway, and Nel recognized the portal for a holoscreen in the center.

The door whispered shut behind her, automated, despite its traditional design. Soft silence pressed against her ears in the wake of all the ambient sounds emanating from the ship. Relief dropped onto her shoulders.

Further exploration showed her a dark bedroom, with a smaller balcony of its own. A bathroom—complete with both cleanser and traditional bathtub—lay off to the right. After a cautious sniff of her armpit, she decided a bath could wait. Maybe it was the effect of the satellite's night, or just travel itself, but exhaustion weighed on her eyes, despite having woken only a few hours before.

Nel retraced her steps to where she'd left her bags in the entryway, and dug through them until her fingers met smooth wood. She carried the two boxes of ashes carefully back to the broad table just inside the balcony and set them down before slumping into one of the soft chairs.

Their contents were secure, the burned, ground bones still contained in their sealed plastic inside the makeshift urns. She chuckled, softly, at the thought of the reactions her father and Mikey would have to being here, countless lightyears away from Earth. They would have liked the view, she decided.

It was humbler than that from the building's front small courtyard, but was ringed in towering trees. And through their boles, she glimpsed the rooftops of what must have been one of the villages Kasanove mentioned.

And Mom will be here too, tomorrow. Perhaps it was because she had carried her father and Mikey with her all this time, but it was easier to imagine them here, than Mindi. She couldn't picture her mother under these alien skies, breathing air that had never blown across proper Earth. *The Recursive* was a strange, almost liminal space, and as odd as it was to see Mindi navigating those halls, it somehow seemed less alien than this pseudo-Earth.

She watched dappled light play across the boxes, the desk, her own space-sallow skin. Something settled between her shoulder blades as she sat overlooking the village below.

Tomorrow she would visit her mother.

Tomorrow she would check on Dar.

Tomorrow she would meet with the *Vīryan* magistrate or whoever was organizing this next stage. But for today she was still. Today, wind sang through the jungle canopy. Today a sun—not hers, but still gloriously warm and pink—set in the distance.

TWO

Shuttles made their way toward the docks in *Vīrya's* underside, mechanical hail over the iridescent sky. Nel fidgeted with her coffee mug as she watched, wondering which one held her mother. Held all the people she'd come to recognize as home without really noticing.

Which one held Mansur's body?

"Heretic."

She still flinched at the sensation of their words, but more from discomfort than any real surprise. It wasn't clear whether they could read her thoughts, exactly, or if thinking was as speech to them. Sometimes, Nel wondered if she was, truly, mad. If Lin's confession to hearing them too was simply some terrible, shared delusion that bound them together, rooted in the hell they'd crossed together. Made together.

Rising with a soft groan, she dropped the mug in the sink with a clatter. The sounds, organic and loud, were a welcome change from the muted clunk of synthetic plastics and aluminum. She rolled her head, feeling the pull and pop of her neck after sleeping crooked in her desk chair. She'd been too tired to wake for dinner, or even move anywhere more comfortable. Even a hot shower hadn't helped. Casting a longing look at her untouched bed, she tapped her wrist.

A digital packet waited on her comm's dash, complete with map and personal schedule. Her own orientation was scheduled for mid-morning, in just under an hour. She let out a soft groan, wishing she had more time to simply settle and get her bearings.

"Nalawangsas and their briefings," she muttered before heading for the door. If she left now she'd probably get there in time even if she took a wrong turn or two. She faltered at the sight of her wheelchair and crutch in the entryway. Her body ached. Her hips and leg burned with all the extra effort of hauling herself around under mostly-real gravity. But her pride hurt more. If Lin had noticed the new cadence in Nel's step, she hadn't let on, and Nel wasn't about to give her the satisfaction of knowing how much had changed. How broken Nel felt.

"Hey comp—I mean, Kasanove?"

"Good morning, Dr. Bently. Did you sleep well?"

"Like the dead," Nel chuckled, her usual humor feeling wan in the wake of horror. "I was wondering when my mother might dock. Or land. Whatever. I'd like to be there."

"Melinda Bently will arrive at 0430 tomorrow morning at which point she and the other visitors will be briefed and settled in the surrounding residences. You would be free to visit around midday—perhaps in time for lunch."

Nel frowned. What did a senti-comp remember of lunch? Or was his enthusiasm affected for his employers? *Is he servant or slave here?* "Thanks," she hastily responded before stepping into the hall. Fresh air drifted from the open arches at the end of the corridor and she raised her chin. Perhaps when their meeting was over she would have the time— and energy—to explore.

After a few glances at the map—a true map!— displayed on her wrist, she turned left out of her room, following the open corridor farther than they'd gone the day before. The row of open arches ringed the entire floor, it seemed, with ramps leading down at each corner, save for the more ostentatious front. She took the second ramp she came to, grateful for the gentle decline and stunning scenery that gave her a reason to walk slowly, aside from her leg.

Soft purple light was cast over everything, different from the ambient blue haze that had lit the evening sky. She paused just before the path led between the thick trees, looking up at the dome. The distant sun peeked above the tree tops and the blue lip of the gas giant slowly disappeared on the opposite horizon. Reassurance edged in at the corners of her mind, at the sight of two orbs in the sky again. *Except this time, we're the moon.*

The path wound gently into the forest—jungle, really, if she was being honest—branching a few times, though each was well marked. The light here was dim, filtered through the dense canopy and the dome high above. With another glance at the map, she hooked right, heading toward the cluster of buildings she could see from her windows. After a few dozen meters she emerged in a small glade, outfitted with worn limestone flagging and a handful of benches.

To her surprise, Zachariah was there, kneeling, eyes closed, on his unfurled sajjāda. His long black hair held more grey in the temples, and his usually smooth, tan face boasted a beard. His eyes blinked gently open as her prosthetic scraped against the stone.

"Good morning, Nel!"

She flashed a smile. "Hey Zachariah. I'm sorry to interrupt."

"You're not. I finished Maghrib earlier, and I was just enjoying the wind. Isn't it beautiful?"

"It is," she agreed. "Strange. But beautiful."

Zachariah rose, carefully rolling his prayer rug, tan hands smoothing the edges meticulously as he went. When he was through, he rose and offered an open arm for an embrace. "Are you a hugger?"

She laughed and nodded, squeezing his shoulders for a moment. She had forgotten he was a good head and a half taller. "Good to see you in real life," she remarked, steadying her uneven gait on his forearm as she stepped back. "May I ask— isn't Maghrib for night?"

"Sundown, more specifically. If I'm lucky enough to have a proper schedule, I choose to pray with my family back home. Others use their own day cycle. And like fasting, if we're under the stress of travel, or ill, there is lee-way." He gestured to the path ahead. "You're heading to the briefing?"

She dug her fingers into the sore meat of her left thigh. "Figured I'd give myself some extra time in case I got wrapped up in ogling the scenery. You'll be there?"

He nodded. "Only due to my previous involvement, I believe. Beyond that, I'll simply be helping the new arrivals adjust for a week." His eyes were gentle and sad as he looked over her. "It's hard, feeling unmoored."

"Preaching to the choir," she muttered with a humorless laugh. "Well, talking to you did me some good. However reluctant I am about it all. I'm sure you'll help these people too. Want to walk with me?"

He lifted the rug in his hand. "You go on ahead, I've got to return this to my apartment. But when they've finished telling us this is all totally fine and normal and not to worry," he chuckled wryly, "I'd love to catch up."

She watched him disappear back the way she had come. *He prays with his family.* They could synch a calendar with Earth's. She'd known people must have kept track, maybe even with some cosmic universal clock wall. *This whole time, it could have been dawn or midnight or summer or fall, I'd never have known.* It probably wouldn't have erased the yawning loneliness in her chest, but it might have softened its sting. First thing after the meeting, she would find out how to synch her comm to Earth's time.

Deep bells sounded from just beyond the trees, making her jump and turn. It felt like a lifetime since she'd heard actual bells. Her comm reminded her that, if she didn't hurry, she'd be late, even given her early start. Grumbling, she set off in an uneven speedwalk.

The meeting was held in a large stone building in the currently empty village's center. Like everything, the village was carved from the original asteroid's surface, but looked nothing like the bleak, pocked surface of Morphose. The buildings were simple, square, spigots sprouting from the roof corners. Like her rooms, most of the space was open air, with swaths of recycled fabric as sunshades. The dwellings weren't big, but they were a far sight better than the apartments on the *Recursive.* Nel searched for a familiar face among the people bustling through the nearby doors in preparation for the new arrivals. Instead, she found loose white and tan clothing that looked halfway between digging clothes and a uniform. *So Vīrya has staff, then.* Logically, it had to have staff, someone needed to tend the trees and sweep the paths and man the recycler, surely, but the idea that this was owned by Lin's family—not the giant conglomerate of IDH, like *Odyssey*—still blew her mind.

"Excuse me, miss," An older man with an open, unremarkable face peered through the door. "We're starting."

Nel grimaced at the honorific and ducked inside after him, making a beeline for the rear-most row of benches. Emilio caught her eye and shoved over, making room for her. She flashed a smile of thanks and plopped down next to him.

The room was bright, though Nel couldn't see a discernable light source. With the wind through the windows, and the smell of distant sunbaked stone, she could almost pretend they were still on Earth. A few rows up and over, Lin sat ramrod straight in her chair. Her eyes were fixed on the displays, tension betrayed only by the rapid tapping of a single finger. She was out of uniform this time, and without bloodstains, but still showed the fatigue of battle.

Nel was seized with the impulse to take that nervous hand, grip it in her until they both were calm. Shoving the idea away as quickly as it came, she nudged Emilio with an elbow. "Do you think they'll address what's happening on Earth? When we can go home?"

Emilio's lips thinned, but he didn't answer.

"If everyone could please settle." A holoscreen hovered behind the man who had welcomed them. Several badges and what must have been his surname decorated his beige, sleeveless jumpsuit. His light brown skin looked suspiciously suntanned and his shaggy hair was loosely pushed back, but not gelled. For someone in uniform, Nel found him reassuringly casual.

He smiled, hands gesturing to the few dozen gathered personnel. "Welcome to *Vīrya*. I'm Dan Huang, First Safety Officer and Alder of the civilian contingent here. If you have any issues I'll be able to help or find the person who can."

"Firstly, *Vīrya* is a residential, civilian moonlet. It currently houses 9,704, most of whom are of the scientific persuasion," he cracked a smile. "As members of the refugee fleet from Earth continue to arrive, however, we anticipate our numbers to increase dramatically. Maps, directories, and other general orientation information can be found on your personal computers. Many of you have already met Kasanove, our resident senti-comp and steward of *Vīrya*. He manages all technical aspects here and is happy to help as well.

"Due to the events that have led many of us here, however, and the dangerous nature of the signal that caused the death of several people, we will still be implementing a station-wide comm blackout. Comms within the station itself are permitted, once your personal devices have been inspected and cleared."

Nel raised her hand.

Huang's eyes settled on her. "I'll answer questions in a moment."

"I was just hoping we could get an update on ah, Terrestrial affairs? I understand the need for a blackout, but a lot of us have been out of the loop since Earth and would probably appreciate some news."

Weariness strained Huang's gentle features. "Earth is still functioning much the same as it was prior to our mission there. Those who were evacuated are listed now as refugees or freelancers."

Nel frowned. "I'm sorry if I'm belaboring this, but my understanding of how you all run things out here is a bit limited and last I checked IDH had its hands in every fucking thing. There's a bunch of other groups though, so whose territory does Earth fall into? Now that IDH is the big bad?"

"We're working to better understand the current situation of Earth, though our abilities are understandably limited with the blackout. I assure you, any pertinent news from Earth will be included in our weekly bulletin. Now, if I could continue?"

Nel snapped her mouth shut and sank back into the seat. It was a half answer, more band-aid over the bullet wound of losing her home, but for the time being, Nel allowed herself relief. The planet was still there and soon she and Mindi could return to Earth. To Jasper Hill. *To home.*

He tapped a button and the holoscreen flickered into a schedule board. "Many will relocate to their previous stations, planets, and ships of residence, or find a new place if returning doesn't suit. Of course, the Nalawangsa family assures me that any who are more permanently displaced are welcome for as long as they need. Most of you will be given work shifts based on your skillset, however there are some who we hope will help us in continuing our investigations. The directory of assignments should be loaded onto your comms..." he tapped his own screen twice, "now."

Nel glanced down at her wrist, eyes narrowed on the list, searching for the kitchen staff. She took passing note of familiar names as she scrolled. Presumably, her role here would be much the same as it had been on *The Recursive,* at least until they sent her back to Earth.

INVESTIGATION
Lin Nalawangsa,
Dar Nalawangsa
Lissa Hugo-Sanchez
Emilio Sepulveda
Annalise Bently

Fuck. "I'm sorry," Nel interrupted, thoroughly not sorry at all, "but Harris is in custody. I'm sure you have to duke it out with the remnants of IDH, and probably involve some space precinct, but do the rest of us really have to be here? Beyond just regrouping and organizing everyone's flights off this rock?"

Her words were biting, more teeth than she really felt, but when she stared at Lin she found teeth were all she had, her fury desperate to sink fangs into the other woman as much as her heart once had.

"Off this rock?" Lin's voice cut through the background murmur that arose with Nel's second interruption.

"Look, I'm not ungrateful to be here and, you know, not have warship guns trained on me for once," she barreled on. Emilio tugged at her arm, but she ignored him. She didn't look away from Huang, but every cell in her body had swiveled toward Lin. Even if she was unable to look at the terrible perfection of her ex-girlfriend, she sure could still yell at her.

"Then what are you saying, Dr. Bently?" Huang asked, lips thin with annoyance.

"I'd like to go home." Her voice cracked over the word. She could barely remember what her house smelled like, or the scent of baking pine needles and the tick of her stove, and the creak of the second stair. But she knew what it felt like to remember those things. To be so familiar with a place its groans and whispers were like her own body's. "I can't be the only one."

The room fell to stillness and out of the hypervigilant corner of her eye, she saw Lin look down at her long fingers, clenched in her lap.

"I'm sure many share your sentiment, Dr. Bently," the alder began.

"You can't go home. No one can, just yet." Lin stood, clearly having collected her imperious thoughts. "I'm aware that out of concern for everyone's mental wellbeing, my brother acted under a degree of secrecy, but I believe we're past the point of such confidentiality being helpful. You're right—Harris is indeed in custody and will face justice for his involvement. But he wasn't acting alone, and there are many people out there who still subscribe to IDH's...values. There are far too many pieces missing still, and we need every hand to help us find them. When it is possible, I promise everyone who wishes to do so, will be aided in returning home. But until then we will keep you safe."

"Safe? You think you're keeping us safe? You've practically imprisoned us on your family satellite."

"Alright, Nel," Emilio interjected, gripping her wrist, "I think you need to calm down."

"I am calm!" she spat, glaring at him.

"Well from where I'm sitting, you're about to cause a level 10 domestic in a rather public briefing and I'm sure none of us really want to be in the middle of it." He stared her down, dark, steady eyes rooting her in place.

Finally, she let the fight fall from her shoulders. "Then send me the Cliff-notes." She shoved out of her seat and stomped around the rear of the room and out the door. She wasn't ready to face Lin, or get back to the proverbial grindstone, but Emilio was right; witnessing her most recent tantrum wasn't fair to the rest of the sorry people still ensnared in the Nalawangsa net.

She was stalking back down the deserted promenade when a call stopped her in her tracks.

"Nel?"

Heat flashed up Nel's spine at the voice, and she tried to force her face into something more polite than disgust. Judging by the sudden frown on Lin's face when Nel turned around, she failed.

"Would you be willing to talk? Maybe try and clear the air?" Lin's eyes were black, filled with every dark secret the universe had yet to share.

Abso-fucking-lutely not. "I appreciate the big gesture and the shiny ships and cinematic rescue, but honestly, it's probably best for everyone if we just...don't. Don't talk, don't see each other. Don't share—" she waved a hand and realized, too late, that it was shaking, "—space."

"*Vīrya's* big, but it's not like I'll be able to avoid you when we're working on the same mission. And," Lin reminded, "we are working toward the same goal."

"I'll make you a deal," Nel bit out. She hated it. Hated every little bit of it. But her mom needed a safe return home more than Nel needed revenge. "I'm bad at saving the world and you've proven you have no interest in doing so. But it's what we're supposed to do. So, I guess we can at least try."

"And after?"

Only Lin Nalawangsa would have the absolute arrogance to ask about "after" when Nel hadn't even agreed to anything beyond a very strained, professional "now." All the confessions and fury and adoration she dreamt of throwing at the other woman clotted in her throat, tangling with one another in some unrecognizable lump she couldn't speak past. Apparently, her grinding molars and staring contest with the remaining emblem on Lin's chest were answer enough.

The officer nodded once, curtly. "Well, you have your deal." Lin backed toward the meeting hall, face strained with what she probably hoped was a smile. It looked more like nausea. "It's good to see you. To know you're alive."

Nel watched her turn and march, chin up, back into the building. It was only when the door clicked softly shut behind, that Nel realized she had never actually answered.

THREE

Nel followed the directions through the now-bustling street. With the uniform architecture and colors, it wavered between compound and village, but in the time it took her to walk from one end to the other, flags had been hung, flower boxes put out, and curtains aired. Cypress lined the promenade, interspersed with stone planters overflowing with vines and vegetables. Like on *Odyssey* and *The Recursive*, lines of light edged the walkways, but here the vibe was more mood lighting than emergency generator power.

She glanced around at the faces, searching for familiarity, and finding only a few. New names, new neighbors. But, already, she saw people introducing themselves, helping one another carry furniture and boxes, laughing over confusion between languages. Life always clawed its way through blast burns and bullet holes. Soon, maybe, it would look homey, each family carving their identity from the matching facades.

"Anna!"

Her mother waved from the narrow entrance of one of the side streets. Mindi's hair was loose, drifting about her face in the faint breeze. She waved again, then jogged the last few steps between them.

Nel let out a sigh of relief as her arms wrapped around her mother's shoulders. "Hey, Mom."

"Hey, honey." Mindi gave a final mighty squeeze and stepped back. "You settle in alright?"

"Eh," Nel wagged her hand in a so-so motion and nodded down the street to where her map said Mindi was assigned. "You? It looks cute."

"A bit English cottage meets villa for my tastes," her mom remarked, pitching her voice low, "but much more space. Come see."

Nel fell into step beside her mom, looking side to side at the colorful array of people and belongings passing through the open doorways.

Like most of the dwellings, Mindi's place was a single ground floor apartment, with an outdoor stairway leading up the side to what looked like a rooftop patio. The walls were whitewashed and smoothed to a stucco-like finish and the large casement windows were flung wide to let in the soft air. Mindi led her inside and set about the almost-familiar motions of setting the rehydrator. "Take a look around, I've only just barely unpacked. Coffee? It's real."

"Please. Thanks." Nel cast another glance at her mother, making sure she was, in fact, really there, before taking a turn around the main room. It was open, the eating area and lounge one large space with a partially separated annex off the back for the kitchen. At least the cooking area was larger than what they'd shared on *The Recursive*.

Mindi had only been allowed a few bags, of course, and though Nel had grown fond of the eclectic furniture they had used aboard the ship, she realized, looking around, that almost none of it had actually been theirs. The carpet had come, and a few other items. New curtains drifted in the windows, and Nel caught the edge of one, rubbing the soft, nubbly fabric in her calloused hand. They were a warm dove grey, echoing her mother's former minimalist style, but somehow working here, too. Like the rug, so very Earth, and yet fitting among the asteroid's carved surface. Like Mindi.

Anger flashed in her chest.

"Anna?"

"What?" She turned, releasing a fist she hadn't realized was clenched around the curtain. "Sorry."

Her mom stepped up next to her, holding two steaming mugs. She pressed one into Nel's other hand with a tired smile. "It's a lot, huh?"

Nel wrapped her hands around the hot ceramic and nodded with a grimace. "Been a lot for a while."

"Want to sit upstairs or down?"

"Down. The jungle is really beautiful, it's just," she heaved a sigh. "Well. A lot."

They settled into the two chairs by the window, Mindi's legs crossed the ankles, Nel's splayed wide, mismatched. The light played across them both, flickering as the trees outside swayed. For a moment, curtains drawn, warm air, the sound of people chatting, laughing, arguing outside, they could have been anywhere. They could have been home.

Mindi's head tilted back, bright eyes scanning the ceiling, then shifting down to take in her daughter. "I don't suppose it's over yet."

"I don't—" Nel jerked one shoulder in a shrug. "No. Not yet. But you should be able to go home soon. I hope."

Mindi's face softened. Under proper light, not the sallow, artificial spectrum of the ship's day-night cycles, there were half a dozen new lines around her eyes. She shifted forward and touched Nel's hand. "Honey, it's not me I'm worried about."

Nel scoffed. "You kidding? Of course you want to go home—this place is pretty but it's not...real. It looks it, but you can feel that it's all just a bit off. You can't tell me you don't miss your book club and your walking group and Aunt Kara and Paula and Tim. Betsy's house in Winooski."

"Of course I miss them, and when the time comes, I'll rush back. But I also have a book club here. Vera and I play cards every Thursday. I can pick up shifts once I'm settled in. It's not home, and

I'll never say it is, but I'm ok. But I don't think you are."

Nel swallowed a gulp of coffee, sputtering as it seared her throat. "It's fine. I'm fine. But I guess I just thought we might be able to go back now. I'm worried about all this shit—stuff, sorry—that I wasn't before. Who's watering my aloe? The thing survived me, so I guess it should be fine with a few years of neglect. Is my truck rusting into the driveway? Or maybe it got sold off to some asshole who smashed it into a tree on that curve on Route 12. I worry about everything left unfinished there. A whole life and I just—"

Mindi's fingers tightened around hers, and her expression grew fierce. "Something we learned, when the virus swept the planet while you were gone, and we were at the mercy of whoever made the vaccines—the IDH I suppose. We can't wait around not living just because we were handed a life we didn't expect. This is my life. Your life. It won't always be, and believe me, I pray that this will all be over soon, but right now we both have to make the best of it. In this new home-away-from-home."

Nel squeezed her mother's hand, head dropping until her forehead pressed against their gripped fingers. "I wish I'd gotten your strength. Bravery."

"Nonsense," Mindi countered, voice dropping back into its usual matter-of-fact tone. "If you were fearless then we'd really have something to reckon with."

Nel chuckled weakly, sitting back.

"Honestly, though, Anna," Mindi promised, "I learned how to be strong watching you. I didn't have an easy childhood, but I think in many ways the world was harder on you. Even if it sometimes was because you dared it to be."

Nel didn't know what to do with that, both an honest assessment and a compliment too high for her to accept. Instead, she looked down at her comm, as if she cared what time it was. A shriek of laughter sounded across the street, followed by a stampede of little footfalls. "So, you, ah, got in this morning? Four?"

"I suppose—it was afternoon for the ship's time zone. I've been running on caffeine, helping sort out the requisitions from the ships and reallocating furniture, home goods, all that, left over from those who departed for other places—stations." Mindi's nose wrinkled. "I will say, I don't know how you get used to the colloquialisms."

"I don't," Nel snorted. "Dar was bitching about how I add 'space' to everything."

"How is he?"

"Stable. I guess. I hate medical terms. So vague."

"Clinical," her mother agreed. "But stable is good. Is he conscious yet?"

"Maybe now. They had him traveling in medical cryo or something. I guess that lowers the risk of stress."

"That's how you arrived," Mindi murmured, looking down, expression suddenly brittle. "After your leg."

Nel blinked. Of course her mother was taking all this in stride. These changes were nothing compared to standing over her burnt, comatose daughter's bedside on an effectively alien spaceship. "I'm sorry. Like, really, really sorry, Mom."

"I'm not. You're here."

Something chimed beside the door and Mindi rose with an excited smile. "That'll be the food delivery. My waistline won't thank me, but I'm so happy to be done with rations."

"Nothing's wrong with your waistline, Mom," Nel muttered, following her out to the street. A young man with a pink-striped afro had parked a small train of hovering cargo platforms and was checking the list on his comm. "Mrs. Bently, I didn't know they put you near us again," he greeted, looking up with a beaming smile. "Aunty Georgia is gonna be happy."

"Until she gets to chapter fourteen, but don't you tell her I said so," Mindi laughed. "Emeka, this is my daughter, An—um, Nel. Honey, this is Emeka Opatayo, nephew to one of my book club girls. He's the one that helped me move that couch when I first got aboard the ship."

"Nice to meet you. Thanks for looking after my Mom," Nel gave an awkward wave.

"Need help unloading, Mrs. Bently?"

"I got it," Nel interrupted, jerked her chin at the other crates stacked high on the platforms behind him. "Looks like you got your hands full with the rest of those."

"Oh you probably have a thousand better things to do," Mindi waved her off, tugging the crate off the small hovering cargo platform.

"I don't think anyone would argue there's something more important than helping your mom unload the groceries," she countered with a chuckle, grabbing the other crate. "It was good to meet you, Emeka."

"You too Miss. See ya around, Mrs. Bently!"

Nel watched him go, wondering, suddenly, where Xand had ended up. They looked about the same age. *I'll look him up when I get back to my room,* she told herself. She hoped he was here, among the trees and open sky, not sequestered in some ship's hospital room without proper light. For his sake. Or maybe she was projecting and wanting a small reminder that at least someone had survived.

Tightening her hands around the crate's handles, she lurched into motion, following her mother back inside. Mindi was already digging into the first crate, eyeing the contents and her available storage.

Nel chuckled and dropped the other crate beside the first with a thump. "Why don't I unload everything onto the counter and you can organize?"

"Good plan," Mindi agreed, throwing the kitchen cabinet doors wide. Soon the counter was overflowing with dry and canned goods and her mother had tackled the cabinet system with the single-minded efficiency of a culinary tactician.

"Here's a bag—looks like quinoa?" Nel remarked, plopping the bag beside another filled with rice. "Holy shit, Mom! Peaches!"

FOUR

When Nel left her mother's apartment, the distant sun was slung low in the sky, almost eclipsed by the swollen curve of the planet above. *Thalassi,* she reminded herself. Though Dar's remark on her not learning the proper names hadn't bothered her, Emilio's dig at her pronunciation of Papadopoulos stung. *Even if he did turn out to be Dar's megalomaniac uncle.*

She rounded a bend and drew up short.

Kasanove waited in the center of the small glade, gleaming cylinder draped in a cloth, like a mockery of a shawl. The reflected sunset dimmed the faint projection of an approximation of his face. He rotated slightly in place, though she suspected his visual sensors encircled his housing. "Evening, Dr. Bently."

"Hey." Nel gave an awkward two-handed wave and drew up beside him. A break in the trees provided a more extensive view of the swirling gas clouds and gleaming arc of the disappearing sun. "Hell of a sight."

"It's beautiful, isn't it?"

"Yeah, kind of is." And she found she meant it. As an archaeologist, she'd grown comfortable with 'strange' not equating to 'ugly,' but the weight of all the terrible things she'd witnessed made it hard to see the beauty. Nel peered through the shields. "So, we're orbiting that planet then?"

"We are." The digital reproduction of his voice was warm, as if delighted by her curiosity. "Have you explored the gardens yet?"

"No. I wasn't sure how, ah," she patted her leg. "Well. You know."

"Everything is fairly level and the paths are accessible to me. It's one of my favorite spots, actually, this time of day."

Nel laughed. "Couldn't you like, I don't know, tilt the whole thing so it was always this time of day? Or something?"

"We'd lose the artificial gravity."

"Oh shit—shoot, sorry," Nel flinched, realizing she should really park her language. "I didn't notice it spinning when we docked—that's how the gravity works, right?"

"It is. During landing it's difficult to see, since your trajectory has to sync with the rotation. Besides, if we maintained the solar reflectors at this angle it'd destroy the plants circadian rhythms, I think."

"Right." She glanced around them. "Where to?"

Two ramps curved down, following the outer wall of the towers flanking the doors. One led into the rear of the manor, to what looked like an intimate outdoor dining area. They took the other, to the right, that wound into a lush cluster of full sun plants.

"My mom would be wild over the plumeria. She always tried to grow them when I was kid but never had any luck. Rocky soils and tough winters."

"I've never seen winter," Kasanove remarked, staring—did senti-comps stare?—out at the expanse of the private satellite. "Though the pictures make it look beautiful."

"It is, if you don't have to go anywhere. Then moving it's a bitch—sorry, hassle."

Humor crackled through his voice. "You don't have to censor your language around me. Goodness knows Dar never did."

"Lin was a bit surprised by my vocabulary sometimes, I think. And my mother has many opinions on it, of course." Nel chuckled. "You've been with the family for a while, then?"

"Indeed. I came to *Vīrya* not long after Lin began studying. I originally worked with Sant's family, though. Before I was integrated."

Integrated. It was odd to hear the term usually applied to her eventual biomechanical prosthetic being used to refer to something so drastic. She shot a glance at Kasanove, humming along beside her. Is this what had inspired Mansur? Watching the utter transformation of his family—what? Servant?

Perhaps Kasanove noticed her look, or the tension steadily pulling on the silence between them. "You must have questions and opinions on all of this. You're welcome to share them with me."

"Silence."

Nel stilled, words faltering into quiet.

"Pardon?" Kasanove asked, spinning with a hum to look back at her. "You look distressed, Dr. Bently."

The observation sent a thrill of fear through her. Senti-comps were human. She had come to that conclusion over the past few months. Despite the occasional HAL-esque eeriness, they weren't computers. They were as fallible as any human. "I guess I just have a lot on my mind," she explained. What else could she say?

"Do let me know if I can help. I'm happy to answer any questions."

Yeah, are all you guys in cahoots with Dar's evil uncle? Polyana hadn't been, Nel mused, and neither had Phil, theoretically. "I'm just trying to make sense of it all. Overwhelming." Nel glanced around the towering trees. How much did the family already know? How much was safe to disclose? Nel suddenly wished Dar had thought to give them a shared story, instead of fucking off into unconsciousness.

She was quiet for another moment, their path winding deeper and darker. The air was only slightly cooler, and the deep shadows lent the illusion of entering some secret jungle. In a way, she supposed, they had. Nel wished briefly she hadn't left her chair in her room. *This is my PT for the day,* she decided. At least Kasanove's pace was closer to a museum crawl than a power walk. After another moment, Nel formulated her line of inquiry and summoned a small amount of courage. "May I ask you about that? The integration, I mean. Or is it considered rude?"

"I don't find it rude. Some would. I think the process, and the science and ethics behind it make many people uncomfortable."

"That why half the time you're hidden away in space stations and control rooms?" Nel asked.

"Yes. It benefits both of us—humans aren't constantly confronted with the reality of what we are, and we don't have to contend with their discomfort at our very existence."

Nel's heart burned with the memory of hatred flung at her for daring to exist as a gay woman. "Yeah, I hear that part for sure."

"I was under the impression that you and my colleague Philos were close. Did you never ask him?" The path branched just before the forest, and they followed the fork into the treeline. It was now dark enough that faint lines of light edged the walkway, casting a soft green-blue glow across the stone.

"Not really. I think I pretended it was because I didn't want to offend him," she hazarded. "But you're right. It made me uncomfortable. I was scared of the answer."

"And you're no longer scared?"

"I'm more curious than scared. And with all the horrific things happening in this world now, I'd rather know the limits of integration. The more I know, the better prepared I am." The image of the mass of flesh and bone in *V Drugoye Mesto* flickered through her consciousness. "Theoretically, at least."

"Then ask away."

With the open invitation, came a wave of uncertainty. Did she even know what questions she wanted to ask? "Integration, as you called it. Is it— is it a choice? Did you each choose to…transform? I apologize if I'm using the wrong words. Just tell me if I am."

"You're not. And the simple answer is yes, of course. There are many ethical theories on digital transhumanism—the technical term behind the integration of a human mind into a supercomputer. But most of us wait until living in a flesh body is," the echo of an expression roved across his physical features, though the digital face remained neutral, "no longer optimal."

"That makes sense."

The canopy opened a bit, just enough to shed pink light across the glade. In the center was a carefully curated birch bonsai forest. Nel gazed at the miniature stream winding through the gnarled black and white trunks, burbling over cobbles turned into boulders by perspective. She faltered over her next question. "Do you ever miss it?"

He didn't answer for a moment, perhaps running through the entire recorded history of his existence. "Often. But I possess the knowledge and processing capabilities to remind myself why I chose this, why I never could have done what I wanted—done what I needed—with the form in which I was born. Missing something that was is not equivalent with regretting my choice."

She regretted a lot of choices—and many things that weren't even her choice to make. But could she say she wished she weren't where she was now?

"I like this fountain quite a bit," Kasanove interjected. "I've always loved *Betula papyrifera*, though they won't grow large in this climate. Our gardener seals them into a cold biome dome for part of the year, to simulate winter. It'd be quite the undertaking to do so on a larger scale, but still I dream."

Nel's shoulders dropped with relief at a far safer topic. "We had a stand of paper birches behind my house. Daffodils too, scattered throughout the roots. I always thought they looked ghostly. In a nice way, though." She cleared her throat. "Thank you. For your candidness. I've always been curious about people. And I'm ashamed that it took a while for me to apply that label to senti-comps."

"Few ever do." He rotated in place until his digital face was in line with hers. "We want you to know you are welcome here. As Dar's friend. As an ally."

"I doubt I'm his friend," Nel snorted.

The delicate digital eyebrows shot up. "Has he spoken more than barked orders at you?"

"I guess."

"Then you're certainly a friend. That boy will order himself into a corner one of these days, if he is not careful." The thin metal extension Kasanove used as a limb unfurled and pointed in the direction of another path. "Are you able to continue on?"

Nel rubbed hard fingers over the seam between her flesh and her prosthetic. She was about to say she could probably do another few minutes, but her comm let out a sharp beep. She frowned down at the readout.

Sender: Jonathan Livingston
Subject: Colab

She shot Kasanova a surreptitious look. Either he was very good at faking it, or her comm was still connected to the untapped Founders' network. Knowing Dar's paranoia, it was hopefully the latter. She longed to open it, but the possibility of a senti-comp—even one as seemingly friendly as Kasanove—reading over her shoulder, sent a thrill of warning up her spine. *Walking. Right.* "Sorry, I still find all the comm notifications distracting. I'm actually feeling a bit run down—adjusting to the new leg and traveling and all that. Would you mind if I headed back?"

"Of course, it's no problem. I'd like to finish my circuit—can you find your own way?"

"Sure thing." She flashed a smile she hoped looked sincere, even through a few thousand photon receptors. "Thanks, though. I hope we can talk again."

"Indeed. Make yourself at home while you're with us. Knowledge isn't proprietary here, and the library is yours to use. There's a smaller study there and you might find some interesting information on my technology there."

"Awesome. I'll do that." An embarrassed flush warmed her cheeks, as if a teacher had directed her to a book on sex ed. She headed back the way they had come, only to turn again. Her nerves jangled and her mouth was suddenly dry. "Hey Kasanove?"

"Yes, Dr. Bently?"

"You guys have any beer?"

A chuckle drifted through the jungle, emanating both from his housing and the tiny speakers that must be embedded throughout the satellite. "I'll send a selection up to your residence shortly."

"Thanks." she let out a rueful laugh before retreating back up the path. The air was gentle, and any other time she would allow herself to stroll slowly through the boles. With her brain churning with the mysterious message and ethics of integration, she couldn't focus enough to even appreciate the return walk. Could Kasanove hear her out here, if he weren't with her? She wanted to like him, but everything in her body told her something big was missing from this puzzle, and it might just be what killed her. She was distracted enough, at least, to make it back to her room without dwelling on the growing phantom pangs shooting from her non-existent calf.

The message passed security or it wouldn't have been received at all, theoretically. *And Samsara's ghosts aren't deadly. Just...clumsy.* The rationalization did nothing to assuage her distrust, nor did the distrust do anything to dampen her gnawing curiosity.

A crate awaited her just outside her door, filled with a selection of a dozen different ales. First sign of conflict and what did she do? Order alcohol. "Yeah, I don't have a problem," she muttered. Hauling the drinks inside, she deposited eleven of the twelve bottles in her cooling unit and slumped onto the plush couch with the remaining beer in hand. Her body ached, strung between exhaustion and anticipation. The ceiling's angled patterns of dim phosphorescence swirled overhead, a mimicry of her thoughts.

The bottle opened with a familiar crack, carbonation fizzing over the mouth before she tipped it to her own. It was skunky and thin but dampened her raw nerves. Before she could think better of it, she confirmed that the message had passed their rudimentary security checks and opened it.

Hey Bent,
Hope you're doing alright. Heard there was some fire and brimstone that we can thank you for. Anyway, I have a client who's worked with you before. They're interested in collaborating on a project. Can't promise big payoffs, but says it aligns with what you're working on.

No hard feelings about the hostage thing, by the way. Was kind of hot, and besides, a bitch has to do what a bitch has to do. Lemme know if you're interested.

Stay cool,
-A

Client? Hostage? Nel glanced back at the sender with a soft laugh. *Jonathan Livingston.* Figures Andy Gull would have a punny alias. If Nel was right, Andy's original client had been Phil, but why wouldn't he reach out himself? Nel's list of ex-coworkers was almost as long as her list of ex-lovers with a substantial overlap, if she was being honest. As a result, many of her former co-workers were on the other side of very burnt bridges.
Like Lin.
She closed her eyes. Every morning, she woke smelling the smoke from that particular bridge

igniting. *And it took Dar's shuttle, Polyana, and my right leg with it.* That was an even more distressing thought to shove out of her mind. Nel's chest turned to fire with the mere idea of the other woman, and she could never tell if the sensation building there was a scream or a sob or actual fucking lava.

Gritting her teeth against the heat, she closed the message down. She should send it straight to Emilio and make it someone else's problem. Whatever they wanted out of her would probably involve both of them anyway, and the security risk was astronomical. If an ally found them, so could their enemies.

Still, the thought of bringing one more piece into this complex puzzle was exhausting. For now it could sit in her inbox. She could keep it to herself for a few days while she thought it over. It wasn't like she intended to reply.

FIVE

A knock came the next evening, as Nel was cleaning up after super. The kitchenette was similar enough to the one on *Recursive* that she managed not to burn too much. She wiped her hands and headed through the foyer. Emilio offered a small wave when she opened the door.

"Oh, hey," she offered, nerves spiking up her back. They had barely spoken since the heated conversation over Dar's unconscious body. Certainly not about Lin or Harris or anything of substance. The week had been too busy, frantic, really, she had told herself. Now, she realized it felt more like mutual avoidance.

"Hey." His smile was tired, but genuine. "I found a back ramp up to the rooftops. Wanna come?"

Nel's shoulders relaxed an inch or two. "Yeah, I really would. One sec." Ducking back to her kitchen, she grabbed a beer from her cooling unit before stepping into the hall.

Emilio glanced at the bottle, eyes crinkling slightly.

"Kasanove did me a solid," she explained, cheeks flushing as she waggled the bottle.

His laugh was soft, but kind. He led them around the corner, past the ramp she'd taken for the meeting. A doorway cut to the left, where a narrow, steeper ramp led up to the topmost storey of the stepped pyramid.

Nel let out a low whistle, turning a slow circle to take in the panorama. "Have to admit it's pretty."

"It is. Found this spot when I took myself on a little tour."

"Didn't feel like bothering Kasanove?"

Emilio's eyes flicked sidelong at her. "Something like that." He eased himself down, one-handed, to sit on the low wall surrounding the rim of the rooftop, swinging his legs over to dangle.

Nel did the same, albeit much slower. When she had settled and popped the top of her beer, Emilio nodded his chin toward the view.

"Figured you'd like it up here. Saw you up on the inn roof enough nights, while your kids were out drinking."

Nel snorted. "Never could miss a good view."

"Lording over the land? Makes you feel big?" he hazarded.

She tapped her heel on the wall thoughtfully. The glass sweated against her hand. Whatever rolled over her tongue was unfamiliar, sour as it was bitter, but it was beer. Beyond, the view approximated summer's sunseet, if Earth had been lit, not by sun, but the belly of a massive emerald-blue moon. "More like makes me feel small. Looking at everyone down there with these complicated lives. Makes my problems feel small."

"I think all our problems could stand to be a bit smaller, these days." He fished a slim, hand rolled cigarette from his breast pocket, along with a battered matchbook. The faded cardboard was printed with the name of his restaurant in Chile.

Nel's brows arched. "Never seen you smoke before."

"Rarely, anymore. They frown on open flames on spaceships, you know." He lit the end carefully before pinching the match tip between his fingers. He held the cigarette out.

She chuckled and ruefully shook her head, holding up the beer. "I think one vice is enough for me these days."

"I used to sneak my father's Kents," he confessed, taking a drag, edges of his eyes tight as he focused on the flavor. Or feelings. Memories. "That's what made me feel big."

The night settled over them, dampening the air, muffling the clink of her beer, the faint crackle of his cigarette's cherry. She couldn't call it a wind, but the air moved, eddying. "So. Harris, huh?"

"Harris." The crows' feet tightened further, and he let out his breath in a long, low sigh. "He was once called Renato."

"When did you figure it out?" she asked, affording him the privacy of looking down, but not that of silence. "I know you said it was while we were on Earth but," she shrugged, "How'd you keep it to yourself?"

"Some of us have a step between thinking and speaking, Bently," he teased. His face sobered and he flicked ash from his cigarette. "It was a slow realization, but I was supposed to keep an eye on him anyway, and the more I watched the more I saw. He had surgical work done, of course, and the years we've been apart have been longer than they've numbered, at least for me. By the time I knew for certain, we'd received word they were extracting us."

"But all that time on the ship. Working with Dar. Why'd you never mention it?"

"I hadn't decided how I wanted to feel about it. And who he is didn't matter," his shoulders lifted in a shrug. "Brother or not, he was our enemy in that moment."

"Cold," she muttered. "Guess I'm glad I'm not on your bad side anymore."

"I said it didn't matter. Not that I didn't love him. Though," he nudged her boot with his, "I imagine you understand that a bit more now."

Nel grimaced. "Wish I didn't."

"Are you angry that I messaged her?"

A frown flashed over Nel's face and she glanced over. "I mean, it worked out."

"Sure. Still, you could be angry. You've been rather uncharacteristically quiet since we got here. Aside from your contribution to the meeting."

Her mouth opened, then shut. *The voices were real.* Of course, she was angry—she always was. But not at Emilio. Not at Dar or Harris or Mansur or even Lin. "It's all just a lot to take in, I think. Maybe I finally reached my limit." The laugh she let out was weak and unconvincing. "I'm sorry. I caused a scene."

He gave her an embarrassed smile. "I could have told you. I think it's about time I started trusting you. You might say it in the most tactless way, but you aren't often wrong."

"Eh," she disagreed.

"Are you going to talk to her?"

"I kind of have to. I mean, we're on the same mission. Or whatever. Our first meeting is tomorrow—I saw you on that list." she petered off, seeing his raised brow. "Oh. You mean talk, talk to her."

He just held her gaze, dark brown eyes amused.

She heaved a sigh. "I don't know. Like, genuinely don't fucking know."

He nodded, still silent, turning to look back at the blue-washed compound below.

"What would you do?"

"You're not me. But," he stubbed out the cigarette, "I visit Harris every day."

Nel's eyes narrowed on him, trying to parse the advice that lay between those lines. The light dimmed, shadows lengthening, crawling further up walls until they engulfed them entirely. The light was odd, too diffuse for proper moonlight, and several shades too blue. The faint lights of the platforms glimmered through the trees, shuttles moving people and belongings from the docking bays.

Nel took a swig, only to find her bottle empty. She suddenly wished for the flimsy cardboard of a six pack, softened in the summer damp. "Guess that's last call," she muttered, rising with a groan, organic knee popping. "See you in the morning?"

"See you then."

She was at the ramp when he turned, backlit by the distant lights of the planet. "She said she heard them too, Nel."

"I know." But it was a whisper.

Nel's first experience with coffee was at the claustrophobic cold brew shop just outside her undergrad campus and was, like most things, to impress a date. She'd hated it until, a few months later, Mikey taught her that just because her heart was black and bitter, her beverages didn't have to be.

She peered into her mug, tilting it toward the low morning light. This wasn't coffee. It couldn't be, this far from proper soil and heavy rain. *But could have fooled me.* After another minute of thoughtfully sipping her comm hummed on her wrist.

Are you coming or on strike until she's gone?

Nel snarled at Emilio's message and, leaving her mug on the table, stalked out the door.

At least this first meeting of the minds, so to speak, was located in the main residential building. Two rights and the third door on the left. Nel hesitated. This hall was the same as Dar's room. She hadn't been able to stomach a bedside vigil with Emilio, though he'd asked if she would join him a few times since landing. Something about Dar, so energetic and full of acid, lying still and silent, turned her stomach. *He's too much like Mansur.* It's what she told herself, when she lay awake in the evening, staring at her ceiling, heart in her throat.

Deep down, however, she knew it was his similarity to another body, beaten bloody, that she'd never had the chance to stand vigil for.

"Nice of you to join us," Emilio remarked from his doorway lean.

She turned, scowling. "I had to finish my coffee."

"You've been up at least an hour," he countered with a wry smile.

"Hey, at least I didn't bring a beer, alright?" She slunk into the room behind him, hating the cornered feeling that arose as soon as the door thunked shut behind them.

It was a personal study, open and airy, despite the low ceiling and dim lighting. The walls were covered in handprints, mimicking countless caves so many lightyears away. But these were handprints she recognized. Nel's fingers shook as she reached out, skimming the rough stucco until she could place a palm over one of the prints. It was narrower than hers, the fingers longer. *Lin.*

"Well, now that we're all finally gathered," a chipper voice interjected. "Introductions."

Nel turned to see the small group collected around a long table. She had noted an unfamiliar name on the list, but frankly had skimmed it until she found the only one that mattered. The one a large part of her wished wasn't there at all.

Lin sat at the head of the conference table, out of uniform and somehow even more intimidating for it. Emilio sat at the other end, hand resting on an empty seat clearly intended for Nel. She plunked down and continued her survey of their current— *temporary*—allies.

"Most of us know one another by reputation, if not by face. But, in the wake of more recent events,

I think we should all go around and reintroduce ourselves." Nel squirmed under the weight of her gaze. "Start afresh."

Fuck that.

Lin leaned forward, deadly hands folding on the table. "I'm Lin Nalawangsa, she/her, former Komodor of IDH, and acting commander of *Vīrya*, in the wake of my parents' absence and my brother's recovery. I specialize in human sociology and the effects of interactions between the Teachers and Terrestrial humanity." She turned, expectant, to the person on her right.

"Hey everyone! I'm Dr. Lissa Hugo-Sanchez, she/they," the next person at the table chimed in. Rich brown coils cascaded from a metal ring perched at the crown of the young woman's otherwise shaved head. "I was tasked with the data analysis of Dr. Patel's investigation on Samsara and I've been working closely with Komodor Nalawangsa over the past few months as we planned for our extraction."

Nel's eyes narrowed on the full lips and brilliant smile, alienation pinching in her chest. *I'll bet you worked closely.*

"I'm an IDH technical officer—former, of course—with an interest in encryption and artificial intelligence. And," she continued, winking one big green eye, "reigning digi-chess champion of Sector 31."

"Not if I have anything to say about that," Emilio drawled, soft enough that only Nel could hear. She caught his eye and he shot her a tiny wink of his own. A wave of gratitude washed over her and she felt her shoulders relax a fraction. Dar might be unconscious, and Mikey might be dead, and Lin was, well...but she wasn't completely without allies.

"I'm Emilio Sepulveda of Los Pobledores—he/him, please—and I'm a bit of un hombre orquesta here. I have extensive knowledge of the communications between IDH and Los Pobledores, as well as the ah," he drew a breath, "motivations of Harris, formerly Renato Sepulveda. Dr. Bently and I have also worked with Komodor Muda Nalawangsa extensively to identify the signal in question during our time on *The Recursive.*"

Nel shifted in her seat, last to speak and somehow feeling all the less prepared. "Hi. I'm Dr. Nel Bently, she/her. I'm an archaeologist, and ah," *I'm an asshole who drinks too much and hears voices.* "I worked on one of the sites of humanity's first contact with the Teachers. I've also been dealing with the mess Harris and Mansur made, which lately consists of following the trail of bodies and blood."

Her words sobered the room, and she tried to ignore the appalled look young Hugo-Sanchez shot her. *Sorry Buttercup, the world ain't all digi chess.*

Lin took over before Nel could further damage the mood. "Thank you, Dr. Bently, for the reminder of what's at stake. We are here because this is bigger than IDH, bigger than the Unified Faction

Mediators. Bigger than humanity. And while many of us have held opposing opinions in the past, I hope that we can set aside animosity and find strength in our differing views."

"Differing views?" Nel muttered. "Sorry if our rules about murder are a bit fucking rigid."

"Rules?" Lin replied, loud enough to make Hugo-Sanchez blink in surprise. "First I've heard of you following any."

"Regarding the murder," Emilio began, brown hands spread wide across the table, as if by sheer will he could keep them focused. Or, if nothing else, keep them from strangling one another. "I think we should step back, determine what each of us has learned since the events on Earth. It may well be that we're closer than we realize."

Nel's gaze slid over to Emilio, chewing on her lip. Pooling their knowledge was good. Necessary. "I'd also like to hear how long you expect we'll all be needed here. I understand what the officer— alder, whatever—said about why we can't go home. IDH has gone rogue, but it's not like there aren't a bunch of factions at odds with one another out here."

"Do you have somewhere more important to be?"

Nel stilled, eyes lidding as the echoes washed over her. *Justice.* Their souls had been ripped away, reformed undying. But they did not call for revenge. "I'm just wondering where it ends. Two lunatics with an overgrown paramilitary tried to destroy the world. One is dead and the other imprisoned. Prosecute Harris. Execute him, if that's what the space-jury calls for, I suppose, but what more is there to solve? You said yourself you were just coming here to bury Mansur."

"Well," Hugo-Sanchez chirped, apparently oblivious to the fact that she was interrupting the tense subtext between Lin and Nel, "There's still the signal, for lack of a better term, that killed a few mission techs and tried to do the same to *Lahifa.* If there's a reason you think it will stop, then by all means, tell us."

Nel shot her a glare, then turned back to Lin. "You first, Komodor."

"Fair enough." She heard Lin swallow, could almost feel the tension in her shoulders as the too-chipper woman took over. "Firstly, I have some interesting updates on the Samsari Gate. I read through the report on the second phase of the Samsari excavation from Dr. Arnav Patel. Originally, the planet had been designed for non-physical life, so to speak. We were aware of the capability of the planet to help transport large groups quickly through wormhole technology, however it was our understanding that we were unable to use it ourselves. Access had been limited to the Teachers alone. Its gate 'setting,' if you will, was converted to its planet form. Mansur used that baseline circuitry for his means."

"Guess that explains how readily you all trusted the damn thing," Nel remarked. "But

Mansur, he wasn't even alive back then—none of you were, even with cryotech, right?"

Lin shook her head. "No. The accounts, they talk about technology like that, about a ring of light, an entire world made of skystone. I think my uncle simply used what they left to us. Took their attempt at connection and tutelage and transformed it into compulsion and totalitarianism. But why didn't the Teachers stop him?"

"We dug through the files—even the ones hidden from most factions—Harris was searching for some super communicator used on Samsara. And he had all this quantum data, proof that we could interact with the universe like the Teachers did. But they never answered. I think they were afraid of what we might do, with access to something so powerful as the gate technology. I don't blame them. The device on Earth was the same technology, and whatever he did on Samsara he wanted to do again there."

"And what about Harris and Mansur's connection?" Emilio asked. "Any light to shed there?"

Lin sighed. "Harris may be currently out of commission, however during our time with IDH it is safe to assume he had systems in place to continue should he be somehow removed from the equation. Despite the clear connection between their project and the signal, I'm under the impression that the signal itself was not of either of the two's making."

Nel's face twisted, but for once she held her tongue. The nature of the signal—the voices that surrounded her thoughts both waking and dreaming—was too heavy a truth for even her to blurt. And she hadn't even found the words to tell Emilio. It was bad enough to hear ghosts. "The same alias Mansur used. Dar won't be happy."

Lin's eyes tightened. "Dar actually knew him. As a child. I was too young to remember much about him, but Dar? Mansur taught him to fly. Taught him to love movement and flight and the pursuit of new horizons. My first real memory of him was the day Ayah cut him off. Forbade him from returning to his home here. I think, now, it was because of his designs."

"And the goal of their 'designs?'" Emilio asked. "I think we've danced around that enough."

Finally, someone asking the right questions, Nel rejoiced.

"I think that's up to Lin to tell us," Emilio rumbled.

Lin's face stilled; her mask turned fragile. "It wasn't discussed, much. Spoken around, more than about. I think Harris knew few would back the project if they knew what it truly entailed. But so many contracted with IDH for the betterment of society, of humanity. After all, it's in the name. And I think, in their way, Uak Mansur and Harris thought they were doing us a favor. Thought they were freeing us, and helping us expand to something better, just as the Teachers did, originally."

Emilio heaved a sigh. "That's the real reason you wanted to come back here. If he lived here, there may be information yet to discover. You could have told us."

Lin's dark gaze swiveled to him. "And risk the rest of these people finding out they aren't safe? Risk the inevitable moles and traitors find out how little we know?"

"God, you people just never learn transparency, do you?" Nel scoffed. "Dar was the same on *The Recursive.* Constantly lying about how safe we weren't." She felt the heat of Lin's glare turn to her.

"Go ahead and tell all these people that there's something definitely trying to kill them in a horrific way. And we don't know enough to stop it. See how that works out for us."

Nel winced. Lin was right and as much as she hated to admit it, she didn't have a better solution.

"What about you?" Hugo-Sanchez chimed in. "What have you learned from your research?"

"I think it may be relevant that our research was conducted with limited resources while running from IDH's war fleet." Emilio drawled, shooting Nel a small smile. "Nevertheless, I believe what we learned is substantial. Initially, Dar and myself attempted to isolate the signal as well, using the data we had along with more that we...acquired."

The corner of Lin's mouth snapped into a sharp smile. "That's how I picked up your trail. Mannu Calabret was never a loyal dealer."

"Calabret aside," Emilio continued, doing a better job than Nel of ignoring the hunt-hungry expression on Lin's face, "With the new data we were able to expand our search time frame." He turned to Nel. "And we came up empty handed."

"I had one of my so stupid-it-works ideas and we were finally able to isolate it," Nel barreled on. They didn't need the details. The truth was still too terrible for her to form into words, into a theory. All that mattered was the trail of bodies to which their search led. "I agree, the signal is, in essence, the byproduct of Harris and Mansur's acts. Through it, we were able to track him."

Hugo-Sanchez eyes got large. "We were able to isolate its location, but you're telling me you were able to determine a timeline? My mapping showed it as more a constant cloud around areas and people that had been exposed to the events. Background radiation."

Emilio nudged Nel, but she shook her head. He sighed, and took the reins, detailing Dar and Nel's excursion to Morphose-131 and their subsequent trip to *V Drugoye Mesto*. Nel half listened, punctuating Emilio's succinct summary with snorts of derision in key places.

It was an uncomfortable secret, her whispers. But they were hers, her terrible, vengeful ghosts filling the stillness around her with purpose and purgatory. They were happier not knowing, she knew. She had been, before her understanding of life and all its forms was suddenly ripped open in violent expansion. If it ever became relevant, she'd figure out then how to tell them Samsara's dead really weren't, well. dead.

"Whatever they were trying to do, resulted in death. I doubt it was the goal—there are easier ways to commit mass murder—but it surely was the result. After Samsara, Mansur fled, where he was picked up by a cargo ship— *V Drugoye Mesto.* We're uncertain as to whether his ship malfunctioned or it was a trap, but regardless, Mansur attempted to do the same thing to the passengers and crew aboard. Only one person survived."

"Have you interviewed them?" Lin asked, dark brows snapping together.

"He's a fucking kid," Nel snapped, "And no, he doesn't remember anything, thank god. He was in cryo. Both his ship and the mining base are literal dead ends."

Lin heaved a sigh and finally nodded. "If that's all the information you have, I suggest we each continue our lines of inquiry—Sepulveda and Bently focusing on the means by which Mansur and Harris were destroying these people, as you've seemingly had a break through with the signal and Hugo-Sanchez and myself trying to determine what the motives were to determine whether it's possible they could still threaten us. I have some key contacts still within IDH who could provide more insight, I hope, should we succeed in extracting them. You have full access to our databanks and library."

"Shall we meet again, perhaps in a week's time?" Emilio suggested. "Compare notes again?"

"Already on your schedule," Hugo-Sanchez explained, smile bright as she typed cheerfully away. "I think we're getting close!"

"Until then." Emilio rose, holding the door open for Nel, who bolted out without a goodbye to either of the two other women. When the door had shut behind them, he looked over at her. "You want to discuss?"

"Not really. I need to think. I might check out the library later this week."

Emilio regarded her for a moment. "You know I'm here, though. When you're ready."

"Yeah," she lied, looking away. "Thanks."

She left him at Dar's door and retreated to the open arches ringing the residential level. Open air had always helped her think, but now, the sheer alienness of the view only served to make her thoughts stutter into confusion. Only reminded her of how little she understood this world. Overhead, the trees swayed in what surely was a manufactured breeze.

"Nel."

Nel tensed, glaring out at the view. The last person she needed to talk to was Lin. Surely she'd gloated enough during their pathetic little summit.

"I know we're," she sighed softly, "at odds right now. But we need to be honest with one another."

"I was honest," Nel rasped.

"Maybe. But I think there's more you aren't sharing. Not even with Emilio."

It didn't matter if the voices she heard were real. Whether they were ghosts or not. If she told the truth, she'd have to face the next terrible truth that she and Lin were linked by something far bigger than Nel's libido and bad choices.

Nel's fingers clenched around the stone bulstrode, new calluses gripping the carved bones of the altered asteroid. Maybe, if she clenched hard enough, the pain would wake her from this terrible fever dream.

"When Lissa mentioned the signal, you had this look. Almost like you wanted to say something. Protest. If I didn't know better it looked like grief."

What a fancy way to say "scared as shit." Nel clenched her fists. "You likened this to Judgement Day. The Teachers to gods." Nel's heart thundered with panic, with dread. "Maybe I fucking converted."

"Don't patronize me," Lin snapped. "It's the same look on your face when I told you I followed Samsara's ghosts to you. You didn't blink, didn't flinch, we're surprised in the slightest." Her voice was nearer now, just a few paces over Nel's left shoulder. If she turned, they'd be close enough to touch. The tension released, the space between them expanding as Lin stepped back, ceasing her interrogation. "Whatever you're keeping from us, you'd best find a way to explain. I don't expect you to trust me. But we're not enemies."

Nel refused to turn, to watch her walk away. *We're not enemies.* But Lin was the last person in this too-small universe Nel was willing to trust. Her comm inbox still burned against her wrist with the knowledge that she could have allies. Maybe even Phil. Answers had driven their team to risk coming to *Vīrya* in the first place.

Before her common sense smacked her upside the head, she tapped the message and opened a reply.

I'm listening.

-B

She sent it into the void and shoved the comm into her pocket, as if by distance she could pretend that she hadn't just made a terrible mistake. Like she hadn't just endangered them all.

SIX

Nel glared at the prison doors, jaw working. *Vīrya's* cells were half a dozen rooms in a smaller seemingly administrative building a few minutes' walk from the residences. She didn't really want to see Harris. She didn't want to listen to his inevitable gloating, or threats, or the placid tone. It was hard to believe she'd once respected the man. But in the days since her rooftop catharsis with Emilio, she hadn't been able to stop thinking about his errant brother. Maybe Lin's insistence that they were on the same side drove her to visit their real enemy. Or maybe all she really wanted was to just assure herself he was imprisoned. That they were safe, at least from him. A part of her, larger than she was comfortable with, wished he'd died in Lin's coup.

But he hadn't, and neither had she, and if Emilio could see him daily, surely Nel could stomach a single visit. *Even if I don't really know what I want to say.* She shoved through the outer doors, showed her old ID to the pair of disinterested guards at the next set, and finally stepped onto *Vīrya*'s cell block. Later, maybe even that night, when she'd run out of reasons not to sleep, she'd wonder why a family estate had a prison at all. But for now, all her focus was on how not to look weak.

"Evening, Dr. Bently," Harris greeted her, voice sipping-chocolate smooth, hardened not a bit by his imprisonment.

If you can call it that. Nel grimaced. His cell was cozy, with a desk and a small washroom off the back for privacy. The bed was small, but covered in a plush afghan. He sat at a desk, an analog journal spread before him, filled with tiny lines of tidy handwriting. "I'd ask if your rooms were comfortable, but turns out I don't really give a fuck."

The corners of his mouth deepened in displeasure. "I suppose it was too much to hope that blast could have burned the attitude from you."

"Nah, just my leg. The attitude runs a lot deeper." His attention flicked to her legs, probably registering which one was flesh beneath the thick canvas of her pants. "I suppose I should have figured that you'd be hard to kill. Cockroaches always were."

"Guess that's why we're both here." She snapped, clawing to maintain control over the conversation. Why had she even come here? What did she hope to gain? She wasn't a jailer, an interrogator, and at the end of the day archaeology was a softer science than most.

"Must we still fear?"

She blinked at the question, one that she'd wondered in less elegant terms, but that now rose unbidden, from somewhere outside herself. Her shoulders relaxed a fraction. She imagined fingers wrapping hers in a ghostly grip. Even here, she wasn't alone. Not really. "You're Emilio's brother, Renato. The one he said he lost to IDH—funny, I assumed you were dead. I'm a bit disappointed. But you said you grew up in Mexico."

He blinked, smile never waning. "I lied. Valladolid is a lovely place. Perhaps it is where I wished I was from. I figured you white girls wouldn't know the difference."

She glared. "That why you did all this? Because poor baby Sepulveda had a boring rural childhood? Because you lost daddy? Cause like, welcome to the club. I might have got a bad attitude out of the whole thing, but you don't see me blowing a bunch of people up. Well," she cracked a merciless smile, "Failing to, really."

"My beliefs are far older than yours, Bently. Casting off the small-minded histories of one's hometown is as old as humanity is. Pushing new boundaries, that's what we evolved to do. That's why the Teachers came to us at all. To midwife us into a new form of being. I do regret that so many lost their lives in our pursuit, but with all science, comes sacrifice. You almost gave your life for Earth. Thank goodness terrestrial humanity volunteered you as their spokesperson. I'd have been worried if they chose someone with sense. This is no different—a few, imperfect, unnecessary lives so that many may live in peace. And if we failed at elevating humanity and instead extinguished our species completely?" His almost benevolent smile turned icy. "All the better."

"Our imperfection is made in your image."

Nausea crawled up her throat, but this time it was her own. "So your little speech, up there on the roof of Spaceport Bakjeeri about how little you thought of us, that was a clue. You were hoping to transform all of us. Like Mansur did to Samsara."

Harris's eyes widened a fraction and Nel nearly pumped the air in victory.

"Oh you thought we didn't know?" The expression on Harris's face was pinched and Nel was filled with vicious victory, thrilled that something cracked his mask, that she reached him, if only to make him angrier. She leaned forward, hands planted on the bars, as much to hide their shaking as to brace herself. Fury flooded her nervous system. *But is it mine?* She'd been fighting long enough to recognize her own anger better than anyone's. And this? This wasn't hers. "Didn't you recognize their voices, their screams, in the signal that took down your whole ship?"

Harris stared at her, face a battlefield between respect and repulsion. A proper human feeling. Or at least, the memory of one. "You absolute—"

"Nel?" The word cut their verbal sparring short.

She glanced at the figure shadowing the detention doorway. "Hey."

Emilio stepped in, holding a tray of food. Based on the smell, it was what they would all eat for supper. *Figures, they'd be just as courteous to a prisoner of war as they would be to its refugees.* "If you've wrapped up your," he gaze moved to Harris, as unreadable and steady as his brother's, "conversation. I'd like a word with Harris."

"Right. Yeah. Sure." She backed up, casting a final vicious grin at the man behind the bars. "Catch ya later, asshole."

Outside, under the dappled light of *Vīrya*'s afternoon, she collapsed back against the building, stone digging at her exposed skin. Her breath came in heaves, gasping as the barrage of emotions ebbed, foreign as the sun above. *What the fuck.* She'd visited him with the intention of learning more or shedding more light onto the ideology they fought. Not gloating, not showing more of their hand than was necessary.

But then, when had she ever been able to control herself, control her fury and indignation and desperation. "If you wanted a spokesperson who could control their tongue, you chose very, very poorly." She muttered. Clammy sweat beaded across her body and she couldn't shake the feeling that she knew less than when she'd entered. "I don't even know why he's doing this. Beyond the science of it all."

"False prophets of true gods."

She snarled and slammed her hand across the noise cancelation of her comm. The relief of silence washed over her, followed by a smaller wave of guilt. The dead—or not-so-dead—needed her. It might have been a mistake to choose someone who was more inclined to rageful rants than diplomacy, but chosen they had, and however ill-suited, Nel was their voice. But she needed help.

"Tomorrow," she lied to them. "I'll tell them tomorrow."

He's awake.

The message arrived later that evening, when Nel really should have been asleep. Instead, she was two beers deep and staring at the undulating dark of the jungle outside. Not bothering with a replay, she grabbed her crutch and rushed from her room.

A few dozen desperate limps delivered her just outside Dar's door. It was open, and beyond the sheer curtain she glimpsed a shadow bent over the blur of the bed. She hovered in the doorway, hand raised to knock. What would she find inside? Would he be coherent? Or had the lack of blood and oxygen done irreparable damage? Would he fly again, speak again? Then the curtain moved and Lin emerged.

"Is he ok?" Nel blurted.

Lin's eyes dropped to Nel's crutch, to her legs, then rose back to Nel's nervous face. She nodded. "He's alright. Or will be, given a bit more time."

Nel's shoulders relaxed a fraction and her breath left in a huff. "Thank fuck."

Lin's smile was small but real. "I guess you two really did become friends."

Nel grimaced. "Not sure if he'd call it that, but. Yeah. I guess we did a bit." Tenuous silence stretched between them. For a breath, it was almost as if the last few months never happened. But they had, as evidenced by the man convalescing in the room beyond.

"Stop perseverating in the hall, Bently." Dar's voice was a ragged rasp, but it was his.

"Guess he's expecting you." Lin nodded toward the half-open door.

"Right, yeah." Nel stepped forward, watching Lin as she turned and swept down the hall. It was late, but she continued past the door to her own room and disappeared around the corner. *Probably seeing Hugo-Sanchez.* She shoved through the curtain, barely taking in the room beyond the sprawling open concept and rich purple and blues. Through a broad open archway lay Dar's huge bed on a raised dais.

Emilio glanced back at her from his seat at the foot of Dar's bed. When she'd reassured herself that Dar was in one piece and his bandages were free of menacing red stains, she limped up to the edge of the bed and sank into the awaiting empty chair. For once she didn't care if the sound bubbling from her mouth was a laugh or sob. "You're ok?"

"Crabby as ever, but he'll be alright." Emilio's face was tired, but his smile was bigger than it had been in weeks.

"You don't mind me here? I don't wanna third wheel you two."

Emilio's brow twitched. "Please. We've had our time." He jerked a nod at the room across the hall. "Besides, his sister has been far more of an intrusive third wheel than you ever were."

"Yeah, I saw her in the hall." Her grimace became a smirk, and she jerked her chin at Dar. "Told you we'd make it, asshole." *Why do I have to be like that?*

"I wasn't sure I would," he countered with a tired laugh. "Next time we're sticking to the plan."

"Next time?" she drawled. "I think I've had enough of being shot at by my ex, thank you very much."

"Heard you almost shot back," he retorted, fixing her with a stare that was just a bit too sharp to be humorous.

She almost rolled her eyes but stopped herself. Maybe Dar had become something of a friend the past few months, but Nel remembered big brothers from her playgirl college days. Just because Lin fired at them both, didn't mean anyone could hurt her but him. *And that probably extends to glove blasts.* "I wasn't going to shoot."

"Looked different from where I was sitting," Emilio interjected, voice dry.

"I'm mostly pissed I missed the whole event," Dar grumbled, shoving at his pillows.

"Yeah, I'm sure your superior attitude would have totally helped the situation. Glad you'll live to torment us all another day." Her attention lingered on his reclined form, noting when Emilio's hand linked with Dar's, brown intertwined with gold. "So, did you tell him what you said when you thought we were going to die?"

Emilio's warm eyes brightened and narrowed on Dar. "Don't tell me you got all sappy."

"Hardly. Nel said we could both do worse, though, if I recall."

She snorted. "Of course, the only thing he remembers is the compliment." Maybe it was the ache of everything she never said to Mikey. Maybe it was the weight of the last few years, or how pale he looked, and the frailness of his chest without the billowing robe or starched collar. She nudged his bed with her knee. "You really scared me back there. Don't know what I'd do without you barking orders at me."

"Thanks for keeping me awake." He held her gaze, then segued, "Speaking of orders, we all really ought to talk about our next steps."

"You almost died—"

"But I didn't, and we're barely safe. So, let's get it over with."

"She's not wrong. Look at what they took out of you." Emilio jabbed his chin toward a clear tube on the nightstand, filled with the metallic trophies extracted from Dar's viscera. He heaved a sigh. "And your sister is way ahead of you. Has a schedule all set up. You need to rest."

"Yeah, consciousness is not the sole requirement of fighting shape. You'll help when you're ready."

Dar shifted, looking around for what Nel suspected was some stimulant to put in his port. He pouted, unsuccessful, but offered a nod. "I'm ready now."

"Compromise," Nel offered. "I'll send you the briefings from our first meeting. And we can talk about holding the next one here, so you don't have to move much. Though Hugo-Sanchez's chipper fucking attitude is enough to make anyone wish they were in a coma."

Emilio chuckled. "She's nice, if you give her a chance, Nel. Even if she's a bit much."

"Hugo-Sanchez? As in Lissa?" Dar asked.

"Oh, you know her?" Nel frowned. For as big as space was, it seemed like a small fucking world.

"By reputation only. She was one of Lin's more recent...interests."

Fire blossomed in Nel's gut, and she let out a scoff that was closer to a snarl. "Gross. What happened?"

Dar's dark gaze leveled on her, unblinking. "You."

She looked away, unwilling to untangle the victory and fury and jealousy that snarled in her chest at his answer. Nel may have been a distraction from a dalliance with the bubbly tech, but that was far outweighed by the fact that Lin then tried to blow up Earth and stalked them through the desolation of space.

Luckily, Dar's comm chimed, saving Nel from having to think of something not rude to say.

"Medication?" Emilio asked, glancing at his own comm for the time.

"Explains why it feels like there's a hole in my chest."

"There is a hole in your chest, cariño." Emilio remarked, voice suddenly soft. He leaned forward and fished a slim vial from the bedside table. Gently, he turned Dar's arm and clipped the medication into the port. His fingers lingered on the seam between metal and flesh.

Nel's face flushed at the intimacy, and she pushed herself out of the chair. "I, ah, I'll let you rest. But it's good to see you. I'm glad you're okay."

He grabbed her wrist, fingers strong. "I don't think I would be if you weren't there."

She let out an awkward chuckle and rose, gathering her crutch. "Probably wouldn't have been shot at in the first place. Think I can drop by tomorrow?"

"Only if you go over the meeting brief with me."

"Promise." She laughed and headed to the door. "Night, guys."

When she had shut the door behind her, she paused, resting her forehead on the smooth stone. She didn't know how to handle his candidness. Maybe Kasanove wasn't wrong about what friendship with Dar looked like. Of all the things she expected to find in the blackness of space, a friend had not been one. She mostly expected extraterrestrials and low-G sex. But between Emilio and Dar, it looked like the universe could still surprise her.

"You should trust them more."

She blinked, unsure whether it was her thought, or the whispers. With signal blocking and the entire satellite screened, she couldn't hear them the way she could on the ship. Words cut through on occasion, but more often it was sensations, ones slightly out of place in the usual maelstrom of anger and frustration and longing.

Closing her eyes, she spread her hands across the rough surface of the door, pressing against the wood. "I'll tell them. Promise," she whispered.

Fluttering filled her mind, swelling with each inhalation. "I think I'm just terrified of what it means that you exist at all. What it means about Harris, about IDH. About the Nalawangsas and this too-pretty paradise." She dropped her shoulders and let the aching wash over her. Maybe all they did, at the end of the day, was magnify her own emotions.

SEVEN

Andy still had not responded, and anxiety was a constant sting on Nel's nerves. She lurched across her room again, happy she could at least pace again like she was accustomed. Wheelies were fun, but she needed the illusion of progress to really get her brain thinking. She chugged the rest of her beer, letting the alcohol burn through her stomach and set fire to her already smoldering nerves.

She'd spent the morning with her mother, done nothing to further research anything, though considering she'd caught Emilio smoking on the roof each time she found herself up there, she wasn't the only one avoiding work. Nel was just thankful that whatever Lin and Hugo-Sanchez were working on seemed to require most of their time. Her secret burned in her throat. Maybe she could just whip out that horrible truth at their next meeting, to make up for all the slacking. Her comm hummed and she scrambled to dig it out of the couch where she'd been trying to ignore it.

Ever play digi-chess?

Typical Dar, no preamble. Nel let the disappointment go, that the message wasn't Andy finally answering. Not bothering to reply, she fished a few extra bottles from her cooler and made her way to Dar's room. The door was open, and she could just see, beyond the fabric, Dar's lean silhouette. For a moment, she let herself imagine his long lines were Lin's, that the draped hood he had taken to wearing was instead a length of dark hair.

Snarling, silently, she shoved the image from her mind and rapped on the doorframe. "Heard you were looking for good competition."

He chuckled, turning as she came in. His movements were slow, but seemed looser, more natural, than when she visited before. He nodded to the drink machine. "Tea?"

"No thanks. Got some Calabret Cloud IPA— whatever that is? I'm kinda impressed."

"I thought alcohol didn't mix with your pain meds?"

She shrugged. "I take them in the morning."

"We gotta get you a port."

"I'd rather not. Though maybe it would make me look cooler. Chicks dig body-mods."

"Typical, tell you something's for your health, you think it's bullshit unless it can impress the ladies." His deft fingers scooped dark powder into a mug and set it to fill with hot water. She watched his movements, noting the shake in his hands and how he braced himself for a moment.

"I'm consistent, at least."

"Speaking of consistency: you promised to go over the meeting notes with me," he reminded.

"There's precious little to discuss," she deflected, moving around the room. It was surprisingly homey. Shelves lined most of the walls, filled with trinkets and art, data cubes and actual books. She paused, gaze lingering on the vial of shrapnel, now in a place of honor beside a tiny bonsai of a plant she didn't recognize and a taxidermy snake with two heads.

"These all the things that have tried to rid us of your attitude?"

He chuckled. "That snake's a *Viperidae astradi bicranius.* I was seven and attempted to keep it as a pet when I found it hiding out past the temple grounds. Bit me for my hospitality. And the plant— *Tanas hopifa*—it doesn't affect most people, but triggers anaphylaxis for some, myself included."

"So, you put it in your bedroom?" Nel scoffed.

"Behind a self-contained microshield," he protested. "I think it's natural to keep the things that threaten you most, nearby. Keep your enemies closer and so forth." His mouth quirked. "So, do you play?"

"Digi-chess? I know a few people who do— did." She glanced over her shoulder with a wince, remembering Paul had been a player. Had he and Dar played against one another? Who had won? "Are the rules the same as traditional chess?"

"I have no idea," he said with a grin. When he was once again perched in the chair opposite, cupping a steaming mug, he raised his voice. "Nove, mind setting up a digi-chess game?"

"Not at all," Kasanove's voice answered from a well-concealed speaker somewhere by the door. An image flickered over the low wooden table between them, slowly forming a chess board and pieces in electric blue and orange.

While the game populated, Nel continued her nosey perusal of his belongings, half-drunk beer dangling in her hand. Her attention snagged on a slim, oblong chunk of metal hanging from an intricate display. Other pendants, and what looked like a few military decorations, hung beside it.

"Lin gave me one of those," she blurted.

"One of what?" He followed her gaze.

"Those pendant things. I mean, it was a bolo, but the metal was the same. Think it was the same design even."

"She did what?" he asked, the game board flickering as he leaned through it, incredulous.

Nel flushed, looking away. "I'm sorry—was it a family heirloom or something?"

"Or something." He shook his head. "They're protection. We each have one, in our family. Not heirlooms, exactly, but more like tradition."

Her brows shot up and she covered her complete ignorance with a long swig of beer. "Protection? Like a talisman? Good luck charm?"

If his eyes rolled harder, they'd fly from his skull from the centripetal force. "It's technology. Taken from the circuitry language of the Teachers. Works similar to an electromagnetic field, but so strong it can protect you from fire, cold, blasts—supposedly even the vacuum of space for a minute or so, though I'm not about to go testing that one the way Lin did. What happened to the one she gave you?"

Protection. She asked me to wear it more. Later, she'd wonder exactly how Lin had tested the device. She sat back. "Um, well."

"If you tell me you chucked it out the airlock in some post-break-up fit, I might just throw you after it. These things are worth—"

"I gave it back."

"Oh, thank the sky," he breathed, leaning back in his own, meticulous version of a slump. "So, she has it?"

"I guess. I don't really know. I yanked it off when she turned me over to Harris. And then I ran. What happened to it after that is anyone's guess. I'd probably still have it if it weren't for shit luck and my pigheaded temper." As she spoke, she realized it was true. She had a long way yet to go, releasing her chokehold on her emotional-support temper, but it was a step. *Admitting you have a problem is the first step.*

"I don't know." He looked down. "I think you had good reason to lose your temper then. Almighty knows I've lost mine over her more than I could ever count. It's something she's good at— pushing buttons."

The digital board between them chimed, having finished its construction.

"Fuck is she ever though!" Nel found the tension in her chest was a laugh. She dropped into the plush seat opposite the pilot and popped the top on a new bottle before setting it on an awaiting coaster. Nel didn't know much about Earth chess, but she was pretty sure the board wasn't twice as tall as it was wide. While the digital pieces she'd glimpsed in Gretatron's office were modeled after starships, each piece here depicted a different character from Hindu mythos.

Nel took another sip, enjoying the fuzziness at the tips of her fingers. "I can't wait to kick your ass." she challenged with a grin.

"You think you're going to beat me?" Dar asked, sliding the elephant shaped pawn forward.

"Fuck no."

"Good. Emilio hasn't let me win once." Whatever filled his mug was a brilliant purple and smelled tart and sweet at once. He took a sip.

"May the best player win." Nel slid her own pawn two spaces forward, trying to recall where and how the other chessmen moved. During his turn she looked around the room, at the various objects on his shelves, anywhere but his face.

Asking would be rude. At least when she was asking because she couldn't stop thinking about Lin. Rather than because she cared about how Dar might feel. "You seen her?"

The edges of his eyes tightened. "Often."

She stared, desperate for more, but knowing it was already tacky to have asked at all.

"She stops by a few times a day between her work and training."

Nel snorted. "Guess she feels guilty about shooting her own brother."

"She didn't shoot me."

Nel's brow arched. "That what you think or is that just what she wants you to believe."

Dar sighed. "Mother of God, you complicate every little thing, don't you?"

"Complicate?" She scoffed. "I ain't the one with my sister's blast burn in my chest."

"Check."

"How?"

He ghosted a finger through the hologram to show his next move, but sat back, staring at her instead of moving. "Nel, sometimes you must choose to feel something. There's no right answer, no wrong answer, no way of knowing if you're making the right choice. Sometimes the proof isn't there. You pick. She said she was trying to smoke screen us. Her glove hit the wall and a hunk of starship blew through my chest. Maybe she was aiming for me. Maybe she wasn't. Maybe she was aiming for you. All I know, though?" He jabbed his chin at the empty chair at his bedside. "She's here every afternoon."

"Yeah, I'll just overlook the tiny betrayal where she left my entire fucking planet to die." Nel glowered at the game, annoyed by how simple he made feeling sound. Even the most basic emotions were hard, let alone something as radical as forgiveness. She would sooner win the digi-chess game as be capable of forgiving Lin. *And I'm definitely losing.* When she spoke, her voice cracked. "Rook to C5....delta."

"Check-mate." Dar watched her thoughtfully. "Are you even going to try?"

Nel let out a soft scoff. *Try at the game or the weapon of mass destruction that's your sister.* She heaved a sigh and took a long pull from her beer. "Two-outta-three?"

Nel lost each of the three games they played, but honestly didn't mind. Dar regaled her with both his and Lin's childhood antics, and Nel shared some of the more ridiculous stories from her CRM days. He was appalled, and she surprised and they'd both laughed longer than any of the stories really called for. She'd run out of beer and an hour later his port dinged a reminder for his next dose.

It was well past midnight, long after their final doomed match ended, mostly out of waning interest, that Nel tottered from his room. Dar was still a vain, determined asshole, but he was the type of jerk Nel could get along with. It was nice, to finally have an evening of peace, however hard won and temporary they both knew it would be. She had not mentioned the message.

The air was cool, eddying through the open halls. Her head spun with her uneven steps. *Or the beer. I'm sure that helps.* A soft, muffled melody drifted past, and she found her feet absently following it, her head tilted to better trace the sound.

The notes cascaded on, dipping toward melancholy, rising with adoration. *Longing.* It was beautiful. She pressed a hand to the cool stone as she listened. Music was never something she was good at, though dancing was fun, and she enjoyed a good campfire ruckus. Violin strings, despite the years of practice her mother insisted on, were more a lesson in futility than anything else, and though playing a guitar would get most people laid, her attempts were embarrassing. Her steps brought her to a dark, open doorway. She couldn't pick out what the melody was, let alone the instrument. A woodwind's wail turned to the rumbling low intensity of a synthesizer.

A single, low light emanated through the curtain, casting long shadows from the elegant figure. And, in the privacy of anonymity, Nel let herself stare. It was easier, without Lin's attention weighing on her like a dying star, when her anger's edges were filed off by alcohol and attrition. She traced the lines of Lin's shoulders, the rhythmic sway of her long arms around what must have been some instrument Nel couldn't quite make out. *I could have loved you.*

I did love you.

Her chest burned, sharper even then the neurological sear of her leg's biomechanical connections. Aching, same as the song, reverberated in her bones. Her hand rose, fingers catching on the too-soft silk of the curtain between them. The song settled into some resolve, and then to stillness.

"Trying to shoot me again?" The question was soft, as if Lin was asking her to come to bed, not blast a hole in her traitorous chest.

Nel flinched, but before she thought better of it, stepped past the edge of the curtain. Deep gold light stretched from a large crystal in the center of an end table. Like Dar's, the space was surprisingly welcoming. Red and peach curtains framed each window, and coarse-woven pillows and blankets draped over the couch and seats opposite. Through an open door to the left, she glimpsed the long table where they'd had their first meeting. The kitchenette beyond was filled with cooking implements and the living area looked like it was, well, lived in.

Lin perched on the arm of her low couch. The usual long braid was undone, her hair longer than when Nel had last seen her, and she wore only a loose crimson sarong. There was no musical instrument in sight.

"I don't mind, you know. Music deserves an audience." Her chin lifted a fraction, but the rest of her lean form remained completely still.

Like a predator, gathering herself to leap. Nel wavered in the doorway. Truthfully, she didn't trust herself past the threshold. "What was it?"

"The song? Improvisation."

"It was beautiful." The compliment clotted in Nel's mouth, and she swallowed hard. "What instrument?"

"Me. My mind." There was the blade-sharp smile. "One of the benefits of augmentation." The zing of flight shot up Nel's nerves. But it was somehow comforting to know that, despite the unexpected softness of her dwelling, Lin herself hadn't changed completely. *I can still hate her, even if her furniture is nice.*

"You got a flute in your ass or something?" Nel raked a narrow glare over Lin's body, telling herself it was just curiosity, just due diligence. Realizing there was no fretwork protruding from Lin's ears, however, she returned to frowning. "So, how's it work? Your ah, magic flute."

"This." Her lip curled at the euphemism, but she turned her head, showing the dark line that reached into her hairline where a tiny silver button gleamed. "Got some adjustments, courtesy of Harris."

Nel gagged at the thought of Harris and Mansur's ideology getting anywhere near Lin's perfect flesh. "Thought those were for gloves."

"It's just a biomech connector. What we choose to connect it too, though, is up to us." Rolling her forearm to display the underside of her arm and palm, she tapped twin minimalist versions of electrogloves. Instead of the usual baleful circle meant for dealing death, however, there was a speaker.

Her left hand trembled upward, and a haunting note trilled through the room, blooming louder as her right hand pulled back and out. It was as if she kneaded the sound from the very air. "The notes themselves come from my mind. Or perhaps heart, would be more accurate. Feelings. It reads the areas of my brain that alight when I think."

Nel gripped the tenuous note humming between them. "It was so...sad."

A strange expression crossed Lin's face and the music died.

She blinked and nodded. "I imagine mine would be too. Maybe with a lot more screaming."

Lin's smile widened. "I don't know. You only heard the beginning of mine."

Nel hovered just inside the threshold, mouth suddenly dry and her heart afire with frustration. At Lin, at herself, at the mountain of wrongdoings that separated them. Then, she faltered, stepped back. "Good night."

"Good night, Nel." A frown flickered across her face, as if she wanted to say more, and Nel almost stepped back inside, told her, please, go on, tell me, tell me more, tell me everything. But the courage withered, and she fled without another word. Only when she was safely locked in her room did she let herself think again.

She slumped over the side of her balcony, panting. Even in the open air overlooking the satellite, her breath was ragged, the air too hot. Overhead, the dome obscured all but the brightest star, swirling instead with murky indigo, akin to the aurora on Earth.

Despite the beers and Dar's recovery, despite laughing with her mother earlier that day, her pulse raced, her thoughts tumbling with secrets. She leaned on the rough stone bulstrode long into the night, unable, or unwilling to sleep. And she was there, still awake, at 0230 when her comm blinked with Andy's answer:

He's gone dark.

EIGHT

"Does it hurt?"

Nel whirled, sweat splattering from her hair. Roving around the satellite served as a good excuse to avoid proper P. T.—and avoid thinking about the meeting later—but the knots in her thighs and burning past the severed end her sciatic told her slacking had finally caught up with her. She wiped a forearm across her brow before fixing the gangly form with a frown.

"Oh. Hey." Annoyance died when she registered it was Xand slouched against the stone banister at the base of the ramp she was climbing for the fifth time.

"Sorry. That was a weird question."

"It's an honest one. And I like that." She shrugged. "It does. Comes and goes. I'd take the pain over the other feelings, though."

His curious gaze eyed the metal and silicone replacing her right limb. She glanced down at the cobbled together prosthetic and the angry, gnarled scars. Her chest still lurched at the sight. But under Xand's almost blank gaze, the sensation was different.

"My mom lost a couple fingers years ago. Accident with a winch. Said she could still wiggle them. Long as her eyes were closed. Used to tell me all the places they wandered off to, now that they weren't attached."

Nel stared at him, then snorted. "Gross. Funny, too, I guess."

He nodded. "The stories were good. Long as you didn't think too hard about it. It's not like I actually believed her. Fingers were down there at the bottom of that shaft with a bunch of broken tools and shit—stuff. Sorry."

"Swears don't bother me. You know I use them enough."

"The psych hollers at me when I cuss." he muttered, looking down at his feet. They were clad in standard issue miner's boots, probably scrounged from the ship where they'd also found him. Either he had some ungainly feet to grow into, or they were several sizes too large.

"Just words, kid. My mom hates when I swear, though." she retorted, trying a smile. "Not a fan of the shrink?"

"No. I mean. She's fine. I just," he shrugged again.

"I hear that. I think my reputation preceded me enough that my shrink knew I'd bite his head off if he didn't let me take the lead."

Xand looked up. "Is he cool?"

"I think so. I mean, for a shrink." she grinned, flexing her legs to relieve the ache. "Not sure if they'd let you switch, but I can ask him if that's something he could work with. If you want. He's from Earth but loves this lifestyle. And so far, has been pretty kind. And he's ah—" she faltered. It seemed wrong to disclose, but she'd do anything to prevent the teenaged mess from becoming, well, like her. "He's a person of faith, too. If that's something you're into."

"I take it you're not?"

"Nah. But I think some of the imagery is nice. Where I grew up the predominant denomination thought people like me—gay people—were all going to Hell." She shifted, digging knuckles into the meat of her thigh. The burn was persistent, almost a bone-deep itch. And that wasn't even counting the sensations that extended below, to where she knew there was nothing. Maybe if she closed her eyes, like Xand's mom, she could still wiggle her toes. "What about you?"

"Gay?"

"Faith," she quickly corrected. "If you want to talk about it. None of my business."

"I don't know yet. About either, really." He turned to flop forward against the stone, kicking it absently with the steel toe of his overlarge boot.

"When I used to look out there, at all of that nothing, I felt really small. And okay with that. I don't feel so alone. So maybe that's a type of god."

"That's a nice way to think of it." She smiled and leaned forward next to him, as much to relieve the pressure from her wounds as for comradery. "Out there mostly scares the shit out of me. No control. Nothing surrounding me. Death on every corner."

His shoulder lifted. The gesture was familiar to Nel already, a little idiosyncrasy that was entirely Xand. "That's the part I like, I think. It's out of my hands. So, I don't have to worry."

She snorted. "Maybe you should be a shrink."

"Nah, I don't think I like people enough."

"That's how I chose my career path—I prefer my people dead."

He tossed her a fleeting frown. "What are you again? A soldier?"

She gagged. "No. I'm terrible with guns. Last firefight I got in I almost shot my ex. I'm an archeologist. Or was. Not really sure what I am now."

"Me neither." He looked down at her hands, hanging beside his. "Do you need an assistant?"

"Ha. I don't even have enough work for myself right now. But I bet someone could find a job for you." Her heart ached at the hope in his voice. He might still be a child in so many of the ways that mattered, but his heart wasn't a kid's anymore.

She thought about asking where they'd put him, so her mother could check on him from time to time. *Or you could check on him yourself, Bently.* She was never good with kids, treating them with the honesty she had wanted at their age. But for the first time she found herself wishing she could be. After a second, she straightened with a soft groan. "My PT routine calls for two more laps. Wanna come with? I could use the company."

His pale eyes lit up and what might have passed as an honest-to-goodness smile unfurled on his awkward teenage features. "Sure. Can you tell me about the weirdest shit you found?"

Aside from your entire community liquified in a ball? She shoved the uncharitable thought from her head before it threatened to leap from her mouth and steadied herself on the wall. "I don't know what you heard about Earth, but we have these big lines cut through our forests and stuff, so we can string huge power cables from the dams and plants where we generate that power," she started.

"That sounds really dangerous."

"I guess it is. We call them power corridors. But some archaeologists spend a lot of time doing surveys out there, before the big machines come through. But because no one's out there unless work's being done, people go there pretty much just to be weird."

She had taken a dozen steps without even thinking. *Maybe this is what I need,* she thought, glancing at the kid. Someone to talk to. Someone to take care of. *Someone who needs me as much as I need them.*

"Space is like that, in the empty corners. Strange. Dangerous. Spent a lot of time in those places." His face grew shadowed for a moment. "Do you think we're safe here?"

"UNAUTHORIZED AIRSPACE BREACH. SECURE SUITS AND SHELTER IN PLACE UNTIL FURTHER INSTRUCTION."

"Shit." Her eyes flew to Xand. She notched her crutch under her arm and grabbed his hand with her free one. "C'mon. We'll keep you safe."

His eyes were wide, face blank, all the snark and bite erased from his stance. But, wordless, he followed her back up the ramp and to her room.

She opened the door and ushered him in, but didn't follow. "Stay here, I'm going to figure out what's up, ok? Probably just more people coming to shelter on their satellite. Maybe Lin and Dar's parents." The lie rang, tinny, between them. Still, she flashed an empty smile. "I'll be right back. There's juice in the fridge. Don't drink my beer."

Her heart was a stampede between her ribs. She limped away, waiting until the door shut between them before she jabbed her comm. "Emilio, what's going on?" She was greeted by static. She tapped again. "Dar?" When she was answered only by static, she tapped the last name she wanted to. "Lin, what the fuck is going on?"

Descending the manor, she broke into a clumsy jog. A second later Kasanove's voice answered instead. "There's an incoming ship, a small, IDH Explorer class. Lin and Emilio are tracking it. Soon as it's close enough, Hugo-Sanchez will scan."

"Is close enough to scan also close enough to fire on us?" She asked, hating that was the first place her mind went.

"*Vīrya* is a residential satellite," he protested, as weak as her reassurance to Xand had been.

"Doesn't mean they won't blast us out of the sky," she reminded, forcing herself to move a fraction faster.

"Asteroid canons have it in their sights. But we're holding fire until we can determine its nature. I have been advised by Lin that our allies are too few to risk destroying the craft."

And too many enemies to risk letting them land unchecked. She kept the thought to herself, wondering when she became a soldier, when thoughts of war and murder and bloodshed became more natural than discussion. *It's not like I was ever good at the latter.*

A klaxon sounded near the lifts, and she glanced up to the wavering lens of the dome. It was so delicate right then, gossamer in the face of colossal elements. A glint, like a titanium mosquito, arced outside the shields. "I see 'em," she relayed. "Man, they're booking it."

"Where are you?" It was Dar's voice this time.

"In the garden, out front. Shouldn't you be resting?"

He ignored her. "You got your suit?"

"Yeah."

"Armed?"

"Yes, why?"

"You're our welcoming committee." Emilio cut in, voice low and serious. "We're dispatching guards as well. I'll meet you on the docks."

She groaned and broke into an uneven run. The ship was plummeting toward the underside of the satellite by the time she was descended to the landing bay. After what felt like a too-quiet eternity in the lift shaft, and a nervous run through the halls, Nel emerged in the docking bay. A team of guards awaited her, along with Emilio. He tossed her a helm.

"Thanks, I feel naked here." she clipped it into place before asking, through the comm, "So what did the scans say?"

"Life signs say someone's on board, but they aren't responding. Not a single signal on record, and they're flying at low power, max speed. Whoever's on board must be wearing a suit, because the thing is flying cold," Emilio explained.

"I don't like this." Nel grimaced, stepped onto the pad with the guards, jerking the sleeves of her jacket out of the way of her glove. One of the guards reached over and adjusted a connection.

Paired.

"Here she comes," Emilio muttered, dropping his weight a bit. The bay doors opened, air writhing silently as the ship careened through. It wobbled, threatening to slide sideways, but its landing lights flickered on, thrusters exploding into action. It slammed into the floor with a crash, snapping one strut and skidding a few hundred meters before thudding into the docking bay walls far too close for Nel's comfort.

A docking crew swarmed the wreck, spraying the sparks and gouged metal with a fire retardant before giving Emilio the all-clear.

"Secondary scanning," he relayed through the comms. "Clear—still picking up signs of a life form. Life support systems negligible. Huge amount of electronic activity though."

"Okay, I really don't like that. Audio blocks on?" Nel asked. It didn't matter that the ghosts meant no harm, death spread in their angry wake. She could relate.

"Affirmative," he responded. "Dampeners engaged. Kasanove?"

The senti-comp's voice boomed through their helms. "All audio communications are temporarily disengaged. Good luck."

Silence. Nel's ears ached in the absence of the white noise, the birds, the wind. The whispers. She wished her hands would stop shaking, wished she didn't feel the discrepancy between her trembling leg and its steady, immovable counterpart. *I feel so weak.*

The ship before them shuddered and jets hissed from its fuselage as it repressurized.

She raised her hand. *Suit: engage electroglove.* Beside her the half dozen guards did the same. Nothing happened. After another beat a message appeared on her wrist:

Jackson and Ki, you've got the exterior. Bently, you and me into the belly of the beast.

She clenched her jaw, watching as the first two broke off and flanked the ship, scanning each corner and exterior holds for any sign of sabotage, weapons, or life. A moment later they gave the all clear and jacked their scanner into the ship's external systems port. A second later the gangway ground open. It wasn't a soldier or sonic death that emerged from the ship, or even a resurrected Mansur. It was roiling cold. Darkness. And silence.

We're up.

Nel followed Emilio as he edged up the ramp, his extended hand blinking as his suit sampled a dozen things Nel didn't understand. Inside, it was utterly dark. He motioned for her to move left while he continued right toward the bowels of the ship. As he turned to go, she grabbed his arm and pointed. Bloody drag marks led up the ramp and across the floor.

He met her eyes, barely visible through the thick glass of both their helms. He didn't have to tell her to be careful. With a tight nod, he disappeared into the cargo bay. Nel followed the blood trail to the rack where one of three emergency space suits was missing. Whoever had piloted the ship hadn't had time to prepare for flight it seemed. Judging by the mess, they may very well have bled out on the way. *Kasanove said life signs.* She crept through the corridor, glancing through the narrow doorways to the shadowed and empty bunk. The trail led straight toward the sealed doors of the cockpit.

One missing suit, but that's a lot of fucking blood. At the cockpit doors. Unlocking now.

Understood. Nothing so far here. Checking the ship's computer now.

She pressed her hand to the door and, to her surprise, it opened without protest.

A single figure was slumped in the copilot seat, sealed in a battered IDH spacesuit. Blood and black fluid splattered its white surface, almost obscuring the glass of their helm, but the blinking lights on their wrist indicated the suit's seal was still intact. Nausea clenched in Nel's stomach at the sight of gore-splattered glass.

One person. Unconscious. Suit intact.

She glanced down to see a large vacuum sealed case with a heavy cable plugged into the cockpits system port. It too, had a blinking stasis light.

Got a case of some kind.

Another tech appeared as Nel was crouching down to examine the box. He knelt beside her, wordlessly plugging a device into the person's suit.

Nel didn't understand most of the readouts as she peered over their shoulder.

Health scanner. I'm a medic.

Emilio's update came through next:

Ship's computer scans come back nominal.

"We're clear, audio comms reengaged," Kasanove announced. A moment later the ship's emergency lights blinked on.

"Blood pressure critical. Pulse weak. Cortisol and adrenaline are high." The medic glanced up at Nel. "Take their helm off for me?"

Nel reached over and unsealed the atmosuit's helm before the terror at what she might see overtook her. Beneath was the pale, bloody face of Andy Gull. Her eyes were half open, unfocused. Her body seized, thick blood spraying from her mouth across Nel's helm.

Andy's helm dropped from Nel's numb fingers, thudding against the floor of the ship. She swore it was Paul's screaming ringing in her ears, seconds before he ripped his own helm off. "Holy shit."

"This is Medic Morris, requesting critical medical transport for one please." He moved quickly, calmly, as if he saw it every day. Lately, maybe he did.

"Bently, what did you find?" Dar asked.

Nel knew it was impossible to smell the blood through her helm. Her nose burned with the metallic tang. Her teeth chattered when she replied, "It's Andy Gull."

Another two medics appeared with a stretcher hovering between them. Morris tapped out an order to Andy's suit, which hummed, then rose slowly off the seat.

Nel stepped back farther, eyeing the levitating woman as her suit eased up and onto the stretcher before settling in place with another hum.

Morris turned to their team. "Let's get her into the medical wing. Hera, run a full workup please. Amanda, you're on brain scan." He jerked a nod at the case beside them. "Do I want to know what's in there?"

Nel grimaced. "I certainly don't but that's sort of the theme of my life lately."

The medic team navigated from the corridor and back out to the landing pad. Even through her helm she caught the distant sound of animated conversation. Hugo-Sanchez must have shown up.

"Need cryomed transport for another two in here, Morris." Emilio interjected, voice tight, even through the muffling comms.

"What'd you find?" Nel asked, not really wanting the answer.

"It's—Lin, you need to be here."

"Mil, what is it?" Dar repeated, clearly done with being sidelined.

"Two adults in cryo. All readout's stable," Emilio explained, clearly for the medical team and not for his increasingly antsy partner. "Lin are you—

"Here."

Their comms switched off. Either Dar was, for once, speechless, or he was looped into their private conversation. More likely the latter. Nel sat back on her heels, seething with FOMO. For all she knew it was yet another dead relative. *Emilio said stable.*

Nel might have been forgotten, but for a moment she had the cockpit to herself. She knelt beside the case, peering at the small panel in its side for a moment. A message scrolled across the tiny data screen:

DELIVER TO DR. NEL BENTLY
FOR SAFEKEEPING.

Nel winced before tapping the button to open it. She ran a cautious finger over the side. It was freezing. A loud hiss emanated from it as the container depressurized. Its lid bounced then rose slowly. Through the roiling fog within Nel glimpsed the pale and hairless face of Philos, senti-comp and former system computer of IDH's largest space station. "Fuck. Kasanove!" she called, unable to keep herself from shouting, even through the comms. "It's Phil. Her cargo was Phil."

"Philos?"

"Out of his stasis tank, or whatever too. He's hooked up to the ship, which probably explains the electrical readings. But looks like he's sleeping."

"Must be in standby," Hugo-Sanchez chimed in. "Can you access him remotely, Nove?"

"The system hard drive isn't big enough for the both of us without a partition—"

"Just figure it out." Dar snapped over the comms. "At least he's on our side."

Nel's eyes narrowed on the sallow, waxy head. *Or he was, last time.* She would have to ask what Andy meant by "dark" in her message. *If she recovers.*

Hugo-Sanchez's arrival interrupted her next thought. A handful of new tech's brought another stretcher—this one retrofitted to support a senti-comp. "We can take it from here. Always wanted to get a chance to study his integration up close!"

Nel made a face and backed out of the suddenly very full cockpit. She watched as they extracted the case, plugging it into the stretcher before disconnecting the cables to the ship.

"What is that?"

Lin stood in the doorway to the cargo area. appeared in the cockpit doorway.

Nel frowned. "Phil. Did you disconnect your comm?"

Lin gave a tight nod, gesturing to the helm cradled under one arm. Her face was lined with tension, lips thin as if suppressing nausea. "I needed a minute."

"I guess he's what she was bringing," Nel replied, too worried to start a fight just yet.

"Not her only cargo." Lin drew in a shaky breath, waiting as the techs left with Phil in tow.

Hugo-Sanchez paused on her way off the ship. "Lin, need anything? You look pale."

No shit, dumb-ass, we all need a fucking break. Nel leveled her glare at the technician, hoping the thought could beam into her perky skull.

"Thanks, Lissa. I'm fine, just tired."

She wavered on the ramp, looking between Lin and Nel. "You sure?"

"I'll meet you this afternoon. Once we get our bearings."

Hugo-Sanchez flinched at the dismissal but obeyed without another word.

"You don't look ok." Nel pointed out.

"My parents were in cryo in the back."

Nel blinked. "What? Are they—"

"They'll both wake up within the hour. Probably." She swallowed. "I don't like this."

Nel looked out the yawn of the ship's doorway. Two cryo tubes were being scanned, probably for the hundredth time. Another team from *Vīrya*'s seemingly endless supply of staff awaited them.

Her parents. What vitriol Nel had wanted to spew ebbed. She recognized the ache in Lin's eyes. The fear. "Whatever it is, we can all find out together."

Lin barked a humorless laugh. "Best case scenario we have a mercenary journalist who was playing taxi to Ayah, Ibu, and Phil, and happened to lose a lot of blood from stubbing her toe midflight. Worst case—"

"Let's not go there," Nel cut her off. "Blood. Weird tech. Unconscious people. Sounds like another Thursday."

Lin stared at her, searching Nel's face for…what? After a second, she reached over and disengaged Nel's comm. "What are you thinking?"

"Honestly? I'm thinking Andy risked a lot to rip him out of *Odyssey.* He was on our—well, my—side before but a lot can change. The more I learn about this tech the less I trust it. And your family's ties to it aren't the best."

Lin's eyes were darker than the dead ship around them. "That's a hell of an accusation to make."

"I'm not making it lightly. About any of them." Dread spun through her heart. "I don't want to believe it either."

Lin's lack of answer was agreement enough. She brushed past, pausing too close to Nel for comfort. "All we can do now is wait for him to wake, and when he does, pray he's still our friend."

NINE

Nel hated waiting. She bounced her leg and glowered at where Lin pored over read-outs at the sprawling table. The library was stunning, and if she could focus on anything other than how fucked they all might be, she would appreciate the two storeys of books, scrolls, displays, and data cubes.

The initial estimate of an hour had dragged into three, and Lin, presumably tired of standing over her parent's cryo tubes, had arrived around the two-hour mark. Dar was tucked into one of the library's more comfortable chairs, head lolled to one side. His skin was waxy and pale, but whatever Emilio had brought him for his port seemed to slowly be doing the trick. Now they both dozed across from one another up on the library's mezzanine.

Despite her avoidance of commitment, Nel had imagined meeting Lin's parents a few times. A spaceship crash and a sentient severed head hadn't featured in her day-dreaming, but the whole affair seemed apropos with the rest of their mercurial relationship.

Lin sat at the head of the long table, shoulders hunched, hands buried in her now tangled braid. Though her eyes scanned the screens before her, she hadn't made any notes for the last twenty minutes.

"You aren't happy to see your parents?" Nel asked.

Lin let out a soft snort. "It's so much more complicated than that."

"Okay, then tell me why," she snapped back. "You can't be pissed that I don't know anything when you won't tell me."

Dark eyes rolled up to fix Nel with a furious stare. "Yeah, you're always so easy to talk to."

"Sorry." Nel looked away. "You're right."

"So are you." Lin shoved away from the table and strode over to a large hologram of *Vīrya*'s main estate. Her long fingers whitened around the edges of the display's podium. Despite the mess of her hair, her electrosuit was fully zipped, back rigid, every line of her tense. "I have so many questions, Nel. They've always been driven. Always on a mission or leading a project or wrapped up in their research. It's not unusual to hear nothing from them for months. When we'd speak, there'd be updates, discussions, never anything personal.

"They were loving enough, I suppose. But if we spoke about feelings, it was those surrounding whatever project we were focused on at the time. More a thesis defense than family bonding. The last time I spoke to Ayah—with any of them—was after Samsara was destroyed."

Nel lifted her chin, getting a better look at the powerful woman before her. It was the first time she heard someone call the planet's change what it was—an apocalypse. "Not even when Dar went rogue?"

"I didn't think anything of it at first. Used to long silences, like I said. Then I thought they were hiding Dar. Then I thought they were hiding from Harris and the truth. And now—" Her voice cracked and her lip curled, though Nel couldn't say if it was disdain at her family or herself. Perhaps both. "Now I think they were hiding from me."

Nel mostly wanted to slap her for being so self involved, but another part of her wanted to assure her that, surely, they couldn't run from someone like her. *But I did. Long before my life depended on it.* "If you haven't spoken to them, you can't know for sure." She faltered on the next, harder, question, fiddling with the words until they emerged as a whisper. "Do you think they're on our side? Or with IDH?"

Lin just stared at the glowing hologram, perhaps looking for the exact spot where everything went wrong.

He's gone dark.

Too many loose threads coiled in Nel's mind, not the least of which was further complicated by the horrific words Andy had sent earlier. She pulled up the message thread, tempted to reply and outright ask what the fuck was going on. *Except she's unconscious now too.*

Emilio straightened in his seat and stretched before climbing down to join them. His face was ashen with exhaustion. He glanced around the room. "Still just us then?"

"Yeah. No word either." Nel reported, before jerking her chin toward the still-unconscious pilot above. "Dar?"

"Drugged him." Emilio deadpanned.

Nel narrowed her eyes, wondering if he was joking at all. There had been a fair number of times she'd wanted to drop a roofie in the pilot's port just for some peace and quiet. "Do you think they're out of cryo yet?"

Emilio shrugged, settling into a chair across from Nel. He leveled his brown eyes on her, frowning thoughtfully.

"What?" She asked.

"While I was on the ship, I did some scans of the personal comms of the passengers."

She gestured with both her hands, as if to say, "and?"

"The security system recorded multiple correspondences with your comm device over the last few days."

Shit.

Lin turned around, finally tuning into the conversation. shook her head. "That's ridiculous.

Nel understands the safety concerns with communication feeds."

Emilio did not look away from Nel.

Swallowing a hefty portion of her pride past the lump in her throat, she nodded. "He's right. I received a message a few days ago. It came from Andromeda Gull, who we crossed paths with on Earth when we were working under Harris and Dr. Ndebele."

"And you responded."

"She was working for Phil the whole time," Nel protested. "And besides, we need allies! Andy helped me on Earth, and Phil's goals never quite aligned with IDH's, at least not where I was concerned."

"I was under the impression that you took Andy hostage," Emilio drawled, expression softening a bit.

"Semantics," she muttered. "I don't know if I can trust anyone, honestly, but if you can go behind our backs and space-text Lin, who was like, literally trying to kill us, then I can do the same with Andy."

"I wasn't trying to kill you," Lin noted, voice low and deadly, but they both ignored her.

Emilio raised his palms in surrender. "Fair enough. But you could have told us."

"I was going to, alright, but then she crashed here, and I figured we could talk about it when she woke up." *There's a lot I was going to tell you.* She looked down, realizing her chance to have control over when and where she'd tell them the truth—all of it, even the hideous bits—had long come and gone. "I'm sorry. This whole thing has been a fucking shit show."

"Dr. Bently, I presume?"

Nel froze, eyes flicking to the figure in the doorway. The small woman bore Dar's bright eyes and Lin's narrow, angled jaw and both of their proud nose, Her mass of thick iron grey hair was shot through with ropes of white. Realizing everyone else had stood, Nel scrambled up and choked out a belated affirmation, "Yeah, hi."

Emilio salvaged what he could of the moment, stepping forward and offering his hand. "You must be Laksamana First Class Tirta Nalawangsa. It's an honor. I'm Emilio Sepulveda. We've been helping your son with his current work."

Nel caught the pointed vagueness to his statement and wondered anew to what events the Nalawangsa parents had been privy. The deep yellow of the woman's choli and saree set off her rich brown skin, but Nel noted shadows beneath her eyes.

Tirta took his hand, shook it. She then cast a raised brow toward Nel. "And you. Dr. Annelise Bently. Your colorful reputation precedes you."

There was no use trying to seem respectable, at this point, Nel warranted. But she could handle polite. "Guilty, ma'am. Thanks for having me; your home is beautiful."

"We weren't aware we had guests until we arrived, I'm afraid. And you've been helping?" She sounded skeptical, and her razor-sharp focus pinned Nel to her spot.

"Where I can, yes. Mostly helping Dar and Emilio. And more recently Lin, as well."

"When you're not transforming my planet?"

Nel stilled. Was it a joke? Condemnation? Empathy? "Ideally."

Apparently, that was the right move, as Tirta's eyes crinkled slightly, and she finally turned her attention to Lin. The komodor was ramrod stiff, one hand still clutching the corner of the map's display.

"Iha." Tirta's head tilted, eyes shining. "I've missed you."

Lin was blinking rapidly, eyes downcast. "I've missed you too, Ibu."

And, for perhaps the first time, Nel truly saw her. Lin and Dar always seemed like privileged overachievers, constantly clawing to be better than the only person who could possibly rival them — each other. *It's not his shadow she lives in. It's her own.*

Tirta watched her daughter for a moment, leaning toward her, as if hoping for an embrace, or even eye contact. When none came, she turned to scan the room again. "Where's Dar?"

Emilio gestured to the reading area on the mezzanine above. "Resting, Laksamana. I can wake him—"

"I can wake my own son, thank you." Tirta raked an appraised stare up Emilio, gave a thoughtful smile, then ascended the curving ramp to the upper level. Nel watched the woman kneel beside Dar, head cocked as she took in his sleeping form, brow creased. *How many times has Mom looked at me like that?*

Feeling like an intruder, Nel looked away and nudged Emilio with her foot. "How much do they know?" she mouthed.

He gave a sharp shake of his head, but any further discussion was stalled by Tirta returning, face a still, reserved mask. "Would one of you like to explain why my son is medicated and bandaged?"

Emilio looked to Nel, who turned to Lin. "Andy brought them here for a reason and this whole charade has gone on long enough," Nel insisted. She might have been the queen of dragging her feet, but that time was long past. "I think it's time we tell your parents."

"Tell us what?" They all turned to see the towering figure of the Brigadir Jenderal himself in the library doorway, eyes like thunderheads.

If the rest of the satellite was paradise, the room Sant Nalawangsa brought them to was purgatory. Though adjoining the larger library, this room was clearly a personal study. Books lined the tidy shelves, and an array of chairs had been reallocated to the space for the unusual crowd. The same projected map of their satellite rotated slowly in the air above the massive, bare deck. There was no dust to speak of—though the idea conjured an image of Kasanove in a French Maid outfit. Nel chuckled to herself.

Lin shot her a glare. "I'm glad you're finding this entertaining."

"Lighten up, Komodor," she muttered. The look on Lin's face could have soured milk, but Nel was mostly just happy no one had tossed her in another interrogation room. "No one's shot anybody. Yet."

The study had only enough chairs to accommodate Sant's wife and daughter, and Emilio took up his characteristic lean on the doorframe. Nel almost settled next to him, but disliked the image it painted that they were two mismatched security guards. Instead, she propped herself by one of the lower bookshelves.

"I'm glad we can all finally speak," Tirta began, diplomatically, "It's been long overdue."

"Shouldn't Dar be here?" Lin stalled.

"Maybe you should have thought about that before you shot him," Nel muttered.

"Excuse me?" Tirta asked.

Lin flinched, looking away sharply, as if she'd been slapped. "I didn't shoot him. He was hit with shrapnel and maybe it was from my blast, but it was hazy and you two idiots were running and I was trying my best to miss, actually. I don't know if I could say the same for you, in the infirmary."

"You want me to fucking try again?" Nel fired back, too exhausted to remember her manners or temper or counting exercises.

"Dr. Bently, I fail to see why you are still here." Sant rumbled. Nel realized her initial assessment had been wrong. Here was the origin of Lin's temper, the single-minded beam of retribution cast from her space-black eyes. "This is a family matter and while our children may have opened our home to all manner of refugees in our absence, my wife and I are here now, and that invitation no longer extends to you. As such, I ask that you return to your room until I can decide what to do with you."

Nel straightened, rage and hurt burning her eyes. This time, though, they were bitterly, overwhelmingly her own. She longed to dust her hands of the matter and jet back home to die in ignorance. Except that was no longer possible.

"Ayah," Lin protested. "She has a right to be here. They both do. And she's telling the truth. Before we all came here, Dar and I were at odds. If you want her to leave, then fine, but I go too."

At odds? Nel almost laughed at the understatement but blinked. *She's defending me?*

Tirta cleared her throat, rising to perch herself on the edge of her husband's desk, as much a shield as he was a weapon. "I believe the preceding events have made us all a bit short tempered and reactive. If Dr. Bently could agree not to threaten the lives of anyone else here, then I think we could listen to what she has to say. Agreed?" Her gaze settled on the archaeologist.

Nel abruptly realized that as firm and thunderous as Sant acted, here was the true spine of the Nalawangsa clan. "Of course. Agreed. I'm sorry I lost my temper—it's something I'm working on."

Lin glanced at her, seemingly as surprised by Nel's apology as Nel herself had been at Lin's defense. "Thank you, Ibu. Do you think you could start from the beginning? Where you've been?"

Tirta turned to her husband, who waved at her, clearly annoyed at being overruled. "Go on, then. The sooner we get to the bottom of this the better."

"Shortly after the whole affair on Samsara," Tirta began, "Sant and I were both contacted— separately, it turns out—by an operative working outside of IDH. They expressed some safety concerns given the loss of life on Samsara. Of course, nothing had been confirmed yet, but people don't just disappear leaving behind a desert. I considered the implications, and of course said I was going nowhere without the rest of my family. Sant and I agreed, but getting the two of you to do so? Dar had radar-dropped by this point, making everything more complicated. And you," Tirta looked over at Lin, eyes gentle in their honesty, "Well."

"He said he had you, alright?" Lin's whisper cracked through the stillness. "He said you were imprisoned somewhere. It took me weeks to search the entirety of *Lahifa.* Even then I was terrified I'd missed someplace. As soon as I realized—"

"You will answer for your deeds," Sant informed his daughter, and this time sorrow laced the anger in his voice.

"'Ga," Tirta interjected, hand coming to rest on her husband's shoulder. "There will be a time to address our daughter's missteps. For now, we do not have the privilege of time." She raised her chin, and the room fell to stillness. "Clearly our plan did not go accordingly. But regardless, our team's efforts to keep us safe took us across three sectors, and I pray they gathered as much evidence as they could."

Sant heaved a sigh, shaking his head. "The last thing either of us remembers is entering cryo on that ship, just before you all left for Earth. Under the guise of helping you, of course. We were told we'd be out in a matter of weeks, and when we awoke, we'd be with our family again, joining the Alkhalaaq resistance. Next we know, we're being woken at home, months later and far from where we were supposed to be."

"Who organized the whole thing? Surely you did security checks."

Tirta glanced at her husband. "We did, and the connections traced back to Los Pobledores. Who our exact contact was, they never said. The voice was feminine. One of the more rural Terrestrial accents, though most sound the same."

Nel rolled her eyes at the ignorance and dared to interject. "It was Andy."

Lin shot her a look that had more edges than strictly necessary. "Why is she your answer to everything?"

"Because she's working for Phil. Or was."

"Philos? Senti-comp of *Odyssey?*" Tirta asked. When Nel nodded, her frown deepened. "If Philos is involved with this rescue—if even he feels threatened—"

"We've explained our side of things, I think it's time you do the same," Sant interjected, heavy gaze resting on Nel. "Perhaps you can help me better understand why everyone keeps threatening to shoot one another."

"Sir, if I may?" Emilio began. When the triplicate of Nalawangsa attention settled on him, he continued, elaborating on the events on Earth during their mission with Harris, and the subsequent flight across the stars. Lin's direct involvement in their pursuit, however, he avoided like a landmine. "While we traveled, Komodor Muda Nalawangsa, Dr. Bently, and I studied the signal first observed during the excavation of Samsara. Through this we were able to make some rather," he faltered, looking to Nel for a life raft, "disturbing revelations."

"Ayah," Lin whispered. "I'm so sorry."

Sant turned to her, dread replacing the anger in his eyes. "What is it?"

Lin drew in a sharp breath, looking to Nel. "I wasn't there—"

"I'll tell them if you won't, but I think it's best if it came from family." When Lin made no move to answer, she barreled into the confession. "We were following the trail of a ship last seen over the sky of Samsara, tracked it across the ah—"

"Castadonna Asteroid Field," Emilio offered.

"Yeah. All the way to a decommissioned mining base. And there we—Dar and I—found your brother Mansur Nalawangsa in the systems room."

Lin finally looked up from her white knuckles. "Uak Mansur is gone. I'm sorry."

Some invisible door slammed shut behind Sant's eyes.

Tirta dropped a hand to his shoulder. "What happened?"

"We don't know—"

"I documented the scene," Nel interrupted. She recognized the determination on the other woman's face, the need to do something. To solve this. "I have photos of everything. And you're welcome to look at them, but neither I nor Dr. Morchek—the mortician aboard *The Recursive*—could make any concrete determination. He was plugged into the base through a port in his skull. Very Matrix, if you ask me." *Lin said you shared films from Earth, and maybe that was one.* Or maybe Nel was desperate for some shared ground.

"His life was not the only one lost, sir," Emilio continued. "With his ship's diagnostics we were able to retrace his steps to his last stop prior to the base. An old civilian hauler—*V Drugoye Mesto*."

Nel cast a glance at Lin, wishing she would do more than just stare, catatonic, at an empty point on her father's desk. "Everyone on that ship had been...destroyed. Transformed. We believe they suffered the same fate as the people on Samsara. Perhaps by the same hands."

"By my brother's hands? And what evidence do you have for this astounding accusation?" Sant leveled the question at Nel, the unfortunate bearer of more unfortunate news. But she heard, under the fatigue and annoyance, resignation. He rose, a veritable mountain of a man. "With ideas like those, it's a small wonder my daughter turned you out on your ears."

"Ayah, listen to her," Lin insisted.

Nel barreled on before anyone could silence her further. "Well, the one survivor remembers nothing, and the only other person who might know is being studied right now and asleep, or..." Was sleeping the right word for Phil, unconscious with his usual synapses thousands of miles away? Nel grimaced.

Lin finally broke her silence. "Uak's shuttle is the only link between Samsara, *V Drugoye*, and the mining station where they found him, Ayah. I'm so sorry, truly, I am. I know he was your family, our family, but the dead deserve peace, and we need answers."

Nel squeezed her eyes shut. Emotions welled up her throat and bubbling from between her teeth. As an archaeologist, she had a duty to the dead. A responsibility to learn their stories and share them, however mundane, however terrible. And, hopefully in sharing, those living could learn from their lives and deaths. By sharing their stories, Nel could grant them a tiny piece of immortality.

Or justice.

"There's more." Nel fisted her hands and cast herself into the line of fire. "More evidence, I mean. This residual energy centered around people exposed to Samsara when it—well." No one raised a voice to condemn or mock her. Nel swallowed her uncertainty.

"The signal?" Emilio asked.

She nodded. "The sounds, voices, they've been trailing me since Samsara. Lin too, I guess. I'm not special, really, I'm just the one who survived. And when I cataloged Mansur's body I heard screaming, pleading, and condemnation. I couldn't explain it. But when we ah, met up with Lin again, I tried to replicate it. Stepped into the airlock, turned off my suit's safety and," Nel's voice thickened, and she dragged her gaze to Lin's shoulders, unable to risk actual eye contact. "The ghosts of Samsara, Lin. I heard them too."

The room fell to silence, and Nel swore even the air itself stilled. "They followed us, clinging to the hope that, because we tried to fix Samsara, we could fix them, too. They tried, in their blundering way, to get our attention. Ringing in Paul's ears to make him hear them. Filling Gretatron's voice box in an attempt to speak. It wasn't an attack on the others who died on the mission, maybe not even on *Lahifa*." Nel admitted, letting out a laugh, more sob than mirth. "Not intentionally. The voices, they're Samsara's ghosts except," she swallowed, feeling the hum of energy coursing through her body, eager, unwavering support. "Whatever happened to them, it didn't kill them. The Samsari aren't dead. Only changed."

TEN

Sant's study exploded into arguments, Tirta attempting to talk her husband down from a growing mountain of incredulity, and Emilio cutting in to temper Nel's terrible revelation. Lin, however, remained silent. Her eyes bored into Nel, who, for perhaps the first time since they reunited, met her gaze. No words passed between them, but Nel finally gave a small, apologetic nod. It was true. All of it, however much they wished it weren't. And Lin knew it.

The family whirled in conversation while Emilio and Nel hovered at the fringes, in perpetual orbit around the anchors of their lives. Each went over and over the facts they'd learned, the terrible truths, and the worse questions brought to light.

"This entire affair has been absurd, and I would very much like to settle into our home, and rest, and revisit this ridiculous set of theories when I've slept and can decipher what, actually, is going on," Sant finally rumbled, rising. "As for you, Mr. Sepulveda—"

"Munashi, actually, sir." Emilio corrected, chin lifted. "IDH may have imploded, but Los Pobladores are alive and well."

Sant leveled an annoyed stare at him but gave a curt nod. "Munashi Sepulveda, then. I appreciate your contributions to my son's research; however I will be taking over from here. Both you and Dr. Bently are relieved of your duties. Good night."

Nel winced as Sant kicked them out in earnest, but this time she went gladly. She hated sitting around and talking forever, and at this point she preferred the dread of the crashing shuttle earlier that day. At least she had known what to do. Had a goal. She slumped down on the arm of a reading chair outside the study door. *And people who trusted me to at least do something.*

Beside her, Emilio scoffed softly and raked his hand through his shaggy dark hair. His voice dropped into soft Spanish. "I don't know whether to be relieved or offended."

Nel barked a humorless chuckle of her own. "Story of my life."

Emilio fixed her with his characteristic thoughtful stare. "You were telling the truth in there. About the Samsari."

"I was." She affirmed, though the look on his weathered face and the ache in his voice told her he believed.

"So your ghosts, they're not ghosts, exactly."

She shrugged. "Not in the traditional sense. And they aren't mine."

"You're their voice, Nel. They're yours enough. And I don't know if they had a choice, but if they did, they chose well." He rested a heavy hand on her shoulder. "We'll do right by them. As much as we can."

"Do you forgive him?" Nel asked, suddenly, turning to stare at Emilio. "Renato, I mean?"

His inhalation was sharp, and his brows so knit that they were almost one over the storm cloud of his eyes. "If he has chosen to go by Harris now, then I respect that. But forgive?" His jaw worked. "I suspect this has something to do with a certain Nalawangsa."

"Two of them, kind of," Nel explained. "Dar says he forgives her. For shooting him."

"They pulled shrapnel out of his wound, Nel. It wasn't a glove-blast that ripped—" pain flickered across his features, "There would have been less damage if it had been, honestly. Why are you so hell-bent on the idea of her shooting him?"

She kicked at the flagging beneath her boots, wondering why his question stung so much.

"I won't call this mess we've been entangled in war, because half the time one side has no idea they're fighting. But we are fighting. And we've been fighting for generations. Maybe it wasn't Mansur and Harris at first, but it's the same idea my ancestors fought against, and all those other tribes thousands of years ago when the Teachers first showed up. We're fighting the idea that someone can decide for us what's best. Someone else."

Nel looked away, feeling chastised, but unsure why.

"And I'm furious with Harris for turning away from what our father taught us, what I tried to keep teaching him. I'm furious that he and Bas and the others got in so far over their heads on either side of this stupid fight that they lost themselves. And no. I don't think I can forgive him yet. But I do understand why he chose his path." Emilio nudged her shoulder with his, gently, pointed. "And I know that what my brother did and what Lin did are worlds apart."

"Maybe I need her to have shot Dar, because then I'd have a reason not to forgive her." Nel whispered, so quiet the words were almost lost among the murmuring ghosts.

Emilio let her sit with the confession but reached over to squeeze her hand. "Forgiveness is hard, Bently. But if you don't do it for her, do it for yourself. Blame eats you alive, held too long."

She was about to answer, to stammer that how could she forgive something so grievous, when Dar stirred on the nearby couch, groaning softly as he woke.

"I'm going to deal with this," Emilio muttered, nodding toward Dar. "You?"

Nel grimaced. "I could tell you I'm going to bed, but I doubt I'll sleep. I'll probably wander around until I find some trouble to get into that distracts from this current trouble we're in."

He laughed softly. "You should try to sleep eventually."

"Will you?"

"When he does, I try to," he remarked softly, indicating Dar, before drawling to the roused pilot, "¿Dormiste bien, Cariño?"

"Do I hear shouting?" He rasped.

Though the commotion in the study had died down a bit, the unmistakable sound of tense conversion still rumbled through the wooden door. "No one likes it when Mommy and Daddy fight," Nel remarked.

Dar blanched, eyeing the closed door with apprehension. "They're awake?"

"We had a little summit while you were out," Nel explained. "It went about as well as you expect. I threatened to shoot Lin again, your dad tried to kick me out, and I dropped a shitty bombshell on everyone. Anyway," she gave a two-handed wave and backed toward the ramp down from the mezzanine. "I'll let you two process this. Gonna take a walk."

She escaped the library before her aforementioned bomb was explained to Dar and set off in a random direction. A glance at her comm told her it was barely suppertime, despite how tired everyone was. The first stop was her room.

Xand was curled on the couch, fast asleep and clutching a pillow. Nel stopped herself from waking him. Someone should get some rest, even if it was just the gangly teen. She dragged the blanket from her bed and tucked it awkwardly over him. He didn't stir.

She hastily ripped a page from her fieldbook and wrote a note:

> *It really was just Dar and Lin's parents. Had some ship trouble getting in. There's food in the cooling unit if you wake up before I'm back.*
> *-N*

Leaving the note on the low, living room table, she slipped back out into the hall. Her steps took her around the estate, down into the dusky bower of the towering trees. Lights from the village beyond cast odd shadows and rays between the boles. It was there, at the mouth of the path, that she wavered. She pictured herself walking down the promenade, bathed in green phosphorescence and blue reflected from the gas giant above. She would wave at those dining on their roofs and patios, laugh as a child ran across her path, and turn, welcome and expected, down her mother's street. They'd eat, outside like the others, and laugh, and speak of nothing consequential.

The soft air swept across her, and as inviting as her imagined scenario was, she took a step back and turned, instead, to the platform that dropped into the mechanical, carved warren beneath. It was hard for her to believe that just hours before, she'd taken this same path, heart thundering, glove powering up. This time, the lights were dimmed for the evening, no emergency bulbs flashing.

Often, the alien world of acrylic windows and recycled air pissed Nel off. But here, the very breeze made her skin crawl—not because it felt fake, or because she could smell the staleness of it, like on *The Recursive,* but because it was convincing. She wouldn't have known the difference had she not seen the lens of the shield above. So, she welcomed the descent into the satellite's mechanics. Here it was honest in its cables and tubes and blinking lights. As alien as the voices echoing through her mind.

She half-followed the signs along the corridors, listening to the not-silence of the air and fluids burbling through *Vīrya*'s arteries. *Maybe this is what a senti-comp's body is. Converted like their brains to bioelectrics.* The hall ended in large double doors, and she cut to the side, into a small service corridor. Left, left, right then left again until she stood against the metal arc reinforcing the asteroid's natural exterior. Pockets of airlocks dotted the curve, waiting for mechanics to perform EVA, or tiny training ships, perhaps.

Nel swayed, legs aching, imagining a childhood here. Playing hide and seek in the hydro recycler, or whatever. Did the Samsari have a childhood like that? *Are some of you children?*

Nel knew the answer, had seen the census reports early in the excavation of the planet.

Samsara was their home, just as *V Drugoye Mesto* had been Xand's home. His infant sister's home. She checked that the nearest airlock had atmosphere and palmed its panel. The door whispered open, then shut behind her. Weight lifted from her shoulders at the stillness.

Nel reached over and rested her hand over the switch on her comm. *Vīrya*'s shielding wasn't perfect, but it did shield from errant signals, solar radiation, and electromagnetic pulses, aside from the moderate protection it offered from physical attacks or accidents. Her comm and electrosuit, still on from the crash, offered an additional boost.

And then there were her mental guards. The decades of common sense and skepticism drilled into her since she was a child. But Nel had never been pragmatic. She was a person of instinct and impulses. More feeling than flesh, sometimes. *Just like them.* Maybe that's why she could hear it. Some kinship born of raw emotion and electricity. It was easier this time, to let them in.

Her eyes lidded and she flipped the switch. It was slow, sinking into static, feeling it skate along her skin like thunder across the expanse of sky. Just a step too sharp to be tolerable.

No words rose up through the swamp of her thoughts. Anticipation was cold fire in her bones. Perhaps like Nel, like the rest of this doomed satellite, the Samsari were listening. Waiting for the bubble to pop.

"My skies..."

Nel turned slowly, feeling the pressure around her like honey. The time on the door's readout panel told her half an hour had passed in what felt like seconds.

Lin stood just outside the door, eyes wide. Her finger was on the airlock's comm button, and the other hand hovered over the entry panel. "They're in there right now, aren't they?" She asked. Nel swore the air between them parted for Lin's words, their wake shimmering in the corners of Nel's eyes. "You're talking to them."

"Listening, more like," Nel replied, voice loud, as if the ghosts surrounding her somehow altered the acoustics. "Think they are too. Wondering what happens next."

Lin didn't answer, gaze raking over Nel's form as if trying to see what she did, what she felt. Did she see the ripple in the air? Or was she wondering what the consequences would be if she dropped her hand lower, pulled the lever and purged the airlock of all its infuriating contents? It was almost welcoming, the thought of allowing virtual nothing to claim her.

But Lin did not send Nel hurling into space. Instead, after a second, she tilted her head. "What do they sound like?"

"Water's warm," Nel invited, "Jump on in."

Lin's eyes grew to dark caverns, and she shook her head. "I—I don't think so." Something flickered over her face, maybe frustration. "I'm integrated. I've been hearing their whispers, words, sounds, but I never dared to listen too hard. And after my new augments and seeing what happened to all the others I—no. I don't think so."

Nel took a step forward, then a second, until, if it weren't for the airlock door, they could have touched. It was the closest they'd been since Nel's glove rested over her chest. Here, Nel was powerful, Lin held at bay by the energy of several thousand ghosts. For once she was in control, and Lin was the one running scared. Energy, white hot and burning, pulsed between them, but Nel would have bet money it had nothing to do with the Samsari. "But you believe me."

Lin swallowed, unblinking, and gave a hard nod. "I do."

The minutes dragged on as they stood, listening, awash with the impotence of waiting. It was only when Nel's nose dribbled blood from the pressure in her skull, that she called it quits. She gave the cushion of sentient air a tiny nod. "Good night, Samsari." It billowed around her, perhaps in an answer, then she pressed her wrist again. Silence shuttered over her and she sagged against the airlock door.

Lin opened it wordlessly, continuing to stare as Nel stumbled back into the satellite proper. "My parent's will come around," she promised.

"Believe it when I see it." Nel snorted. She flexed her legs with a groan and headed back up the corridor. "See you in the morning, Letnan."

ELEVEN

The walls of the library's second floor were covered in maps. Some of planets, others of star systems, and still more perhaps of buildings and satellites. Nel limped up the ramp from the mezzanine to the more intimate second storey ringing the room's open center. Several carrels and alcoves led off from the main room. She had spent the night alone, and her morning, too. After carrying out her P. T. exercises, she headed past Dar's room and Lin's, both eerily silent. The library was as well. Wherever the Nalawangsas were, the message was clear—Nel was not included.

As she limped along, she eyed the antique tomes crowded around the railing. Most were what looked like resin models encasing their digital versions. Nel paused by one, peering closer. It was a text from Iceland, one used for luck during childbirth. Flickering in a gentle scroll along the glass beside it were the sequences of the DNA samples lifted from the placental blood splattered across its whisper-thin pages. She shivered. A large platform—like that displaying *Vīrya*'s layout below—was next. The center was filled with a brilliant full color holo of a lush planet. After a second, Nel recognized the structures beneath its translucent surface. *Samsara*. Her head dropped and her eyes stung, overwhelmed with sudden, borrowed grief.

"That's a particular favorite of mine."

Nel whirled, almost falling in her surprise.

Today, Tirta Nalawangsa was wrapped in the soft folds of white and cream, offsetting her skin, a shade darker than either of her children. Her eyes were the brilliant brown of a flooded riverbank.

Nel fought the urge to do something as foolish as bow and held out her hand. "Ah, good morning. Laksamana, or—I'm sorry, do you still go by that? With IDH and all—"

"Like my son I've chosen to continue to use my titles until I have something more fitting with which to replace them. From you though, I think I'd prefer Tirta, if that's alright." She offered a gentle smile, one Nel felt would be directed at a skittish animal. Maybe a puppy.

"Sure. You can call me Nel."

Tirta took Nel's hand, turning it over to examine her palm thoughtfully, soft fingers tracing the callouses. "Welcome to *Vīrya*, Daughter of Earth."

Nel swore the satellite shifted under her feet. The words sounded closer to an incantation than a welcome. "Thank you. I really appreciate it. Though I know we're rather uninvited."

"Oh, don't listen to Sant, he's all bluster. I appreciate your dedication."

Lin had said Dar took after their mother, and she after their father. Nel had barely spent an hour with both collectively and agreed. She could trace Dar's irreverence all the way back to the woman before her with her eyes closed. "It's an honor to meet you. I've heard a lot."

"Have you?"

"Compared to everyone else."

"You looked us up on the database."

"I assume you did the same with me," Nel countered, seizing her only defense.

"I did." Her round features softened slightly. "I'd heard you speak first and think later."

Nel's face flamed with embarrassment. *Off to a great start.*

Tirta gestured to the walls stretching between the tall, narrow windows. "I also heard you like maps."

Nel followed her gesture with her eyes. The collection was beautiful, a personal Alexandria. "I like knowing where I stand."

Tirta met her gaze, thoughtful, observing. "And where do you think you stand here?"

Nel looked down, checking to see where her mismatched feet rested at that moment. Perhaps it was the mother in Tirta that pulled the honesty from her, or the fact that she seemed content to meet Nel where she was, without the incredulity or disrespect her reputation earned. "I think I'm a necessary inconvenience. Were it not for the Samsari—" she cut herself off, remembering belatedly, that those were Tirta's people. "I've been on the business end of scrutiny when it comes to the parents. This is next level, even for the family of someone I was, ah—"

"Fucking?"

Nel choked on her surprise, which brought a proper laugh from Lin's mother.

"Sant and I started much the same way. I didn't have time for relationships, and certainly not his level of romance. We were friends until I realized he wasn't going anywhere no matter what I tried. So, we married. Sometimes I think Lin forgets her parents weren't always paramours."

Nel scrubbed her hands on her thighs. This wasn't anything like she imagined it would be. *And that's okay.* "Well, both your children are quite the powerhouses. You have a lot to be proud of."

"Those are kind words for a woman who left you and your planet to burn to death."

Nel froze. She turned slowly, as much to give herself time to think as to keep from toppling over. "I'm sorry?"

"Sant is, like many men, fragile and too stubborn for his own good. He adores Lin with a singular devotion. So, like Dar, I protect him from what Lin often is: a complicated, deceptive creature."

"You got the details of her time in IDH. When we were running."

"From her, yes. I hoped it wouldn't be the case. We pulled back from IDH after the events on Samsara—we knew what it looked like, as did Dar. All we could do was pray, pray that our children would survive it. Of course, by that point we were in cryo, anyway. Luckily, my network is as far reaching as IDH's and far more personal." She offered a hand, soft and motherly and filled with steel. "Last night, when I was looking through everything, I heard your message to Earth."

Nel flushed, dropping her hand. "Got a bit flowery there. About to die and all that."

"That's when I understood why Dar invited you, and why you probably thought it wise to come—and I'm grateful to meet the woman that so thoroughly wrecked my daughter's world."

Nel winced. "Look, about the bad influence. I didn't realize a lot about this world—"

"She needed it. She has had everything in the world handed to her and worked herself ragged trying to prove she was worthy of it all. That's where we failed, I think. In telling her everyone deserves those things, she forgot she does too. I'm just sorry she didn't listen to you more."

Nel chuckled. "I wasn't aware she listened to me at all."

"I doubt she listens to me either." Tirta breathed a long, thoughtful sigh. "She's always been a bit of a beautiful, if distant mystery to me."

Me too. Nel couldn't answer. She hoped Lin would come around, hoped her promise to help was genuine and not yet another ploy of Harris's. She feared it, too, feared the work they would have to do to repair the shattered thing between them Nel had once dared to call love. The battered spark so fully engulfed in the furnace of her anger.

"If you're able, may I show you something?"

"Sure. I probably should get some more steps in." Nel agreed, though her muscles ached and her back still twinged from too many years digging.

Tirta frowned at the phrase, but either already knew about smart fitness tech on Earth or didn't care enough to ask. Nel guessed it was the latter. They left the library through a side door, taking a long, switch backing ramp down the side of the estate's pyramid. Tirta's steps were slow enough for Nel to keep up without issue, and graceful enough to seem unintentionally so. The mid-morning sun was brilliant, bright enough to hide most of the gas giant's swell, save for a thin crescent of brighter blue.

"It's beautiful," Nel admired. "If a little strange."

"That's how I felt when I first saw it."

"Dar said Brigadir Jenderal Nalawangsa built the jungle for you?"

She smiled, and Nel recognized the playful teasing expression that sometimes crossed Lin's face. "He did. He worried I wouldn't agree to marry him otherwise. But the rest of the satellite existed well before Sant met me. *Vīrya* was built by my husband's grandfather. There were gardens before, of course, but nothing like this." Her delicate hand swept across the view, and her face grew pensive. "My family was comfortable on Samsara, but it was nothing like this. It was an adjustment, coming here. Leaving my home planet. That's why he made the jungle. So, I wouldn't be so homesick."

They emerged at the base of the pyramid, and Tirta led them away from the village and main elevator to a small single level building holding nothing but a second, much smaller transport platform. While as utilitarian as the corridors down to the docking area, these were brightly lit and whitewashed, the cables and tubes affixed high on the ceiling and out of the way.

"Welcome to *Vīrya*'s internal systems." Lin's mother gestured at the double doors that opened before them at the bottom of the lift. "It was a base of operations for an IDH hub before the organization outgrew it. As such, it had substantial infrastructure—engineering, chemical, and medical laboratories, for example. But much of the underbelly was going unused, so the departments that weren't decommissioned were relocated here when the satellite turned private."

The walls changed to large acrylic windows and bright, clinical lighting. Tirta watched Nel as she leaned on the rail along the wall to peer into the series of rooms beyond. Labs that would make the CDC envious stretched on either side. Many were dimmed and unused, but a few dozen scientists worked away inside the largest three. Maps of circuitry and prototypes of every human physiological system were arrayed, in part or in whole, across the benches.

"Holy shit." Nel gaped. The prosthetics she recognized were gleaming, as much art as they were functional. She watched a flesh kidney, cupped against a mechanical adrenal gland, filter thick, crimson blood. On another bench two people compared the functionality between grown nervous tissue and a spider-silk net of manufactured wires.

"The Nalawangsa's might be known for their diplomacy now, but my in laws were innovators when it came to biomechanical systems and technological integration with human physiology. My son tells me you do not have an integrated prosthetic."

Nel glanced over with a frown. "I mean. The whole integration bit still kind of skeeves me out. But I do wish I had something more useful than this thing." She patted the borrowed limb. A pang of guilt shot through her chest. It had served her well. It had done its best. "No offense, old girl," she muttered.

Tirta's face softened with a concealed smile. "I can imagine integration feels a bit alien to you."

"Invasive, might be a better term." *After all, your daughter's really fucking alien and I had no issues integrating with her.* "I've seen many dangerous tech issues since getting out here. Seems reckless to make something a part of my body when it could be hacked or whatever. Like what happened with Grettatron—sorry, Kapten Greta Wagner."

"That was a tragedy. Her and Dar's former companion."

Nel glanced over sharply, eyes narrowed. "He said you never knew about Paul."

Sorrow flitted over her features. "He never told us. That doesn't mean we didn't know. We let him have his privacy, and tried to figure out why he didn't feel it was safe to tell us."

"Gotcha," Nel looked away.

"Did you tell your parents about the people you dated?"

"I ah," She frowned. "I rarely brought anyone back. They met more than a few women I introduced as friends and we all just pretended for a bit. Things are different down there. My mom knows about Lin though."

"She's staying with us, yes? Your mother?"

Nel gave a tiny nod, suddenly picturing Lin and her family having dinner with Mindi and fought down a wave of anxious nausea. In a desperate effort to avoid fulfilling that hideous prophecy, Nel pointed at the bioengineering beyond the window. "So, some of that is actual tissue—was it donated?

"Actually, less complex systems can be lab-grown," Tirta responded, not acknowledging the clumsy topic change. "We can grow mostly the larger organs and those already predisposed to regeneration, like the liver. Entire limbs, for example," she paused, glancing down at Nel's leg, "contain too many integrated tissues to be fully grown yet. And there are still many who opt for mechanical augments, whether for logistical or personal reasons."

Logistical. She recalled Jem's comment about how they needed to work off their own life-saving augments. "I gotta ask: how does payment work out here? I was told by my biomech tech, who helped me with this unit," she tapped her prosthetic, "that it was like, debited to our service at various jobs? It seems so nice, just to have it put on a tab, so to speak but it got me to thinking—how is that any different from indentured servitude? Like, 'Here's your new liver, have fun working it off for the rest of your life, sucker.'"

"It isn't."

Nel stared.

"At least, when you put it like that. But contracts can be transferred or petitioned to be canceled entirely. And there is something for anyone to do. Those who aren't physically able, can still run our systems. Those who aren't mentally capable of system-managing can be companions to others, and make art. At least," she frowned, "that's how it was meant to be."

Nel hummed, gaze still poring over the feats of godliness just behind the quarantine windows. She missed running. She missed walking without her crutch. This was a carrot, offered by the deadly philanthropy of the Nalawangsa matriarch. *Wonder what the stick is.* "I guess I'll be finding out for myself here, pretty soon. I assume that's why you brought me here?"

A small smile eased over Tirta's face, approval, perhaps, of Nel's conclusion. She gestured to a circuitry map one of the techs was testing. "That could be yours. If you want it."

"So, where's the catch? You can't tell me this is just a gift. I know those were a lot of pretty words, but is my contract to your family? Cause that's a weird dynamic."

"Well, you may be reckless but you're not stupid." Her face took on the hard, calculating stare that Nel had come to know as Lin's battle face. "I want a favor in return. I give you that state-of-the-art integrated biomechanical prosthetic. And in return, you save my daughter."

"Laksamana—Tirta." She sucked a breath in hard through her nose. "You think she's still on Harris's side?"

"You don't?"

"I—" Nel actually, thought about it before blurting that, yes, of course she thought Lin was a double-crossing psycho. Because she didn't. She may have held the woman at glove-point in the heat of their reunion, but now? She almost wished Lin was evil or their enemy. It would make it so much easier to hate her. "No. Not once she explained everything. It hasn't crossed my mind since, I guess."

"Good." She gave a small nod. "Then we agree."

"Ignoring the fact that there's no way I'll be capable—if you don't think she's still in cahoots with the nutcase, what do you think she needs saving from?"

"From herself. I give you this, and you help her, work with her, do whatever is necessary to keep her from eating herself alive with the guilt of being on the wrong side of science, even for just a moment."

Nel scoffed. "You could have the best scientists and soldiers here to help you with this mess—and the best therapists to help with Lin's perfectionism. Why me?"

Tirta stared at Nel for a long, quiet moment. The insulated windows prevented even the beeps and scientific discussions from disturbing the dry air within the corridor. "The device on earth, that would have ended it all. It was never meant to have an override. It was programed later, to be disengaged by a single override code. Yours. Next time you speak to Lin, perhaps ask her why."

The bottom of Nel's stomach dropped to her battered boots. She very much wished she could sit without falling in a heap at the woman's feet. "What?"

"I don't know what you said or how you did it, but you got through to her. My daughter might be back here, among family, but her heart is still lost among the stars. But because of you, I know she's capable of coming her way back to us." Tirta's brown hand covered Nel's. "So, what do you say?"

Nel looked from the strength of Tirta's features to the delicate fabricated nervous system being tested on the other side of the glass. *Saving Lin.* It wasn't something she even thought was necessary. Nel's mind lingered on the image of the young woman's dissociated stare the day before, listening to her parents learn exactly how far she had fallen from grace. And the terror in her eyes watching Nel bathe in the voices of the not-quite-dead. Nel heaved an exasperated breath and extended her hand. "You have a deal."

TWELVE

With her eyes closed, Nel could almost imagine proper sunlight warmed her face. Bitter coffee coated her tongue, and her muscles ached. Somewhere, children shouted and friends called to one another. The whisper of pages turning underscored the other sounds and Nel smiled. She pretended she was on the screened-in porch of their summer rental. Lake water dried on her skin and her mother was reading the latest Tosca Lee thriller while her father commenced his annual reorganization of the dilapidated shed.

"She find her sister yet?" She mumbled, rocking her head to the right to aim the comment at her mom.

"It's her nephew that's missing in this one," Mindi corrected, "and she hasn't yet. But Anka was pissed the other day when I asked how she was liking it, and she's a fast reader. Might not be a happy one, this time around."

Nel blinked her eyes open, rocketed from her memories by the foreign skyline of stone and jungle. She sighed, and chuckled. "They're dark thrillers, I wasn't aware happy was an option."

"Hey, we had a romance last month," Mindi retorted.

"With her stalker!"

Mindi shot her a look over her readers. "Like you can talk."

Nel pulled a face and fished another beer from the stash under her mother's table. It had been a blessedly quiet two days since her promise to Tirta. She passed a distracted Emilio in the hall that morning and had yet to see Dar since his parents' arrival. *Asshole is probably off talking about starship engines and forgot entirely why we're here.* It was a bitter thought, and one she wasn't proud of. After all, she had been the one dragging her feet—foot, rather—for most of their time on *The Recursive.*

As much as she enjoyed the respite, she was itching to know if anything, seriously, anything had happened. Hopefully someone would at least tell her if Andy or Phil had awoken.

"I like this," Mindi remarked, sliding a boney finger between the pages and looked thoughtfully out over the view.

Nel cast a sidelong glance at her mother. "The, ah, satellite, or..."

"Sitting here with you, listening to the world around us. It's peaceful. Meditative." She heaved a soft sigh and turned to look at Nel fully. "But it's not you. I barely see you since we got here, and now you're lounging on my rooftop for hours at a time. For God's sake, Anna, it's like a teenage breakup around here."

Nel grimaced and sat up to protest, except the world spun a bit and her heart hurt and she needed a shower and Mindi was way too right. "Yeah. Kind of fucking is."

"Anna," her mother began, about to correct her language, surely, but she turned it into a soft laugh. "Lin?"

"Her whole damn family. Since they showed up it's been the Holier-Than-Thou episode of the Big Ego Show and I'm so over it. Lin is the one I've seen the most of, which really doesn't help me feel anything other than furious. But," the words caught in her throat and she let out a strangled scoff, "I still promised her mother I'd keep her safe."

"Excuse me?" Mindi frowned, lips pursing in displeasure at this news. "I haven't even met these women and you're making promises?"

Nel groaned and dropped her head in her hands. "I don't know what I was thinking. Her mom—" Nel switched to a pretentiously mocking tone, "—Laksamana First Class Tirta Nalawangsa, dangled a fucking carrot for me and I ate it right up. Promised I'd 'keep Lin safe from herself' in exchange for a proper prosthetic. How can I tell her not to feel guilty for her choices when I can't stop blaming her for them?"

Mindi listened as Nel petered into silence, then asked, gently, "I'm not saying I like her or trust her, frankly I'm tired of seeing her break you to pieces every other minute. But maybe forgiving her would save you too, honey. You don't have to like her. You don't even have to see her again when this is all over. But that anger will come with you. Blame hurts the accuser just as much as the guilty, when we hold it too long." She flashed a wicked smile. "I, however, as your mother, am capable of blaming her for all your heartache forever, and plan to do just that."

Nel sorted. Her comm buzzed, interrupted her next thought and she glanced down. "Speak of the Devil—Oh shit."

"Anna, really?"

Nel expanded the message and tilted it toward her mother.

Updated Personnel Assignment
Bently, Annelise, PhD.
Relocation: Data Sanctum Sapta, Satellite
Vīrya

"Oh shit is right," Mindi muttered, setting aside her book. She tried to roll her eyes, but the expression was dulled by her concern. "I suppose you'll be racing off to start an argument?"

"Start one? This message is an argument in itself. First I've heard of this. At least it looks like it's still on *Vīrya*. Maybe they've finally made headway. Or just decided to remove me entirely.

Put me in a cell right next to Harris." She shoved herself out of the chair and scooped the beer from under the table. "I'll talk to you later, give you any updates with my one allotted phone call."

Mindi lifted her cheek to accept Nel's peck and fixed her with a stern look. "Maybe these very important people could deign to meet me before they send you back into danger, hmm?"

"I'd let Harris have me before I went to that dinner party." When Mindi's stare narrowed, she held her hands up in surrender, backing toward the stairs. "Alright, alright, I'll ask. Promise!"

She tucked the beer beneath her arm and jabbed her comm as she forced her weaving steps into some form of sobriety. "Kasanove?"

"Yes, Dr. Bently?"

"Is Dar in his room?"

"Indeed. I'm afraid he's with Munashi Sepulveda and Dr. Hugo-Sanchez at the moment. Would you like me to tell him you called?"

"No. Thanks. I'm just gonna head over there." She was furious they met without her, that they were sending her at all.

By the time she reached his door the beer had sweated through the side of her shirt and her brow was greasy with sweat. She propped her crutch against the wall and pounded the door. Silence. "Look, I asked Kasanove, I know you're in there. You can't send me on a fucking mission and—"

Emilio jerked the door open.

"—not include me in the briefings," she finished with a grumble. She looked from Emilio to the couch beyond where Dar and Hugo-Sanchez sat, bowed over some blurry holoscreen. Nel grimaced at Emilio and muttered, "Guess I've been replaced."

"Just because you're incapable of maintaining more than one friendship at a time, doesn't mean everyone is, gaucho," he responded, but did her the kindness of keeping his voice low. Turning, he called to Dar, "You owe me that drink. She's here."

"Not fair, I bet she would be," Dar retorted.

"You bet she'd come in with guns blazing. I bet she'd be here and be all dejected."

"I'm about to not be here at all if this keeps going," she interrupted. "When were you going to tell me that I was being shipped off?"

Emilio glanced at Dar, whose expression remained sincerely blank. "What?"

Hugo-Sanchez looked pained and rose. "I think I'll see myself out."

"Why, was it your idea?" Nel accused, jabbing a gnarled finger at her. "If so, you better stay right there."

"Bently," Dar began, heaving a sigh. "Stop making a scene, and just tell us what you're pissed about this time."

That took the bluster out of her sails. "Sorry. I'm just tired of people making decisions about me, without me." She limped to the end of the couch furthest from the too-bouncy tech expert and slumped into the cushions. "I got a notice on my comm that I'm being sent to another part of the satellite. Data Septum something."

Dar's frown deepened. "Data Sanctum Sapta?"

"That's the one. Don't even know what it is, but that's where I'm supposed to go. And if none of you know about it, then I guess I'm going on my own."

"Not entirely. I'm not supposed to be able to see stuff at this security level but..." Hugo-Sanchez tapped away a series of notices on her own comm before enlarging the screen. "Lin's going with you."

"I can't," Nel protested.

"Those are your orders," Dar corrected.

"Dar, look I get that you adhere to logic and reason, and orders are like, your kink or whatever—" His dark brow twitched in a way that, if she were into dudes, would probably have had some sort of effect beyond annoyance. "I don't think these are orders I can follow."

The room fell silent, and neither Dar nor Hugo-Sanches would look at her. Emilio, however, leaned on the counter in the kitchen, staring at her, unreadable.

"Okay, say I do go. Why is she coming too?" *Because you made a promise.* She had no idea this was what Tirta had in mind. "She might be an anthropologist, but she's more of a soldier. And a war criminal."

"Well, she's also family of Mansur. You know, my family's other war criminal." Dar snapped. "And she has far more insight into any of this than you do."

"And I thought the Bentlys were dysfunctional..." Nel muttered, unable to argue with his point.

"Honestly, Nel do you really want to start down the qualifications route?" Emilio asked softly.

She blanched. "I guess my biggest qualification is surviving it all."

"And you could say the same about Lin. She saw Samsara too. She endured Harris's orders for months, even after realizing he was wrong. "

A shudder went down Nel's spine. Running across the stars from Harris was bad enough. But living with him? "Fine. I'll try, alright? I'll do my best."

"Bently, your best—"

"She agreed, Dar." Emilio remarked.

Nel finally ground out, rising with a lurch. "I can't believe your parents would hinge our only chance at answers on my personal domestic hell."

Dar's door hissed open, admitting Tirta, followed a second later by Lin. Their mother's face was unreadable, beyond a crease of displeasure. It matched the new fine lines Dar's face had grown over the last few months.

Lin herself was shrunk into a corner by Dar's kitchenette. Both graceful hands were clenched at her sides. With a lingering look at Nel, Tirta turned to Hugo-Sanchez. "Lissa, it's lovely to see you again. How're your fathers?"

"Both doing well, thank you. Da is still doing cartography, of course, and Apa finally retired earlier this year. We'll see how long he can actually relax." Hugo-Sanchez chewed on the end of her tidy twisted curls. She'd tugged them from the tie at the crest of her head and was now massaging her scalp, absentmindedly.

"Good to hear. We're grateful you could help us with this unfortunate situation."

Lin's ark eyes bored into Nel's the second she made the mistake of looking up. "You saw the assignment?"

"Assignment, like you had nothing to do with it."

Tirta's eyes were narrowed on Nel, perhaps hoping to silently remind her of the promise she had made.

Maybe I'm saving her sorry ass with tough love, alright?

"I actually told them it was a bad idea." She let out a tired, humorless laugh. "Expected you to be packed and halfway to the shuttle launch by now, trying to escape."

Nel grimaced. "Not like I even know where I'd go."

"Hasn't stopped you before."

"Last time I had a hostage to make arrangements for me." The joke hung between them, funny, if not for the biting tone with which she said it.

"Well, that hostage is dead now," Lin muttered.

Nel stilled. Here she was complaining about having to work with her ex, and Andy would never work again, never laugh or breathe. "When?"

"Late last night. She was shot sometime just before her flight here." Lin explained.

"Ibu, I'm sorry, but can you explain what's going on?" Dar leaned back to look at his mother, still hovering in the doorway. "Where's Ayah? Why are you sending Lin and Nel to Sapta?"

Tirta laced her fingers together, nodding to the available cushions on the broad sectional. "May I sit?"

"Yeah," Dar waved dismissively, before repeating, "Where's Ayah?"

"Thank you." Tirta took the seat next to Nel, offering her a small smile. "Your father is currently questioning Harris regarding Samsara and Mansur. I wish we could find some reason why he was indoctrinated by his own twisted version of alien mores." Tirta murmured. "Alas, we must content ourselves with learning the how of his monstrosity, and not the why. Regardless, Lin and Nel will be on the first transport out tomorrow morning. Your assignment is to search the data sanctum and catalog any findings. Due to both your experiences with Mansur and Harris's...designs...we felt it was best that you two be the ones to undertake this responsibility."

Nel glanced at the information still displayed, forgotten, on Hugo-Sanchez's comm, assuring she had the correct name before embarrassing herself further. "And how does Data Sanctum Sapta play into this?"

Tirta bowed her head. "Good question. Data sanctums are derived from similar technology to Samsara, and Sapta was—"

"Uak Mansur's training ground." Lin interrupted. She leaned forward and brought up a map on the display of Dar's room console. Nel peered closer. Most of the satellite was labeled, from the recycling systems to the back corridors, to the personal rooms of the highest family members. *Figures, Sant and Tirta's room is the top of this pyramid.* Nel almost chuckled at the thought of her and Emilio drinking and smoking just above their precious sprawling balcony. The topo aspects indicated there was a clearly human-built series of buildings far to the narrow end of the asteroid. It was to this spot that Lin pointed.

"To cut to the chase," Lin continued, "That is Sapta." Her eyes were mostly fixed on the schematic of *Vīrya*, but the split-seconds when they weren't, they were on Nel. "It's abandoned."

"How can a place be abandoned on a satellite?"

Lin flinched. "Easy. Everyone makes a pact not to go there." Her voice was strained with regret.

"What is it?"

"An old family place. That's all," Dar protested. "Just because Uak Mansur—"

"It's a temple." Lin's voice was quiet, but her words struck silence across the room.

Nel looked between them. "A temple to what?"

"The Teachers. There are thousands, scattered across the galaxy. Samsari shrines. Places where we were able to communicate with them."

Nel sank back into the couch cushions, only to recall Tirta was sitting far too close to warrant such casual posture. "Right. So, you and I are going to an abandoned temple to see if your uncle left his, what, secret notes just lying around on the pews?"

Lin's lip curled. "More or less."

Tirta clapped her hands together and rose. "Survey equipment along with food, water, cooking supplies and so forth will be taken care of, so pack just your personal effects. *Vīrya* isn't big, but the temple is a solid day's journey away, so I suggest you both prepare and say any goodbyes this evening."

Goodbyes. Nel bristled at the word. All the other times she'd been whisked away in this strange universe, she hadn't had the time for farewell. And as innocuous as this mission seemed, her stomach churned at the thought of something so formal as a goodbye. "Guess that's my cue," she stated, rising as quickly as her leg allowed. "See you losers in the morning."

Trita followed her to the door, hooking her arm with two elegant fingers as the archaeologist made to leave. "Dr. Bently."

Nel paused, staring at the floor until she could school the glare from her features. When she finally met Tirta's gaze, she hoped her expression was suitably blank. "Komodor."

"Are we still—"

"Yeah. Doesn't mean I have to act happy about it."

Tirta's brows rose, but a smile softened her surprise. "Indeed. Rest well. We'll see you tomorrow."

"Yep." Nel cut the conversation with a curt nod and left the room. The door clicked closed behind her, shutting out the family, and Nel sank against the wall, eyes stinging with the familiar sense of impotence that came from Nalawangsa orders.

She fired off a message to her mother saying she'd be by in the morning before slinking to her room. It was still tidy. She barely had enough belongings to make it messy, and certainly hadn't had the time. Her chest ached, heart longing for the mess of her office bookshelves, the rows of cool rocks and un-provenience d artifacts, the squelch of mud under her toes when the swamp behind her house flooded the backyard every spring.

"The only mess here is me." She groaned and swung open the door to the cooling unit. A single beer was left in the plastic container within. Well, it wasn't like she'd be able to bring any with her, and whatever the mission entailed, it would be best done sober. *Like it or not.*

Feeling responsible, she fished the bottle from the case and popped the top. A deep pull, then a second smaller one, and she felt the tension intching up her shoulders relax a fraction. Then she perched herself on the arm of the couch and awaited the knock.

When it came, half an hour later, Nel's eyes were heavy and her beer empty. A small part of her had hoped it would be Emilio. Or maybe even her mother. But when she jerked the door open, she realized there was never anyone else it could have been.

Lin was beautiful, in that infuriating effortless way she always was. Nel slammed the door. She leaned against it, pressing her forehead to the cool stone as if that might help, hands branched on either side as if for impact. Fire burned in her gut. Agreeing to help Lin stay on the mental straight and narrow was easy when it was Tirta asking, when the juicy reward of a better leg was dangled in front of her. But with the gravitational stare of the woman actually before her, Nel forgot all reason, forgot diplomacy. *Try. You promised you'd try.* Even filled with fury and indignation, she had to admit that slamming a door in someone's face wasn't professional.

Nel drew a loud breath through her nose and jerked the door open again. "What."

Lin didn't say anything for a moment.

Was she, too, imagining another time, another universe when they were separated by only a meter of sun-warmed stone and not lightyears of mistakes? "There a reason you showed up?"

"Well, I just wanted to let you know that I, well," she faltered and Nel almost wrote down the date and time. *First time Lin Nalawangsa is at a loss for words.* "I would have made them send someone else. If there was someone. But Dar's not well enough to go and Sepulveda's insisting on staying here. He wants to be on Harris's panel."

"And Hugo-Sanchez?"

Confusion flickered over Lin's face. "Why? She's wrapped up figuring out what's going on with Philos. Besides, she's not been in any of this as long as us."

Nel chewed on her lip, wondering whether Lin forgetting about the tech officer was purposeful avoidance or genuine. She muttered, "Well I can't go then either. I have to wash my hair that day."

Lin stared at her for a moment longer. "Ibu got to you, didn't she? She asked you to come. You'd be pitching a way bigger fit."

Nel clenched her jaw. "Don't you think your family's asked enough of me?"

"I think we've asked far more than we should and you gave far more than we deserved. The Nalawangsa's have demanded too much of a lot of people, actually." She looked across the open room beyond, through the open balcony doors. The low warm light cast her beautiful features in bronze. "You could have refused."

"She made me an offer." Nel sighed. "You still want me to help?"

"I do. You have expertise and skills that I don't, you've witnessed the aftermath of Harris and Mansur's actions closer than I think any of us want. This mission isn't over, it's true, but you can be. No matter what my mother said."

It was tempting, and a larger-than-not piece of her desperately wanted to return to her boring, normal life. *But even if I did, how would I return to it?* "I'll help. Don't know how, of course. But I'll help."

She expected a toothy, victorious smile, but Lin only nodded. "We're on the same side. I messed up. Alot. After this—if there is an after—I will atone for what I've done in the name of IDH. But for now, will you allow me to try and atone for what I've done to us, to you?"

You said you'd try. Nel opened her mouth but found that, for once, she too was speechless. This was the promise that, in her deepest dreams, lingering just past the point of wakefulness, she wished to hear. In those dreams the words cooled her anger, extinguished the fire raging inside her. Real life wasn't a dream.

"What you do has always been your choice," Nel answered, angry, and not sure why. "I can't promise how it'll make me feel, or if it'll change anything."

Something gleamed behind Lin's eyes and Nel found herself almost hoping it was determination. "That's enough for me."

THIRTEEN

The far side of the estate was more overgrown, the verdant tangle divided only by a handful of stone paths. Nel hadn't slept, instead spending the time packing and, once dawn arrived, she headed to the village to see her mother. Now, with mid-morning fast approaching, she slung her duffle onto her shoulders as a backpack and notched her crutch beneath her arm. Though the added weight made her thigh and hips ache, it was welcome. With the sun climbing the dome and the faint whisper of wind it was almost like her trek from the Antofagasta airport. Longing twinged through her chest.

The path wound past a large cork copse and ended at a stone-flagged clearing. An empty hovering transport—like the one she and Dar had used on Morphose, but half the size—awaited. Dar himself was seated at the helm, hands resting in his lap and staring at some point far beyond the asteroid's horizon.

Nel knew that look. Swinging her duffle awkwardly down, she plopped it on the transport's cargo area, before shuffling over to sit beside him. Birdsong and a breeze bustled through the clearing, bringing the scent of bacon and warm bread. Nel pulled in a long lungful then glanced over at him. Her mom always opened the floodgates with a trickle of innocuous talking. "Temperature fluctuations, right? That's how we get a breeze?"

"Aided by fans for additional atmo-recyling." Dar's voice popped with disuse. His attention dropped to his hands. "I see his face, sometimes, when I sleep. And sometimes it's dead, and sometimes I just wish it were, because how can someone talk, when their eyes look like that. And worse of all, sometimes it's not his face, but Paul's, or Emilio's or yours or Lin's."

Nel didn't have to ask whose face he originally meant. She saw the same one, crystalized eyes through cold-atrophied lids, a man whose immaculate preservation was in mockery of his victims' unrecognizable change. "We're getting close," she lied. "We certainly have a lot more information now, and with your parents—"

"They don't really get it, though." He heaved a sigh, rocking his head back to stare up at the swollen arc of the dome. "Gods above, it's like being a kid again. They sweep in and take over and think they know what's best."

"I think they're trying," Nel shrugged. "But I know what you mean. It's hard to explain to people who had the privilege to sleep through the whole thing."

"Kind words considering they sent you on a mission after kicking you out of the meeting." His usual drawl was back, barely.

"Your mom's been more transparent than you and Lin together, just so you know. I'm on Team Tirta right now. We've got a club. Ordering T-Shirts and everything."

Dar chuckled darkly. "That tells me how well you don't know her, is all."

"I mean, you're all a little intense and overdramatic, but it is neat, to see someone's parents. To see a premonition of what her face might look like. When she's older."

Dar shot her a pointed look, which she deftly avoided. "Why do you think I've tried to keep my dalliances far away—my father's hairline is the last thing I need them to see."

Nel laughed softly, scanning the long, straight path ahead, cutting deeper into the jungle to what, she presumed, was the data sanctum. "We're going to be okay, Dar. You know that, right?"

He lapsed into silence.

"The dreams you're having, with our faces dead instead of Mansur's. They're just dreams. I have them too, and others that are hard to shake in the morning. But we're all gonna get through this, some way or another."

"You an oracle now?" he teased.

"No, but my gut isn't often wrong."

"Seriously, you make the worst decisions—"

"I didn't say I listened to it, alright," she snapped. "But it's gotten me through this, alive if not in one piece. And I'm telling you, whatever is down there—" she jabbed her finger down the unassuming path for emphasis, "—is the next piece to this ugly puzzle." Maybe it was more her desire for progress so she could finally go home, more than any gut-instinct pull. But she didn't need to admit that to Dar.

He flashed her a thin smile. "Thanks. It's hard to be grounded. Been flying since I was tall enough to see the instruments and reach the yoke. Even if there was nothing to do, there was some place to go."

"The illusion of control," Nel remarked sagely. "I know that one. Just, you know, beater cars as a teen rather than starships." She nudged him with an elbow. "Besides, all the shit we find gets sent to you all to analyze, so you'll probably be the first ones to see any breakthroughs."

"How generous. Look, Nel," Dar began, then faltered. "I know this won't be easy, you working with her, but I'm grateful. My sister is complicated. And stubborn, and way, way too clever for her own good. For any of our own good. You might balance that out."

Nel let out a soft chuckle. "Your mother said the same thing, more or less."

"Well, she's right. Lin made a lot of mistakes, and she will do penance for them. Try to see both of those things, alright? Not just the former. Forgiveness." Dar's face was so still he seemed to have been paused. Then the corner of his mouth twitched. "The names of the ships in her rebellion fleet."

That made Nel glance over. "What do you mean?"

"*Lihifa. Ndum. 'Asaf.* They all mean some form of regret. Or longing. The absolute performance of it all, I'm almost envious. That whole fleet was an apology to you."

Nel rolled her eyes, shifting, wishing this topic didn't make her chest feel as if her heart flamed within the cage of her ribs. "If that's the case, it's gotta be for all of you, too, as much as me. More than me."

Dar hummed, noncommittal. "Do you remember what I told you, before?"

"Maybe she shot you and maybe she didn't?" Nel hazarded.

"And maybe it doesn't actually matter."

Nel stared at him. "It kind of does, though."

He gestured to his own chest. "I have a hole blown through me either way. And I can choose whether I also have a hole blown through my family." His face cracked into a familiar calculating grin. "Besides, when my sister is wracked with guilt, she brings me my favorite snacks."

"Well, I'll say the same thing I said to your mother and to the war criminal herself—I'll try."

"Thank you." His attention flitted to somewhere behind her, and his open expression shuttered before he muttered to her, "Be nice."

Nel turned, confused until she caught sight of the pouf of curls making its way down the path. Hugo-Sanchez's whistle had an incredible range of notes, and Nel would have been impressed if it weren't for everything else she detested about the woman.

"Morning!" she called over with a flash of bright teeth. Emilio trailed behind her, holding a few small industrial looking cases. "I got your tech gear all set here. I can bring you up to speed now if you'd like. I gave Lin a tutorial last night."

I bet you did. "I'll check it out once we're onsite. I learn best in the field," she responded instead. *Look at me, keeping a whole entire opinion to myself.* "Thanks, though."

Dar dragged himself from the pilot's seat. "Help her load up, will you? I've got to check in with Mil," he explained. "About the mission."

It was obviously bullshit, but Nel let it slide. It was nice to see someone else exploring vulnerability for once. Or it would have been nice if he hadn't left her to the chipper wolves. She rounded the end of their transport and pointed to the waiting pile of boxes. "All these?"

"Yep!" Hugo-Sanchez gave another grin and lifted one. For someone her size, she was deceptively strong, and Nel felt another twinge of annoyance.

She attempted to bury her attitude by grabbing the next crate and dropping it into place with a thunk. "How's Phil?"

The tech gave a shrug. "Still in stasis. I've run so many tests, and Kasanove is burning through his RAM helping out. I'm afraid we might need to pull power from the rest of the system. But, honestly, none of this makes sense."

"No shit," Nel muttered.

Hugo-Sanchez shot her a look, the closest Nel had ever seen her to something other than peppy. "I'm dating someone else, Dr. Bently."

Nel grimaced, shooting a look to where Emilio and Dar were holding a hushed conversation. "TMI. I'm so not interested in you."

Hugo-Sanchez heaved a sigh and pushed another stack of smaller boxes into place before facing Nel squarely. "No, but you are interested in Lin. I'm not your competition. Couldn't be even when I tried." She met Nel's gaze, chin up. "That's why you're so mean to me, I assume."

"It doesn't matter. You can date whoever. And I'm mean because that's just how I am." *You've been a colossal dick, Bently, and you know it.* Guilt crawled up Nel's throat, along with something else she didn't dare name. "Sorry. That's not fair." she sighed. "I guess I'm sick of seeing everyone know more than I do about this world, and this way-too-extra family." *And Lin.*

"Oh, stars, so extra, right?" Hugo-Sanchez let out a squeak, hand covering her mouth, before losing her battle and letting out a loud cackle, drawing a surprised glance from the two men. "Like who has a family satellite? Why couldn't they settle for a private shuttle like normal people?"

"Or a turn of the century bungalow." Nel couldn't help but crack a smile. It was a relief, she admitted, to let down her hackles a bit. Maybe she had enough to fight without dragging Lin's exes into her line of fire.

Hugo-Sanchez sat back, smiling a bit, seeming to read Nel's mind. "You can think I'm too bouncy, and I can think your attitude is juvenile, but let's let it go for now."

"Fine," Nel rolled her eyes. A tiny sense of relief hit her, as if she'd set down a weight. *She's still way too cheery.* "I'll pick someone else for my daily antagonist."

Hugo-Sanchez tittered, but the laughter died when the aforementioned Lin appeared at the end of the path, electrosuit fully fastened and a travel case slung over her shoulder. Ignoring everyone else, she strode to the transport and tucked her bag in one of the few remaining open areas before raking a concerned look over the whole. "This all we're bringing? I know the systems were never disconnected but we don't even know if the structures—"

"We packed everything, bunsó," Dar said softly, walking over, his gait a stiff ghost of his usual saunter. "Just the fragile stuff is going with you. Got collapsible shelters, portable recyclers in case the system scan was wrong. Tried to think of everything since..." he grimaced. "I wish we could all go."

Lin offered him a fragile smile. "Like you've ever willingly roughed it."

Nel snorted, remembering the pilot's demeanor when on Morphose. "Last time Dar and I camped out it was a symphony of attitude," she cut in. "And that's coming from me."

Lin's smile strengthened a fraction and she cast a sidelong glance at Nel's boots. Her voice dropped until only they could hear. "I thought you were washing your hair."

Nel shrugged, ratcheting down a strap over the packs and crates spilling over the cargo area. "Eh, I remembered bad hair is kind of a queer hallmark."

Lin turned, still not meeting her eyes, pausing as if about to say something, then shook her head, and settled into the pilot's seat.

Their comms all chimed in unison and Dar took a step back. "Go-time, team."

Nel wavered a moment before tugging Emilio into a one-armed hug. "We'll be in contact, I'm sure."

"Good luck," he murmured into her shoulder before pushing her away. "Try not to kill each other again."

Nel made a face and opened her arms to Dar. "You cleared for hugs?" The way he flushed told her that he and Emilio had probably been disregarding certain doctor's orders. Still, her squeeze was gentle when they embraced and it was all too soon that she was climbing into the seat next to Lin and offering a wave goodbye. *Don't call it that.*

The electric hum of the craft and the manufactured rush of wind through the open vehicle made conversation blessedly difficult. Unwilling to have the mission fall into awkward silence just yet, however, Nel remarked, "I was looking at the itinerary. It's about half a day across the surface, right?"

"A bit longer," Lin called over the noise. "Four hours at max speed for this guy, but it'll be closer to six with this much weight. We can unpack the equipment and get our bearings tomorrow, but we should make it to camp in time to at least get our sleeping situation set up."

"Sounds like a plan." *This is so awkward.* Nel nodded and cast her gaze out at the surrounding forest. There had been mention of the structures awaiting them, but she hoped there was more than one collapsible tent. Sharing with Dar on Morphose was rough enough. *If there's only one bed, I'm sleeping in the evil temple.*

For the next several hours, the jungle hummed past, clusters of towering trees broken by smaller paths or occasional clearings and buildings. As the day wound on, however, these breaks in the surrounding forest occurred less and less. Soon, the arching canopy converged above and the cold light that dappled from above dimmed. Their conversation was infrequent, and usually only triggered by Nel asking about spots on the map readout or, even less frequently, Lin pointing something out.

Despite the smooth path, Nel's shoulders and back ached from holding herself stiff to avoid touching the woman beside her. An hour had passed since they last saw any outbuildings or cabins when the road itself abruptly changed. Two stone pillars flanked the sides, and the tree cut narrowed. Beyond the markers, the surface was rougher, no longer tidy grey bricks. Instead, it seemed to have been carved into the asteroid itself, and rose, winding and narrow before disappearing into the trees.

The transport glided to a halt just between the hewn pillars and the engine quieted to a faint hum. It was closing in on evening, the blue planet above descending quickly behind the dense tree cover. In the rising darkness, Nel could barely glimpse the landscape ahead, but caught the hulking hill cutting across the planet's belly.

"Well," Lin sighed.

Nel glanced at her when she didn't continue. "This it? The map says we have another three plus kilometers."

"We do," Lin clarified, "But this guy won't be able to go the rest of the way. These are just residential models, the more militaristic ones—" she stopped herself and swung down. She unclipped her bag from the pile of boxes before typing a series of commands into the transport's computer. "We're going to have to hike from here."

Nel groaned softly. *I can't walk without limping; you expect me to fucking hike?* Embarrassment was bad enough, but in front of Lin, Epitome of Grace? She climbed down too, jaw tight against the impending pain. Tugging her own bag free, she began unfolding her crutch and tightening its bolts. Shame stung her eyes, and she blinked rapidly to keep her sight from fogging. With her crutch secure, she cast an assessing gaze up the path ahead. It wasn't a boulder scramble, but it wasn't the level paths near the estate, either. Beneath her steadying hand, the vehicle's engine dropped into a lower gear, and it headed back the way they came.

"Oh, Nel, I should have realized..." Lin waited at the head of the trail, staring at Nel's crutch and leg. She reached into her pocket for a bioflare. She squeezed her fingers into the soft center and the cube began to glow. "Your limp..."

"I'd rather not go there, honestly."

"I can probably carry extra."

"Don't." Nel grimaced at the thought of Lin jogging up the trail with a few hundred pounds of bags and boxes just for Nel to lurch along behind her. "There's no way you could carry that and besides my bags add some balance."

"No, but—" Lin began to protest, but Nel pointed at the equipment cases at the woman's feet.

"You can carry that, though." She swallowed her pride. "Either that or you're carrying me when I break an ankle and drop all the fragile stuff."

Lin opened her mouth as if to say something more, but her cheeks flamed and instead she shouldered the equipment. Nel gripped her crutch and followed her into the darkening press of the jungle.

FOURTEEN

"Minute," Nel collapsed unceremoniously onto a boulder. The estimated hour of hiking had lengthened into a horrific two and was closing in on the first half of a third. Ahead, Lin peered around the next bend before nodding and picking her way back down to where Nel sat.

"The site shouldn't be far ahead." Lin hoisted Nel's pack onto her shoulder with a soft, "Oof."

"Thank fuck," Nel muttered. She waved Lin along, renewing her grip on her crutch. Relief numbed her steps as she ducked into a rough-hewn tunnel for the final dozen meters. Nel stopped in the mouth of the tunnel and let out a low whistle.

Where the main estate was sprawling and effortless in its tidy, manicured balance with the jungle, this place either had been let go to seed, or the engineers never bothered to fight back the jungle in the first place. What had once been a presumably open courtyard, intimate in its size, was ringed by low buildings carved from the walls of an ancient impact crater. Fallen trees splayed over the edge from where they had eroded in, and vines snaked between rocks and over doorways and windows. The U of buildings ended at the foot of the tallest crag, where another stepped pyramid was tucked in the curve of bedrock. Reaching out to the tunnel's walls, Nel brushed a hand over the pockmarked surface, recalling a different asteroid. *Hopefully this one has fewer creepy bodies.*

Lin grunted, dropping their personal effects into a tidy pile in the middle of the courtyard. Nel flopped down among the bags with a groan. "Well, that was a lovely stroll."

"No kidding. At least the way back will be downhill."

"Downhill always hurt my knees. Getting too old for this shit." Nel grimaced. "The rest of the equipment here?"

Lin jerked a thumb over at the larger boxes resting in a corner. Already a fallen branch rested on the pile and pollen dusted its surface.

"Jeeze, sci-fi nature works fast around here."

"Jungle's a jungle, even in space," Lin pointed out. She rummaged through the pockets of her jacket and produced two protein bars, handing the archaeologist the less squashed one.

"Thanks," Nel answered, and she meant it.

"We can start with these, then have proper food once we're done. There's a kitchen, across the way, and if the common area is intact we can use it for studying anything we find in the Sanctum. But I have no interest in sleeping there."

Nel followed her thumb's jerk to the lidless stare of the bunkhouse's dark, empty windows and chewed on her snack. As much as camping made her body ache, she wasn't sure if she'd ever feel safe sleeping within the oppressive temple buildings. The protein bar wasn't much better than terrestrial ones, but it did wonders for her energy and mood. Popping another bite into her mouth she asked, "Where's the shelter? I can tackle that if you deal with warmth and food."

"Rest a second, I'll get the boxes down."

I'm not a fucking invalid. And, as much as sitting for a minute sounded nice, she knew if she stopped moving now, she'd be down for the night. She wolfed down the protein bar and sent a ping to the rest of the team back at the estate.

To: Vīrya *Mission Control*
Made it to Sapta. Setting up tomorrow.

There was an immediate response to them both from Dar, but Nel left it unread, instead rising with a groan to help Lin maneuver the only crate marked "FRAGILE" off the larger transport. "So this is a place of worship?" she asked, typing in the passcode on another crate holding their larger camping equipment.

"It was. Over time, though, my father's family began to view the Teachers from a more scientific lens. Most of the factions out here do, but there are some that still interact with them spiritually. Or did, before they disappeared. My uncle was one of the few who were more…devout, I suppose, for lack of a better word. He spent most of his time here when he was home, and turned it into more of a research outpost," Lin explained.

Nel shuddered, watching Lin's tense profile. She almost asked whether Lin considered herself devout, whether the whispers she didn't dare listen to felt more like disembodied static or divine messengers. *She called it Judgment Day.* Nel supposed it didn't matter if you believed in gods when they came to kill you. "Researching what, how best to destroy humanity?"

Lin's scoff was low and humorless. "Apparently. But, at the time it was how the Teachers existed and how they came to be. It was easier to get readings and analyze them out here, away from most of the electronic systems of the satellite." She rocked back on her heels and surveyed the growing chaos of boxes and bags, making a tally with her long fingers. "We have two personal tents. Warmer. A case of rations—they might send more if we're out here longer. Purifier for the water if the facilities don't work."

"Right." Nel grabbed the two lightweight shelter cases, relieved to be useful. "I'll get these up. You said that the building by the path was a kitchen? Why don't you check it out, see if we have drinking water?"

She watched as Lin wordlessly hoisted the rations and water equipment and headed toward the building. Inside, her graceful silhouette flitted against the blue light from the brilliant bioflare. It was easier to deal with Lin when they had a shared goal, lists of tasks to keep them fed, warm, safe. *Maybe that's all a relationship is, at the end of the day.* She shoved the feeling away and set about unfolding the shelter.

The shelters were easy, popping up quickly, despite how Nel's limbs shook after the near-constant rattle of climbing. The tents were smaller than the one they used on Morphose, and lacked the hard casing needed for pressurization. Still, they were sturdy and, most importantly to Nel, there were two of them. Despite the vague chill pervading the courtyard, Nel broke a sweat hauling rocks over to use instead of trying to drive heavy spikes into the asteroid's hard silicate. Dropping the last stone in place, she tugged off her overshirt, grateful she hadn't worn her electrosuit for the hike. With the organic stickiness of sweat and natural air, the strain of her tank top, the burn of her muscles, she could almost pretend to be in the field again.

"We've got running water, a rehydrator, cooling unit, and a big table." Lin reported, appearing in the kitchen doorway.

"Good. Just about done here." Nel glanced over her shoulder, ratcheting the last straps down. Lin's eyes lingered on her shoulders, tracing the new muscles and roving down to the marbled scarring up both forearms. She blinked rapidly and focused on Nel's handiwork. "Wow, you made quick work of those. Where'd you learn to do that?"

"Morphose. With Dar." Nel explained, voice suddenly clipped. She was angry that Lin dared to look at her with hunger, and moreover, Nel was angry that she liked it. "Base didn't have enough atmosphere to stay in, so we just camped. Plus, killer sound and all that." She yanked a zipper closed, frowning at the thick filmy fabric in her hands.

Pain flickered over Lin's face. "I'm impressed you managed to get him to camp on an unshielded asteroid, must have been a good team. He can be a real baby."

Nel scoffed. "Baby is right. I don't know if he'd agree about the teamwork. But we did what we could."

Lin gestured to the tents. "Which one is mine?"

"Pick. We have the Presidential Rooms and the Penthouse," Nel joked.

"No honeymoon suite then?"

Nel was too startled to remember her rule against eye contact with the traitorous woman. Lin's eyes were fathomless and for a breathless moment, Nel almost leaned forward, almost threw every grievance to the wind.

With a huff, Nel tore away, and limped away to grab her bags. Not bothering to let Lin choose, Nel barreled into the nearest shelter and dropped her bags, breath coming in heaves. *We're barely civil and she fucking flirts?*

Yanking her sleeping kit out, she threw together the low cot, desperately trying to control her heart rate. *God, she pisses me off.* A plush sleeping bag covered the cot, and her duffel could be tucked beneath. A tiny collapsable set of shelves went beside, able to hold her dopp kit. Shaking hands set the two tiny boxes of cremains there, beside her bed. With her tent mostly set up and no more excuses for emerging, she followed the rich savory smell coming from the kitchen.

Like the rest of the exterior, the kitchen was carved from the asteroid itself. The furnishings were beat up, and surprisingly analog, save for the cooling unit and rehydrator. Lin had produced another glowing cube and set it in the middle of a large stone-topped table. "Lights don't work—too long without nutrients and the bacteria die, I guess."

Nel hummed, picking up the glowing cube to examine. Shadows flashed across the walls as she turned it over in her hand. "These are nice, though."

Lin finished stirring a pot that smelled surprisingly like SkyLine Chili and scooped two large portions into waiting collapsable bowls. "Not much but it's hot."

Nel took the bowl she offered and closed her eyes sniffing the fragrant steam. Lin had already poured them each a tall glass of water and Nel settled onto one of the long benches alongside the table. "So, what's the plan?"

"I think we should take tomorrow to get the equipment set up, take stock of what they have here. Plan to tackle the rest. No sense rushing in headfirst just to have something blow up in our faces."

Nel snorted, patting her augmented thigh. "Why not? Always worked for me."

"Has it?" Lin countered, softy, though, as if she hadn't really meant to say it aloud. Her dark eyes lingered on Nel's body. "I'm sorry I pushed you. We all should have realized the transport might fail."

"I could have spoken up." Nel took an over-large bite. It was indeed an imitation of Skyline, if one dehydrated the beans for a decade and used protein blocks instead of beef. "Food's decent."

Lin wrinkled her nose. "I've never been a fan of chili. Beans in general, really. But it's warm."

"Well, if this is your only experience with it, yeah, I bet you wouldn't be a fan." Nel chuckled. "My dad's family was from the Midwest—the central part of the USA—and they made chili like this, sweet, with cocoa powder. Always reminded me a bit of mole poblano. Ever had mole?"

Lin nodded. "Once, when we were visiting my mom's family on—" She winced, barreling past the pain point of Samsara. "They had a neighbor who was a recent immigrant from Earth. She cooked a lot of wonderful dishes."

Nel let the conversation rest. The bioflare between them was bright and far more welcoming than the sinister glow of the warmer when she camped with Dar. Their spoons clinked softly against the dishes and glasses thunked on the worn stone tabletop among a delicate host of other, human sounds. The forest crackled with life outside the ring of light and her body ached, far more than after any walk-over for archaeology. *I missed this, though.* Soreness and soil and the night chill. She frowned at Lin's empty bowl. *Company.*

"It was the explosion." When her voice cracked through the silence, it startled them both. "My limp, I mean."

She felt the weight of the other women's attention fall across her shoulders. "In Chile?"

"Yeah. Dar's shuttle. Harris was there, trying to use Polyana. I blasted him, but he triggered the quarantine and the shuttle blew. My arms were burned a bit, from the glove-fire. Emilio and Dar had to wait until the shuttle's integrity was compromised enough to break in. By that time part of the frame had already collapsed." Her voice was abruptly raspy, as if the smoke from that explosion still clogged her throat. "Anyways, it was a shitshow. I wasn't conscious when it happened, or at least don't remember it."

"And your leg was broken?"

Nel traced the faint outline of her prosthetic. "Mid-femoral amputation."

Lin leaned back as if she'd been slapped. It was her turn for her voice to break. "Nel, I—"

"Don't." Nel glared at her. "Don't you dare. I can take it from Zach and my mom and even Emilio, but I won't take pity from you." She swallowed hard. *I don't think I could survive your pity.*

"I'm going to fix this, Nel. I'm going to track down every horrible thing Harris did, then I'm going to make him regret the choice to ever work with Mansur." Something in the blackness of her eyes ignited.

Nel looked away. She was unable to stomach the promise, but not out of doubt. Nel believed her, and Lin's vows were far scarier than any failure.

Holding the same phosphorescent cube overhead, Lin edged through the common area. It was long, with shelves and desks along the back wall, everything covered with dust. Nel stared blearily at the map on her readout, comparing it to the actual floorplan of the place. Dawn had come far too early for her exhausted body, and as they had silently prepped a cold, easy breakfast, her muscles and joints were a brutal reminder that forty was closer than thirty. Even with the protective press of her electrosuit, she felt wrung out.

"Just says 'Common Room' on here." Nel reported, eyeing the covered desks. She recorded it all, spinning in a slow circle so her suit's scanner could add the additional data to its schematics. Then she followed Lin through the nearest doorway, grateful that the mission provided enough topics to keep them from each other's throats. The next series of rooms were clearly both for decontamination and for bathing.

Lin tried one of the showers, shrieking and dodging away when the pipes banged and doused her with rusty water.

Nel's smile cracked wider, and she wet her hand just to flick more water at Lin. "Don't know if I'm gross enough to shower in water that looks like septic."

Lin made a face at the archaeologist, flicking her sodden braid at her before wringing it out. "It'll run clear after a minute, but I'm glad we have actual drinking water. We brought decon tabs at least, for that worst case. Bunkhouse next?"

"Bunkhouse?" Nel asked. "Just what kind of research—"

"Temples have priests, do they not?" Lin countered, trying the knob in the next room. For a temple to technological gods, the building's infrastructure was surprisingly analog. The knob turned, but the door wedged against something heavy on the other side. The playful nature of splashing each other died, drying Nel's mouth and erasing Lin's smile. Lin shoved it with her shoulder to no avail, then stepped back, hand rising to point at the latch.

"Woah," Nel protested, snapping her own hand out to grab the other woman's wrist. "Let's try something else before we go blasting shit. Preserving evidence and all that."

Lin faltered, eyes flicking to Nel but not dropping her hand.

"I would prefer we wait to shoot anything until like, day three, ok? My fucking nerves, man." Nel shook her head and dropped into a clumsy crouch once Lin's reactive glove was down. "Hinges aren't on this side, but if you shove it again—" Lin did so wordlessly, and Nel peered through the narrow crack that appeared on the hinge side. "I could try to tap open the pins from here. Looks rusted as all hell, though." She rocked back to look up at Lin. "What about the windows? Think we could just crawl in that way?"

Lin gave a sharp nod and dropped back, weaving their return through the showers and common room. Neither spoke until they were back outside. Nel tried to ignore Lin's nervous expression by scanning the long bank of the dorm building. It was the largest, long and low, stretching the width of the courtyard across from the temple itself. The same carved, square windows dotted its exterior wall, but most of these, Nel now saw, had shutters that were tightly locked.

"Lin, if that door is blocked from inside, and these windows too—"

"There's got to be another door." Lin interrupted.

"Or this," Nel peered over the tall sill of the last window. Here the shutters were shattered and knocked open. It was dim inside, and she squinted but, aside from the faint lines of dust motes lit by the tiny cracks in the other shutters, nothing moved. She knelt again, cupping her hands on her good knee. "Here, I'll give you a boost."

Lin looked between Nel's offered palms and the hungry dark of the window before clenching her teeth and climbing up and through. She landed with the faintest of thumps and her head popped out a second later. "It's clear."

Nel grabbed her proffered hand and scrambled until her belly rested on the sill. Graceful as a beached seal, she inched inside before dropping with a far louder whump.

Lin's light seemed unwilling to reach too far. Rows of cots lined the walls, each separated by printed bio-plastic screens. However manufactured the weather, it was clear time still had some effect, the bioplastic slumping in places and sun-bleached in others. The door to the washing station was barricaded, two cots thrown against it and a chair wedged under the knob.

"I don't like that," Nel remarked, voice suddenly a whisper. Turning, she saw the shutters, too, were latched shut. The one through which they had gained access was truly broken, and the edges of the shattered wood, scorched.

"Glove blast," Lin observed, brushing a tentative finger along the damage.

Nel turned a dial on her own glove and raised it. "Documenting," she explained when Lin shot her a look. "Why we're here, right?" She turned in a careful circle, snapping stills and recording video as she did. The cots were mostly stripped, and the cubicles devoid of personal effects. Nel skirted around the privacy dividers, dropping to her knees with a quiet groan to check under the beds.

"I found his office." Lin called softly from the far side of the room. The end of the room opposite the door was a larger, private bunk with one half as an office. While all the other areas were relatively sparse, aside from the clear attempt to barricade, this was a disaster. Drawers were pulled out, books—actual books!—were pulled from shelves, pages torn free.

"Looks like things have changed a bit from the schematics."

"What, you thought destroying the world would only require a big button?" Lin quipped, but the joke faltered on her strained tone.

"Well, terrestrial humans have managed to try to destroy themselves since we could pick up rocks, I've learned." Nel peeked under the translucent film covering some equipment on the shelves and remarked, "Shit. All of this abandoned? I know community colleges that would kill to get their hands on this stuff." She tugged the sheet farther away to reveal an array of instruments.

Wires, radios, comms, and speakers were piled on some, with others holding more traditional biological equipment like microscopes and petri dishes.

"Here, I'll get this side." Lin helped her lift the sheets away to document the equipment in its current set up. Abandoned was the right term, apparently. Slides were left out, notes scribbled on pads, and even a desktop cooling unit had been left open.

Nel scanned the books and data cubes on the shelves. "Same stuff here as in any office—clinical texts, desktop gizmos." Nel remarked. She glanced between the Newton's Cradle and Lin, safe to stare so long as the other woman didn't notice.

One of Lin's delicate fingers lifted a silver ball then released it. Her dark eyes watched as it clacked into its companions, knocking the opposite one into motion. "I always liked those."

Nel continued her perusal, turning to look over the naked cot. She froze, eyes fixed on the sheets balled on the floor. The fabric was sallow, and stained with dark, rusty brown. The fluid had clearly sat on the stone beneath awhile, as the floor too was stained. "Lin."

"Is that—" Lin began, but Nel interrupted her with a curt nod.

"Yeah. A lot of it." Nel crouched, remembering the stains on Xand's ship. She let out a weak chuckle.

"This is funny?" Lin asked, voice strained.

"No, I just was remembering, when we were documenting *V Drugoye*, I found a stain and got all flipped out just to learn it was barbecue sauce." She shook her head ruefully. "All the tech in the world and I still make an ass of myself."

Lin's smile was faint, but there, and Nel mentally congratulated herself on breaking the tension. She snapped a series of photos and then scraped a tiny piece into her suit's analyzer nozzle. She grimaced at the readout. "Yeah, blood. Type AB pos, if that makes a difference."

Lin hummed thoughtfully, dropping smoothly into a crouch. "We can compare it to the database of people present whenever this happened. But there's thousands of people on *Vīrya* at any given time."

"That's a start, I guess. There a record of the people stationed here?"

"Should be, if they were here in any official capacity and not," Lin gave a faint smile, "a conjugal visit, so to speak. Besides, we don't even know if it's related."

Nel lurched to her feet to scan the room again. It took a minute to get her annoyance under control, and when she did, she bit out, "I've done nothing but find blood and guts and bodies in the wake of your uncle. And this is his creepy ass research outpost, so I'm gonna assume whatever blood, guts, and bodies we find here probably are related."

"Wishful thinking, I suppose." Lin's voice was tiny, so soft Nel almost felt bad for being angry.

"I know." Nel heaved a sigh and scanned the room again. "At least whatever happened was fast enough no one had a chance to clean this place out. I think I might go through these books once everything is documented."

Lin frowned. "We can just scan them and search via the database. It'll be faster, and Dar can run the programs while we keep cataloging."

"Right. I just work better without digitizing sometimes." Nel cast a glance over her shoulder. "I can take care of the desk and books, if you want to check out the equipment some more. You've a better chance of recognizing anything out of place. It's all weird tech to me."

Lin edged toward her way out of the room, a strange, pained expression on her face. Nel followed, helping to remove the cots and chair from the door. "I'm going to get the water system purged, then I'll look at these. Meet back up for lunch?" Lin offered, still wavering in the doorway.

"Appetite might depend on what else we find," she joked, darkly, fiddling with her suit's settings to scan the room. Dread was still a weight in her gut, but at least now she had something to do, a job, a way to fight back. *Or just a way to make them shoot you in the front, and not the back.*

While the rest of the satellite's surface felt like a museum or sprawling estate, this place was entirely different. There was a feral pallor overhanging them, something ancient and terrible. Nel had spent countless hours in cemeteries, in memorials, and handling remains. Every place had a presence, even if it was simply stillness. This was not still, nor restful. *It's furious.*

The light dimmed as she peered at the shelves, recalling what Kasanove had said about learning more about senti-comp tech. Bound tomes—textbooks, mostly, she realized—lined half the shelves. Cubbies behind the desk were filled with circuit boards, energy cores, and a host of things Nel was pretty certain were from some episode of *Star Trek.*

Like the other desks she'd encountered, this one had a spot to project a screen. Making a mental note to have Lin check it out, she tilted her head to browse through the books. *Make Your Own Neural Network* by Tariq Rashid. *The Emotion Machine* by Marvin Minsky. *Wetware: A Computer in Every Living Cell* by Dennis Bray. She took pictures of the shelves before flipping through a few to check for any handwritten annotations. Kasanove could procure digital version to search the published contents, but Nel was no stranger to adding her own commentary to what she read. Mansur, it appeared, was no such man. She took the Bray and a dense looking monstrosity titled *Final Frontier: Digitizing Consciousness,* which had a promising looking glossary that even a troglodyte like herself might be able to decipher.

Next, she checked the single large drawer in the desk itself. *Locked.* She palmed the handle of her trowel and wedged the tip into the drawer's mouth, prying until the jungle-softened wood gave way. Inside was a tidy stack of slim journals, bound in sturdy, plain grey canvas.

Carefully removing the stack and setting them beside the books, she slipped what looked like the newest journal from the set. They were actual paper, and the tiny, careful writing—legible even in script—was done in faded black ink. *Handwriting?* She peered closer, realizing she seen so little of Lin's handwriting—or really anyone's. IDH provided few opportunities to write so much as a post-it longform.

Flipping to the middle, she found more of the tidy, almost engineered handwriting. Diagrams were sketched in margins, and brackets, asterisks, and footnotes—seemingly to the author themself. She glanced behind herself, as if the satellite's security system—as if Kasanove himself—was watching and began to read.

> *The largest difficulty with Clark's ideas regarding matter transference is the concept of consent—the root of it, I understand. It's a key flaw in the theories of digital transference. [expound upon this in previous chapter after discussion of Clark's own prototypes.]*
>
> *Consent. Did we ask consent of the creatures we brought with us during our*

first interstellar voyage, as new and unformed as ourselves? Did we ask consent when we domesticated the fauna of every world upon which we set foot? What is transference but superior breeding? Ultimate domestication: where we sculpt the intent of, not maize or bovines, but of ourselves.

Nel tossed the journal across the desk, wiping a swath through the layers of dust and pollen. She didn't recognize half the terms. But she knew a monster when she saw one.

When she was back in her shelter that night, with the openings carefully shut and light dim, Nel sprawled across her cot with her reading list. She turned *Final Frontier* over to stare at its cover. It was stylized, in the way the outdated science textbooks of her undergrad years often were, with circuits photoshopped to look as if they merged into organic neurons. Or they were actually connected. How the fuck did she know, at this point?

Her eyes lingered on the author: Phillip Clark. Probably the same "Clark" referenced in the journal she'd snooped through that afternoon. She thumbed through to the backmatter, skimming references and indexes so thorough her dissertation was rolling over in its much-deserved grave. There, at the back, were photos and bios of each contributor. Her stomach dropped to her mismatched feet.

Even wearing caustically 70's sideburns and without the distortion of a few dozen liters of brackish water, she would recognize Phil's handsome, if unremarkable features.

> *Dr. Phillip Clark,*
> *Associate Professor*
> *University of Quantum Studies*

> *Dr. Clark is at the forefront of artificial intelligence development. Recipient of the IDH Grant for Superior Computing Theory for his prototype DIQI—Digital Intelligence Quantum Interface—he hopes to collaborate with the Nalawangsa estate's Artificial Intelligence Military Laboratory on their newest project. When not "plugged in" to the digital worlds of his own making, Dr. Clark enjoys hiking with his partner, Grace, and their mastiff, Angus.*

Her eyes ached from staring at the tiny handwriting, and her heart thrummed, loud and certain against her ribs. It was different from the more honest bio she had read on *Odyssey*, clearly before whatever fall from grace mentioned in the other. A girlfriend. A mastiff enthusiast. A tenure track. How had this man, full of life and so utterly normal, ended up decapitated and piloting an entire space station?

FIFTEEN

The pervasive jungle humidity was barely lessened inside the dark, cloying rooms. Nel inched along the shelves of the office, snapping photos as she went. Her comm let out another buzz and she bit back a sigh of annoyance. *I thought this was supposed to be an isolated mission.* Dar, Hugo-Sanchez, and Lin had been going back and forth for the last two days discussing how best to penetrate the sanctum itself, and Nel was about ready to just walk up to the damn thing and knock.

Lin's fingers flew across her comm screen with brief periods of stillness while she went back to staring into a microscope waiting for them to reply, muttering about wishing they had an assistant.

Turning so Lin wouldn't see, Nel dialed back her own comm's notifications and returned to doing actual work. She, too, wished they had someone else to help, but that was more to act as a buffer between the two of them. The bench before her was a mess, covered in broken glass slides with a haphazard line of menacing jars along the wall. Biology was never her strong suit, but she appreciated where it overlapped with forensics and anthropology. Thankfully, most of the intact samples and slides were labeled. The other shelves had been her focus for the previous days, but today she would finally tackle the main desk itself.

After each photo, she typed out what the artifact was, the date and time, its context, and anything else of note. A boxy piece of equipment sat on the cart beside her. With a touch of her finger, it produced a sturdy plastic bag printed with the artifact's provenience. With careful, gloved hands, she lifted the next slide into the bag and set it into a box labeled with the bench number. It could have been tedious, but she found it meditative. Most of the physical research notes were destroyed from two decades in the damp weather, but she cataloged those anyway in the off chance anything could be extracted back at the estate.

The top of the desk was documented, and she dropped to a crouch with a quiet groan to check the drawers along its face. She pulled it open, grimacing as the slides screeched with rust. A few blessedly sealed clear boxes awaited with what she really hoped was someone's lunch and not experiments. Lifting the first one out, she documented the hideous contents before peering closer to try and make sense of them. "Gross."

"What is it?" Lin asked, curiosity in her eyes.

Nel made another face. "Someone's nineteen-year-old bologna sandwich, or Frankenstein's senior capstone."

Lin tried to hide her smile, rising to come look at Nel's find. "I wouldn't care at this point, I'm so bored of looking at endless microtech and wetware." Her smile died as she crouched down to look at the thing properly. "I have no idea what the tissue is, but that looks like a test integration. "

Nel shuddered, not wanting to get any closer, but dying for a break in the monotony. "That circuitry," she noted, eyes narrowing. When she looked to Lin for confirmation, the Komodor's face was pale. "It's the same as the protective shields your family uses, isn't it? The pattern at least."

Lin shot her a look of surprise.

"I saw one of Dar's, in his room and he flipped shit about you giving me one. Explained what they were." Nel couldn't weather the storm brewing beside her. *You gave me a family heirloom. To protect me.* "I didn't ask him about it at the time but if I had this during the shuttle explosion—"

"There are a lot of factors but, yes. It's likely you'd still have your leg." Lin bit out. "I'm sorry."

"I gave it back to you," Nel deflected, voice hoarse.

"And I made you run." Lin lapsed into silence, letting the room fill with awkwardness and the faint distant hiss of the machines around them. She returned to her own work, face unreadable.

Nel turned away, unsure if she was more scared by the terrible things between them, or the apologies. She documented the next experiment, which looked much the same, making a note to extract some of the tissue for testing. If integrations hadn't creeped her out before, seeing decaying flesh on the other end of a mess of circuitry might have done the trick. "Dar said you liked to test the shields."

"He really was in a sharing mood, I see." Lin let out a soft scoff. "It was only once, really. Twice if you count Lago Medusa, but it's not like I would have drowned right away. I swam out and manually triggered it, to see how deep I could swim. And the other time I told you about—I spacewalked."

"I assumed that was with a suit," Nel shook her head in disbelief.

"Just the electrosuit and the device. I guess I wanted to see how far I could push it. See if I could," She sighed, frowning, "feel something I guess."

Nel watched her for a moment longer, wondering if anything could actually frighten Lin Nalawangsa. *Her uncle's monstrosities, apparently.* It made their adversary that much scarier. "How do you stand those things?" Nel asked. "Integrations, I mean. I'm supposed to get one but the whole idea freaks me out."

"With what you've seen, I understand why." Lin made a face. "Honestly, I try not to think about them."

"When'd you get it?" Nel bent over the third experiment's tiny label while she scribbled a few more thoughts in her fieldbook.

"Twelve."

That gave Nel pause. She straightened, frowning. "You were a kid."

"Easier that way, I guess. A lot of the IDH kids got them younger. Dar did his at nine. But he had a lot of fevers. I think it made it easier to treat them."

"That's a big choice for that age. Maybe I'm just projecting. Puberty was a nightmare, I can't imagine choosing to add one more permanent change to the mix."

"It's not a choice. When, maybe. But not whether. Not if you're in IDH."

"You were a fucking kid. You weren't in anything, regardless of your parents' jobs—"

"The factions out here aren't just jobs, Nel. This is space. The people your parents work for own the metal you walk on, your water. They own the literal air you breathe. There are hundreds of ways of life, but you gotta pick one. And until you're old enough to, your parents pick for you."

Nel swallowed, then turned back to her work. "It isn't that different, when you put it like that. Not sure any of us have a choice about our upbringing in the beginning. But I'm sorry. That's no way to live."

It was hours before they finally retreated from the office lab, and Nel was relieved that most of what they found was inert and uninteresting. Except, with the oppressive weight of the jungle, and the forgotten flesh in the drawer, Nel wondered what they were missing, and what awaited them in the bowels of the temple itself.

"How long have you known Phil?" Nel asked vaguely. They were both seated at the kitchen table, Lin fixated on her comm's display of what looked like genetic code. Nel had Phil's book spread before her, not really reading, but staring into the light in the center of the table.

Lin frowned, barely looking up. "Philos? We didn't actually meet until I was a teen—I returned from *Odyssey* and he had been transferred to the ship we flew on. Eventually Dar took it over when he graduated."

"And he was already," she grimaced. "Well, integrated?"

Lin frowned. "He was. But he'd known my family before that. It's not common to still be involved after their integration, but I guess they made an exception. There were studies done and apparently people find it upsetting."

"Fucking creepy is what," Nel muttered. It was then, night muffled by the alien moonlight cast through the windows, that Nel recalled Lin's expression when they found the blood stained sheets. Horrified, sure. But she didn't look shocked, or surprised. In fact, if Nel had to guess, it looked like Lin had been expecting it. *What else is this family hiding?* She pulled up Phil's database entry, scanning the very sparse vital statistics:

> *Phillip "Philos" Clark*
> *Age: 57*
> *Age at Integration: 39*
> *Current Station: Unknown*

Nel looked back up at Lin and their eyes met over the display. He had been integrated when Dar and Lin were children, probably just before his transfer.

Lin's eyes narrowed and she turned her head to see what Nel was reading. "Why? What did you find?"

"A book. And Mansur's study notes." She cleared her throat. "That night, when he showed up bloody at your house, before your father asked him to leave…whose blood was it? Was it his? Phil's?"

"I thought he crashed his ship. He was a terrible pilot." Lin minimized her work, leaning forward on her folded arms. "What are you getting at?"

Nel heaved a sigh. "This book, Phil wrote part of it. Before he was," she drew her fingers across her own throat. "It started me thinking about Polyana, and Kasanove, and Ada, and all the other senti-comps out there and who they were before.

Why they chose to integrate. I spoke with Kasanove when we first arrived and asked about it."

"God, you're nosey." Lin remarked, but her tone was gentle.

"Maybe that's a good thing." Nel heaved a sigh. "I know Dar found it hard to think about how much Mansur changed since you two were kids. How no one recognized what he was doing. But maybe he didn't change at all. Maybe Phil was his first experiment."

Lin snorted. "Phil was the first documented senti-comp, but as far as I know it was his own research. Besides, no one starts their studies by converting an entire person."

"Okay," Nel reasoned, "maybe it was somewhere in the middle, but my point stands. I think the horrific things Mansur and Harris did were inspired by whatever happened to Phil."

"Senti-comps run our biggest systems up here. If people start thinking it's us versus them, how do you think it'll turn out?"

"I don't think it's us versus them. I just think that there are an awful lot of senti-comp books in that office and this guy is all about doffing the hideous yoke of physical existence. Why not start with his childhood friend?" Nel's heart pounded. She wasn't sure of her own theory until it spilled from her mouth, but now the thought lay naked between them. *We won't even have a chance to kill each other out here. We'll be too busy trying not to die in a hundred other horrible ways.*

Lin's face had a sheen that Nel guessed had nothing to do with the jungle's humidity. She stared at the light, now, as if the answer would materialize in the swirling phosphorescence if she simply looked long enough.

Pulling up the map for Data Sanctum Sapta, Nel thumbed through the growing directory of rooms and buildings. There, below the pyramid itself, was a series of unlabeled rooms. She rubbed the scars stiffening the meat of her palms. "I think we should go into the temple."

"We haven't cataloged everything here, and besides, it's just where we used to commune with the Teachers—"

"The sooner we're done here, the sooner my mom and I can go back to our little rock and you can jet off to do whatever billionaires do out here. Assuming we survive." Nel heaved a sigh. "I don't want to go in there either, but it's why we're here. Let's see if there are more maps or documents of what used to be under there, then dive in."

The Komodor swallowed hard, jaw set. "I know you're not wrong. But I'm just terrified of what it means if you're right."

"Mansur's dead. Very dead." Nel slid her rough hand across the table until it was inches from Lin's. "What harm can he do?"

SIXTEEN

The first sound came just after midnight. Nel sat bolt upright, holding her breath. Her heart hammered in her ears and she shifted to the shelter door, opening it a fraction. A muffled thump sounded from somewhere near the pile of supplies.

"Lin?" she hissed.

The other woman's shelter door opened, and Lin's dark eyes met hers. She tilted her head toward the sound, eyes narrowed in question.

Nel shrugged and held up a finger to tell her to wait. She finished fastening her leg and grabbed her trowel, just in time to see Lin disappear into the dark. *Dammit.* A voice that wasn't Lin's shrieked, followed by the crack-sizzle of a glove blast as Nel scrambled past the shelters.

"Lin, what the—" Her gaze lighted on the ungainly figure cowering among the mound of their cargo crates. Lin stood, glove raised and eyes blazing. A small crater smoked on the ground between them.

Without thinking, Nel grabbed Lin's wrist in iron fingers, twisting until the weapon pointed at Nel's own heaving chest instead. "You're fucking kidding me. You gonna shoot a kid?"

"Kid?" Lin's eyes were huge, her entire body trembling and were it not for the teen recoiled at her feet, Nel might have cared.

Shoving the woman's shaking arm away, Nel dropped to her knees beside the boy and reached out a cautious hand to touch his shoulder. "Xand?"

Lin's expression grew horrified. "You're telling me you know this man?"

"Yeah, actually." Nel patted him awkwardly on the shoulder. "This is Alexander Petre Damascus, from *V Drugoye Mesto*."

"*V Drugoye*, that's the one that—" Lin thankfully thought better of whatever she was about to say and settled on a frown. "That still doesn't explain why he's here."

"She's got a point there," Nel glanced over at the kid. His face was streaked in dirt and sweat, and maybe a few tears, but he looked none the worse for wear. "You hungry? Thirsty?"

He jerked a nod, trying not to look at Lin.

"Come get cleaned up a bit and we can talk." Nel rose with a groan and offered him a hand up and a smile. "Better make it a good one."

Lin faltered into step behind them as Nel ushered the kid into the kitchen and squeezed the cube on the table until it lit. She pointed to the sink and cranked the water on so he could wash his face and hands before popping their leftovers into the warmer for him. Lin hovered in the doorway, watching Xand drench the floor and counter as he washed up. Nel glanced back and caught her eye, jerking her head at the table with a pointed look. Sheepishly, Lin sank into the spot closest to the door.

"Here," Nel tossed the kid a dish towel and set the bowl of soup on the table along with a glass of water. Xand was thinner, she noted as he sat, and now looked closer to a drowning victim than a healthy boy, but puberty was never kind.

He sat, arms braced around his food, but he didn't take a bite, just staring at Lin seated at the other end of the table.

Nel followed his gaze. "She's fine, just looks evil. She mostly only shoots at me. Eat, then we can talk."

Lin glared at her, but pointedly sat back and began scrolling on her comm, probably looking up the kid's stats on the database. It did little to make her look less scary, if Nel was being honest. Xand was a noisy eater, and he made quick work of the soup and gulped the water, and the second glass when Nel got up to refill it.

"Better?" she asked.

He gave a nod, looking between the two of them.

"I think we've stalled enough," Lin pointed out.

"Empathy," Nel reminded her, but turned to the teen. "Ok, hit me. What brought you out here at midnight?"

"I didn't leave at midnight," he pointed out, turning to Nel and, much to her secret delight, totally ignoring Lin. "I left a bit after you. I saw the mission posts and thought maybe I could help. You said you were stressed out, said you needed help and that it had to do with my ship." His brows curled together. "I'm sick them all looking at me like I'm either gonna bomb the place or take a spacewalk without my suit. All they got me doing is seeing psych and watching the littles back there and they're just snot factories and the babies—" he grimaced, but there was a haunted look behind the expression.

His sister. Nel gave him an awkward smile of encouragement. "They don't always think before assigning jobs."

"It's not like anyone's gonna miss me."

"I'm pretty sure they will," Nel remarked. "I'm surprised they didn't send out an alert."

His smile was sly. "Oh, they did. Easy to erase them though."

Lin frowned, unable to continue her act of indifference. "I'm sorry, you erased them? And what bulletin did you see? This is high security we're talking about and if a child can see anything there's been a huge breach."

"He's a man when you shoot at him, but a kid when it comes to your security?" Nel pointed out.

Xand tossed her an eyeroll with all the unconscious arrogance of adolescence. "Your security is good. I'm just kind of really smart. About computers. Hacked in just to see what was really going on, because no one tells anyone anything, especially me. Saw the bulletin about some mission and then Dr. Nel messaged that she was going away for a while."

Lin was typing furiously on her comm, probably running the security breach up the flagpole.

"I'm glad you're 'kinda really smart,'" Nel began, "But security is to keep people safe."

"To keep them controlled, more like," Xand muttered. "You said maybe I could help. When I saw you before you left."

"Nel?" Lin interjected, her black brows arching.

"I didn't mean like this!" Nel countered, scrambling. "I thought maybe once things died down he could find a way to help with—oh fuck it."

"I don't care why you've suddenly grown a soft spot," Lin countered. "First thing in the morning I'm getting Transport on the comms and sending him back to his parents."

Xand's expression shuttered and before Nel thought better of it, she grabbed his clammy teen hand. "He doesn't have parents anymore, Lin, thanks to your fucking uncle. He has me and a whole gaggle of doctors. But that's it. Besides, you were saying yourself you wished we had the budget for an assistant. He can handle the basics and knows more than a bit about engineering and computers, clearly. And I bet he can cook," she shot him a glance, "Right, Xand, you can cook?"

"Sure," he agreed with perhaps the least convincing lie Nel had ever heard. "Do it all the time."

"There you go, he can cook and assist with the non-dangerous stuff."

"Danger?" Xand's voice perked up and Nel shot him a glare.

"We're not discussing it." Lin countered. "Get him to bed and I'll deal with it in the morning."

The boy looked between them, dejected. Nel offered a rueful smile. "She's right about the morning." Giving a cursory scan of his gangly frame, she pointed to her tent. "That one's mine. Why don't you change into a spare set of my clothes and take the cot? I'll get things cleaned up here." *And have the discussion Lin is avoiding.*

The boy nodded then lurched toward Nel to grip her in a sudden hug. She gave him a nervous pat on the head before stepping back and shooing him toward the shelters. He slumped out of the room, and she waited until she heard him shuffle into bed before easing the kitchen door shut. With the open windows it did little to muffle any conversation, but it gave the illusion of privacy. She leaned back against the door and crossed her arms to stare at Lin. Her heart was a stampede in her chest. "You shot at a kid, Lin."

"It was a warning! I wasn't going to shoot him," Lin snapped back. Her eyes had the wide, wild look from before, and Nel almost wondered for a second if she was frightened.

"I've heard that before," Nel muttered. But she, too, had mostly meant it, when she parroted her excuse for holding Lin at glove point.

"I didn't know it was a kid, I didn't even know if it was a person or..." her face twisted in a mask of despair. "This is no place for a child."

Nel couldn't really argue with that, but it wasn't a place for adults either, for any decent people, really. She heaved a sigh and flopped into the seat across from Lin. "It's not gonna look good if you send him back and he says you almost shot him."

"Don't be manipulative, you know it was a misunderstanding and I was protecting us." Lin's voice cracked and her skittish stare turned to her still-shaking hands. "What's the deal with him?"

Nel frowned. "It's all in the notes—lone survivor of *V Drugoye*. Found him when we were salvaging."

Lin hummed. "I know what the notes say. And what you had to see. And do. But I was asking what the deal was with you two. I didn't think you were a kid person."

"I'm not. Never was any good with the students. But he's fucked up, and I don't want to fuck him up more." Nel dropped her head into her hands with a groan. "I'm sorry. I know you weren't trying to hurt him. But I just..." she trailed off.

"You care about him."

"I see myself in him," Nel finally admitted. "I'm no good at communication, or patience. But I'm good at broken. And seeing horrific things. Besides," her eyes narrowed on the dishes on the table, the smear of food that was so close to what Xand's family turned into. "You see what he has, you're not really a kid anymore."

Lin's fearful expression softened into familiarity, into understanding, but she did not speak. Nel watched her and wondered what Lin had seen by Xand's age, out in this cold vacuum, what her world told her was normal and okay. *How scared do you have to be to shoot at a child?*

Nel didn't sleep. She could have chalked it up to being relegated to the barely padded floor of the shelter, or the faint clammy chill that filled the jungle in the small hours of the morning. Maybe it was the fact that Xand snored, or that she could hear Lin pacing in the kitchen long after she went to bed. Nel stared at the boy bunched up on her cot across the tent. With her eyes lidded, and her brain addled with lack of sleep, she almost saw the ghostly movement of air around his form.

"Did you bring him here?" she mouthed against the dark, wondering if Samsara's ghosts could hear her like she heard them, without true speech.

When dawn came, she gathered her suit as quietly as she could. She crept into the washroom and took a short, tepid shower before drying and donning her suit. As she was toweling her two-toned hair, she noticed the door to the bunks was ajar. She stilled. A soft sound, almost footsteps, almost sighing, drifted from the room beyond. Whatever was waiting for her had surely heard her clomping about trying not to slip on the water-slick stone. She edged closer and gave the door a careful nudge. It swung open to show her Lin, seated at her uncle's desk, sobbing.

"Shit." Nel opened the door fully and came to stand in the office doorway. Lin's arms wrapped her knees as she stared at the Newton's Cradle on the desk. The spheres clacked softly into one another. Her face was botchy and her eyes puffy. "Hey," Nel began, ducking her head to try and get the other woman's attention. "What's up?"

Lin shook her head and carefully wiped her face before checking her comm's time. "I'm sorry. It's time we start the day, I suppose. There's coffee in the kitchen, I made it last night when I—"

Nel reached out, fingers resting on the other woman's comm. Maybe if she didn't touch her skin or her suit, warm from her body, it didn't really count. "You were scared."

Lin blinked wetly and looked up. "We need to get to work."

"When you fired that warning shot last night, it wasn't him you were seeing, was it?" Nel prodded.

"I have to message the transport team," Lin deflected. The wild look was back in Lin's eyes, shadowed like Nel's, shadowed like Xand's.

"I figured." Nel straightened and backed up with a sigh. *So much for stopping her from hating herself.* "I'm sorry. I was angry last night, and I know you wouldn't have—"

"I don't." The confession was tiny and terrible and sat between them on the desk, uglier than the stains on the floor. "Behavioral Therapy and Community Reintegration."

Nel frowned. "What?"

"What I'll be doing after this. If we survive, like you said yesterday, when we were talking. I won't be 'jetting off' anywhere, as you put it. I was on the wrong side of this war and after this, I'll be atoning for the choices I made."

Nel swallowed hard, heart hammering again, the way it did when she hung between fear and something far more complicated. "Mansur is doing his best to turn us all to monsters. Let's not help him, alright?"

Lin's nod was stiff, her jaw tight, but it was followed with a faint, strained smile. The fragile truce between them broke as a loud clatter sounded from the kitchen. Her eyes narrowed and

Nel tossed her an awkward placating smile before bolting out of the creepy office to see what Xand had done. She cut through the courtyard, tossing her towel over the line they'd strung across the space and ducked into the kitchen.

What she saw made her stop so quickly Lin, a second behind her, collided with her back. Heat spilled over Nel from where their bodies touched and she sprang away, as if burned. The table was set for three, and Xand was scraping reconstituted eggs onto plates. The cooking area was a disaster, but it smelled glorious.

"Fuck—I mean, man, that smells good." Nel praised, popping a few packets of orange juice into the rehydrator as a treat. It tasted fine, and she told herself the little chunks were pulp. "Never could get the eggs right on *The Recursive,* got complaints all day whenever I tried."

"Just gotta add spices and stuff," Xand explained. "Hides the weird dehydro-tang."

Lin sat silently at the same place she had last night, as far from the boy as possible, eyes large. When he handed her a plate with a wary look, she flashed a tiny smile and whispered her thanks.

Nel passed around the juice and grabbed her own plate. "I really appreciate this, Xand."

He seemed to stand a little taller and dropped the pan into the sink with a clang. Lin flinched but tried a shaking bite of her food.

"It's good, thank you," she began, once they were all seated. She finished another forkful before clearing her throat and gripping the edge of the stone tabletop. "I'd like to apologize, Alexander, for last night."

Nel stilled, but didn't dare look up, lest she startle the humility from the room. Beside her, Xand's bouncing leg and tapping fingers stilled, too.

"It's Xand. And s'ok—"

"It's not okay," Lin corrected. "Before we came here, I was working for the people hunting Dr. Nel. The people who hurt your family. I knew it was wrong and I was trying to get out, but it was difficult, and I saw what happened to those who betrayed IDH so I had to be careful. I know I don't have to tell either of you how dangerous they were. It's not a good excuse, but it is a reason. I came here to help end what they were doing, to maybe try and make up for what I saw, what I did. And I think, in the dark, not knowing you, I forgot that. I forgot I was here, on *Vīrya*, and among more friends than enemies. And I'm very sorry I scared you."

Xand shuffled, taking a large bite and chewing loudly, before bobbing his head. "Uh, thanks. Sometimes I see stuff differently too, in the dark."

Tension bled from Nel's shoulders, just a bit, and she let herself relax enough to finish breakfast. The eggs smelled better than they tasted, but they tasted far better than most of what they'd been eating for the last few days. When they'd finished,

Xand got up and cleared the table and slumped over to the sink to start washing.

Lin watched him for a moment before flicking her attention to Nel and nodding to the door. The archaeologist followed her out, wincing at the sound of dishes. "Thank goodness that stuff is meant for travel, otherwise it'd be shattered by now," she remarked.

Lin laughed softly. "It's nice, not feeling like we have to sneak around lest something horrible jumps out of the woods at us." She checked her comm again and glanced up at the brightening dome above. "I'm going to message the team, but I think we have as much information from the labs as we're going to get, aside from waiting for the analysis. Once we're in the temple itself we could boot up the subsystem and see if any data survived." Lin grimaced, following Nel's nervous look toward the temple. "I'll talk to the team about Xand and our mission today, if you get the equipment together."

Nel sighed. "Go easy on him, alright? He's dealt with enough." When Lin agreed, the archaeologist retreated to the lab.

Half an hour later, she had managed to stock the small hover-cart they'd use for the exploration into the temple itself. She tightened the straps on her wrist, hoping she'd have no reason to use the glove synced to her system. Her toolbelt was filled with the portable bag printer and a dozen tiny picks and tweezers, along with Dirt-o-mancer. She was adjusting the larger equipment on the transport when Lin reappeared, looking refreshed, hair damp and tightly rebraided.

"Just about ready, here," Nel reported.

"Thanks." Lin nodded to where Xand was poking around the vine-covered stones. "Transport team is coming in four days for us, or to drop off more supplies if we're not finished cataloging. They'll pick up Xand then."

Nel's brows shot up, as surprised by the impending end of the mission as she was by Xand's extended stay. "Four days? That's the earliest?"

"There's enough room in the shelters." Lin finally answered. "And I told them there wasn't a rush. We could use the help."

Nel shot her a surprised smile. "What do you mean?"

"Exactly what I said." Lin bit back.

Despite the tone, Nel caught a softness around the other woman's eyes as they watched the teen try to balance on one of the larger fallen trees. "Maybe he is still a kid. Despite it all." Nel chuckled, watching as Xand slipped and plummeted with a yelp.

Lin's eyes narrowed as the pile of gangly limbs untangled and he leapt back into action, giving the trunk another go. "Don't make me regret this."

SEVENTEEN

Damp stone pressed in from all sides, and what little light filtered through the dense canopy did not reach within. Lin went first to work the unlocking device, and Nel, equipment trolley in tow, came after. The lights from their suits bounced and arced with each step. Steep stairs led down from the courtyard, ending perhaps a storey beneath at a large, plain door. They had left Xand above, in the safe confines of the courtyard, to pack what they had already cataloged in preparation for the impending pick up. His excitement at being allowed to stay on, even for just a few days, may have been contagious, but the feeling faded the farther down they climbed.

The ramp ended with a tall, narrow door and simple circuits inscribed the lintel and jambs. Lin let out a long breath through her teeth in anticipation and pressed her hand to the circle in the center of the door. A hum, a soft *thunk* somewhere within the structure, and the stone parted into four segments, each retreating into its respective wall.

Within, darkness swirled. Nel watched the air, wondering if some day she would recognize each eddy of the Samsari as she could faces. Alongside her, Lin wavered on the threshold.

A shrill buzz sounded from both their comms and they jumped. Nel gripped the handle of the hovering equipment cart breathing to calm her frayed nerves. She nodded to the baleful entrance still awaiting them. "Once more unto the breach?"

Neither spoke as they stepped into the darkness. The organic sound of stone underfoot, and a distant dripping of water filled the space, and, judging by the unmet reach of their light, and the faint echo off hard walls far ahead, it was a large space indeed. Nel dragged her attention from the dust motes disturbed by their passing to the map readout above her comm. The layout—if accurate—was geometric in design, with a dozen concentric square storeys descending beneath the largest and topmost, open floor. The map contained precious little information, beyond the vague labeling of the upper levels.

Hall Of Worship
Communication Hub
Meditation Room
Storage

Beyond that, they were unmarked. Nel started her scanner again, letting its radar ping softly to itself as she spun in a slow circle. The image was grainy and showed a series of benches ringing a gleaming pool. A tiny trickle of a stream sent phosphorescent ripples across its surface. "Guess we found where the lights went," she muttered to herself. A low dias stood in the center of the water with what resembled a small podium. Beyond that, the room was empty.

Nel raised her atmohelm light and began a circuit of the room. The benches were plain, carved from the same stone as the building itself, and despite the horrifying images conjured by Nel's imagination, deserted. Roots crept from the trees far above, curling from the ceiling, around the seats, and across the circuitry carved in the floor and walls, as if nature itself, the very universe, wanted to rewrite the purpose of the room.

When Nel turned, she found Lin standing in the room's center, light cube resting on the podium. Except, now Nel could see circuits and speakers and diodes crisscrossing its surface. Lin cast her gaze to the ceiling, features lit from the discarded cube. A tear dribbled over the rim of her eye and for a moment Nel expected it, too, to glow.

"Centuries ago," Lin swallowed, voice rising like prayer in the darkness, "in the eons of our ancestors, our people came to meet the spirits of the all-knowing, and it was through these great teachers, that we came, in turn, to know the universe."

Nel drew closer, pulled by the magnetism of the other woman, or perhaps the gravity of faith. "That's beautiful."

Lin nodded, still searching the swirling darkness. "It was our litany, in IDH, for a long while, especially in places like this."

"And the last you heard was just before Samsara went dark?" Nel prodded.

"More or less. I think it was him. I think they were so appalled they abandoned us to our bespoke doom."

"I guess I'd block Mansur too, if I had the chance." The archaeologist reached a nervous hand to the podium's angled corner. "Do you think they'd answer, if we turned this thing on?"

"No." Lin's eyes cast downward. "I would hope, but I'm afraid they won't come back. That we've gone too far for their forgiveness."

Nel hummed noncommittal. "Creatures as powerful as that, if you fucked up it's kind of on them, for not teaching you better, you know?"

Lin's face was hard, furious almost. "Do you think he could have killed them? Uak Mansur?"

The press of stone above oppressive. "I wouldn't want to give him more credit than deserved," she joked, but the humor soured to fear in her mouth. "I'm going to finish this scan then head down to the next level, if you're ready."

Lin seemed loath to pull herself away.

"Hopefully the rest is empty." It was a hollow hope and one that denied their need for answers.

Exploration continued, both photographing and tapping out notes in otherwise relative silence. The next level was accessed by a steep ramp descending from the rear of the prayer room to the next space down. Here, too, the lights no longer worked, and the glow from their helms cast alarming shadows. At the base of the ramp was another door, which Lin unlocked in a similar fashion. The air was a fraction cooler, and rows of stone columns reached back into the darkness.

"Data banks," Lin explained. "I'm going to run a scan, see if there's anything we can salvage."

"If you don't need help, I might head down to the next level. Says it's a meditation room?"

Lin winced. "Be careful. I don't trust anything down here yet."

"Don't worry, I'll start shrieking if there's more death and destruction."

"Never had a doubt," Lin muttered, but her shaking hands as she gave Nel one of the kits off the cart said that the joke wasn't funny.

Another ramp, another door, and Nel stepped into the dark press of the temple's third room. The level beneath the data banks was smaller a fact made more extreme by the tightly packed lab benches. Her helm's light swept over plastic sheets draped over hulking shapes on the stone table tops. Everything was tidy, clearly prepped for storage long ago, and Nel was partway through her perusal of the benches when she caught sight of a faint glow near the rear of the room. She edged closer, fingers tightening on her trowel's handle. The translucent cellulose sheet blurred the details, but on the rearmost bench was a standby light, blinking slowly into the darkness. Trembling fingers drew back the protective sheet, and she saw a plain computer portal, complete with a node for holoscreen projection.

Groaning softly, she tapped out a message to Lin.

Something's on down here.

Moments later, Lin came gliding down the ramp, steps whisper soft across the dust. She stilled next to Nel, one hand reaching out, stopping just short of touching the archaeologist.

"You're alright?"

"Yeah. Just found this."

"This room is supposed to be empty. None of this," Lin spun in a slow circle, taking in the equipment, "is supposed to be down here." She jabbed a device into some tiny port in the bench itself and typed a few codes. "There's power, probably generated from some of the deep cells I found upstairs. There's way too many for just a typical setup, even a laboratory one. I'm just going to see." She spun a dial on her device and the holoscreen jittered to life.

It was a perfect hologram of the device that nearly destroyed Earth. Nel's heart leapt up her throat. *It's a hologram, nothing more.* "Is that—"

"Yes." Lin jerked a stiff nod. Her eyes narrowed slightly. "Except this. And here." Her finger roved across the surface, trailing distortion in its wake, while Nel squirmed at the idea of Lin getting anywhere near that close.

"You think it's a prototype?"

"I think it's the original," she murmured back. "The one that we" her grimace deepened, "that you stopped had additional ports, hookups to convert the lower frequency of Earth power to what we use up here. Our systems need a lot more hertz."

"How do you even know that?"

She shrugged, eyes still wide and fixed on the schematic glowing between them. "Part of learning about our human cousins is learning about the differences in tech. And Lissa taught me a few things, when we—before."

"When you were dating, you mean?"

"Yes, then." Lin's attention flicked up to her, then back down. "This one is from Samsara. The center of it."

"It's the conversion part, that turns it from a planetary form to the transport, right?"

She tilted her head as if a different angle would provide answers. "I wonder if it's something more. He destroyed the people on Samsara—where this was found—and then sent Harris to do the same on Earth. When I realized you were right about it, I assumed it was just a giant doomsday device. A bomb, or something to broadcast the signal."

"But the signal was the Samsari."

"I know. I think this is what made them, Nel. I think this device takes physical forms and remakes them into—" her face paled and her jaw clenched, as if biting back vomit.

Nel couldn't really blame her. The only thing worse than the ghosts, was the failed attempt to make more of them on *V Drugoye Mesto*, and that point was arguable. "What's a gate but a massive translator," Nel guessed. "You claim he was devout, or obsessed with them, in the very least. And those notes of his that you found, they've the tone of a madman. Harris even admits it—they wanted to turn humanity into the Teachers. Or some abomination thereof."

Lin held her gaze for a moment before blinking and dropping her attention back to the device in her hand. "This is enough to analyze for one day. I'm going to get this data on our system— carefully—and we can take the afternoon to go over it all. At least we know we're headed in the right direction."

"Good plan. I'll take some pics of the equipment, in case there's anything new." She was reaching for another sheet when Lin's soft voice stopped her.

"I'm sorry, Nel."

Nel turned, frowning, and trying not to admire the planes of Lin's face in the hologram's light. "What?"

"You raced across my mother's imploding planet with me." She swallowed hard. "The least I could have done was help you try and save yours."

"I ah," Nel cleared her throat, "I heard you did. Help, I mean. With the override code."

Lin flushed, twisting her long fingers together. "I knew if anyone would make it that far, it'd be you, out of sheer fury. I altered the kill-switch, just in case I was wrong."

"What a batshit idea."

"It worked."

Nel met her eyes over the glowing image of humanity's doom, and found there was a smile on her mouth. "Guess we made a better team than either of us realized."

The survey took the better part of the day, and both Lin and Nel were quiet when they emerged from the temple. Once they had both washed up, they found Xand whipping up packets of red curry protein.

"There was a message," he blurted as Nel and Lin entered the kitchen.

Nel let out a soft groan and dropped to sit on the nearest chair. "Message from who? Dar?"

His eyes were wide with excitement, and he jabbed a finger at the stone mouth they had just exited. "That place got a message."

Nel turned to stare at Lin, hoping for Xand's sake, her face didn't give away the horror in her gut. "Nothing came through either of our comms."

"No, I mean, like a while back. I was looking at the data banks you loaded into the mission files—"

"And what did I expressly ask you not to do?" Lin growled.

Xand drew back, trembling, but a second later clenched his jaw and stood his ground. "And Dr. Nel said you needed help. Maybe you lost an uncle, but I lost everyone." He turned on his heel and stormed away into Nel's tent, wiping furiously at his eyes.

"Dude," Nel groaned at Lin. "Could you just can it with him?"

"With what we're dealing with, that level of security breach could ruin us. You want him to lose all of this as well? Send all of us into oblivion?"

"No, but I think we're past that point. It's not hacking if he's invited. Besides, the ghosts— Samsari, whatever—haven't killed either one of us yet. Maybe they have more control. Plus, he doesn't have any augments. I'll go talk with him, okay? It's not like we can keep him out with firewalls or however you do it. Might as well harness that brain and make it work for us."

Lin's lips thinned and she drew a long breath through her nose. "Fine, but he's going to have to ask, first."

"Of course." Nel nodded toward the tent. "I'll talk to him, you finish dinner. And after, you can apologize. Again."

Lin's face wrinkled further, but she nodded and dragged herself over to the now-burning meal.

Nel limped to where soft sobs emanate from her tent. She peered under the unlatched shelter door. Xand was curled in a ball on the cot, shoulders shaking. She let the door fall shut behind her and lurched over to sit at the end of the cot. She dropped an awkward hand to the bare ankle sticking out from the too-short pant leg. He didn't jerk away, and she took that as a good sign.

He sniffed, wiping the snot bubbles on his face. "I'm sorry I messed up again."

Nel shook her head, trying not to wince at the boogers. "We're not angry. Just worried. There's a lot about this whole mess we still don't understand, try as we might. If you got into something we haven't cleared yet it could be really dangerous."

"I just want to help." Another sniff and snot-wipe. "I want to try and do right by them."

"You will. I promise. Lin and I are going to go over what you found and the other data too, tomorrow. But for now," she gave the ankle a firm pat, "Why don't you ask first. Deal?"

He nodded wetly. "Deal."

"Can I do anything for you right now?" She asked.

He tucked his arms closer to his chest. "Can I just be alone for a while?"

"Sure thing. Thanks for dinner and checking the data." She stood and slipped back out of the tent, closing the door behind her before heading back to the kitchen. The food was ready and after several minutes, a quiet Xand joined them.

Aside from the murmured thanks, however, no one spoke as they ate. Once supper was cleaned up and both Lin and Xand were focusing on their own evening routines, Nel crept away, to the sanctum entrance. Her hands moved over the rough stone rhythmically, scarred fingers digging into the nooks and crags. It felt so much like pumice, like limestone, dips and hollows and protrusions. If she closed her eyes, shut out the brilliance of Thalassi's blue belly, she could have almost been on Earth.

With Lin sending things off to the rest of the team—to Lissa, probably—and Xand watching some space station reality show, she had a moment of peace. *Well, solitude, at least.* She released her body from its rigid attempt to hide her disability and limped across the temple courtyard. It was never truly dark on *Vīrya*, but the dense trees and towering stone shrouded the ground in shadows. She took the steep sanctum ramp and came to a stop at the bottom, steadying herself on the hewn doorway before picking her way over until she could sit at the edge of the gleaming pool.

The water was made mercurial with the changing, pulsing lights. Grateful to have a moment without the oppressive cling of the electrosuit, she eased off her boot and sock and lowered her foot into the cool water. She groaned. There was nothing like wild water on the feet after a day of work.

Lying back, she felt the scrape of stone against her bare shoulders. Her past self never would have believed where she would end up. She could bitch and scream as much as she wanted, but the fact remained that, three-odd years ago when Lin asked her to follow her into space, she made a choice. She signed papers, whether or not she remembered.

Nel was no stranger to following a cute butt into new job opportunities—and leaving them just as fast when a different cute butt appeared on the horizon. Archaeology was a small world, even out here it seemed. But, try as she might, she wasn't able to keep her head down until everyone was distracted by the new drama du jour.

And, Jem aside, she had mostly ditched that habit the moment she stepped into space with Lin. She inched closer to the pool until the water lapped up her remaining knee. *I don't even know where Jem ended up.* She felt guilty for not looking, for not wondering beyond a cursory thought when they first arrived, and even guiltier that she was relieved Jem hadn't reached out either. As usual, everything else ceased to exist once Lin was in her sights.

It wasn't just Jem. It was Nel's house, her truck, her Friday night drives down to Black Pond

Brewery to hang out with her old undergrad buddies—the ones whose hearts she hadn't broken, and a few who had managed to get over it. She was lucky to have someone like Mikey argue for her to be up for tenure, and luckier that, even after his death, they gave her an offer.

One hand gripped a loose stone, feeling the bumps before tossing it into the water with a plunk. *Why did I throw it all away to come here?*

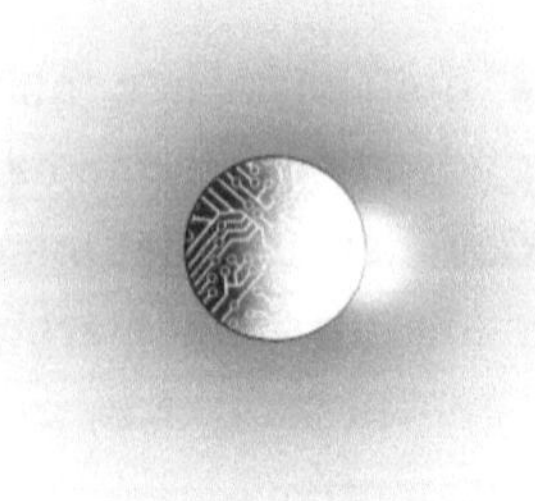

EIGHTEEN

"Dr. Nel!"

Nel groaned, throwing an arm over her eyes. Eager field school students were bad under normal circumstances. But this early in the morning?

"Dr. Nel!"

"Ask Dr. Servais, please." She stretched, absently wondering why her back hurt so badly. "And for the love of god, stop shouting."

The sound of rocks crunching, and the faint acrid scent of rehydrated eggs drifted over her and she opened one eye with a grimace. A boy's face bobbed above her head, greasy hair dangling around his shadowed face. "Dr. Nel, did you fall? Are you okay?"

Xand. Vīrya. Lin. Mansur. Oh. "Fuck, shit, I'm sorry Xand. What time is—" she blinked at her comm and tried to sit up. Her back was tight, spasms echoing through her lumbar as she lurched upright.

"It's morning. Komodor Nalawangsa asked if you were up yet, and that's when we realized neither of us saw you go to bed. Figured you and her were—"

"If you finish that sentence I'm taking your lunch money," Nel grumbled. Taking his offered hand she levered herself upright. Apparently, she had fallen asleep with her foot in the water, and it was now pale and wrinkled. She made a face, but didn't bother drying it off, just scooped her boot and sock up and limped after the giggling teen.

"Nel!" Lin rushed from the kitchen when they emerged into the courtyard, eyes wide in panic. She stopped short of grabbing the archaeologist, hands flexing just inches from Nel's shoulders. "What happened?"

Nel waved away her concern, trying to ignore the heat that bloomed between their skin. "Sorry. I went down to the temple pond to clear my head and must have fallen asleep. Everything okay over here?"

"Yes, I just thought…" Her words turned to a soft, straggled sound. "I was just worried."

"Sorry." With a sigh, Nel stretched, rolling her neck and shoulders. "Think I can grab some breakfast before we get back to it?"

"Of course." Lin's dark eyes followed her across the courtyard and into the kitchen. "You're alright though?"

Nel gestured to herself with the spatula, annoyed at the scrutiny, and piled rehydrated eggs onto her plate. "It'll take more than that to shake me, these days." She shoved some bites in before asking, "What's the plan for the day?"

"I was hoping to spend today combing through the data sets. Making sure we didn't miss anything before we go farther."

Nel polished off her eggs in as few bites as possible, both for the flavor and speed, then followed Lin across the courtyard. "I'll take a look at the footage, if there's anything."

"Luckily it only archives changes in the environment, so you don't have to scroll through years of empty rooms." Lin nudged the door open and gestured for Nel to lead the way into the common room.

Nel eased down onto one of the seats. "Where's the boy genius?"

"I have him going through anomalies in correspondence, since he was so eager." One long delicate finger tugged the security footage from her screen to Nel's.

"Did you apologize to him?" Nel asked, eyes narrowed.

"I did. Did you explain to him why it was a problem?"

Nel nodded. "He's trying to help, but I think I made it clear he needs to ask before doing shit like that again."

"You know, children up here don't listen any better than they do on Earth," Lin teased softly. "Ask Ibu." She stared thoughtfully at the screen before frowning at Nel. "Don't turn him into your mirror."

Nel frowned. "Mirror?"

"Like Dar does. He always has a person to reflect everything he's not back at him. Someone whose ideas and choices he can shoot down. You were his mirror on *Recursive* I'd bet. Paul was for a time even. But mostly it was me." Her jaw tightened, words heavy enough Nel expected them to leave ripples across the screen. "Everything we did as children was a test. It wasn't acknowledged, and sometimes I wonder if it was even intentional. But Dar and I competed, neither ever really winning, I think. Expected to model our parents' different cultures, but raised in a dysfunctional, enmeshed version of both."

"I wonder what Emilio is to him," she mused.

Lin frowned. "What's Emilio got to do with it?"

"They're, um…" Nel faltered, realizing that Dar had ample opportunity to tell his sister about his relationship, and clearly hadn't. "They've been working together a lot. Lots of exchanging…ideas."

"Next you'll tell me that they're roommates." Lin's eyes lidded, but her expression was fragile. "I wish he'd told me."

"It's not like he told me, I just happened to be standing in the middle of them when Dar decided to process grief in someone else's mouth." Nel explained with a grimace.

"Sounds familiar," Lin remarked, before nodding at the work between them. "Let's get this over with."

"Yeah, that's enough about your brother's tongue." Nel nodded and started up the videos, resting her chin in one palm while the footage played.

The screens showed the lab rooms and kitchen, but not the bunks, probably for privacy. The footage had been compiled from the year before Lin recalled Mansur arriving bloody at the family estate, all the way up until after his passing on Morphose, just to be safe. People came and went from the kitchen, most wearing long, sleeveless robes with stiff, high collars. From what Nel could see, there were three lining colors, probably denoting ranks. *Vīrya* had a personnel manifest, on which the temple's residents were displayed, and though Nel picked out the more notable figures on the footage from their included ident photos. It was dull, if she was being honest.

A round, Black man—Dedicate Jom—wearing one of the few red-lined robes, frequented the common room. Data cubes filled the shelves, with a smattering of analog books as well, though Nel couldn't make out any titles. She took a still of the clearest frame and made a note to Hugo-Sanchez to enhance the image. Maybe they could determine if any notable titles were missing.

The kitchen was a hub of activity, busiest around the evenings. Half a dozen men and women flitted in and out, laughing, or sharing quiet conversation. The food seemed plain, often colorless, with a single dish. Though she understood the lack of cameras in the private areas, she wondered if the bloody cloth could have had an innocent origin. Any suspicious activity, she flagged, but there was very little beyond…wait. She leaned forward a bit more, squirting at the hazy recording.

One of the younger priests, a woman listed as Jenna Kim, crept into the kitchen late one evening, about a month before Mansur's fateful bloody appearance. She snuck through the room, leaving it dark, and began preparing something, pulling a small packet from her robe toward the end and sticking its contents into whatever she made. The next morning during breakfast, she reappeared, pulling a messy, leaning birthday cake from the cooling unit and delivering it, triumphant, to Jom.

Nel flopped back with a sigh. *False alarm.* But damn, did that cake look good. As the days spun out before her, she caught a few lingering looks and brushes of hands, and wondered if the "priests," as Lin had called them, had the same romantic restrictions as many sects did on Earth.

Then, someone not in robes arrived. Though younger by a good decade, the impeccable Nalawangsa taste and bearing was unmistakable. Mansur swept into the common room, arms out embracing Jenna. It wasn't a romantic gesture, Nel realized, as he pulled away and ruffled her short hair. He faced away from the camera, only the edge of his jaw visibly moving as he spoke to her. She laughed, then looked down and grew serious, maybe even castigated. They left through the door to the courtyard. Then, for another long few days, there was nothing. No activity, no people, not even the regular lights rising or dimming. Nel made another note, then checked the manifest during those dates.

Transfer of all Personnel to Level 161

She scanned the list of all the names, noting their new departments, most elsewhere on the satellite. *Tirta said they expanded the interior of Vīrya, perhaps this is when.* Then, fourteen days later, Mansur appeared again. This time the lights stayed dark. He and a strong looking white man dumped most of the data cubes and books into crates. They moved quickly, speaking little from what Nel could see. She paused the video, peering at the stranger's face. The pit in her stomach yawned wider. His cheeks were rounder, and his head topped with thinning brown hair. But there, under the hair and vitality and despite the extra 200 odd pounds of body, she saw Phil.

She made a note for Hugo-Sanchez to check the face against the *Vīrya* database. But that was formality only. Over the course of the next few days, she watched as they left the bunk house in the early evenings, disappearing for most of the night, before reappearing looking haggard just before scheduled dawn. The manifest still claimed the site deserted.

One particular morning, Phil strode back early, on his own, shouting something over his shoulder. Mansur stormed after him, hands moving wildly. They were stained in dark red and yellow fluid. He reached the other man, hand gripping his shoulder, but Mansur was shoved away.

"Lin I think—" She opened her mouth to tell Lin, but she stilled as the video continued. The argument went on, Phil shoving Mansur again, harder, Lin's uncle staggering back with a snarl before his fist rose. Phil turned on his heel and fled into the bunk house. Mansur stalked outside and both men were gone from the footage for another few hours. Mansur's last appearance was just after dawn, dragging something large in bloodstained sheets. Days came and went, and then seasons. The site was left to the elements until she and Lin arrived, years later. "Oh, fuck no."

"What is it?"

Nel enlarged the screen and turned it around, though certainly murder wouldn't be any less clear. "I think your uncle murdered Phil. Or," she swallowed the acid rising in the back of her throat, "helped him on his way to be integrated."

Lin watched the footage, face stoney, looking away when she saw the sheets. A strange series of expressions flickered across her usual stoicism. "Senti-comps don't usually keep too many memories from before. I know Kasanove said he couldn't recall anything past first awakening afterward."

"Could Mansur have erased Phil's memories somehow?"

"Probably. Or just the trauma of your friend doing that to you."

"And why is there blood on him before this?" Nel scrubbed a hand over her face. "Our timeline is: he does this—that's when you recall him showing up covered in blood—and spends the next however long studying elsewhere. Then at some point he travels to *Odyssey of Earth* and from there to Samsara and the *V Drugoye Mesto*. Where he does his nasty thing."

"We know he meets Harris, though whether that's on Earth or *Odyssey*, or even after that point, I have no clue."

"I don't get it." Nel glared at the holo. "He succeeds with Phil, though whether that was his plan all along or improvising, I don't know. And then he succeeds again on Samsara. More or less. But he was so successful on Samsara, how did he fuck up so hard on *V Drugoye*?"

"Why do you think it was a mistake?"

Nel made a face. "The Samsari were fully transformed. The bodies on *V Drugoye* were still very much there. At least, more recognizable than my stomach could handle. What went wrong?"

"I did it." Xand's voice cracked from the doorway.

NINETEEN

"He didn't fail on *V Drugoye*." Xand spat out.

Nel swung about in her chair with a wince. "Sorry, I didn't mean for you to hear that."

He hovered in the doorway, eyes as anguished as when Nel first met him, cowering in *The Recursive's* infirmary. "He did everything right. I'm the one that fucked up his plan. I'm the reason they're all dead."

Lin looked between them, panicked. "What do you mean?"

Nel waved at her to hush. "You were in the wrong place at the wrong time, Xand, that's all. The person to blame is the monster whose idea this was in the first place."

"How did you mess up his plan?" Lin shifted, clearly trying to make herself look approachable.

Hard when your whole family looks like the man that ruined his life. "Do you remember more, now?" Nel asked, hoping she didn't startle him back into silence, or the easy-going dissociation he affected most of the time.

"They want me to talk about it in psych, but I don't see what good it'll do. Doesn't make it hurt less. So, I mostly pretend like I don't remember. I didn't at first, but some of it's come back." His voice dropped lower with his shoulders. "He said his name was Moksha. We didn't pick up people, usually. But our systems were old, and we didn't have the money for real repairs. And he offered credits. Wouldn't have risked going out of our way to help someone otherwise. The first week there he was real polite, joked with everyone, even held my little sister at dinner so Ma could eat." His expression was stiff, each word twisting his feature further into a grimace of grief. "He held her. Rocked her."

Nel wanted to press her arms around him until he remembered he wasn't there anymore, but safe and here. *But is "here" even safe?*

"He said he was just a retired merchant, had a string of mechanical bad luck. It was the second week, and he kept asking my Da about the ship's system. At first it was just normal questions, stuff you'd ask an engineer to make small talk, I suppose, if you knew enough. And then the questions got weirder. I don't really remember what it was, exactly, but he said something and my Da just looked at me across the table. I'd only ever seen him look like that once before, when our trajectory went faulty and we flew into the path of a comet."

His face was still, save for his mouth, eyes focused on a distant point just past where Nel's hand rested on the desk. "Da said there was an issue with the power draw on Moksha's ship. He'd offered to go through it all, get him flying again, but Moksha was very touchy about it...." he trailed off for a moment, eyes roving over the items on the desk. "It's good to be a kid, sometimes, people don't really pay attention to you. One night, I was bored so I snuck into his ship and poked around. Honestly, I was hoping to just find some extra ore cubes, or something better to read than the same ten novels and my dad's engineering manuals. But I found this...thing. A big sphere with all these circuit lines."

Nel tapped a few commands on her screen to pull up her photo of the holo-schematic in the temple. "Did it look something like this?"

He backed up, colliding with the doorframe and jerked a nervous nod.

She minimized the image and reached out a hand. "Want to come sit?"

He lowered himself carefully into one of the chairs by the door and swallowed hard. "Anyway, I knew that was the power draw. I know enough about computers to know it wasn't anything good. I was gonna flag him. But he caught me. I keep thinking he might have just let us go, left us alive, if he hadn't caught me."

Nel's heart burned with his inclusion of himself with the dead. She knew that ache, the strange feeling when someone passed that, for a while at least, you stepped beyond the veil with them and had to continue, only partly alive. "Is that when you ran?"

Xand nodded. "I heard him coming, ripped a random piece off the thing and ran. I wish I'd stayed and fought him. I guess he didn't chase me long, cause by the time I got to the ship's command core the whole thing was flickering with some massive power draw. Then the whole ship went dark, just enough juice for me to find an escape pod and jet."

"That's terrifying, Ale—Xand." Lin offered. "Do you recall what the piece looked like?"

He frowned, reaching into the pockets of his borrowed baggy pants. After a moment's fishing, he leaned forward to hand it to Nel. Even she recognized the circuitry.

"It's like the device your family has, like the bolo you gave me." She flipped it over to look at the other side before handing it to Lin. "Or, at least partly similar."

The woman bent over it, turning it over and over as she examined the pattern. "I don't know enough to say what its purpose was, but you're right, it was perhaps styled after those devices. I'll get it scanned and to Lissa right away." She paused and looked back to Xand. "Your cryo report says you didn't enter the pod for another week."

He lifted his shoulder in a quiet shrug. "I figured once he was gone, they'd get the systems back online and see the escape shuttle was launched. Come get me. And as the days went on, they didn't. Eventually I realized they weren't going to. We're taught to self-prep, with a ship as old as ours. In case of emergency. So, I climbed in and hoped someone would rescue me. And if they didn't, well at least I'd be asleep for the end."

Lin scrolled through their data readout thoughtfully. "Is it okay if I keep this for a bit? I'll return it after, if you'd like."

He nodded his head. "I didn't know what else to do, kept it as a reminder, I guess. That I should be dead."

"Well," Nel offered, "Maybe it'll help us bring justice to your family. And maybe try talking about any of this with your counselor?"

He made a face. "That shit only helps when you don't know why you can't sleep. Or why your heart keeps beating too fast. Or why you keep dreaming about people liquifying before your eyes, or your baby sister screaming and screaming and—" his voice choked into silence.

When she was certain he wasn't going to try and finish that god-awful sentence, Nel tilted her head. "You need tools, not reasons, huh?"

"I'm tired of sympathy. I don't need someone else making sad-eyes at me to tell me what I lived through was awful."

Lin scooted forward, head dipping to try and catch his focus. "What was her name? Your sister?"

"Ezmat Maria Damascus. She was three weeks old. They hadn't meant to have another, not on a hauler with our limited resources. My mom always said she must have been born for a reason. That's why they called her Ezmat. Meant for greatness."

Lin murmured something Nel didn't recognize, but she lowered her head and whispered a cobbled prayer of her own.

"Thanks for talking to us, Xand," she murmured. "I'm sorry. About what you saw. About the hurt."

"Thanks for not trying to bullshit me like the psych team."

"Language," she muttered, but offered him a grin, ruffling his hair. Suddenly his arms were around her, squeezing tightly, and his face was buried in her shirt. Wordlessly, Nel's arms locked around his thin shoulders, her chin resting on his head. Her eyes met Lin's from over his mop of brown tangles. The tension between them suddenly seemed so small in the face of the teenager's grief.

So what if they'd each almost killed each other a few times? They were still here. So were Dar and Emilio and Mindi and Lin's parents. But for the boy in her arms there was only Alexander Petre Damascus, age 14.

TWENTY

"They postponed our extraction," Lin announced, by way of greeting.

"Good morning to you too," Nel muttered. With a long gulp, Nel downed the glass of orange juice Lin pressed into her hand. "The device?"

"The device," Lin affirmed. "They want us to go into the temple again, check the remaining levels, and do preliminary scans only. If we find anything of note, we can be more detailed."

Nel glanced sidelong at Xand where he slouched at the table, distractedly scrolling through his comm's holoscreen. "Xand, would you mind prepping the computers and scanners on the cart for us?"

He nodded and headed across the courtyard to the lab. When Nel was certain he was out of earshot, she turned back to Lin. "What do they think we're going to find down there?"

"They don't know, which is why we're going. I just wish we had the team we did on Earth." Lin rolled her eyes at Nel's raised brows, "Not the exact team, obviously. I just mean, more hands. Ones that don't belong to a traumatized juvenile hacker."

The coffee steamed and Nel stood, staring at it for several silent moments before she remembered she had to actually drink the caffeine for it to work. She finished it off in three scalding gulps. "If he wasn't here, we wouldn't know about the other device," Nel countered.

"I know." Lin nodded toward the temple. "You finish breakfast, I'm going to get our suits prepped."

"Don't think breakfast will help much. I'll join you once I give Xand a hand." She wondered if her lips would crack from the sheer fakeness of her smile. "Hah, Xand-a-Hand."

Lin blinked at her and turned back to her comm screen. "Whatever you'd like."

Twenty minutes later, they descended once more through the temple until they reached the next locked door. It opened like the rest. Beneath the lab was a smaller, empty room, and beneath that, the same. The stone floors were coated in dust, their beams cutting across vacant walls.

With only the final, smallest level left, Nel was beginning to wonder if they had missed something entirely. *Or missed our chance at finding the truth.* Perhaps Mansur had brought the rest of his projects with him, carrying the same evidence that would condemn him to his lonely outpost damnation. Still, they let the scanner record what it needed before descending once more, leaving only confusion and footprints. "Just one more to go."

"I don't know whether to be relieved or annoyed," Lin confessed.

"Careful what you wish for," Nel muttered.

"I know. Everything we learn is more horrible than the last, but there's so much we have yet to figure out, and so little here, beyond confirmation that Uak—that we were doing something terrible."

Nel glanced over at her sharply. "You didn't know this is what they were after. Ultimate betrayal aside, Lin, I don't think you're him."

Her answering smile was fragile, but there, nonetheless. At least they had graduated to meeting each other's eyes on occasion.

See, Tirta, I can be nice. Nel straightened her shoulders and nodded toward the final door. "Let's see if you just jinxed us."

Lin crouched by the door and set the electric lockpick against the stone. Nel craned her neck to watch as the screen cycled through a few dozen settings. Instead of a click, the device let out a series of distressed beeps. Lin sat back on her heels, looking up at the ceiling with a sigh. "It must be some setting this thing doesn't read. I'll have to ask Lissa if there's been updates to the software or—"

"Or," Nel prodded, casting her suit's light farther up the door to the thick stone frame, "It's not that kind of lock."

Lin followed the beam of Nel's light and stepped back, almost tripping on the last stair. Symbols scribed the height of the doorframe, no longer the utilitarian circuits of above, but swirling over the massive block of the lintel in electric filigree. Under the bioflare's overbright glare, the copper set within the markings gleamed as if newly inlaid. The language was the same as on Samsara, but here at least no one had warped the meaning. Near the bottom on each side, about a meter from the floor, the circuit was broken.

Nel peered at the gap in the stone on the left side. "Looks like an entire chunk is missing here," she felt the edges with her gloved hand. They were smooth, clearly having been carefully carved. But whomever had last locked the temple door had clearly taken the missing pieces with them. *Or destroyed them.* "Yours is missing too?"

Lin nodded, peering closer. "I'll send some images to Dar and see what he says. We might be able to get in by the afternoon. Maybe our parents have insight."

Nel hated waiting, hated the strange impotence that came with needing everyone else to look at their findings, analyze this, algorithm that, asking if they could search the lab, if they could check the temple, if they could breathe. "It's just a circuit, right?"

Lin looked up from her rapid typing with a frown. "Yes. Power would flow through the missing piece, then the rest, probably tripping the pins as it goes, and completing the circuit via the other piece."

Nel grinned and tugged her trowel from its holster and crouched with a soft groan. A naked copper end shone where the piece would fit. Carefully gripping the less-conductive wood handle and praying the electrosuit gloves were as insulated as they claimed, she pressed the metal tip to the exposed wire and angled the tool until the side of the blade connected to the copper in the engravings. She jerked her chin toward the right door jamb, grin widened to teasing. "I dare you to stick your finger in there."

"I've heard that before." Even in the dark, Lin's pupils widened a fraction farther, though whether it was from fear or something else, Nel refused to guess. "Are you sure about this?"

"Not really, but it's worth a try." Nel shrugged, "Besides, it's not the most dangerous thing I've put my hand in lately."

Lin drew a long breath in through her nose, then knelt fluidly and disconnected the wires from the lock pick, clipping each end to complete the circuit. A faint hum filled the air, felt more than heard. The stone around them shuddered and the door rumbled slowly upward.

"Open sesame," Nel muttered, unable to hide her victorious smile. A second later, she frowned. "Wait, if I take my trowel out will it shut?"

"Didn't think ahead?" Lin leaned over her and wedged a slim strip of metal from her own kit to replace the connection the trowel made. She glanced at Nel, still too close for comfort. "Not anymore."

"The rest of you think ahead for me," Nel muttered. "But, you wouldn't have gotten in at all without me."

"Guess it's good we're together, then." Lin's face was so close, eyes darker than the room beyond and just as hungry.

Nel couldn't tear her gaze away, couldn't breathe anything but the air already warmed by Lin's lungs, and for a shaking moment she felt herself pulled forward, mouth inches away from Lin's. Dust swirled in the deep, damp darkness, and they stayed, passing warmed breath between until the comms beeped with some question from the team.

Right, mission. Nel tore herself away, sucking air like a drowned woman, and staggered upright. She wondered if not for the interruption, if Lin would have kissed her. *Would I have let her?* Shoving the traitorous musing deep into the back of her mind, she renewed her grip on the cart and trundled into the room before she could make another mistake.

The schematic was terribly wrong. Level 8 was not an overflow storage section, as the label claimed. Though the space was, indeed, no larger than the apartment Nel and Mindi shared on *The Recursive*, tanks lined every inch of the walls, a moist curio cabinet of putrefaction. Despite most of the temple having been on standby for years, this space was still filled with blinking lights, filters on some of the jars whirring, and somewhere deeper in the room, just beyond the reach of their lights, Nel thought she heard pumping, burbling fluid.

"Found his shelves of nastiness," she called over her shoulder. Lin followed her, letting out a soft groan as she took in the specimens. "This is going to take forever to catalog."

"No kidding." Nel moved slowly along the shelves, wiping dust from the labels to record their contents. Some contained the ivory lace of nerves and plexi, others segments of brain matter.

> *Supraclavicular, exceptional*
> *Limbic lobe, atypical*
> *Intercostobrachial, typical*
> *Parietal lobe, typical*
> *Trigeminal, typical*
> *Cerebellum, atypical*
> *Frontal lobe, exceptional*

Judging by the sheer number of specimens, typical and otherwise, there were organs from at least a dozen individuals, if Nel was making a conservative estimate. The next set of shelves held gleaming data cubes, each labeled with timestamps and titles. Nel tilted her head to read a few and abruptly wished she hadn't:

> *Vivisection of interior ventral spine.*

Nel followed the low biomechanical sounds to the rear of the room. Her uneven steps faltered as she stared at the monstrosity before her.

An exam table protruded from the wall, tilted slightly to allow fluids to drain into a bucket at the bottom. A body was strapped on its surface, padded leather buckled around each wrist and ankle, as well as a strap across the abdomen. Tubes were embedded at arterial points. Its naked skin was taut and shiny from overhydration. Brown hair dotted the pale chest, clustered at his groin, and dusted his forearms. But the worst part was the gleaming metal capping the severed stump of his neck.

"Oh fuck, no." Nel staggered back, reaching back until her hand gripped Lin's forearm, as much to ground herself as to get the other woman's attention. Nel knew by the iron grip of her long deadly fingers, that Lin saw. The sheets balled on the floor were presumably those missing from the rooms upstairs, and these too, were stained.

Even after years of desiccation, she saw the shattered humerus, the stoved in ribs, the putrid stain across his stitched belly. Somehow, in the stark contrast between the surgical curation on the shelves and the violent, savage wounds of the man before her, Nel found she preferred the honesty of the latter. Whatever had been done to him had clearly preserved the flesh almost perfectly. Warning sounded in the back of her head, but couldn't isolate it from the dozen others screaming through her gray matter. She lurched to her feet and reached for him.

"Nel, it could be covered in toxins—"

"He, Lin. Not it." Nel lifted one forearm, twisting it incrementally until she could see the tattoo along the flexors of his forearm. A mastiff, in the traditional style with a banner beneath. *Angus.* "Lin Nalawangsa, meet Dr. Phillip Clark. In the flesh, as it were."

"Charmed, I'm sure," Lin whispered back, dark eyes fixed on the foreshortened throat. She wiped her mouth clearly fighting back the urge to jettison her rehydrated breakfast as Nel reached out again. "Can you stop touching it—him?"

Nel's bare palm pressed to his sternum. The flesh was clammy beneath her hand, but not cold. And, thready through atrophied muscle and bone, came the faintest of tremors. *Thump-bump. Thump-bump.* A strangled whine dragged itself from her throat. Her wide eyes met Lin's. "He's alive." She glanced back at the gleaming cap on the severed stump of his neck. "Biologically, at least."

"I might—" Lin clamped her mouth shut, eyes squeezing closed. Her sharp inhalations were loud against the background sounds of burbling fluid. The Komodor turned, and a wet splat heralded another addition to the biological horrors.

"Should we bring him with us?" Nel asked when Lin ceased heaving behind her.

Lin grimaced. "No offense to Philos, but the last thing I want is that," she gestured to the not-quite alive figure, "in our camp. Besides, even with Dar and Lissa's help, I don't trust myself to plug all that back into the right ports."

"It just feels wrong to leave him here. Now that we know."

"I know. Stars, how are we going to explain this?"

"I'll run the scans, use the porta-morgue or whatever this thing is called. Do my forensic thing. Could you—" she faltered, wondering what Lin could do that would keep them both busy, from thinking too hard.

"I'm going to go through the computer hub here, download what I can. While you," she waved the rest of her own sentence away, refusing to put the sight before them into words.

"Lin—" Nel swallowed hard.

Lin's hand brushed over Nel's, the readouts casting an electric starfield against her dark eyes. "I'll be careful. You too."

"Oh him?" Nel coughed a weak laugh. "Me an' him go way back. Old buddies."

Lin stepped backward in the direction of the lab computers, seemingly unwilling to turn her back on Phil's form. Nel remained. She set about documenting everything. Her mind fell into the trance of work, methodical, meditative.

In the absence of a "why," her thoughts strayed toward what must have transformed Phillip Clark into Philos, what rendered almost four hundred adults and children into a single, incoherent mass of mutilated flesh. What ripped away the souls—for lack of a better word—from the Samsari and reformed them into sound. The idea of the machines hissing and bubbling through their campsite during the night made her skin crawl. But could she leave him there? Did Phil even know his body still existed?

Could they reattach him? His head, stitched atop the atrophied body, haphazard and hideous like Mansur-stein's monster. *Please, for the love of fucking science, let Phil not be a part of this.*

Except, he was. Willingly or not, the proof lay slick and supine before her, condemnation in the form of yet another body, albeit one that still breathed. *I'm not sure that makes it any better.*

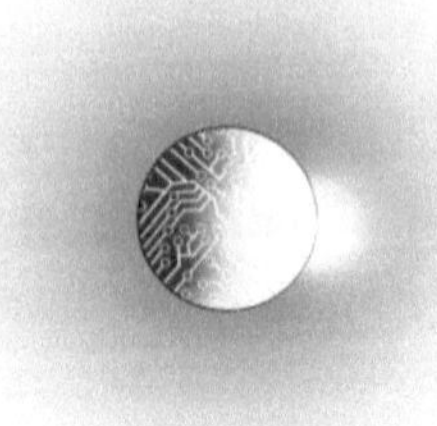

TWENTY-ONE

Humidity rose from the leaves, insects buzzing just far enough away to become white noise. In the kitchen Xand clattered as he washed up from dinner. The comms, silenced, flickered with conversation as the team back at the estate ran through a thousand possibilities, each one more terrible and insurmountable as the last. Both Nel and Lin ignored them. Nel turned the piece of the device that Xand had pilfered over and over in her scarred hands. Lin stared into the rough stone table, unreadable beyond abject dread.

Neither had told Xand the details of what was found, but their faces had, perhaps, been enough for him to know not to ask as he made them dinner. Nel couldn't have said what it was, her mouth filled with the stale laboratory air, and the imagined taste of blood. Lin rose first, wordlessly disappearing into the washing station across the courtyard.

"Dr. Nel?" Xand's usual drawl was fragile, and when he sat at the empty chair across from her, his fingers picked at the ragged skin around his nails. "Did something happen?"

She swallowed, forcing herself to look up at him with a faint smile. "It's just heavy work. Archaeology often is, finding justice for the dead."

Xand swallowed, clearly not believing the lie. "Are we gonna be okay?"

"You tell me, Mr. Kinda Really Smart." The teasing fell short, however, and she heaved a sigh. "I don't have to tell you that there's a lot of fucked up shit in this mess. But I think, as terrible as the answers we keep finding are, the fact that we're able to have answers at all is a good sign. Gives me hope. What about you, did you find much looking through the computer data?"

He lifted a shoulder. "Some, nothing that means anything to me. Just a few signals coming in over the years. I forwarded them to the rest of the team, though."

She smiled, this time properly, and squeezed his wrist. "Thanks. It makes a difference, having you here. Having you taking care of things while we're down there. I like coming back up here to find life waiting for us."

He didn't smile back, just stared at his hands. "What's gonna happen to me when we go back?"

"Hard to say, but I'll argue that you should stay with us. Research assistants always held the whole project together, in my experience. You can't get rid of me that easily."

This time, he smiled back. "I'm gonna finish a few more scans before the next *Hack This* episode airs, if that's okay."

She nodded, gave his arm another squeeze and headed across the courtyard for her own shower. Lin's tent was dark, and the shower rooms were wet, but deserted. Did Lin feel as isolated as she? *It's not like either of us can really put what we saw into words.* At least, not ones that meant anything, that captured the dread dragging at their guts.

Leaving the shower room lights off, she stripped and stepped under the tepid water. Rolling her neck did little to loosen the decades' tense muscles, but the cascade of water soothed her. Soap, rinse, then another soap in an attempt to wash the terror from her skin. It didn't work.

She dried, donned her tank and cargos, then hung her suit in the sterilizer. She was reattaching her leg when she heard the straining notes of music. It drifted across the stone like fog, and she followed it across the courtyard until she stood at the sanctum's dark mouth. The overgrowth seemed taller, late in the evening and the shadows cast by the planet's belly, overlong. The song was longing, aching, unmoored.

Nel tried to avoid Lin outside of their forced proximity of work, but each time they spoke, the words strayed dangerously close to the event horizon of forgiveness. *And that's why it's so hard.*

She'd never considered herself someone with a death wish, but she imagined it might look different from her mother's perspective, perhaps, or anyone who saw the aftermath of Nel's head-first rampage through life. But danger or not, they had to work together and based on the thunder between her ribs, Nel's heart felt that was scarier than the headless man in stasis beneath their feet.

Nel checked that Xand was still in the kitchen and focused on his computer. She watched the display's garish light flicker across his face. Distracted, eyes wide as he absorbed his show, he looked like his fourteen years. She headed to the sanctum door and descended into the temple itself.

In the muffled night, the ghosts' footsteps were easier to hear. They still sent a thrill through her limbs, but it was a familiar one now, as if a gentle hand brushed up her spine. She let them usher her down, down, into the nestling darkness of the prayer room. Lin sat in one of the pews, tan skin luminous against the black interior. She wore her casual clothes, electrosuit left open under her blouse. Her elbows were crooked, hands gliding loosely through the air.

Nel watched for another moment, letting the sound wind to its conclusion.

Lin's eyes opened and her cheeks flushed when she saw her audience. "I'm sorry. I didn't mean to disturb you."

"You don't disturb me," Nel whispered, half hoping she wouldn't hear.

Lin's mouth twitched, then curled into a smile, playful, so familiar it was like the curve of Nel's own spine. She reached beside her, eyes never leaving Nel's, and produced a large dark bottle with a flourish. "Mansur had good taste in one thing, at least."

Nel's eyes narrowed. "I don't know if my problem is bad enough to trust his booze."

Lin chuckled. "Well, based on Dar's stories from his pilot academy days, what happens with a whole bottle of 37 Year Kan Dressu is pretty scary."

"That whiskey's as old as me." Nel couldn't help her faint laugh. "Depending on who's counting."

Lin stood, cat-quiet, and nodded toward the pool at the center of the room. Nel's uneven steps followed her down the narrow stone path without question. The Komodor folded herself down to sit with her back against the podium and patted the stone beside her. Nel hovered for a moment then lowered herself to the dry circle of rock. The windows far above showed a clear sky, lit with little other than planet-light.

"Moon's pretty," Nel murmured.

Lin hummed in agreement, gaze cast far beyond the pregnant orb in the sky.

"What, no comment on how technically, we're the moon?"

"Technically," Lin dragged the word out. "We're a moonlet. But, either way it's beautiful." She tilted the bottle back, eyes narrowed in concentration as she swallowed, then handed it to Nel.

It was smooth, with a tail-end bite that ached with familiarity. It washed over her tongue, then burned a path down her throat.

Lin's fingers brushed hers as she took the bottle. "Your clock's wrong."

Nel glanced down. "It's EST. Zachariah showed me how I could sync my comm to Earth time. I keep track of local time too, of course, but this makes the ache a little less."

Lin stared at her own comm for a silent moment. "Mine's always local time. I never know where my parents or Dar are. Or whether they're waking or sleeping. It only matters what I'm doing, where I'm going."

"Lived like that for a while. Doing contract work. Following whatever grant I could. It's lonely," Nel confided. "Drank like this a lot then, too."

"It's some kind of sin, I think," Lin remarked, looking down at the label, "to drink something this fancy out of the bottle."

"Eh," Nel shrugged. "I think there's something poetic about it. Reminds me of a funeral."

"Or wedding."

Nel gripped the bottle by the neck as Lin passed it back. "Haven't been to as many of those, lately." The stream burbled through the crack in the wall, cutting a glowing curve between the benches before spilling into the deep pool in the center of the temple floor. Nel rolled up her pant legs and doffed her boots, before dipping her foot in the water with a soft appreciative sigh. Lin followed suit, setting the ripples alight as her long calves dipped beneath the surface. Nel felt Lin's gaze on her, undoubtedly tracing the scars where her frostbitten toes had been carved away, where metal and wires met burn-gnarled flesh.

"I wish I had been here."

Nel fought the urge to shrug. "I'm glad you weren't. I think I had to do it solo, you know?"

"Me too. I'm sorry, Nel." The words were soft, gentle as the water lapping at their legs. Lin's attention was still on her prosthetic, but soon rose to Nel's face. The archaeologist swallowed and looked away. "I'm sorry about all of this. We really destroyed your life."

"Eh, I do that to myself enough anyway." She cleared a sudden rasp from her throat. This time she met Lin's gaze. "I'm sorry too. I expected you to know everything about your own world, when I know so little about mine. I was too wrapped up in being misunderstood that I misunderstood you. You are so alien and powerful, it never occurred to me that you could be a pawn too. Even," she swallowed and repeated, "Even with Mikey. You said they were hunting you that night. That they would have killed you too." Nel turned, frowning a hole into Lin's hand, unable to look her in the eye. "I'm glad they didn't."

Lin looked away, eyes haunted, and Nel abruptly wondered if Lin wished they had.

Nel swallowed hard, expecting shame to overwhelm her. It didn't. Instead, she felt lighter. "I wasn't a very good girlfriend."

"You were good at some of it." Lin cracked a tiny smile. "You were right though. There were things I didn't know, but there was a lot I didn't share. I was so fixated on what I wanted to see I missed the truth about IDH. I wanted it to actually work for our betterment. I wanted it to be this incredibly benevolent force among all these factions. I knew you would run, if you discovered you were trusting lies."

"It wasn't the lies I was trusting, Lin." Nel frowned, nudging broken stones into little piles with her scarred hand.

"I figured that one out a little too late." Lin stared, and Nel let her. Let her gaze weigh between them, insistent, until she wondered if her chest would implode. The words sent an ache through Nel's chest, an ache that felt like farewell, that thudded, too definite, over the tiny, nameless hope that had unfurled in the past weeks. *Is it too late?*

Lin's head tilted back, her eyes tracing lines of copper on the vaulted ceiling that surely meant something to her, if not to Nel. "I wish it was like it used to be, wish we could just tap a button and be connected to the Teachers, like I do with Dar."

Nel hummed in agreement, taking another pull. As much as she listened to the Samsari voices, they were rarely forthcoming about the details of their demise. "A lesser sum of greater parts."

"Hmm?"

"It's what they told me. The ghosts." When Lin's expression remained unreadable, heat flushed up Nel's face. "On *Lahifa* you said you heard—"

"Whispers. Footsteps. Not conversations." Lin shook her head ruefully. "Background chatter, almost, sounds when there was no one else there. I thought it was stress, then that it was Harris waging some psychological warfare on me. Then I thought it was your ghost. That you had—" she grimaced. "The screaming was the worst, for me."

Nel looked away. All her months on *The Recursive,* running from Lin, she never thought the woman's relentless search was partly due to fear that Nel died. "Me too. About the screaming. Thought I was crazy, honestly. Thought I might have lost my mind along with my leg. I heard it in my nightmares. Couldn't explain it to my mom, didn't have the heart to tell her everything we've seen. Even when I saw the readouts with Emilio and Dar, even when there was proof staring me in the face, I couldn't really shake the feeling of insanity that comes with hearing fucking voices. Until you said you heard them too." Nel wet her lips, chest heaving at the admission.

"What else do they say?"

"Depends. 'You unmade us.' 'Now we are this.'" Nel swallowed past the sandpaper in her throat.

"But mostly they just beg. I heard them all around his body when we found him."

"Did they tell you anything about him?"

Nel frowned, glancing at Lin for as long as she could stand. Her mouth grew dry at the memories of Morphose, of *V Drugoye Mesto*. Body after body, Masur leaving a trail of bloody human breadcrumbs. *One. Two.* She braced herself against the cool stone of the podium, knuckles white around the whiskey. *Three.* "It's not like they know why he did it. Or probably even how." Maybe it was the growl in her voice, or the words themselves, but Nel watched the pain flicker across Lin's face. It had been so long since she had watched anyone so affected by her words or emotions that, for a second, she enjoyed it.

The Komodor's attention bounced around the hewn walls, as if searching the whorls of sentient sound for salvation. "When did you realize what they were?"

"After you caught us. After Dar collapsed. After I tried to shoot you. They'd been talking to us, begging us. I figured maybe someone should listen."

"Hear them now? Breathing?"

"Justice."

"It's so much more than breathing," Nel promised. She could feel them, pressing in, billowing across her skin like fog. She swore she saw the air puff and whirl with Lin's every exhalation. "This entire temple was made to talk to them, right?"

After a beat, Lin nodded. Nel reached carefully for Lin's wrist. Lin's hand darted out, gripping the archaeologist's fingers like a vise. Then, glacially, she moved Nel's hand to the comm's controls. First, Nel toggled off the cancelation system, then, hands still joined, Lin guided her to the stone disk set in the podium. With a touch so gentle it was almost a caress, Nel activated the sanctum.

Goosebumps rippled up Lin's bare arms. Her pulse flashed in her throat as her lips parted. It was pain, certain, unyielding, but it was the burn of existence. Life. Unerasable. Irrefutable.

"Fractured."

A gasp puffed from Lin's parted lips. "It's beautiful."

"We are not beauty. We are not whole."

Voice steadied by the vengeance of the dead, Lin asked, "Do you know why he did this? What you are?"

The air rippled.

"We are many. We were you, until he forged us into this. Into one. Into all. Into nothing. He fashions himself as our Teacher, but we are not the taught.

"He can't hurt you anymore," she promised. "And I'll do everything I can to fix this. To make it so no one ever does this again."

"Broken most by how we are reformed."

"Yes, I know. I'm so sorry, I'm so sorry." She was shivering now, almost seizing, and her eyes rolled, pupils contracting to pinpricks. Tears welled in Nel's own eyes, blurring the image of the other woman, Lin's hands gripping tighter.

Nel swore electricity buzzed through the pads of her fingers, humming from the electromagnetic field arcing between her and Lin. If that buzz had a dial, she'd crank it to eleven. There was a mission to focus on and Xand was just over the hill. *But...*It wasn't safe and there was the literal Earth-shattering betrayal. And hunting her through the asteroids. *But...*

Lin was complicated, and Nel was chaos.

But I don't give a fuck.

Nel turned with measured movements, afraid that, with one false move, the satellite itself would tip into nothingness. As if the gravity between them anchored the universe itself. Lin's breath came in heaving gasps and when she fixed Nel with a stare, her black eyes were wide and wild.

"Could—"

"Yes." Lin's reply ignited the air between them.

Nel lunged, shoving the bottle aside and slamming them both to the ground. They hit hard, leaves and rocks crunching beneath them, but Nel devoured Lin's yelp with a kiss. She yanked Lin's suit zipper down, shoving a hand under the electromesh to cup warm flesh.

Nel crawled down the other woman's body, kissing, licking, biting, groaning, worshiping every familiar mole and fresh scar. New circuitry lined both arms now, bisecting biceps and deltoids, joining between her sharp clavicles to slice up her throat. Nel dragged a nail down the ink, wondering if she tore enough would Lin return to who she had been when they first pressed their bodies together after a different horror, under a different starscape. Part of her knew that no wound would be enough to fully excavate her from Lin's starborn body, or Lin from Nel's Earthly flesh.

Beneath her night-chilled hand, Lin's core was a furnace. *Good,* Nel decided, *Let her fucking burn.* Thalassi's reflected light washed them both in turquoise. Lin's pupils were blown from excitement or fear and Nel found herself hoping it was both. She wanted touch, wanted pleasure, wanted Lin. But most of all she wanted to be the reason for every hitch in Lin's breath, for every muffled moan and stolen shudder. *I want to be the one that lights the match.*

Adrenaline surged and Nel rolled back on her heels, to stare down at Lin's trembling body, burning. Victorious. The woman beneath her was undone, and Nel wondered if she would ever be satisfied until she had unmade the woman as thoroughly as Mansur had destroyed the Samsari.

One long finger trailed along the lines of Nel's titanium thigh, the light blooming faintly with Nel's still-pounding pulse. Lin's glassy eyes roved over Nel's still clothed body, but when the archaeologist reached for her again, the floor beneath them shuddered.

Screaming, singing, tearing in every fiber of her mind. Lin surged upright, and Nel reached to tap the cancellation again, to close out the torrent of sound and sensation. Electricity sizzled through the air, followed by the scent of ozone burning. Then a voice, not Kasanove's, not Phil's, one Nel didn't recognize, thundered through the satellite's comm system.

DOWNLOAD COMPLETE.

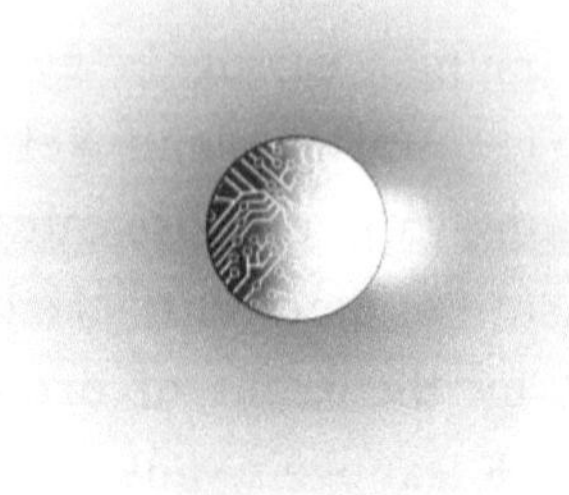

TWENTY-TWO

Pain flooded Nel's body. An overwhelming push of foreign fury and her own terrible dread. Her ribs ached with the effort of sucking air into her lungs, her muscles spasmed with random jolts of adrenaline and exhaustion, a dark mimicry of the orgasm she had wrung from Lin seconds—hours?—before. Something hot dribbled down from her ears and when she swiped it away her hand came away bloody. Beside her the same thrashing wracked Lin's fever-hot body, her eyes rolling worse than before. Nel gripped the komodor's wrist in panic-firm fingers, jabbing madly until the cancelation chimed brokenly.

"Lin!" The voice crackled through their comms. "What the fuck? Bently!"

The ringing in Nel's ears faded a bit, enough to recognize Dar's voice, to recognize it was laced with panic. She fumbled with her comm until she could answer. "We're okay, what—"

"Your vitals!" He snapped response pitched almost to a shriek. "Your suit's been pinging for the last forty minutes!"

Forty minutes? She blinked in a useless attempt to focus her vision. *That can't be right.*

When Lin finally seemed able to breathe again, enough to reply to Dar, Nel staggered to her feet still holding the other woman's wrist. She didn't register what Lin said, only that it shut her brother up enough for them to gather themselves. Nel slammed her boots on and dragged them from the still-shaking stone, limp forgotten, mission forgotten, everything forgotten save for Lin and Xand and her mother and their precariously small team across the asteroid. As they emerged, Nel shoved Lin toward the tents, heaving out an order. "Xand, now." Then she hauled herself up the stepped side of the temple itself until she could see over the ridges of rock and undulating jungle canopy.

It was the early hours of dawn, judging by the dimmed glow of the estate in the distance. One by one, in a wave emanating from the temple's epicenter, the lights flickered then extinguished. Within moments, the asteroid was reduced to rain-slick rocks gleaming like silver under the starshine. It would have been beautiful were it not for the brutality of what Nel was certain awaited them in the dark. Fabric rustled beside her, but she didn't turn. She lifted one arm and felt the comforting warmth of the Xand's shoulder as he notched himself under hers. Fingers, familiar as her own, slipped into her hand on the other side.

Not a single light shone. The landscape was awash with the reflected light off Thalassi's blue swell, but shadows deepened behind the pale skeleton of *Vīrya*'s architecture. Darkness bled across the satellite. She swallowed the fear enough to speak, and asked, softly, "The voice we heard—"

Beside her, Lin jerked a nod, but Nel didn't need to see. Just as she had known when she first looked on Mansur's face, that he had done it, she knew now, beyond the hitch in her gut and the leaden weight on her chest, that it had been his voice booming from the sanctum. Her grip tightened on them both.

"We've been operating under the assumption that Mansur failed whatever experiment he attempted on Morphose." The truth rasped its way past her gritted teeth. "What if he succeeded? What if he's alive?"

"Alive? Nel, his body's in our morgue."

"And if bodies mattered how could thousands of Samsari be whispering in my fucking ears?"

"We're done here." Nel decided. "We're going back, fuck the rest of this research. Whatever happens next we're deciding as a group, together." She didn't need to say she wanted to see her mother, that the two of them should be among family if the worst happened. "Xand, you're with me, let's get the essentials packed. Lin, you able to radio for extraction? Cause I ain't hiking all the way back, ghost-uncle or not."

Lin gave another fear-sharp nod and brought up the screen of her comm. Nel tried not to think too hard about why the holoscreen seemed to flicker in and out, blurry with pulses of static.

Wordlessly, she led Xand back down into the crater to pack. They had finished dismantling the shelters when Lin reappeared. Her eyes were bright, almost manic, and her hair was still in disarray from Nel's raking fingers what seemed like a lifetime ago. "You get through?"

"I did. Dar's sending a transport out."

"There power for that?"

"Most of them still have a few hours of charge. We'll probably have to pull the rest of the fuel cells if we need to go any farther, though. He'll be here by dawn."

Nel wished he was there already, that they didn't have hours to deliberate over their impending doom. Thankfully, it took the better part of the two hours to pack what they could and stack the rest in the protection of the common room. Xand had piled all the personal bags and crates in a tidy heap, and Lin was setting the last of the equipment in its cases. Nel secured each with a buckle, ears trained for the sound of the approaching transport. Still, she was surprised when the alarm on her wrist chimed fifteen minutes until dawn. The light hadn't risen. With no power, how could the solar reflectors function? Nel grimaced. If they were going to die, she'd rather be able to see it coming. *If we can see it at all.*

When Lin emerged from the common room looking exhausted, Nel flashed her a wan smile. "Is all the equipment stashed for now?"

"It is. The data banks are here though," Lin answered, patting the crate on top. "We'll at least be able to analyze that much." Her eyes were downcast but flitting over the flagging as if reading their potential next moves. "Let's get this up on the ridge, make it easier for Dar to get close enough." Her attention flicked up to Nel. "Mind doing a final sweep?"

Nel obeyed wordlessly, stepping into the claustrophobic press of the common room first. There was so much she wished they could study further, so much yet they probably could learn. But with what time? When she had finished, she emerged once more into the now-deserted courtyard. Like during the blackouts on *The Recursive,* she hadn't realized how much noise the satellite made until its system was down. She sank onto the tree that, just a week ago, Xand had been clambering across and dropped her head into her hands.

Did we do this? Whatever inevitable download had been waiting for them, Nel knew that their hands triggered it. And try as she might to tell herself it was finally something they could fight, she couldn't shake the guilty weight on her heart.

A shuffling sound rose from just ahead and she glanced up, expecting Xand. There was nothing, in the darkness, just the open mouth of the Sanctum. Her eyes narrowed, and she heard it again. It was not the soft footsteps she had come to recognize as the Samsari echoes. It was not Xand's casual slumping, nor Lin's perfect, dancelike approach. This was lurching, wet, followed by a long, metallic drag. Her heart quickened, stinging with the nearly constant flood of adrenaline. *Mansur, is that you?*

She surged to her feet and took off across the courtyard, following the faint sounds of Lin's orders and Xand's nervous griping. Already, electric engines squealed overhead and Nel worked a blunt finger against her ear, brows up. Nets dropped a moment later and Xand happily climbed into one, transferring each crate from Lin's hands to a spot secured to the webbing.

"Just those and that'll be the last of it," Xand relayed. He stared at her, then followed her gaze to the woman signaling to the craft above. They lurched into the air, swinging as a winch hoisted them up, up, into the belly of the craft.

The soft wind rushed past the open sides, and the jungle canopy whipped by. Gleaming limestone rose from the verdant swath ahead. Xand's muffled chatter drifted from the front and Nel let her head rock back against the shuttle's frame. Desire and fury and terror washed over her mind, thoughts whirling in a tailspin.

Turbulence jostled the shuttle an hour later as they descended. Ground crew swarmed around the craft, their work illuminated by helm-mounted bioflares as they unloaded the equipment and their few personal effects.

"Lin?" Nel limped down the ramp after her. When the other woman turned, she drew closer. Nel raked a shaking hand through her hair. Already the evening before was fading into a dream, fuzzy and neon, a bubble outside the rest of their reality. "Are you okay?"

Lin's lips tightened, hoisting her bag onto her shoulder. "It's not just about that. It's about everything. I've known pieces of this terrible truth for a while. Longer than I'm comfortable admitting. I just wasn't prepared for how terrible it was."

Any other discussion was interrupted by the sight of Dar picking his way across the landing pad. Lin rushed to him and Nel watched her halt, uncertain, until Dar rolled his eyes and pulled her into a wincing hug.

A large, warm hand settled on Nel's shoulder as she bent to lift her bag. "¿Cómo te va?"

She let the bag drop and spun, arms locking around Emilio wordlessly. "No sé."

He returned her embrace, and she felt his shoulders rise in a sigh. "Here too. It's been hard going."

Emilio watched her shoot another frustrated glance at the Nalawangsa siblings, already heading back toward their estate. Xand hovered next to one of the transport's landing struts.

"Hey buddy," she called over. "Mind giving me a hand?"

His face lit up and he rushed over, happily taking her larger bag. Nel waved away Emilio's amused, raised brows.

"I'll help you drop this at your room, then it's back to Lissa's lab to get us all on the same page," Emilio informed them ruefully. "Business first, unfortunately."

Nel made a face, but fell into step between him and Xand. "Never thought I'd miss the office pizza parties, but would it kill them to have snacks? As good as your cooking was, Xand, I was hoping for a home cooked meal. I'm starving."

Emilio chuckled and met her eyes over Xand's poof of hair as Nel drew up at her door and fumbled with the keypad. "It's good to have you back."

"Getting tired of these aliens?"

"Most of them, at least," he agreed, and Nel's shoulders flamed with envy at the softness in his tone. He and Dar made it look so easy to reach across the gulf of culture in the name of love. Lin was complicated. And Nel was furious. And there was very little middle ground Nel could see in the chaos between them. *Especially when doom comes knocking in the middle of the one activity we ever agreed on.*

The corridor to her room looked much the same as it had during her nightly wanderings, shadowed and cast in blue, but her comm told her it was mid-morning, despite the lack of sunlight. An incongruity that snagged her focus, that brought her back to nights on the Vicuña y Las Rosas rooftop, the hungry darkness of the northeast corridors, the protracted dusk of *The Recursive.* Still, when she palmed the lock to her room, the door opened and the space within was not the sucking maw of space or gnashing teeth of the wilderness, and looked the same as it ever did.

Xand deposited their bags at the foot of her couch and turned back with a sad smile. "I'll head back to the dorms, let me know what happens?" He faltered, looking up at her with his big brown eyes. She saw what he wanted to ask, what she wished she could answer. *I don't know if we'll be okay.*

"Bullshit, kid, you're coming too." When his eyes lit up, she chuckled. "Leave your things here, if you want—there's too much room for just me and I've gotten used to your snoring." Nel shrugged and pointed at the couch. "Unless you'd rather go back to the dorms?"

He shook his head quickly. "It's probably for the best I go. Someone has to keep you to from embarrassing yourself, and besides, I probably know more about tech than Dr. Lissa does anyway."

"Give you a nickel if you say that to her face and I get to watch." Nel ignored Emilio's rolled eyes and jerked her head toward the manor proper. "I could use one more person who doesn't think I'm a nut."

Emilio chuckled at that and led them back down the hall. "Speaking of crazy—how was it working with her?"

"Eh," she begins, almost parroting that it was terrible, that she was glad to be done with it. But was that true? "Weird. Mostly just weird."

Before she had to answer another, worse question, however, they arrived at Lissa's open office door. The room was lit with half a dozen bioflares, casting the rough stone architecture into cold relief and when she stepped in on Emilio's tail, the conversation died. Nel was no stranger to being unwelcome in a room, but she did find it rude that when faced with Mansur's newest evil plot, she was still A Problem. *Priorities, people.*

The entire Nalawangsa family ranged about, Dar resting in a chair, Lin leaning against the back like a dark Angel of the Annunciation. Their parents sat across the low coffee table from them, and the rest ranged about, sitting or not seemingly as their nerves allowed.

"Dr. Bently," Sant bit out. "I see you're still on the team."

"Sorry to disappoint," Nel tossed back with a smile. "What can I say, I'm an altruist."

"Speaking of surprising guests—would someone care to explain why there is a child here?" Tirta asked.

"Xand," the teen announced, stepping forward with an offered hand and open face. "I was assisting Dr. Bently and Komodor Nalawangsa at Data Sanctum Sapta. I also collaborated with Dr. Hugo-Sanchez on the technical side."

Strange pride flashed through Nel at his professionalism. *It's not like he learned it from you.*

"Oh stars, you're DrugoyeDatalord?" Lissa bounced from her seat beside Tirta to vigorously shake Xand's hand. "I had no idea you were so young! I really admired the encryption system you used on that last transfer," she continued, towing the boy over to the open seat next to hers, jargon flowing. Nel used the diversion to cover her escape to the stool between Emilio and Dar. When she sat, Lin glanced over.

"Datalord?" she asked with a tiny smile.

"C'mon, everyone has an extra cringy handle when they're a kid," Nel whispered back.

Tirta cleared her throat. "If we could turn to the matter at hand?" The matriarch's gaze swept over Lin's hard lines, her fragile shoulders.

Nel had almost forgotten the reward for her clandestine promise to the Nalawangsa matriarch. Had it been enough, what she'd done to help? Had it been enough to save the juggernaut of determination and self-critique? Did it matter, at the end, whether she got a new leg, if there was no Lin to keep up with?

Tirta settled herself on the arm of her husband's chair and folded her hands in her lap, the picture of collected, careful, power. "Let's begin with the asteroid in the room. Most of us were asleep last night when, at approximately 0200, we experienced a catastrophic power outage, which is still underway. Dar, you said you witnessed the anomaly on the feeds?"

He nodded. "I was up, waiting for my next dose, and was scrolling through what the team sent over, when all the screens flickered. I thought it might have been an unexpected solar flare, as far as our star is, but they stayed like that for a solid hour. Cycling through static. All downloads ceased, then all tertiary functions then, well." He gestured to the room and the surrounding darkness beyond. "That's when I reached out to our field team. The vitals of Lin's suit had gone haywire shortly before the initial anomaly."

Wasn't the only anomaly last night. Nel shook away the flush that rose when she thought back to the sight of Lin panting beneath her. She felt the weight of the woman's stare on her, even now, drilling into her bones from her perch on her brother's chair.

"With this level of outage," Hugo-Sanchez interjected, "I can't get into the database, let alone analyze anything. Thankfully Phil has remained on a dedicated branch circuit and is isolated from the rest of the satellite's big iron."

"I'm sorry, iron?" Nel asked.

"Mainframe," she clarified. "His backup power is keeping him safely in stasis. Got another cycle before we need to start worrying. I assume we will have evacuated by then?"

The room stilled.

"We have generators, solar ones, of course, but they won't come online until we can get the reflectors up and running," Tirta explained.

"Air?" Xand asked softly.

Hugo-Sanchez nodded. "Trees, the natural cycles of the jungle should keep us breathing long after the generators are up, thankfully. We still aren't sure what caused this—"

"I am." Lin's breath was deep and long "I think it's time we all face the truth. Dr. Bently—Nel. I was rattled, altered. You were more aware than any of us when it happened. Why don't you explain?"

Nel wasn't in the mood to have all eyes on her, not with the terrible nagging guilt that they knocked over the first doomsday domino. "We were discussing the Samsari voices—the signal— and I wanted Lin to hear them the way I do, thought maybe she could understand them better. Thought if only we just asked them, or asked the Teachers, what the hell happened. What Mansur was after, if they knew. So, understanding that the

Sanctum's original purpose was to basically do just that, we turned it on."

Sant drew a sharp breath in, but before he could condemn her, Nel barreled onward. "But they were clamoring, and saying all the usual terrible things they do. And then a big booming voice—one I didn't recognize—said 'Download complete.'"

"We heard it too," Tirta offered softly. "Though what it meant is less clear."

"You recognized the voice, though, didn't you, Ayah." Lin asked her father, their cavernous dark eyes mirrored in one another's faces.

"I did." His voice sunk low with defeat.

Nel cleared her throat. "If we could get Kasanove to explain, or access—"

"Kasanove is dead." Lissa intoned.

Lin's eyes widened and she glanced at Nel then back at her parents. "How?"

Dar was the one who answered. "The power surge, I guess. Or whatever it was that was downloaded. Maybe the signal—"

"It wasn't them," Nel defended. "It wasn't the ghosts. I'd know. They haven't hurt anyone intentionally."

"We're not suggesting it was." Lissa looked down at her clasped hands, more withdrawn than Nel had ever seen. "After the outage I went into my lab to see if he could boot the systems back up. I found him floating in his tank, every connection corroded and burnt. There are safeguards in place, I don't understand."

"Were you able to save whatever he was working on?" Tirta asked.

Lissa's curls bobbed with her nod. "Mostly. He was helping me with analyzing the readings and pure chronospacial information. We determined Mansur's original plan was to use the senti-comp processing on *Odyssey* and the gate of Samsara to convert Earth. Probably all the folks on the station too."

Lin jerked a nod. "The marks Nel and I saw all over the consol, he made them to use the planet's original form. Harris said he found a way to allow us to connect with the Teachers again. That it would protect us from whatever new danger the universe spit at us. I think he hoped to use it to transform Earth's inhabitants. All of us, eventually."

Nel let out a soft scoff. She desperately wished there was someone who knew just a fraction more than they did, and was suddenly grateful that she'd had enough such people around her thus far. "This might be a too-soon comment, but with Kasanove gone, if there was power could Phil be installed? Assuming we wouldn't be risking the same fate for him?"

"Too risky," Dar argued. "At least at this juncture."

"It takes days to prepare for that kind of transfer, and we don't have days. If we're lucky, we have only hours." Hugo Sanchez's face was uncharacteristically blank.

"So, what now?" Xand piped up, startling them all.

Tirta acknowledged him with a small nod. "Crews are working on getting the generator systems prepped, and Lissa and Dar are focusing on getting any information from the system, and Phil of course. And," she heaved a sigh, "the rest of us are trying to brainstorm."

Through most of the conversation, Nel had kept her attention on Sant. His eyes were deeply shadowed and the fine fabric of his shirt was rumpled, hanging off shoulders that ought to be broader. Still imposing, but Nel found she pitied him more than she was intimidated by him. She waited until he looked up and met her eyes.

"Sir?" she interrupted softly.

His mouth opened, probably to snap something at her, but then shook his head. "I keep hoping it was just a power surge, that perhaps the plan ended with his death."

Nel shook her head. "With all due respect—and I mean that, sir—if Mansur's plans ended with him, I doubt very much that we would all be sitting in the dark right now." She sighed, rubbing an exhausted hand through her grown-out dye job.

Sant's face fractured, the way Lin's had in their train car, a mask so hard and unyielding that it had no choice but to crack. When he began to speak, the most Nel had heard since he stormed into the library, the room hushed, letting his low words roll like thunder through the stillness. "We knew Mansur's research wasn't the type of work one brings up around the Bambanti feast table. But, the history of science is filled with terrors as much as victories. Perhaps even more so. There were times we argued over it, times we heard him shouting through the comms, heard Dr. Clark shouting back."

Tirta's sculpted brown hands cupped his shoulder. "It's not your fault, my chandra."

"I never thought he would move so far past the philosophy of the matter, so far past good, past ethics. At least, that's what I told myself. Then, Dr. Clark happened. They were friends, off and on, as tempestuous as the rest of Mansur's relationships. He helped Mansur, but his love was for the philosophy of it, not science. When we learned that Dr. Clark had been integrated, it broke us. We were told it was an accident, what happened to him. After that, the sanctum was decommissioned. My brother never returned."

"I've read some of his notes—the ones I could stomach," Nel mentioned softly, when she was sure his account was through. "Consent is the cornerstone of the senti-comp tech, at least in Phil's teachings. But your brother's work reminds me of the Teachers, coming to Earth assuming they know best for us. Consent doesn't matter to Mansur when it comes to 'bettering' humanity," Nel pointed out.

"Indeed." Sant's jaw tightened. "I am learning just how deeply we failed my brother, now."

"I'm more inclined to believe he failed us," Tirta corrected, but her eyes were soft. "Each of us has combed through the data, and I imagine many of us have done so on our own time, too. There is precious little we've found about the methods, or whether such a thing could continue in his absence."

"Until last night," Dar amended. He craned his neck to look up at his sister. "Why jump from senti-comps to reversing death?"

Nel shrugged. "It's not about reversing death but avoiding it entirely. Humans, everything we do is about death. Avoiding it, revering it, seeking it, overcoming it. Look at those devices your family—"

Lin's face drained of color and her eyes flew wide. "His stasis shield. If we get enough power we could see what his last life readings were. We could find out what killed him."

"Mansur? He didn't have one." Nel recalled.

"Of course he did," Lin snapped.

Dar shook his head. "I looked for one, when she showed me his body."

Nel frowned into her palms, as if their calluses held the answer. "I spent way too long cataloging every inch of his deposition. There wasn't one."

"Maybe that's why he died. Or it could have destructed. Burned out by whatever ended him too?" Tirta asked.

"What're the odds, though?" Nel looked between them. "Man as terrifyingly clever as he, just up and forgets a lifesaving device. Unless...'He unmade us,'" she quoted.

Hugo-Sanchez leaned forward, eyes bright with curiosity. "I'm sorry, what devices? You're talking about a portable stasis shield? Those are incredibly rare and expensive."

Lin's cheeks pinked.

Nel snorted. "Well, apparently if you're private-satellite rich, your whole family can have them."

"Everyone we loved, technically," Lin answered, her heavy gaze holding Nel's a breath overlong. "But yes. Many of us integrate them into our prosthetics. You're less likely to just, forget it at home. Or drop it."

Sant rumbled, "I fail to see where this is going. Why the stasis circuits matter at this juncture."

"Because that circuitry has been everywhere Uak Mansur has," Lin explained. "The sphere at the center of Samsara, the one Harris retrofitted on Earth."

"The one he used to kill my ship," Xand interrupted. He dug the piece from his pocket, picking lint from the sharp metal edges before handing it over to Sant's wondering hands.

Nel stilled. "His head."

"What?"

"He had this big thing integrated with his fucking skull—it'd be pretty metal if it wasn't so terrifying. He replaced his occipital with this great big device. And I didn't think anything of it, beyond you know, 'gross' and 'what fresh hell' but now I wonder: could he have integrated the device into that?"

"Any advanced biomech is conceivably compatible with stasis shields. If you have the resources." Hugo-Sanchez remarked, staring at the Nalawangsa parents with seemingly a new perspective. "They're fascinating, I had the opportunity to study them during my undergraduate capstone. It envelops you in a type of forcefield, holding your body in stasis. Like cryo but less stable. Then it sends out a digital readout of your last living state to the nearest emergency services—if other paired devices aren't chosen or nearby—so if people get there in time you can be saved. It can hold someone suspended for a good while, up to a week."

Nel swallowed past the lump in her throat, skin buzzing with the whirling of the ghosts, warm with the fecund hum of understanding. The thought that bubbled in her brain since she saw the cable embedded in Mansur's occipital, burst. The bloody, twisted path they had tracked led to one place. "And if your last state of being is, in fact, digital?"

Lin's eyes widened, staring at the device in horror, as if she expected it to thrum to life, like Phil's still-beating heart. Her face ramped from sober to terror, and perhaps only Nel could see the shift, but it made her want to reach across the wrongdoings and anger and take her hand. "The download. You mean—"

"It can be done—I rebooted Polyana with a thk file." Nel's hands flexed into fists. "Everything we've found—Phil's past, the people aboard *V Drugoye Mesto*, the Samsari voices, they all point to him transcending physical existence. What if he was the next stage? The shield sends a readout of your state. A few tweaks and it's calibrated for the quantum level. He didn't send out an SOS. He sent himself."

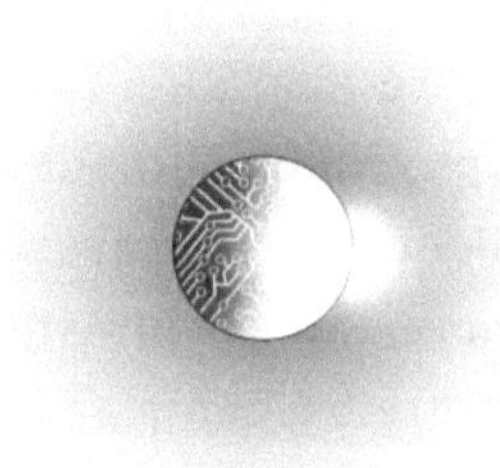

TWENTY-THREE

Whispers eddied in the wake of Nel's realization. For once, no one argued. For once, Nel wished they would. She would give everything to be wrong, for Mansur to be dead and gone and the only threat safely locked in the *Vīrya* prison. Nel met Lin's eyes in the dim light and did not look away.

Lin gave her a tiny nod and it was she who finally broke the silence. "Ayah, what now?"

Sant's hand tightened on Tirta's delicate fingers. "We've deliberated on what he did long enough. We must turn to what we assume he must be trying to do next. We have teams working to manually raise the reflectors. I can only assume that if Mansur is in the system, we must stay isolated from any outside contact. Effectively a system quarantine. Luckily, without a physical or digital connection, it's impossible to transfer him elsewhere, and we saw how difficult it was for him to do the latter initially."

Nel's jaw clenched. She didn't trust the word impossible. "All ships grounded then?"

"Indeed, Dr. Bently," Tirta answered. "There are a thousand small things our staff will work toward that will ensure backup plans and when we have more details on that, we will share them."

"For now," Sant looked up at his daughter, perched, as if poised for flight, and his son, still weak, still bandaged, "We should spend what time we can with family." He rose slowly, still clasping Tirta's hand. "Let us plan on meeting again this evening, after dinner. The current time is," he glanced at his comm, "1038. Let's keep the local comms to a minimum as well. Save what power we can."

Nel's chest ached as Lin helped her brother to his feet. When they passed, Dar reached a hand out to capture Emilio's.

Lin glanced at Nel. "You can come—"

"My mom," she interrupted. And it was true, but a flash of fear shot through her body at the thought of being included. She had spent so long on the outside of this alien world, this complicated family, that she wasn't sure if she knew how to be on the inside. "I'll see you later?"

Lin slipped a hand around her wrist, then released as quickly as they had touched. "Later," she promised.

Nel was left with Xand and Hugo-Sanchez. "You got family here?" she asked the tech expert.

"A sister, down in the village," she explained with a tiny smile. "But she's got her husband and kids, and I'd rather work on this."

"You sure?" Nel hesitated. She wasn't about to invite her to Mindi's, but it felt wrong to leave her to her work.

"Promise. I'd rather keep busy, and if I look at those kids I might just lose it." She straightened and shot Nel a wink. "Now shoo, I got an evil sentient virus to stop."

Nel let out a short laugh and raised her arm. "Alright, c'mon Datalord, you heard the woman."

Xand was quiet, eyes wide and hung with deep shadows. She gave his shoulder a squeeze before leading them down the hall and out of the estate.

Darkness was a shroud, and Nel realized anew exactly how much noise *Vīrya* made. Soft outside air drifted across their faces, cooling Nel's damp cheeks. She glanced over as they walked and cleared her throat. "How you doing?"

"Dunno. Fine." His tense expression belied the words, however, and they didn't speak as they crossed through the dark village and drew up outside Mindi's door.

"It's not often you bring me another mouth to feed," Mindi remarked when she opened the door to find Nel with the nervous teen in tow. "Let me guess, you're the Mister Damascus that my daughter has been telling me all about."

"This is my mom, Mrs. Bently. I didn't tell her anything bad, promise." Nel assured with a chuckle.

"I'm Xand." He looked between them, expression hovering between pride and worry as he held out a hand for Mindi to shake. "I can go back to the cantina—"

"Nonsense." Mindi shook the boy's hand with a smile and ushered them in, but fixed Nel with a curious stare.

"Why don't you go wash your hands." Nel watched him turn the corner to the bathroom before pulling her mother into a tight hug. "It's good to see you."

"You too, honey." Mindi's arms were thin, but warm around her shoulders. "My neighbors showed me the bulletin. Brought over that glow-cube thing too. Did you find answers?"

"Eh, not the ones we'd like. But headway was made." Nel made a face, pulling back. "Do you mind? About Xand?" She asked.

"Of course not." Mindi scanned Nel's appearance, looking for any sign of injury before ducking into the kitchen. "It'll have to be leftovers, the stove won't work."

Nothing works. Nel followed, shucking off her boots before slumping onto the stool by the counter, staring into the depths of the bioflare for a moment. "Xand followed us out there. Actually helped a fair bit, if I'm being honest." She watched her mother deftly pull out a covered tray. It was incredible how well she had adjusted. She moved around the kitchen like she had been there for twenty years, not a handful of weeks, as if the ingredients she used weren't cricket flour and recycled water from a thousand asteroid residents' piss. "What'd you make?"

"Biscuits. Had to tweak your grandmother's recipe a bit—butter is not easy to come by out here—but I think they're alright. I was never great at them anyway, though your father always said they were just as good as hers."

Nel snorted. "Not when they came out like hard tack that one time. Remember Casey grabbed one and used it as a puck on her back yard rink? Thing's probably still there."

Mindi swatted at Nel's arm. "You keep insulting them and I won't save a single one of these for you."

"More for the kid," Nel joked. "Bottomless pit, that one."

"That boy looks like he could use some proper food." Mindi slid the bowl of cold biscuits onto the counter. "When am I going to entertain your errant woman?"

"She's not mine," Nel snapped, chopping at the salad greens a little more aggressively than was necessary. *They told us to spend time with family.* She knew what that meant, but didn't have the heart to tell her mother. The most she could manage was a tasteless joke. "And maybe when we're not about to die. Again."

Mindi straightened, hands resting on her hips as she surveyed her daughter's face, attempting, perhaps, to find a clue at how she was supposed to receive the news. "I see."

Perhaps she would have said more, but Xand reappeared, sliding onto the bar stool beside Nel. "Thanks for having me, Mrs. Bently. This looks really good." He pointed to the rest of the toppings. "Want me to do those? Unless there's something else?"

Mindi smiled approvingly. "Someone taught you well. I always told Anna that the best thing to hear was 'what can I do to help.'"

Xand looked curiously at Nel. "Is Anna your name, Dr. Nel?"

Nel wagged her hand with the knife. "Like how you could go by Alex or Xand, I could go by Anna or Nel. But Mom's the only one who is allowed to use the former."

"Copy that," Xand grinned, and it was a little bit stronger than before. They fell into anticipatory quiet, Mindi adding sauce to a platter of protein slabs. Xand's contented chopping filled the dim kitchen, and Nel scooped the salad ingredients into a big bowl. Nel gathered the place settings and headed to the table by the window.

She squeezed his shoulder as she passed behind the teen. "Thanks buddy." Moving around the table she carefully set the forks and knives and napkins, glancing up for a moment when she was done. Mindi was listening to Xand detail his favorite spices to liven up protein, face soft. Xand's mop of brown hair was getting longer, and Nel absently wondered if she should offer to cut it. *Maybe we can make an appointment when this is over.* Her heart tightened. This was no time to be getting attached, especially to an orphaned teen who would probably be placed in some fostering situation soon. Hopefully the foster system here was better than those on Earth.

Nel tore herself away from her musing to serve the protein steaks. The three of them settled around the coffee table, helping themselves to portions as the chatter began anew. Mindi asked Xand careful questions, and Nel relayed the lighter anecdotes from their time on *Recursive* or at Sapta. Outside, there were no golden streetlights to mark afternoon, and the impotent reflectors were still housed in the asteroid's augmented hull.

They moved to the couches with tea—Lady Grey for Mindi, chamomile for Nel and Xand—and the topics turned nostalgic. Xand's eyes lidded as he took in the comfort of surrounding voices and soon, he curled on his side, head resting against Nel's leg, snoring. Mindi fell silent, watching her daughter fiddle with the kid's hair. Perhaps it was the tenderness, or perhaps it was the looming sense that, whatever the end would be, it was close, but Mindi asked, softly, "Do you know what you're going to do, after all this?" She took a slow sip of her tea.

Nel didn't answer for a moment, cradling her own steaming mug in one scarred hand while the other continued its twirling of Xand's brown locks.

The steam smelled of camomile and confessions. *Will there be an after?*

"I can barely think past tomorrow." But the thought of afterward felt as ephemeral as the sensations in her new leg. She always assumed she would return to Earth. To her ranch in Jasper Hill. To her blue Nissan Titan and swampy backyard. The gap in her resume would be filled with enough lies to get some teaching gig or state job. She hadn't considered a life beyond soil under her nails and cold beer on a sweaty day. And try as she might, she could never picture Lin there.

There's beer here. And sweat. And even soil, sometimes. But even during the academic year, she was home as much as she wasn't. Maybe that's all home was, a place she returned to in between running. "I couldn't say, about her."

"How was working with her?"

Nel glanced up with a frown. "Fine. We didn't kill each other."

"Anna, honey, I know you too well to think anything you're involved in could be 'fine.'"

Nel grinned sheepishly. "It was good. And awkward. We both got some stuff off our chests. But I'm still mad. And she's still, well, alien." *Not too mad or alien for you to fuck her, apparently.* But Mindi didn't need to know that.

"Do you think she'll still be in your life?"

Nel looked down. How could she explain the churning in her chest? How close she came to actually shooting at Lin. "She's trying so hard to apologize, to do penance for her choices and everyone seems willing to forgive her. Honestly, her every action feels like a giant attempt at an apology."

"An apology to you?" Mindi had her research librarian face on, eyes bright over the tops of her glasses.

Nel heaved a sigh. and turned her attention back to the sleeping teen beside her. "There's this pressure to forgive her, love her, and I know if I can't, it makes me the asshole. I can't just decide one day that I'm over it. She hasn't made up for it yet."

Mindi hummed thoughtfully, looking down at her mug of tea. "If she did, Anna would you move the goalposts again?"

Nel glared at her almost-drained tea. She couldn't even answer that question for herself, let alone aloud, to her mother. Hating Lin was as inevitable as loving her, and as inescapable. *And is there really a difference at the end of the day?* Either way, Nel's entire being was consumed by Lin Nalawanga.

It was hours later, the three of them dozing in the stillness, when the klaxon screamed across the darkened asteroid. Nel scrambled up from where the three of them were dozing to see a single ship blasting from the satellite's underbelly. The sound went on for a moment before faltering into silence. The muffled feeling of the small hours drained, replaced by buzzing dread. She reached over and tapped at her comm to check the time. It didn't respond. Her frown deepened and she tried again. Nothing. Maybe her comm had just had enough of her bullshit. Maybe it retained too much moisture in the humid jungle air. *Maybe this is how we die.*

A second later a thunderous knock pounded on the door. Xand's eyes widened and he curled up on the seat, a snarl of anxiety. "Dr. Nel—"

She shook her head. "I don't know. One sec."

The knock came again, and Nel jerked the door open a fraction, bracing it with her boot, as if she could keep their doom at bay with her Red Wings. The smell of plumeria, of ozone muffled her thoughts. *Lin.* And the smell of smoke.

Lin stood outside, chest heaving and eyes caverns in the dark. "Thank the stars."

Nel didn't open the door any wider, but she relaxed a fraction. *Guess it's just my doom, then.* "What happened?"

Her eyes flicked to some place just behind Nel and the professional mask crept back over her strained features. "I'm sorry to intrude, Mrs. Bently."

"I'm no stranger to midnight emergencies," Mindi assured, voice tired. "Why don't you come in?"

"Thank you." Lin stepped inside, hands clenching and releasing repeatedly in a useless attempt to channel her nerves. Nel turned to take in her mother in the dark kitchen, Xand perched on the stool eyeing Lin with his sleep-vacant eyes, and Lin herself hovering as if stepping off the foyer carpet was akin to stepping out an airlock. It was fitting that this was the way she introduced Lin to her mother, in a doom-dark room. *Right, introductions.*

"This is my mom, Mindi Bently." Nel brushed past Lin, daring to place a hand on her shoulder to usher her forward too. "And, Mom, this is Komodor Nalawangsa. Lin. This is Lin."

Lin surged forward, offering her hand and a nervous smile. "Mrs. Bently, it's lovely to finally meet you, though I'm sorry it's not under better circumstances."

Mindi cast her an appraising look and took the hand. "It's good to meet you too, I've heard a lot."

Lin blanched, but set a bioflare on the counter between the four of them. "I'm afraid this is all I can offer as a gift at present. I'm glad to see you've found another."

"Candles were always a traditional hostess gift back home," Mindi offered before asking, "I still have a carafe of coffee from yesterday. It's not warm but, well."

"I ah," Lin's hand went to her port, but then she gave a small nod.

"Not enough coffee in the world for what we're about to discuss, I imagine," Nel muttered. She looked over at Xand. "You okay to stay? You don't have to—"

"I have to survive it, though, right? Might as well know." His face was blank, but she recognized the fatigue in his shoulders and stepped behind him to give his shoulders a squeeze.

Mindi poured them all a mug of coffee—real, honest coffee, even if it was cold—and hovered over Lin's mug. "I'm sorry, how do you take it?"

"Black, thank you," Lin answered.

Like your heart? Nel had the sense not to say it aloud, but when Lin met her eyes over the rim of their mugs, she realized she wasn't the only one thinking it. "So, end of the world?"

Mindi shot her a disapproving glance. "Let's let the woman have a moment to collect herself. It looks like she ran here."

Nel realized that, yes, Lin did look disheveled, breathless. *Just how I like her.* She slammed a mental lid on that thought before leaning on the countertop next to Xand, staring at the inconceivable sight of Lin drinking coffee beside her mother.

Xand looked between the three women before asking, softly, "Are we going to die?"

"Of course not," Mindi comforted.

At the same time Nel squeezed his hand. "We're gonna do our best not to."

Lin didn't answer at all. She took a slow sip of the coffee, almost succeeding in hiding her wince at the cold bitterness. Clearly the estate had better quality. "You heard the shield alert?"

"We did," Nel confirmed. "Big old screech right before you got here. I almost wondered if it was warning me you were about to show up."

"If only." Lin let out a single soft laugh. "A ship left. We had called all the staff in, of course, to be with their families in case—well."

Mindi's attention snapped to her daughter, eyes narrowed.

Lin stared into her coffee, pale face mirrored on its surface. "They're doing a sweep now, to be sure it wasn't someone panicking, but all bodies are accounted for. Dar and Lissa can't get into the logs with the power down, but I guess she's linking up some batteries from the..." she looked up to see everyone but Xand with a glazed expression. "They're working on it. As soon as they know where he's headed, we're sending a team out after him. Maybe, with any luck, we can stop him."

Nel's jaw worked. "I'm sorry, how can a spirit, or whatever we want to call him, pilot a craft? I get that the Samsari can like, possess tech or whatever, but I don't have to be a pilot to understand there's a big jump between messing up someone's high tech smart watch and flying a starship. Did he take over Kasanove's little podium or?"

Lin shook her head. "We don't know."

Nel clenched her hands, fuming and frantic. How could they still have so many questions? "Is there something I can do?"

Lin didn't answer for a moment. "Do you still want to help?"

Nel's eyes bugged. "If I didn't want to help, do you think I'd be on this fucking rock right now? No, I'd be home and probably dead but blessedly free of stupid questions like that."

Lin winced. "You've done nothing but complain the whole time and talk about going home! Maybe I was trying to give you a break."

"I complained because no one told me all the details!" Nel's body flamed with fury that this wasn't over yet, hurt than she was still excluded from the solution, from the conversation, and from Lin's innermost thoughts.

"Anna," Mindi began, softly.

"I was trying to protect you!" Lin snapped back.

"Oh yeah, pretend it was for my own good. You're a regular white knight. Sir Fucking Lies-a-lot."

Lin's expression pinched. After a beat, she pressed her palms to the counter on either side of her mug and slid away from the table. "If you want to help, then you know where to find us. Thank you for your hospitality, Mrs. Bently. We'll let everyone know our next moves as soon as we figure them out."

Mindi followed her to the door and offered a hand. "It was nice to finally meet you. Perhaps next time will be under better circumstances?"

Lin shot Nel a pained glance. "Perhaps." She gathered her vest and paused at the doorway, before closing the door behind her.

Nel couldn't keep herself from watching Lin go. She strode to the door that Lin had just shut, bracing both her hands against the wood, grimacing. Frustration bubbled in her gut, popping with angry heat.

Mindi fixed her with a stern glare. "I can't say whether I like her or not, but I can say that was absurd."

"Mom—"

"Small wonder you've never pinned one down."

"Oh I've pinned—"

"Absolutely not, Annelise Bently. Not in front of me and certainly not in front of the boy. If I have to hear one more foul thing out of your mouth," she drew a breath and broke into exhausted giggles. "Really, 'Sir Lies-a-lot?' God, Anna, I at least expected better puns from a librarian's daughter."

Nel frowned, but the bubbles were now her own laughter, and she slumped against the counter in hysterics. "Shit I really am insufferable!"

Xand was making an effort to smother his own laughter, but soon he, too, succumbed. He leaned his head against Nel's arm when she squeezed his shoulder.

"Sorry buddy. You haven't been getting me at my best lately."

"It's ok, Dr. Nel. It's nice when grown-ups don't always try to act perfect around me."

"No one is perfect," Mindi promised him. "We just get better at hiding it."

"Well," Nel interjected, "Some of us, anyway." She heaved a sigh before fixing her mother with a narrow glare. "What's with you defending the woman who almost got me killed a bunch of times."

Mindi's brows rose in a silent "touche," and smile smiled. "Because she managed to not actually kill you every one of those times and well," she fixed Nel with a pointed look, "I've never seen you so invested. So, I'm willing to ignore her crimes if that's who you want."

"Crimes can be hot," Xan piped up.

"As far as I'm concerned, you think nothing is hot, okay?" Nel made a face and turned back to the open window, staring through the darkness into which Lin had disappeared.

Nel's entire career was built on curiosity, searching for humankind's potential among their ghosts, speculating where they all might be headed based on the paths already walked. And those questions were personified in Lin. The puzzle of her past, balanced by the potential of her future.

Somewhere in the bowels of the satellite worked Dar, Emilio, Lin's parents. Even Hugo-Sanchez. And here, waited Mindi, and Xand, lives already so shattered by this high-tech family feud.

He lost his entire family to a fucking techno-ghost. She had nothing to bitch about in the grand scheme of things. "Shit, I gotta go apologize."

Mindi wiped her eyes, still chuckling. "Is that something you're doing these days?"

"Better late than never." Nel heaved a sigh and grabbed her own overshirt. She hovered at the door. "Mom, would you mind if Xand stayed?"

Mindi shook her head, eyes soft as she looked at the boy. "Not at all. I heard you were really good at digi chess, Xand. I have an old traditional board if you'd like to try that."

"I'm sorry mom. I love you. But I—you really think this is the right thing to do?"

"I know. I love you too." Mindi leaned closer to her over the counter. "I know you. And right or wrong, I know in your mind this is the only choice. I've always trusted your gut. It's about time you did too."

"I don't know if I want to forgive her. I mostly really want to fight her. Scream. Make her realize what she did."

Mindi presented her cheek for Nel to kiss and the archaeologist let out a surprised laugh when Xand gave her a tight hug. "C'mon, kid, I'll see you soon." He nodded, but his big eyes were fixed on Nel, and his jaw was tight.

"I'll be back. Promise." She forced the words out, even though they both knew that if Nel thought survival was guaranteed, she wouldn't need to run in the first place.

"I know. Go get her, honey."

Nel flashed her two thumbs up and set out across the suspended satellite.

Terror.

Justice.

The whispers drove each thud of Nel's boots. She swung by her rooms to don her suit, grateful it was clean and at least partially charged. Hopefully her body's friction and motion would do the rest.

Death.

Vengeance.

Once dressed, her next stop was Lin's room. Empty. Dar's was the same. *C'mon, ghosts, show me the way.* She drew a breath, hands out, shaking. Even through a thousand layers of asteroid and shields, she knew where Lin waited, her entire body was drawn to the precise degrees. *Of course I still can't decide if I want to fight or forgive.*

Retribution.

Her comm, awakened with the minimal charge of her electrosuit, pinged.

Docking Bay K 72

Nel sent a silent thanks to Emilio and broke into a jog.

She was panting by the time she got there, but they were waiting. It was a smaller ship, barely twice the size of the short-range shuttles. Helm-mounted bioflares cast bouncing blue glares across the satin sheen of the metal as a handful of ground crew toted banks of fuel-cells over from the other grounded crafts. Lin was tucked in the far corner of the bay, holding a muted conversation with her parents. Not wanting to intrude—or draw Sant's ire—she slipped into the open cargo bay of the ship. It was skeletonized, everything unnecessary stripped away to lengthen the life of their borrowed fuel. Dar already sat in the cockpit, scanning the shuddering readouts and making careful calculations about fuel and speed and goodness knew what else. Emilio stood over him, brown hand resting on the pilot's shoulder in silence. When he looked back and met her gaze, his eyes softened in a tiny smile. "You made it."

"I heard there were explosions. Couldn't miss it." Despite the humor, her voice was low, not wanting to disrupt Dar's concentration. "Where we headed?"

Emilio's expression darkened again. "*Odyssey of Earth.* The ship he took wasn't a long-hauler. Not short-range, either, mind, but given the fuel reserves he took it's within this sector. Lissa worked enough of the details out based on the schematics you two found at the sanctum." He glanced at her. "They worked their technological magic and got enough power going."

"That should be the last of the cells. Lissa's on her way with Philos." Lin announced, striding up the gangway. She stopped, speechless for once, when she saw Nel, suited and waiting beside the other two. Her mouth moved, then her eyes darted to her brother and the Los Pobledores leader, and she stayed silent.

"I owe you an apology," Nel offered. "It wasn't you I was angry at. Well," she tried a smile, "maybe just a little. Anyway: room for one more? I know taking down a big evil ghost guy doesn't really call for bad jokes and pushing buttons, but thought maybe I could still help out."

"You're a walking natural disaster." Dar snapped. Too distracted for it to be actually mean.

"Hurricane Bently, at your service." Nel snorted. After a moment she looked up.

Lin's expression softened slightly, enough for Nel to see the woman through the cracks in the facade. "There might be a few buttons."

She chuckled, trying to remember why her ribcage felt as if something very, very heavy had been pressing on it.

Dar dialed in another few numbers on the console with a frown before nodding and sitting back, satisfied. "Fifteen. Well, assuming Lissa gets here soon."

"Speak of the devil," Lissa sang, jogging up the ramp pushing a cart with Phil's transport case. "I'll get him set back here then you should be good to go!"

"You're not coming too?" Nel asked. As much as she didn't want to listen to Optimist's Greatest Hits the whole way, the woman was supposedly a tech genius. *Second only to Xand.*

Hugo-Sanchez's coils swung as she shook her head. "They need me here, especially without a senti-comp. Lots of transfers to do, once we're sure it's safe to bring everything online." She hesitated, glanced at where Lin spoke with her brother. "Take care of her, will you?"

"In between trying not to die myself, yeah."

"Phil and Andy chose you for a reason. Remember that." Another hair-bobbing nod. "Take care, Dr. Bently."

Nel looked around wishing there was something she could do to keep busy. Noting the passenger seats and harnesses just behind the cockpit, settled into one, as much to rest her already aching leg as to stay out of the way. She caught Lin's eye but when she opened her mouth to speak, however, Tirta stepped into the cargo bay.

"It seems we're ready. It's time." She stepped up to her daughter, one hand pressing to her brow, the other to her nape, eyes closed. She murmured something, a prayer, a promise, and dropped a kiss to Lin's upraised brow before slipping away to do the same for Dar and Emilio.

Nel looked down, wishing she could name the writhing in her gut something other than dread or doom. She jumped when Tirta's warm, dry hand dropped her hers, then gestured to her face. "May I?"

Nel nodded wordlessly, lifting her chin as the woman performed the same gesture and verse. When she was done Nel asked, "For luck?"

"For safety." Tirta tilted her head to the side in equivocation. "Thank you, Dr. Bently. For everything you've done for us. For her. When this is over, a leg will be the least we can do. I wish we had time now—"

Nel waved her words away. "Wouldn't really be the time for a test drive anyway. I'll try to bring back the rest of me."

"Well," Tirta glanced at the rest of them, hand reaching back to grip Sant's as he appeared behind her. "Until then."

"I'll be with you on the comms as long as I can. As long as the battery power lasts." Sant himself went straight to business, detailing their launch procedure, which Nel tuned out, still unable to pull her focus away from Lin. All too soon, however, Sant was embracing his children and shaking Emilio's hand. He turned to Nel, face as unreadable as his daughter's. Finally he offered his hand. "Dr. Bently, you have my gratitude."

"Thanks. Good luck, sir. We'll do everything we can." She drew a deep breath and settled back in her seat. "See you on the other side." She leaned her elbows on her splayed knees, looking up when Lin settled into the seat across from her. The komodor folded her hands together, observing Nel, unblinking. Doors slid closed, shutting them in stillness. The craft shuddered as the engines kicked in. Lights bloomed then dimmed, power siphoned only to the necessities.

Lin stared, and Nel did not look away.

A thousand expressions flitted over Lin's features, eyes narrowing, softening, lips twitching into almost a smile, almost a sob. The force of their flight shoved them back against their seats as *Vīrya*'s belly opened and they rocketed into blackness.

Still, neither looked away.

Their gazes were a beam between two worlds, two sides, two lifetimes, invisible save for the way the air eddied, as if their souls were two halves of a binary system. Perhaps it was the loss of gravity, perhaps it was the spacecraft leveling, but something settled in Nel's body, a subluxation sliding back into place.

TWENTY-FOUR

The flight would take 19 hours, by Dar's calculation. The first hours were spent bringing everyone—namely Nel—up to speed on the mission, but try as she might, the archaeologist's thoughts kept sliding off the details. Dock on Odyssey. Dar and Emilio would go on to Samsara, to disable the obvious tool Mansur would try to use. Simple. Then Nel and Lin would reinstall Phil so he might use the space station to erase the evil ghost himself. Easy.

Nel wanted to vomit.

It didn't help that everything was marked with the giant asterisk of "unless Mansur catches us." She paced the small cargo bay, drawing deep breaths in through her nose in an attempt to calm her nerves. She hadn't slept since the night before last and fatigue dragged at her shoulders. Still, how could she rest when Mansur was so far ahead of them, when Earth was once again on the line? How could she sleep when Lin was in one of the tiny bunks on the other side of the thin metal walls? She doubted Lin was sleeping either.

Dragging a hand through her hair, she about-faced at the end of the long cargo bay in the ship's center and headed back toward the cockpit. On her way up the ramp to the seats, she caught Emilio's eye. Like hers, his expression was shadowed and dull.

"Gaucho," he murmured, patting the seat next to him.

She crumpled into the chair and shook her head. "How are you guys so calm?"

"Well, Dar used most of his effort flying this thing. Now I must keep an eye on the autopilot system while he sleeps. It helps to have a task. And I just think of what waits for me, after this."

"I assume that's also involving him?" she teased, jabbing her chin toward the sleeping pilot in the cockpit. One hand draped limply over the yoke.

"Perhaps." His smile was gentle. "After all this? There's a little restaurant in a village south of Antofagasta. I think I might retire there. For a while at least."

She tried to smile, too, but her cheeks were suddenly damp. "Why am I scared, Emilio? I've done this—flying into the maw—a few rounds now. I feel like I haven't been this scared before."

He hummed. "Our brains do funny things. Make us forget the fear and pain just enough so we could do it again, if we have to. Is it dying, that frightens you? Or failure?"

"I mean, both, I guess." She frowned at the old calluses and new scars on her hands. A map of everywhere she'd been. A promise that there were more places, yet, for her to go. "Honestly, I don't think dying would be the worst. Last time I almost died I just got to hang out with my dead best friend and besides the worms and stuff, that was okay."

Emilio glanced over at her. "You saw Servais?"

Her cheeks flushed with heat. She hadn't meant to tell anyone that part. "I know, brains just fire at random when we go. Just signals and all that. Anyway," she continued, stretching the word so long she hoped he would forget what she said entirely. "I think it's the failure. How much longer?"

He brought up the trajectory, swiping away several insistent looking messages. "Twelve hours. It'll take eleven minutes to dock, assuming he hasn't taken over the system yet. Then we'll head down to Samsara to disengage what we can. We're flying in the dark, I'm afraid."

"Es al lote." There were so many assumptions, so many what-ifs that Nel could hardly see success on the other side.

"Sí po." He reached over and pressed his rough, warm hand over hers. "You should rest. Take comfort where you can."

Last time I "took comfort" we ended up with an evil spirit haunting the satellite. "I will. You too."

She shoved herself upright, glancing back at him before she tottered toward the bunks. "I'm glad you're here."

"Y tú, Bently. I'll see you tomorrow."

Nel forced herself to go to the bunks. There were enough for a dozen people, Nel supposed, centered around the main area designed for eating, cooking, and socializing. A bed waited for her just past the kitchenette. But she hovered, instead, just outside of Lin's room. Why was this how they were?

You.

Lin had delivered the apology of a lifetime at Nel's muddy, shitty boots. She had done everything in her power to make up for a betrayal that could have cost Nel her planet. *But it didn't.* She glanced through the dark porthole in the door, imagining the delicate form of the Nalawangsa daughter. *"She programmed it for your code. Yours alone."* Was that betrayal? Or the only help Lin could give Nel while under the pressing scrutiny of Harris? Did it matter? She jumped when the door she was half leaning on slid open to reveal Lin's tired eyes and stress-messy hair.

"Couldn't sleep?" Lin's voice was mist drifting across the cold metal around them.

Longing bubbled from Nel's burning bones as she recalled the exhaustion on Samsara sifting through bonedust, the sleepless nights on the train, the night on the rooftop in Chile when Nel's life was forever altered with a single starswept kiss.

She didn't speak, only reached across the eddying air between them, hand offering, trembling until Lin's arm uncoiled and closed the gap. Palm touched palm, marking one another in time, handprints on a cavern wall.

Lin stepped back, pulling Nel in after her like a magnet. The room was lit by the ambient light filtering through the tiny, reinforced window. Nel didn't care. She let the other woman draw her in, down, to sit beside her on the narrow cot. "There's another few hours before we get there."

"Yeah." Nel's voice scraped its way from her tightening throat. "You scared?"

"A bit. You?"

Nel jerked a single nod. "Nothing new, though."

Lin's lips quirked. "You've been so strong and angry and brilliant, I was starting to think nothing could shake you."

"You're the one who spacewalks for fun," Nel pointed out. Her brain splashed the imagined image of Lin stepping into the void. Dar had said he thought it was curiosity.

"Better than the alternative." When Nel tossed a questioning glance at her, she continued. "Instead of launching myself into the sun just to feel the burn, I swore I'd just step into space, untethered, to feel the potential of the vacuum around me. Instead of falling desperately in love with every human being I encountered because of how unique and interesting and so very strange they were, I studied us. Where we came from. Who we were before this. Why my ancestors made the choice to step into the stars. And why yours chose not to. But when I watched you storm out of Jerod's, all fury and feelings I was overcome. I wanted to excavate everything that you had ever been, every perfect mystery of you, and learn who you would be, what you would do with these strong hands of yours."

Nel looked down, realizing their palms were still pressed to one another. The expression burning in Lin's eyes was raw and instinctual and so very, very human. "Remember in Bakjiri? I said we can't help when someone gets under our skin? Well you did. More than any Chilean soil or parking-lot beer. It's like you took over and now I don't even recognize myself enough to tell whether it's you or me in there."

"Sometimes, maybe, it's both," Lin offered. "I know what you mean, though." Nel frowned, peering through the dim light at the planes of Lin's impossible face. Her black eyes were luminous voids that Nel's sense of adventure longed to dive into, just to see how far they went. "I've been impossibly tangled in someone. So much that I broke every rule I set my life by."

Nel opened her mouth to argue: see, wasn't it terrifying? But Lin's expression wasn't terror. It was certainty, it was longing, it was unbridled devotion. "Me. You mean me."

"Nel, my life's trajectory has been permanently affected by only three things: bearing the weight of my family's name; the implosion of the planet my mother called home; and you."

"I'm sorry. I never asked for that." Nel shook her head, not disagreeing, but hoping the movement might shake the fog from her clamoring thoughts. This type of conversation she would usually have drunk, if at all. Fuck knew why she even started it sober. "My entire life I've been this bonfire of anger, raging to be enough, to be seen. Not to be the best or the brightest and fuck knows not the nicest. But simply enough."

Lin tilted her chin, shifting closer. "I would have told you, but I was scared. I would do terrible things for you. I would do anything and everything for you. And if you weren't ready to bear it, I couldn't let a fraction of it out. When you said you loved me on the carrier we had been shot at, screamed at, bombarded with fire and smoke. I couldn't trust that you would mean it later."

"You're not 'enough,' Nel. You're my everything. My utter end."

Nel's free hand rose, pressing Lin's mouth into silence. She couldn't articulate what Lin's confession did to her, only that it ignited in her chest and mind. Her lungs billowed. It wasn't anger, or even fear, beneath the flames, but, oh, did she burn with it. It was faith. Faith in everything she set her eyes upon. Faith that humans were beautiful and terrible, insignificant and oh, so magnificent. And none were as furious and fathomless as Lin Nalawangsa.

Nel drew a slow breath, in through her nose, letting it fill her lungs with an icy burn. None of it made sense, not even with all the shards of their piecemeal confessions scattered before her. "I told you a thousand years ago, just before you broke my heart, that you were my north star. My super nova. My guidance in this black, breathless mess of space. I know things are about to blow up. Again. And, if we make it out of here, I'm starting to think they always will." Nel's voice threatened to shred itself on the blade of her honesty. "But I still mean every last word."

Lin's lips ripped free of her silencing palm and slammed against hers, a collision of heat and sweetness and desperation. Nel's hand raked through Lin's hair, gripping her by the nape. The other slid up to grab her throat, the way she'd imagined all those months ago when they were still playing at enemies. Then she pulled away, her fist, wrapped in black strands, dragging Lin's head back until they could look one another in the eye.

"I need you to hear something. Before, well." And Nel didn't know whether she meant before they fucked, or before they died, and it didn't really matter in the end, because in the shadow of the corrupted *Odyssey,* both seemed equally inevitable.

Agony flickered across Lin's face, a shadow over her naked hunger, but she let herself be held limp in the grip of Nel's scarred hands. "Of course."

"If we get out of this, I'm going to need some," she barked a desiccated laugh, "space. Time. Go back home. I don't know for how long. Maybe forever. Maybe just for loose ends. There are some things I need to think over, and I mean truly, bare feet buried in soil, think. And I can't think straight when I'm with you. I lose track of where each other ends."

Lin jerked a nod, brittle and desperate at once. "I understand."

"I'm not done," Nel snarled against her mouth, a threat to draw blood. "You found me in Chile. And in Oromocto. And on Samsara when it collapsed, and on *The Recursive.*"

Lin stilled, save for her ragged breaths. "I did."

"After I've dealt with what I need to, after you've done your behavioral reintegration for your crimes, after I've figured out what's next, I thought," she almost choked on the request, "maybe you could find me again."

It was only then that Lin dared move again. She closed the space between them slowly, one hand slipping under the hem of Nel's tank top. Her touch trailed across Nel's body, pausing at each new scar, new bruise, new augmentation, all the while Nel's hands didn't loosen. There had been enough space between them to last a thousand cryo-lengthened lifetimes. She wasn't about to let there be more.

The heat building between them tugged a groan from Nel's chest. Blood flushed her skin, tightening between her thighs. Whatever inhibitions tethered her before now evaporated and she pressed forward, chin tilting to capture more of her with every kiss. Her mouth peppered Lin's throat, then dipped to the hollow between her clavicles, the valley between the gentle swell of her breasts.

Nel finally eased her rough hands over the surface of Lin's perfect brown skin, cataloging each change with touch. She dropped a kiss into the hollow at the base of the other woman's throat.

Earth was in the crosshairs again.

Everything might end in a big, fucking boom.

But for a merciful minute none of that mattered. The horror and hope fell away from her shoulders, and she wanted nothing more than to let herself fall too.

Nel yelped as Lin surged back, tossing them both onto the bunk, dragging Nel on top of her in a tangle of low gravity and sheets. Salt and the tang of clean skin sparked along Nel's tongue when she closed her teeth over one brown nipple. She grinned against Lin's softness when the other woman yelped. "Too much?"

"No," the word trailed off into a gasp as Nel moved to her other breast then down. She crawled past her navel and down, burying her nose in the trimmed tuft of black curls. "I could just live down here," she confessed before continuing with tiny sucking kisses.

One arm pinned Lin's bucking hips. She tasted of salt, of sugar, a fruit so heady and alien Nel would gladly have starved if she never could taste her again. Her tongue moved in time with her curling fingers, merciless, stalking Lin's climax like she'd stalked Nel through the stars. Lin's hips bucked and sweet musk flooded Nel's mouth. She glanced up to watch Lin's expression. Her head flung back, hair tangled beneath her, chest heaving with shuddering moans.

After a panting few moments, Lin leaned forward, kissing the wetness from Nel's face. Lin tugged Nel's heavy cargo pants down past her hips and paused. "It doesn't matter if we win tomorrow. It doesn't matter if we die." Lin murmured against the pulse flashing in Nel's throat.

Buzzing at the back of Nel's skull told her Lin's fingertips brushed over the titanium of her prosthetic, gliding up Nel's metallic thigh, her palm's heat leaving prints on the satin finish, fingers digging against the exposed biomechanical sensors of Nel's leg. Sensation zinged up Nel's nerves, a flash of fire that left her gasping.

"Sorry—"

Nel grabbed her hand and shoved it against the lines of buzzing electricity. The sensation drowned out the flickers of phantom pain, burned away the background hum of anxiety and dispair.

"It doesn't matter how long you're away; I cannot tear you free from my flesh, my soul." And though Lin's words were violent, Nel couldn't find a lie in them, not when she sunk beneath all the waves of emotion crashing in her throat, not when she breathed them in, let them drown her. Lin pressed the heel of her hand against Nel's center while her other hand tap danced over the lines of overclocked sensors. "It doesn't matter where you go or how fast you run, Nel Bently."

Nel's center of gravity pitched, the heat behind her sternum yanked toward Lin, the pull so great it seemed to suck the very air from Nel's lungs. A lifetime of feeling insufficient, and now she was breathless from the sheer force of being wanted, desired, reduced to a David before the Goliath of Lin's desire. *Consumed.*

The grip of those deadly hands was the only thing that tethered Nel against the exposed-nerve blaze of her fear and anger. Every step into the heat she took, there was Lin, never more than a step behind.

"I run just as fast." Lin's fingers curled. Nel's head slammed back, thudding against the ship's side. Lin held Nel's shuddering body against hers, pressing her tight between the cool sheets and her own hot skin. "And I will always find you."

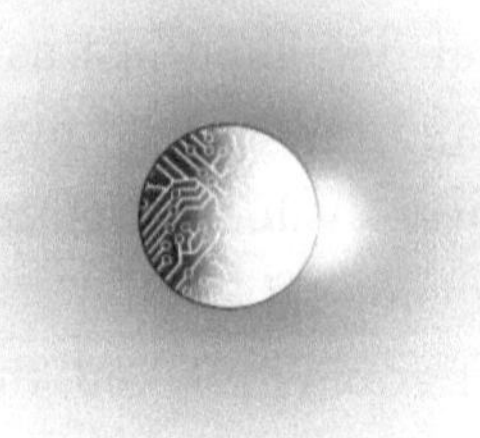

TWENTY-FIVE

"Going dark." Dar's voice cut through the sweat-warmed sanctuary of Lin's bunk. Nel groaned and pulled Lin's long lean body against hers, until she could bury her nose in the other woman's sex-tangled hair.

Lin winced. "My legs are jelly. How am I supposed to brace for docking?"

Nel heaved a sigh. "Guess we'll flop around all ragdoll and hope for the best." She finally wobbled upright, her own limbs more than a little loose. "Worth it, though."

"Indeed." Lin sat up on the edge of the bed. She rolled her suit on, smoothing its contacts to her tattoo. Seriousness underscored the dreamy expression on her face. "Thank you, for your forgiveness."

Nel swallowed her rising fear and gave her hand a squeeze before reaching for her leg. "Thank you for waiting for it." She struggled with the battered connections she'd torn off the night before.

"It was a prosthetic, wasn't it?" When Nel glanced up with a frown, Lin clarified, "That my mother promised you, if you helped us."

Nel huffed a laugh. "Yeah. But not for working with you guys. It was in exchange for you. Keeping you from going off the deep end."

Lin's brows rose as she zipped up and began fiddling with her augments. "You agreed to that?"

"Well," she shrugged, "Regardless of how I felt about the rest of things, it wasn't exactly out of my way. Caring about you." She tested her weight on each side. *A little uneven.* At least it was harder to tell than in her well-worn boots. She crouched again, flipping open the panel on her biomechanical quad before jabbing Dirt-o-mancer's tip into the height calibration screw.

"Here. Try this."

Nel glanced up from her crouch. Lin held out a leather wrist band equipped with a slim multitool. Nel flipped it open to see a dozen prosthetic adjustment tools, along with a few higher-tech items including a pocket electromag lock-pick and toposcan among a few less familiar pieces.

"This is awesome, where can I—"

Lin's delicate hand flipped it over to display the tooling decorating the exterior of the band. A slim rectangle of metal engraved with the now-familiar personal stasis shield circuitry, plus an entirely decorative design of a pointing and margin trowel, crossed at the neck. "It's yours. Terrestrial leather even."

Nel whistled low, thumb rubbing circles across the gleaming hide as if she could knead sense from the emotions colliding in her chest. "Where'd you come across that?"

"The leather's from a little shop in Tersa Eth where we picked up your trail." Lin looked at her sidelong.

"You bought me a gift when you were hunting us down?" Nel chuckled. "Guess I'm not the only one with conflicting feelings."

"Why do you think Harris put me in charge of hunting you? He didn't care the reason, after a while, but he knew I wouldn't let anything get in my way." She flashed a smile. "The tool is from the *Vīryan* labs, and modeled off of one Arnav had for his chair."

Nel clapped her hand over Lin's, sandwiching her fingers between her calloused palms. They stayed there for a moment longer, space-black eyes meeting earth-brown. "It's perfect. Thank you."

The ship's lights dimmed, then went out entirely. In the dark, Nel made a face, then followed Lin out the door. Dar was already seated in the cockpit, yoke held loosely in his hands.

Emilio's eyes crinkled when he watched Nel leave the same room as Lin, but he had the decency not to make a scene. "T-60," he relayed, knowing their first question.

"Anyone hailed us?" Lin asked, folding herself into the copilot's chair.

"No, nothing. Last contact was with Lissa seven hours ago. All good back home, at least. They'll be online again by the time we—well. Soon." Dar grimaced, not looking away from the instruments. "There she is."

The massive metal curve of *Odyssey of Earth* swelled out of the darkness as they drew closer. Nel frowned, head tilting. Before, it had looked like a network of lights. Now it was almost indistinguishable from the surrounding void. "It's dark."

"Sorry, next time I'll make sure my evil genius spirit uncle leaves a fucking light on," Dar grumbled, voice taut. "IDH fell out of fashion, so to speak, and most personnel moved to join their families elsewhere, if they had them, but there was still a robust crew after the transfer of power. There should still be—"

Something hurtled out of the blackness, colliding with their windscreen and everyone let out a collective yelp.

Nel's eyes widened as she caught a glimpse of space-frozen flesh and vacuum-blown eyes. "He's already there," she growled. "Mansur blasted them out the fucking airlocks."

Dar let out a pained whine. "Alright, suit up and strap in. We're going to have to go in cold, VFR only."

Nel glanced at Lin questioningly to see her face a mirror of Dar's distress.

"Full spacesuit. He's shutting everything down, including life support. Mansur can't know we're here. I'll help you get yours on."

Nel trailed behind Emilio and Lin to where their suits hung at the fore of the cargo bay. She brushed a hand over the comm on her wrist, powering everything down as she was instructed. "It feels wrong. Silencing the ghosts. I always get a twinge of guilt."

Lin's eyes were soft. "We'll get them justice, Nel."

The archaeologist didn't answer. This wasn't the time for promises. She donned each layer as they did, letting Lin's careful fingers check each seal as she did so, until the sounds were muffled, then shut out entirely.

Pairing.

"Comms?" she mouthed pointing at her wrist.

From within her helm, Lin shook her head. "Nothing except emergency life safety systems." Just as quickly her voice cut out and the static from the open line clicked off. *Suit: disengage all non-vital systems.*

Confirm: system override, all non-vital systems disengaged.

Suit: confirm.

All the readouts disappeared from her helm display, along with the screen of her comm. Nel laced her clumsy gloved fingers with Lin's and let her lead them back to strap into the seats. The running lights flickered then went out followed by the emergency lights. Then the passive air and life support and finally the instrument panels. They were encased in darkness. Dar, now suited too, gripped the yoke, Emilio's hand ever-present on his shoulder as they glided toward the extinguished space station. Far distant, glowed Samsara's ring of metal.

Tiny shifts, the smallest movements corrected their trajectory as the space station grew and grew in their view. There was no way Nel and Lin would be able to traverse the long gangway from the docking ring, not without being noticed, and Nel began to wonder if they'd be able to dock successfully at all. If Dar would be able to start the engines again. If he and Emilio would make it to Samsara. *Way, way too many what-ifs.*

Nothing stopped them as they drifted past the docking ring, however. Ships and shuttles usually dotted the ring like piglets against a mechanical sow. Now it was empty. Their speed became suddenly obvious as the imposing curve of the station grew larger. Dar's arms shook with the force of maintaining their trajectory. *We're going to crash, we're gonna—*

Dar yanked on the yoke and the ship banked hard, their momentum careening them closer and closer until the ship thunked against the hull, bouncing off, back toward the empty expanse from which they came. They came to a drifting stop a few dozen meters from the austere steel. Lin flew into action, freeing herself from the harness and reaching for her brother. Their gloves grasped, and she leaned down, helmets tapping silently.

Nel extricated herself as well, touching gloves with Dar and Emilio. She raised the tint of her helm just enough that they could see her parting wink. It was easier, somehow, to say goodbye without words. *See you on the other side.* And she hoped, harder than she ever had before, that it would be true.

Lin unclipped Phil's case from the cargo webbing. The 0-G walk to the cargo door of the ship gave Nel way too much room to think, to fear, to listen to the visceral sounds of her own breath, her own heartbeat. It was over far too quickly. Lin clipped the tank to her belt and gave her a tiny nod before palming the door release. Air writhed, sucking at their suits as the door slid open. Then, just as suddenly, it stopped. Lin pointed to a button on Nel's suit and then at the expanse of *Odyssey* before them. It was huge, there really wasn't a chance of missing it, but Nel abruptly wondered if this was how she would die. *Suit: engage propulsion.*

She grabbed Phil's other handle and pushed off into nothingness.

The propulsion from the magboots pushed Nel along, weightless, free. She craned around, staring at the shuttle's belly, tiny juxtaposed with the colossal space station. And beyond...beyond was black, inky and hungry and indescribably massive. The tank's handle tugged at her as Lin guided them to a small service hatch and latched her boots onto the curved metal. Nel only half watched as she set to work on the manual controls. The rest of Nel couldn't look away from the view behind them.

Their ship drifted farther, revealing the expanse behind. Nel found her chest was almost too tight to breathe, that her very skin seemed to vibrate with the enormity of space. Then, she let go. For a breathless moment she was completely untethered, nothing save the suit between her and oblivion. Just Nel, alone. The sensation was exhilarating and horrifying at once. Her laugh was loud in the pressurized helm, and her cheeks damp. She turned back to see Lin, face illuminated by starlight, smiling.

The woman extended a hand and beckoned. The gravity of their situation, of their relationship, drew Nel back until she slipped through the open hatch and into a different sort of darkness. She made sure Lin nudged Phil's tank inside and glided in afterward. The hatch closed with no sound, and the first hurdle was over. *Now for a hundred more.*

Suit: Disengage propulsion. Disengage mag boots.

Disengaged.

The corridor was just large enough for them to walk abreast, and for the taller Lin to stand without scraping the dome of her helm. Nel wished her suit could display the usual environmental readouts, but save for its essential functions, powered by her own friction and battery, it was just that, a suit. Lin raised her own wrist and read through its readouts swiftly before tapping the screen to enlarge the map and pointing to a snarl of infrastructure squiggles on the outermost layers of the station.

Nel reached over, jabbing at the center of the station with one blunt glove finger, offering a questioning frown.

Lin nodded, then shut down her comm entirely. She pointed left, right, left and left again. For now, at least, they could keep to the main halls. If they hadn't already crept through *Odyssey* while being hunted, Nel would be worried. Except that first time, there had been power. And air. And despite most of the station's security personnel looking for them that time, a genocidal, omniscient ghost was infinitely scarier. Worried didn't begin to cover it.

They set off into the dark. Three dozen steps and they made the first turn, onto an identical corridor. Another ten and the second turn. This one brought them into a larger hall, though still utilitarian in style. Still, no lights, and seemingly no air. Only the gravity, generated by the station's mechanical spinning, was still in place. At least when they used shielded comms and text communications, Nel had still been able to fire off stupid questions and poor-taste jokes. Now, without the outlet for her anxiety, she felt like she might implode, suit be damned.

What if they didn't power Phil down right?

Lin led the way through the next score of turns before she halted. Nel almost collided with her back in the dim light and shuffled to regain her balance before looking over Lin's shoulder to see why they stopped. Lin's shaking, suited arm pointed into the shadowed stretch of corridor ahead. A lump, darker than the surroundings, lay crumpled on the floor. *And we have our first body, folks.*

Nel pressed a hand to Lin's shoulder, then slipped past her. A meter from the body, she knelt, scanning the floor for any sign of blood or fluids. Nothing. She reached out, wishing she could scan the form for any sign of life or trauma. *How quickly we learn to rely on tech.* Instead, she grasped what felt like a shoulder and rolled the person over onto their back. Her yelp resonated off the interior of her helm.

The person's entire face had been stoved in. Bloody tissue and brown fat, pink bone shards and smeared gray matter, beaten into a pulp and unrecognizable save for the location atop the person's bruised neck. The lividity was still bright, red enough that Nel wondered how long the person had lingered before finally succumbing to their wounds. She forced down bile.

There was no augment, no metal or wire that had ripped itself free of their face. This had been done by something else. Someone else. She tugged the thin vest from the victim's shoulders and draped it over what was left of their face before rolling back onto her heels and standing. When she turned, Lin's face was colorless and she seemed unable to look away from the remains.

Nel nodded toward the hall. They had much farther to go, and surely other bodies would be waiting. *Let's not add ours.* With renewed grip on Phil's tank and renewed terror spurring them on, Nel and Lin cut deeper into the station. If Nel thought the corridors were monotonous her previous times aboard, now they were indistinguishable. Despite the squeeze and press of the electromesh on her flesh, her body had never felt so bone-achingly cold.

Another two silent turns and Nel drew up, pointing to another hatch, this one unlocked, and cast a questioning eyebrow to Lin. She frowned back, not understanding. Nel's sigh was too loud in her helmet as she mimed them jumping in, arms splayed as she pretended to fall, then land.

Lin quickly shook her head, making a series of movements that Nel didn't understand, but that ended with her drawing her finger across her throat. That one, at least, was clear enough for Nel to drop the line of questioning. Maybe without power there would be no way to stop. The had just passed the marker for a residential section when a tiny chime sounded at the back of Nel's head.

Suit battery low.

She grimaced. The thing might be charged by her own movement, but countering the space-frigid temperatures and lack of oxygen apparently took more power than their museum-crawl through the dark space station generated. A moment later the suit chimed again, battery fine.

Cold crept into her bones at the realization. Her suit had malfunctioned on Morphse too, oscillating between low and charged the closer she came to the body. They already know Mansur awaited them, but now her body knew, too, at its most visceral level. *He's here.*

They followed the curve of the hall and this time Nel was the first one to see the next body. Two, actually, Nel realized, noting another, smaller form on the floor a few meters away. *Please don't be a kid.*

The first set of remains was pressed against a service hatch marked for emergency use only, the hatch's bolt was crushed into the locked position. Nel brushed aside hair to peer at their face. They were young, light brown skin frozen to the metal door, expression a rictus of cold fear. Nel squeezed her eyes shut for a second, then looked lower. Their torso ended at the ribcage. *I see.* The other form was not another body, but their lower half, torn away as they tried to escape. Nel didn't know which would have been worse. At least it wasn't a child.

It was pointless to try to close frozen eyes, or cover them as she had before, but she let the hair drape back over their final stare before returning to Lin and letting her lead them past the gruesome landmark.

You will be remade.

Nel stilled. The whisper came from the back of her mind, like the battery warning. This one, however, was filled with malice. She grabbed Lin's hand, but when the other woman turned with questioning eyes, Nel realized she hadn't heard it. Not yet, at least.

For once, Nel wished for a countdown. Tech was terrifying, but when the danger was something out of Carpenter, she appreciated its security. Instead, she was forced to mark the time by counting her steps, counting the levels through which they descended, noting how the air roiled faster, more frantic, as they drew closer to *Odyssey's* center. *Except there is no air,* she reminded herself. But lo, there was movement, as if something passed through the surrounding vacuum. She let her eyes linger on the swirling.

We will be one beast, perfect and without pain.

Lin's hand tightened around hers and she realized this time, Lin heard it too. If Mansur continued to hiss sweet nothings into her brain, Nel was tempted to shut her entire suit down and just hold her damn breath.

Their final push through the dark, frigid levels brought them to the innermost shell before the forest. Bodies littered the floor, people piled atop one another in a gruesome dash to safety. Most were frozen in their clawing attempt at the door, crushed beneath their comrades. Others were slumped in despair. All were dead. A red swath cut through to the door itself. Blood froze in puddles where those blocking the way had been rent apart, a gorey path carved by a genocidal Moses.

They were almost there. Just the forest, and whatever awaited them in Phil's chamber. Just two tasks, insurmountable. Nel inched along the bloody trail to the door, wishing they had the time to pay respects, to cover the dead. But there was a tipping point in war, in disaster, where the deaths were too great to be honored until after the killing was done. *Let's just hope we're doing the killing.* It hadn't occurred to Nel until then that, whether he deserved it or not, when faced with Mansur there would be no option for mercy.

There is no need for mercy, when we are all one people.

The voice was the yank of vagus nerve pain. Nel had run headlong into the meat mass that was Mansur's idea of "one people." She was all set on that. Lin knelt beside the door, pumping the manual latches, dialing in the emergency lock codes, steady because there was no choice. The door unlatched, blasting open with the pressure within, and they were scrambling through, both of their shoulders straining as they yanked it shut behind. Phil's tank dropped unceremoniously into the vines on the ground and Lin's rushed fingers dislodged her helm. Nel followed suit, panting in fresh, forest air. She flopped against the wall on the other side of the door, flexing her hands.

Lin leaned back beside her, hair a snarl of black snakes, eyes wide and wild and Nel wondered if she had ever seen something more beautiful. *Maybe she's born with it, maybe it's Mansur.*

Trees towered around them, higher than Nel could have imagined, vines and leaves blocking any sign of path. "It's a fucking jungle."

"Over-production of heat. All the processing power Phil was using to solve this. Before Andy kidnapped him."

"Head-napped, maybe?" Nel hazarded with a weak laugh. "This place is way creepier in the dark and cold."

"The dead don't help it, either." Lin grimaced. "I never expected to miss the chimes as the doors opened. The worst ones were on *Promise*. Dar's ship."

"That the one that blew me up?" Nel asked.

Lin winced. "No. That was just one of its shuttles."

The tension around her eyes sent a twinge through Nel chest. "So, ah, what sucked about the *Promise's* doors?"

"Dar said he was too busy to change the defaults, but he secretly liked the sound. If it was just us he'd jab a finger at the right time, as if he was using psychokinesis."

"Or the Force," Nel laughed, then sobered. "Wait. Do you guys actually have telekinesis up here?"

"You tell me," Lin answered, narrowing her eyes and crooking one finger at Nel, as if to draw her in.

And Nel did feel a tug, the constant pull that drew them together, closer and closer until a single breath couldn't fit between. The ground shuddered. The pseudo-sun above flickered.

"We have to go on," Lin whispered, looking up at the glowing orb that housed Phil's interface. "We need to keep the suits on, just in case."

"I know." Nel relished the air while she could. "Is yours—"

"Yes. It's been malfunctioning since the first body. The battery reading keeps fluctuating. And I heard a voice."

"It's him," Nel murmured. She staggered to her feet, dragging Lin upright before fishing her machete from her backpack. Her fingers flexed around its handle.

What if we can't erase Mansur?

Nel cracked a smile, gleaming with all the teeth of the several thousand dead that lead them there. Then she would push buttons until everything blew.

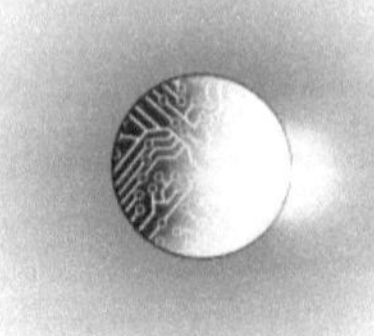

TWENTY-SIX

Sap and loam littered Nel's space suit as she drew up just below the access to the CPU. She jabbed the machete into the earth and braced her hands on her knees, panting. Lin staggered up behind her, arms shaking as she set down the tank.

"I get it now," she rasped. "I get why you have such a bad attitude."

"Rude." Nel answered. "Why?"

"Because hauling that damn thing all the way here—no comms, no hover-tech, no nothing, is really frustrating. I'd be grumpy too if this was my entire life."

Nel snorted. "Thanks. What's Dar's excuse then?"

Lin giggled, the mirth fading quickly in the humid air between them. She swallowed, glancing up at the glowing sphere high above. "Just one more door."

Nel wiped the blade of her machete off on her thigh and slid it back into its sheath on her pack. "So how we getting up there?"

Lin pulled what looked like an automatic crossbow from her own bag and cranked it back. She latched Phil's tank to her waist again, gesturing for Nel to do the same, then held out her arm. "Hold on tight."

Nel hoisted the tank in one arm, so it wouldn't swing wildly beneath them, and snaked her other around Lin's waist, gripping one of the thick straps on her suit. Their faces were so close, for a breathless moment, and Nel suddenly wished to drag them both down into the dirt, to tear their suits off, death be damned. Lin dropped a kiss on Nel's lips, then fired the grappling bolt into the access tunnel high above. While they'd been unable to communicate, Nel had wished to speak, but now it seemed there were no words worthy when you might die beside one another.

They hummed upwards, coming to a swinging stop just beside the hatch itself. Lin cranked it open and hung on while Nel clambered through, hauling the tank up next, then Lin last. The door clanged shut and both stilled, wondering why Mansur was waiting to retaliate. The clean-room hallway stretched on, the final length that lay between them and victory. Manufactured atmosphere hissed across the floor. Another bump, a beep and the door to Phil's room opened.

Darkness, whirring. The air around them shuddered and the sinking feeling returned to Nel's tightened gut. There was no way they'd made it this far, no way that he didn't have something planned. Orange standby lights bloomed beside the consol, then faded, pulsing against the dark. "You handle the systems. Life support, Samsara, all that. I'll get him jacked in, alright?"

Lin's gaze lingered on her for a protracted moment, then, wordless, she turned to the bank of instruments. "You did this before."

"With Polyana, yeah." Nel dropped her pack at Lin's feet and hauled the tank to the dark, empty port. She knelt and opened the case, squinting against the condensation that spilled out. The glass tank slid out easily and landed on the platform with a thud. She fiddled with the wires, double checking that they were untangled before replacing the stasis cables with the system connections one-by-one. When all but the final one was set, she glanced over her shoulder. "Alright, all cybersystems go over here. Just the last one."

She could almost hear Lin's eyes roll. "Bringing up the mainframe now. Last conductor now."

Nel's hand shook, extending the final wire over the port. She pressed her forehead to the tank, breath fogging the acrylic in the chill of the room. "C'mon Phil."

In the stillness, Nel heard a shift, a drag. Footsteps were nothing new, after all the ghostly sound had echoed around Mansur's body. But her mind was arrested by the memory of the steps she heard just before their extraction from the sanctum. Then, too she had comforted herself with the lie that they were the only three there. But listening to the lurching approach from the computer center, she was reminded that it was, indeed, a lie. She glanced at Lin, to see if she heard it too. Desperation stripped the performance from the Komodor's face.

Another step, another drag, another breath. Now, she was sure it was behind her. Nel clenched her jaw and tried to turn. Her feet tangled in the cables and she slammed into the floor. Her skull cracked against the freezing metal of Phil's stand, stars exploding across her vision. "Fuck!"

When she blinked her vision clear, someone stood over her, blood-slick, sallow flesh, steaming in the chilled room. Gleaming titanium capped her attacker's truncated throat. The stink of formalin and organic fluids washed over her a second before hands wrapped her throat. It dragged her upright as she flailed, elbows jabbing into the naked torso. Ringing overtook her ears. Or maybe she was screaming, maybe it was Lin.

Suit battery critically low.

She scrambled to regain her footing but her boots slipped on the slick floor. *Where did the blood come from?* she wondered before registering the warmth trickling down her nape. Clammy hands tightened around her trachea. Her lungs seized, trying to suck air that wouldn't come. Why had she left her trowel in her pack? Skin came away under her nails as she ripped across the tattoo on her attacker's arm, red ribbons striping his filmy flesh. Her still-sparking vision darkened at the corners, hyoid straining under the crush.

She heard the ramping buzz of a glove powering up and panicked. A glove blast could fry the entire system. The quarters were too close. Adrenaline hit her veins. She twisted, blocking Lin's line of fire and dug into the metal on the body's neck, working her fingers under its rim, cursing her short nails. Blood sprayed across her, salty copper in her mouth and coating her suit. The body slumped to the floor.

"Guess we know how he flew here." Nel remarked, still gasping. When she met Lin's eyes, they were filled with terror.

"You blocked my shot."

"You would have fried the system," Nel panted.

"He was going to—"

"Doesn't matter. Power on, Lin." Shoving Phil's headless body aside, she lunged for his tank and connected the final wire. The fluid in the tank sloshed still, Phil's head bobbing in a way that was funny, if your humor had been forged in explosions and body counts. Nel chuckled weakly.

Soft plastic tapping sounds came from the instruments as Lin typed out commands and codes, face lit with unforgiving light.

"It's not working," Lin's words trailed into a groan. "He did some hard reset, it looks like, screwed up a bunch of background processes. What about over there?"

Nel turned back to look at the small panel displaying the biomechanical data from Phil's tank. "Nominal here."

"Let me try something." Static shrieked through the speakers, the larger screen overhead flashing bright, then gold, then bright, and Nel squeezed her eyes shut against the pain. Sound popped and everything went dark. Their breath was loud in the otherwise silent room and Nel tried to blink afterimages from her eyes.

At the base of the tank, a single green light blinked.

"Phil?" she whispered.

"Dr. Bently?" The almost-human voice rolled through the room as, one by one, lights flickered back on, systems powering up with a whir. The main screen displayed its usual image of Phil's face, moving with expressions and speech in a way his physical one never would. "What are you—" he stopped, programs probably cycling through a hundred updates. "I see."

"It's Mansur. He took over the system."

"Yes. I can feel him. He," the image of his face flashed to screaming, jaw overextended for a moment and the speakers glitched to a digital howl before returning to normal, like a hidden frame in an old film. "He gained remote access to Samsara."

"Is there anything we can do to stop it?"

"Maybe. I need to think."

Nel's stomach twisted. The man had countless banks of memory and processing power. If he needed time to think, they were in deep shit.

"I WILL REMAKE YOU."

The screen flashed again, now a face Nel recognized from her nightmares, grinning. *Mansur.* The whirring increased, auxiliary fans kicking on as the two consciousnesses warred over the system.

"I HAVE CRAFTED MYSELF IN THE IMAGE OF OUR GODS. I HAVE BROKEN TIME AND SPACE TO BRING HUMANITY INTO LIFE BEYOND DEATH, LIFE BEYOND PAIN. NO PREJUDICE WHEN WE ARE ONE BEAST."

The temperature rose a degree, though their breath still fogged and Nel wondered if feeling would ever return to her hands. A flicker and Phil's avatar reappeared.

"He's trying to force me out. Lin, reroute the overcurrent connection to the processing banks. Move the tap on Transformer 43 to its third position. Bently, I need you to—" His image flinched, superimposed for a moment with Mansur's before Phil returned. "Why can I not access the auxiliary emergency drives?"

Lin did as she was told, scanning the numbers on the myriad ports, tugging the plugs out and sliding them into place while Nel craned around, squinting against the blinding, flickering light as his screen was repeatedly overtaken. Phil's body had lurched from the instruments behind her.

"There's a shit ton of cables disconnected from a section labeled AUX-CPU," she relayed.

"WE ARE THOUSANDS. MADE ONE."

The voice was now overlaid with countless others before snapping back to Phil's usual Mid-Atlantic accent. "Please reconnect—"

A scream split through the air, each of the tiny speakers that lent depth to his digitized voice projecting a slightly different pitch. It went on, and on, but Nel got the gist, diving for the disconnected bank. She glanced at the cable tips just long enough to register the color before jamming them into their coordinated ports. Everything went black again for a tense second then the lights returned. Lin reached for Nel's hand, her lips blue.

"Is that my body?"

Nel shot a horrified glance at Lin. *It's not like I can lie to a supercomputer.* "Look, Phil—"

"I've really let myself go." A zing of humor shot through the audio before dropping back to business. "He's taken over most of my vital processes, but there is a manual override that should blow the system."

"OVERRIDE?" the other voice cut through. The display faltered again, this time for longer as Mansur gained more control of the system. "YOU THINK YOU CAN OVERRIDE THE DIVINE? THE PERFECT? THE TEACHERS MAY HAVE BEEN FIRST, BUT WE WILL BE BETTER. WHOLE. I SEE NOW WHY THEY RAN: WE ARE TOO POWERFUL IN THIS FORM."

Lin pointed at a single black point in the constellation of circuits. Ice crystals rimmed her black eyes. The override switch had been smashed, the connections crushed in like the face of the first body.

"It's like the doors at the sanctum, if we just gotta close it, anything will do." Nel dug through her pack where she'd left it at Lin's feet. Her fingers found the wood-warm handle of her trowel. Through the flash of swamp green and system-failure orange, she caught Phil's electric eye. "Right Phil?"

"Correct, Dr. Bently. Without the circuit closed I cannot start the system purge." Phil explained, a second before the sound boomed again.

Beeps. Whistling air. The background hum of Mansur's murderous electric manifesto. Last time, it had been her choice, made alone in the dark, billions of lives resting on her. She wished suddenly that they had sent Hugo-Sanchez, the tech expert, or Zach to therapize Mansur into a guilt-ridden self-destruct. But they sent Dr. Nel Bently, expert at anger and blowing things up. She tugged her trowel out and swallowed her fear.

"Don't you dare," Lin hissed.

"I know. Close the circuit this way, there's no way we'll make it to the escape pods in time? Or what, the countdown accelerates? Some reason that after all the shit we've been through, now that we're finally within spitting distance of peace and quiet and a normal fucking life, we won't make it."

"Something like that," Lin whispered.

"It bypasses the emergency life safety system, Dr. Bently." Phil explained. "This room has shielding, temporarily. But to truly wipe the system, that too will go down. Otherwise we could never be sure if it worked."

"When you say wipe the entire system…" Nel looked over at him. When first faced with the last vestige of Phil's humanity, she had questioned if there was any humanity left. Someone so changed, who lost flesh and blood and all recognizable form, like the doomed souls on *V Drugoye Mesto*. The weight of borrowed circuitry and silicone cupped the end of her right thigh. Other than a few trillion terabytes and one fancy-ass fish tank, what was the difference between her and Phil, really? "What about you?"

"The circuit must be closed when I bring the purge program online in T-30 seconds. Not a moment later." She swore she saw the memory of a smile flicker across the waxy surface of his preserved features. "All systems: go. Godspeed, Nel Bently."

Lin gripped the archaeologist's forearm in her deadly fingers. The console's glow cast the copper of her features in electric verdigris. "Think about this. We could still make it out. If we run."

0:28

Thirty seconds. Thirty seconds to save the world. Nel rolled her sleeve up to look at the wrist cuff Lin had given her just hours before. "These are a shield, right?"

"They're small. Enough to protect against fire, drowning, a vacuum for a short period..." she trailed off as Nel stepped closer, gripping Lin's hand, squeezing the shield device between them until the metal bit their laced fingers. "It's only meant for one person. And when the station blows—"

0:17

"What's one more explosion?" Nel rasped. Her throat stung with the fire she once called fury. "You wanted to walk into the sun, and I've been burning since my first breath."

Deadly, delicate fingers buried themselves in Nel's hair. "So, we'll burn together."

0:09

"Hey, Mansur," Nel shouted. The speakers boomed and cracked with acknowledgement. Dirt-o-mancer's tip was poised above the crackling circuits. "Go to hell."

0:00

Nel pressed her brow to Lin's and drove the trowel home.

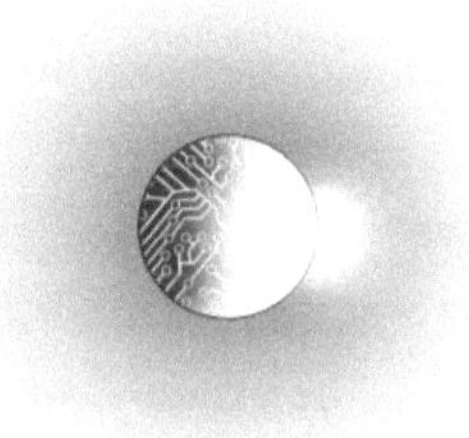

TWENTY-SEVEN

The swamp at the end of the road buzzed with biting life. A record brood year of cicada screamed from the oak grove and the hot scent of pine soaked the still air. Nel watched her lawn grow higher and higher, grass choked out by clover and horseweed. A half-drunk red ale dangled, forgotten, from her hand. Sweat stained her gray tank top, and the toes of her one bare foot dug into the silty ground. The other foot, gleaming titanium, the best the Nalawangsa name could buy, was tucked under her faded folding camp chair.

Even when the sun had set and the mosquitos swarmed, her glazed eyes stared, unseeing, at some point beyond her property's edge. Try as she might, to gather all the pieces of herself that blew apart four months before, nothing fit together quite right. The memories of waking after their rescue, of the long flight home, cryosleeping next to her mother, were blurred, as if some part of her life had truly ended when *Odyssey* exploded. Now, she was piloting someone else, though a life she only half recalled.

Her first few weeks back, she barely slept. Nel paced the house. Rearranged her office, the pantry, and every living room bookshelf and donated half of their contents. She applied to half a dozen CRM firms. Two of the firms never called and a third low-balled her.

But as time stretched on in the summer heat, like taffy, she found herself just...staring. Half an hour lost in the whorls of her scratched cherry countertops, another in the dance of insects over the stagnant water out back. She would blink back to awareness in the dusk, an entire afternoon swallowed by the emptiness in her chest. Mindi's messages piled up, sharing where she was on her book club trip around the world. Check-ins from Zachariah came too, and she even answered a few times—he was stationed on Earth now and expecting a child—but lately she would just watch the answering machine as his messages grew more concerned, then less frequent.

Instinctually, she knew the others must have been just as broken. She pictured Emilio pausing as he wiped down the Padrito's counter, thinking of his brother, or Dar, unable to bring himself to fly quite as fast. She pictured Lin, perfect and terrible, working off her time under the heat of a far distant sun. Sometimes, she wondered if any of them had survived at all.

When one of the firms she forgot she had applied to requested a video call, Nel found herself staring into the middle distance in silence when they asked about her most recent workplace. Afterward, they agreed it probably wasn't the best fit. *I guess there are gaps in more than just my resume.*

School busses chugged up the crest of the road and college kids outnumbered the townies in Jasper Hill's bars. September went, and with it the liminal late summer days. October arrived, more cold rain than colorful foliage. Wet autumn wind groaned over the knoll, rattling her weathered front gate in its latch. And despite pages peeled from the wall calendar, Lin did not come.

It was finally Annie's bright voice materializing in her voicemail, that paused Nel's stupor enough to warrant a response. It took two weeks for her to find the energy to dial. The numbers had changed, and Nel's fingers seemed clumsy as she typed them in. Even the ring sounded foreign, so different from a comm chime.

"Hello?" The bright voice was the same, if maybe a bit more tired.

Nel froze, staring at the unfamiliar reflection in her hall mirror.

"Hello?"

"Uh. Hi. Hi, Annie," she stammered out. "It's Nel. Dr. Bently."

"Holy shit, professor!" The tone shifted and Nel wondered if Annie had even expected a response. "Long time, no see. How you been?"

"Yeah, been a bit. Crazy how time flies." Nel hesitated. Right, this is when she was supposed to ask about the other person. "Been good, ah. Up and down. You? Last time we talked was…How you been?"

Annie's laugh was soft, perhaps confused. "Same, better than bad, you know? Look, I'd love to catch up properly. I gotta finish this report tonight, but what're you doing Friday?"

"Friday?"

"The sixth. Day after tomorrow," Annie prompted.

"Um, let me check," Nel answered, staring at her pathetically blank calendar as if plans she'd made four years ago would leap out and bite her. *Who even put up this year's calendar?* "Yeah, I'm free."

"Want to grab a beer? There's that spot that opened up on Maple, next to the old theater. You been there yet?"

"Ah, no. Haven't had the chance. Looked good though," she lied. She'd have to look it up later and brush up on the local news before they met. "That sounds fun."

"Awesome! Meet you there at say, seven? Grab a bite too?"

"Yeah, Friday at seven's great," Nel agreed, when her brain translated to military time. "Can't wait, it'll be good to see you."

The line clicked and Nel wasn't sure if she'd said goodbye, or just cut the call. The reflection holding her cell looked perhaps a little bit more like her, when she squinted, with greasy hair and gray sweats. "Fuck, I need to do laundry."

Rain had turned to fat slush by the time Nel swung her Frontier into the sloped parking lot of Clatter Shack Distillery. It was an old building, one that had been the VFW last time Nel went. A new porch and half a dozen columnar outdoor heaters gave the place a facelift. Nel tromped through the mounding slush, wincing at the added chill from her metal leg—hidden under black jeans and an almost too-tight pair of old boots.

Inside, it was loud and warm, the lights low, and Nel scanned the crowd for a mass of dyed curls. There, in one of the booths near the door to the porch. Nel edged between the tables, giving her awkward two-handed wave when the other woman looked up. "Made it."

"Shit!" Annie surged to her feet, work boots planted, rocking them back and forth as they embraced. "It's been way too fucking long!"

Nel laughed, wondering when Annie's language had started to sound like hers. "No kidding. You order yet?"

"No, just got in. Here's the drink menu."

Nel peered at the menu, eyes glazed as she read down the names, and when Annie rattled off an order at their waiter, she mumbled, "same." Maybe Emilio was right, and she needed to try reading glasses.

"Some things don't change, eh?" Annie chuckled. "I bet you can still drink me under the table."

"Slowed down a bit," Nel answered. Her gaze slid over the table, rolling half-heartedly over Annie's shoulders, her face. She was older, just the underside of her hair dyed now. A puffy vest topped a flannel in classic archaeologist fashion. Nel could barely remember what Annie's body looked like, underneath. "You look good."

"Thanks," Annie smiled, but there was a shadow to it, and she didn't return the compliment. "Here we go!"

The waiter delivered two fogged pints and two snifters of what Nel presumed was the Clatter Shack's own small batch. She knocked back a deep chug of the beer then let out a long, appreciative sigh. "Haven't had this one before. It's not Black Pond, but pretty good."

"Bring the crew here a couple times a season, if we're working in the area."

"Where you working these days? Last time it was at PANUS, right?" Nel tried to remember.

"Yeah, stayed there another year, but they wouldn't make me full-time. I was digging in Yucatan when the pandemic hit, and the blackout. After that got sorted I got tired of lean winters so I headed over to CNE-Arch."

Nel frowned, scooping a hunk of mayo up on her fry. "Where's that out of? Don't remember the name."

"South Monson, actually. James Carlsbad started it up a year and a half ago. Been a bit slow, but things really picked up after we won bids for the energy contracts. George's actually there too." She hesitated then tossed out her offer. "They'd take you on, you know. Not sure what they'd give you specifically, but our wages are competitive."

Nel had known the offer would come. It was surefire, even for someone who burned as many bridges as she crossed, that an old friend or friendly ex would offer work at some CRM firm. She'd even wondered what figure they would throw out for someone with her experience. But hearing it on Annie's tongue somehow made the idea no more tangible.

"That's assuming you haven't totally hung up your trowel."

My trowel is buried in an exploded space station. "Thanks, Annie. I'll think about it. I'm not quite sure where I'll pivot to, just yet."

"How was your sabbatical?"

Nel frowned, realizing that must have been the party line about where she'd gone. *Sabbatical.* Sure, most professors traveled for theirs, taking the time to do field research, but it was such a stuffy word for what she'd experienced since she left USNE. She cleared her throat, realizing she hadn't answered and lied, "Busy, honestly. What about you? Ever think about returning to academia?"

Annie shrugged with a rueful grin. "I'd like to teach at some point, but I was hoping to sync it up with when I had kids. But that ship might sail soon."

"We'll you're still in your twenties, still young," Nel reassured. "There's plenty of time left."

"Thirty-three."

"Hmm?" Nel frowned, glancing up over the rim of her beer.

"I'm thirty-three. Be thirty-four in January." Her smile stretched, suddenly strained.

Their conversation faltered, and Nel found she was unable to fumble up the pieces. If she'd ever had tact, it was burned up with her trowel. Instead, she looked down, thumb subconsciously rubbing a circle around one of her new leg's ports.

"Where'd you go, Dr. Bently?" The words were soft, all brassiness set aside.

Nel dragged her attention from her aching limb across their half-finished dinner and up to Annie's too-honest eyes. *She was there for you. No questions asked—well, not many. She saved your life.* There. That was someplace to start. "You, ah, you saved my life. With the canoe. Thank you. I never did thank you for that."

"I'm sure you would have made it. But I'm glad to have been a help." Annie's eyes were still over-wide. "You were working with them, weren't you? The Emissaries."

Nel's heart burned. The events that utterly changed her life were different here. While catastrophic in the moment, they no longer impacted the Earthly day-to-day and so diminished to history, headlines. "Is that what everyone called them?"

Annie didn't answer, perhaps holding her details hostage until Nel offered an answer of her own. But there wasn't one. Not one Nel wanted to share, not an honest one. She finished off her beer and leaned back before asking, "Did they kill Dr. Servais?"

"No." Nel shook her head. "It was their drama, maybe, but no. That was one of the Los Pobledores' guys. Not Emilio, though, he's become a good friend, actually." *Emilio. Last she might have heard on the news, he died.* She cleared her throat and segued clumsily, "You seeing anyone?"

Annie laughed. "Here and there. Job doesn't make it easy though."

"You're telling mc," Nel chuckled too, and felt something loosen a fraction in her chest. "Do you remember when that girl brought her boyfriend to field school years back. God what was her name?"

"Claudia? Claire? Something like that? What a disaster!"

"Cleo!" Nel recalled, grinning now. "And he didn't know she'd been cheating with that nerdy kid until he got there."

Annie giggled into her whiskey, raveling the field story like an old knitting project, and when that one was through, Nel remembered another, and then Annie, back and forth as their drinks disappeared and chowder bowls were replaced with coffee mugs. The music had slowed and the crowd more or less dispersed when they tottered out into the cold, damp parking lot.

"My tolerance isn't what it used to be," Nel noted with a wry chuckle, slipping a bit in the slush as they paused by her truck.

"Want a lift?" Annie's voice went soft again, and her hands tucked deep into the pockets of her pink vest. She looked cozy.

Nel glanced between the blue of her truck and Annie's silver coup. "I'll be alright, but glad I stopped at two."

Annie pressed closer, full body warm and alive. Nel let her eyes lid, breathing in the scent of sandalwood perfume and rye. Part of her missed this. The weight of another body. Shitty weather. Cold metal at her back as someone kissed her up against a car in a bar lot. She rested her forehead on Annie's shoulder for a beat then straightened, pulling back from the allure of her old ways. "I'm gonna pass."

Annie's face fell, but she didn't drop her kindness. "No problem. I had fun last time, but friends is cool too."

"Friends are what I need more of, turns out," Nel chuckled. "Thanks."

"There someone else?"

"Kind of. In the not-fair-to-you way." Nel looked up. "I hope so."

Annie's smile returned, teasing now. "Well, I guess some things do change after all." She took a step back holding up her keys. "Sure you don't need a ride? No strings."

Nel nodded. "I'm good. Thanks for this. I think I needed it more than I realized."

"Anytime. Really. Season's slowing down soon. Maybe after the holidays we could do it again. Maybe I'll bring George and James."

Nel watched her go, leaning against the sobriety of her truck's cold door. She wanted to see Annie again, of course she did, in the way that she wanted to get a job and move on. In the way that it was expected of her. But there was very little Nel wanted anymore. It was as if her life had imploded under the gravity of her experiences, and now it drew everything—every thought, every whim, every moment she and Lin had ever shared together, into its sucking void.

When her hands were numb and her head clear—clearer, anyway—Nel climbed up into her truck. The road was a starfield at lightspeed as her high beams caught the freezing rain. Nel took the road slowly, picking her way home as new businesses and old houses drifted past in the dark. Her truck door was loud when she slammed it shut in her driveway; she limped up her front stairs and switched the porch light off. The bed was cool and wide when she fell into it, exhausted, but unable to sleep.

Still, Lin did not come.

TWENTY-EIGHT

Heavy spring rain splattered against the newly painted ranch, soaking the winter-brown yard and swelling the banks of the swamp. The rooms were empty. Shelves bare. Bright squares marked the southern yellow pine where carpets had lain. Wind, warmed with impending spring, swung the plastic sign beside the mailbox. Nel stared at the bold black letters.

Under Contract.

She hadn't even met the buyers, knew nothing about them beyond their names and that one had just been hired as assistant professor at UNNE. Not for anything so poetic as anthropology, of course, but some type of advanced mathematics.

Nel nudged open the fridge door and slid in the beribboned mixed pack of Black Pond's beer. A bottle opener magnet and the paper it held were the only remaining evidence that one Dr. Nel Bently had ever graced 517 Bear Road. She slipped the airline tickets from beneath the magnet and dropped the keys on the counter

"Gaucho." Emilio's arms tightened around her shoulders before he stepped back to survey her. "You look well."

"Nothing an open bar won't fix," she drawled, clambering into his old black Tiggo.

He grinned but let her ride in peace. The Chilean autumn was a nice escape from the long months of grey New England winter, and she tipped her face up to the sun with a smile as the road swung them through the hills heading into town. Aside from erosion and a handful of newly built properties on the outskirts, very little had changed. They descended into the village proper and Nel's gaze caught on the pull off to Los Cerros Esperando VII. Guava had grown over it now, barely visible and certainly not drivable. It felt overgrown in her memories, too.

She rolled her head over to look at Emilio. His skin was darker from the summer sun, and the lines he gained during their last few years were a bit softer now, and more familiar. "Thanks for picking me up."

"Bus stop isn't too far for me, and the kid makes it easier to step out."

"How is he?"

"Good. The studies keep him out of trouble, mostly. How long do you think you'll stay?"

She smiled. "A few days. My flight out isn't until the 17th."

"Good," he repeated, looking at her sidelong, but he didn't pry. He drove them down the main drag, such as it was, and pulled into the narrow alley driveway beside his restaurant. He turned the key and sat with her as she listened to the engine tick. "Need another minute?"

"It's just strange, being back after everything."

"It was for me, too, at first." His warm broad hand settled on hers and squeezed. "Xand might kill me if I keep you any longer though."

She shook her head with a soft laugh and got out, swinging her duffle onto her shoulder before following Emilio up the back steps and into his apartment. She'd barely stepped over the threshold when a projectile of limbs and messy hair shot from the door down to the restaurant and slammed into her.

Xand's arms were hard around her and after a second, she realized he had to lean over to hug her now. "Señor Sepulveda said you'd be by."

"Sorry it took me so long, kid," she said, hugging him back before stepping back to get a good look at him. He was a good four inches taller than when she last saw him, and his hair was longer, half-pinned up. The Chilean summer sun had down him good, too, she saw. "I missed you."

His smile was watery, but he blinked a few times and glanced over at Emilio. "I'm gonna finish up downstairs, 'fore Max takes over. She's staying for dinner right?"

Nel laughed. "A couple of dinners, yeah."

He wavered a bit in the doorway. "You'll be here when I get back?"

"I will." She squeezed his shoulder. "Promise, this time."

Emilio showed her to the guest room and Nel breathed a tiny sigh of relief. She really was getting too old to take the couch. For the next hour she got settled and showered off the film of long-distance travel. Clean and dressed in cargos and a fresh tank top, she found her way to the small balcony jutting off the kitchen.

The screen door clapped as she shut it behind her and took a seat in one of the empty metal chairs. Emilio already lounged there, a hand-rolled cigarette dangling from his weathered brown fingers. The familiar walls of Emilio's restaurant hadn't suffered in his absence, run perhaps by the same systems that had kept her mortgage current.

Emilio pressed a sweating bottle of Austral Calafate into her hand. "Better?"

"Better." She took the bottle and popped the top. "I'm glad most of my problems these days are solved by a shower, food, and alcohol. Thanks for having me."

"It's good to see you. We've missed you."

"Not that Dar would say so." She chuckled.

"Well, he'll be here in a few minutes, you can ask him yourself."

"Still can't believe you convinced him to take a terrestrial job. Even if it's at ALMA," Nel marveled. "Didn't see him as roughing it down here with us dirt-kissers."

"I think he enjoys the challenge. He's home most weekends, these days." Emilio's smile turned sly. "Besides we'll both be headed to *Vīrya* in a few months."

"No shit. For a while or…?"

"Just a few weeks. We're marrying, Dar and I. It'll be a small affair, just family." He glanced at her. "I was hoping you'd come."

Her heart swelled and her throat burned. "Yes. Yes, I'll come. Holy shit. I'm so happy for you." She leaned her head back against the plaster of the wall, jaw aching with her smile. *Just family.* "Thank you for thinking of me."

"Well, my brother was the other choice but he's rather busy."

She wrinkled her nose. ""So, what're you going to do with him?" she asked, watching Emilio's face for any clue.

"Harris or Dar?"

She snorted. "Harris. I can use my imagination about what you and Dar get up to."

He heaved a slow breath, shaking his head. "They've allowed me to advise his rehabilitation council, but understandably, I'm not technically allowed to help in the decisions themselves."

"Too lenient?"

"Too strict."

Her brows rose. "I always thought you were the good cop to Dar's bad."

"Don't insult me, I'd never be any sort of cop." His expression softened and he nudged her with an elbow. "Remember, we're a bunch of outlaws and degenerates."

She snorted. "So, little brother goes to rehab?"

"Essentially. If he chooses to. It's rehab or a labor station. Or the monks, I suppose, but I doubt he'd pick that life."

"The fucking monks. Did you ever figure it out, where he went bad?"

Emilio finally looked over at her, rich skin lit with the bright gold of the sun, of their sun. "Bad? Harris is complicated. And hurt. And angry. And, if I'm honest with myself, he always was. Our father raised us enmeshed in Los Pobledores lore. We learned about the Mapuche, and Chileno culture, and the colonizers. But we also learned about Los Pobledores, and why our ancestors stayed, when others fled. Just like Ranato—Harris—and I. Two sides of the same story." He heaved another breath. "He will go somewhere to learn how to change his actions. He will regret them, or he won't, he'll reform, or he won't."

Nel hummed in thought. "I'm not sure I'm as generous. But I get it. I'm more understanding of it now, after everything that happened."

He's gaze slid over to her. "And where will Dr. Bently go, after this?"

"Thought about traveling the world, like my mom. But there's something calling me out," she waved her can at the golden sky, "there. Same thing that brought me here a decade ago."

"Mystery?"

"I guess. Got enough money saved from my house to just, coast a while. There's a one-way ticket burning in my pocket to a place called Restu-Yol. Apparently one of the first non-terrestrial place humans settled thousands of years ago."

His brown eyes warmed. "Looking for someone in particular?"

She knew who he meant, without asking, but instead she took a long sip of the cold Calafate. "Myself, mostly."

"Do you still hear them?"

"No. I think I do in dreams. Them and Phil and Mikey and all the ghosts we've collected. But nothing real. I'm ashamed that it's a relief."

"Lending your voice to the dead is heavy work, being their emissary to the living. They were lucky to have you."

Her vision misted and she swallowed hard. "Nah. I'm the lucky one. You and Dar and Xand, you have no idea what you three mean to me."

Emilio's eyes crinkled and he ashed his cigarette into the ceramic dish. "I have some idea."

"We're doing drinks after this," Dar called, letting out a soft hiccup. Clearly, he was more affected by terrestrial alcohol than his usual port usage. "Heading to Jerod's."

"It's an invitation," Emilio clarified. His cheeks were pink and eyes even softer than usual, one arm wrapped under Dar's. "Xand's old enough to be on his own for an evening and your bus won't leave for another few hours."

Nel's vision misted at the sight of them, and she thought her chest couldn't hurt more. "You go on ahead. I was going to poke around town for a bit. See what's changed."

Emilio's gaze lingered on hers, understanding burning between them. He saluted her with his drink and escorted Dar down the stairs, singing something softly as they went. Nel only caught a few lines, but thought it might have been Violetta Parra.

Her bag was easy to pack, and goodbyes were easier unsaid. *And they aren't goodbyes, anymore. Just for-nows.* The tickets were in her passport and she slung the duffel over her shoulder, leaving a short note on the counter beside the mate gourds.

It was inevitable, the path she walked. The dry earth of Chile's soil ground under her boots as she hiked. Darkness edged the road as she hiked out of the town and up, through the narrow clefts. The scent of lapageria hung in the cool air and she lifted her face to the star-swathed sky.

Guava spilled up the trail and across much of the site now, but Nel picked out the shape of the line of rocks easily, glimmering in the moonlight. She set her duffle at the base of the nearest one and climbed the last few meters to the crest of the hill. The golden lights of the town twinkled below and Nel wished she could hear the music at Jerod's. Maybe Dar and Emilio were dancing.

Nel did not turn at the whisper soft footsteps following her trail up to the site. She would recognize those cat-quiet steps anywhere. She imagined Lin's electro suit responding to her accelerated heart rate, squeezing against the press of impending emotions, warming to comfort her shuddering skin. Skin that, in another lifetime, was Nel's to caress, to protect, to have and to hold.

"Evening, Komodor Nalawangsa."

Lin stilled, then crossed the last distance between them, folding down beside Nel's sprawl.

"Was starting to think you wouldn't come," Nel whispered.

"I'm sorry I didn't come sooner." She shifted more, pressing closer to Nel, shoulder to shoulder, staring at the sky. "I knew once you came here, you'd be ready."

Nel shoved the dirt in her boot toe. "How'd you know I was here?"

"Dar."

"Traitor."

"Are you mad?"

"No. For once." She let out a soft laugh. It was so much more than that. *I would have waited forever.* She knew it down to her bedrock bones, a truth buried beneath shame and sorrow and a thousand apologies so complex that she couldn't figure out those she deserved and those she owed. It was all she could do not to wish the howling distance between them was smaller.

She watched Lin for a protracted moment. "Look," she held her wrist out, nudging Lin's comm awake with her watch. "We're finally on the same time cycle."

Lin held her gaze, mouth curling into a smile. "We were when we first met, too, you know."

"So." Nel rocked her head, enjoying the rough bite of the stone. The Milky Way was a sparkling swath across the southern sky and Nel picked out a single gleaming star. *"See that star? Somewhere between here and there."*

"So," Lin whispered back.

Nel pressed their sweat-streaked brows together, fingers tracing the raised lines of electroink on Lin's throat. Warmth uncurled, a frond in sunshine, brought forth in the wake of a wildfire. "Do you wanna get out of here?"

Lin's gaze settled on her shoulders like electromesh. An agonizing beat passed between them. "Our time cycles will be out of sync again," Lin whispered.

"Earth is my home. Its bones are mine. She's not going anywhere. So, what do you say?" Nel's heart pitched over the event horizon of her black-hole eyes. "I'll keep track of where we've been, you keep track of where we're going."

Lin laced their fingers, kissing each of Nel's knuckles. Her touch wasn't lustful, but reverent. Careful. As if she were the first woman to press her lips to the archaeologist's scarred hands. As far as Nel's heart was concerned, she may as well have been.

Nel rocked to her feet and grabbed her duffle. "Course, my flight has a few stops along the way. But I figured the long way around just means I get to see a bit more of the world. Your world."

"Nel–" Lin surged to her feet, face a wolf moon of desire and delight.

"The bus leaves for Antofagasta in fifteen minutes. You could grab your things. It's not like you ever really unpack." Nel reached a calloused hand out to grab Lin's hand. Grab her heart. "Fifteen minutes. We could make it if we run."

A smile exploded across Lin's lips. "Race you."

END

ACKNOWLEDGEMENTS

The end of an era. Nel has been with me for a decade, and with her I sweat, and swore, and dug. Now I find that as her story comes to a close, I, too, am hanging up my trowel. I've faced my own—perhaps less explosive—battles alongside Nel and neither she nor I would be the same without the incredible support I've had over the last few years.

Thank you to every archaeologist I've worked with over my career, for your stories, and your silliness, and your kindness. Thank you to my amazing group of friends that I've found while digging—Kate, Moira, Nadia, Audrey, Jackie, and Meche, to name a few.

Thank you to the lovely writers who have cheered me on from the sidelines. To Marissa—I wish our friendship could have weathered the world. Thanks for being my biggest fan when I was just starting out.

Thank you to my small but mighty family—my mom who taught me to love literature, and to search for a story, and my dad, who shared the stars with me.

And to Brad, thank you for being my partner in adventure and always running just as fast.

ABOUT THE AUTHOR

V. S. Holmes is an international bestselling author. They created the BLOOD OF TITANS series and the NEL BENTLY BOOKS. *Smoke and Rain*, the award-winning first book in their fantasy quartet, became an international bestseller in 2018. *Travelers* is also included in the Peregrine Moon Lander mission as part of the Writers on the Moon Time Capsule. In addition, they write game content for Stone Blade Entertainment.

As a disabled and non-binary human, they work as an advocate and educator for representation in SFF worlds. When not writing, they work as a contract archaeologist throughout the northeastern U.S. They live with their spouse, a fellow archaeologist, their dogs, and own too many books.

www.vsholmes.com